THE ATMOSPHERIC RAILWAY

Shena Mackay

THE ATMOSPHERIC RAILWAY

New and Selected Stories

Jonathan Cape
London

Published by Jonathan Cape 2008

2 4 6 8 10 9 7 5 3 1

Copyright © Shena Mackay 2008

First published in Great Britain in 2008 by
Jonathan Cape
Random House, 20 Vauxhall Bridge Road,
London SW1V 2SA

www.rbooks.co.uk

Addresses for companies within The Random House Group Limited can be found at:
www.randomhouse.co.uk/offices.htm

The Random House Group Limited Reg. No. 954009

A CIP catalogue record for this book is available from the British Library

ISBN 9780224072984

The Random House Group Limited supports The Forest Stewardship
Council (FSC), the leading international forest certification organisation.
All our titles that are printed on Greenpeace approved FSC certified paper
carry the FSC logo. Our paper procurement policy can be found at
www.rbooks.co.uk/environment

Mixed Sources
Product group from well-managed
forests and other controlled sources
www.fsc.org Cert no. TT-COC-2139
© 1996 Forest Stewardship Council
FSC

Typeset in Bembo by Palimpsest Book Production Ltd, Grangemouth, Stirlingshire

Printed and bound in Great Britain by CPI Mackays, Chatham, Kent ME5 8TD

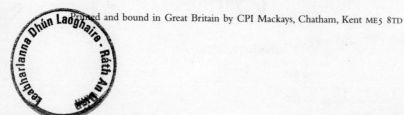

For Christie

CONTENTS

The Atmospheric Railway

The train carrying Neville back to Hampshire was formed of ten coaches and was scheduled to divide at Eastleigh, where the front five carriages would proceed to Poole, while the rear five branched off towards the New Forest. The journey had been faster twenty years ago, he thought, back when Eastleigh was still famed as a railway-building town. It was a Sunday night in January, and he was on his way home after spending the weekend with his cousin Beryl. Neville, retired but for a couple of directorships, uxorious and slightly tubby in his soft red jumper and checked scarf, felt a certain relief at the thought of re-entering his own dimension and leaving the past behind. He had travelled up on the Friday and they had done a lot of walking in the streets, cemeteries and parks of south London. The idea of researching their family history had been Beryl's and, in late middle age as in childhood, Neville found himself following Beryl's lead. Neither of them had any siblings and they had grown up in the same street almost like brother and sister. They were orphans now. Neville's wife, Faith, had suggested that Beryl's interest in the past was an attempt to establish her own existence because she had no children. Faith and Neville were the grandparents of three. Perhaps there was something of atonement in it too, Neville thought, but did not say. Beryl's father, his Uncle Frank, had been a photographer whose shop exploded one night in a pyrotechnical display which lit up the neighbourhood.

The fire destroyed not only many of their own family pictures but a whole local archive, a portrait of a community, its schoolchildren, celebrations, funeral rites, sporting events, commerce and industry. Frank Graham had been more than a portraitist and wedding photographer and he took, for his own interest and pleasure, pictures of houses, shops, churches and parks, streetmarkets, deliverymen and their horses, children at play. What a museum the Frank L. Graham Photographic Gallery might be today if the stock

I

had survived, what a rich resource for other family historians. There had been suspicion of an electrical fault in the darkroom, unstable chemicals or the spontaneous combustion of celluloid, but the cause of the fire was never established. Forensic fire investigation technology was not so sophisticated then as it is now. It happened when the cousins were in their early teens, secret smokers both; Beryl had two pairs of keys cut and sometimes in the evenings they sneaked their friends in to the shop to drink cider. On the night of the fire Neville was at the cinema, and Beryl had gone round to a girlfriend's house. Neville had often wondered if she really had been at Susan's.

This morning when he was shaving in Beryl's bathroom, Dusty Springfield's 'Goin' Back' came on her angelfish shower radio. The bathroom was white, with flashes of blue and green glass and turquoise towels, but as he stood in front of the art deco mirror, Neville saw, with a pang as sharp as the scent of apple blossom talcum powder, the room as it was in her parents' time. The walls were tiled black and white, there was a pink Armitage Shanks bathroom suite and a candlewick pedestal set which always rucked up under your feet, a wonky bathroom cabinet, and a Mabel Lucie Attwell print with the verse which began: *Please remember, don't forget, never leave the bathroom wet . . .*

When he came into the kitchen, where Beryl was sitting at the table in a white towelling robe, the radio was on there too. He knew that at home, Faith would be propped up on her side of the bed listening to the omnibus edition of *The Archers.* 'It's all a bit Nigel Pargetter's Great Uncle Rupert, this digging up the ancestors,' Neville remembered her saying.

'Were you listening to that song? I think I might have it played at my funeral,' said Beryl. 'So take note, please.'

Neville imagined a coffin, with a little tremor, beginning its stately glide along the rails and passing through the closing curtains: *'Catch me if you can, I'm goin' back.'*

'Noted. Except I'll snuff it before you do. Being three months older, and . . .'

Neville patted his stomach in the bathrobe he'd found hanging on the bedroom door. He put his hand in his pocket and pulled out a lipstick. Beryl held out her hand and he dropped it into her palm, and she opened the pedal bin with her toe and tossed the lipstick in. Neville noticed a vein like a small violet on her bare ankle. His own were in a much worse state. Beryl's toenails were painted vermilion. Their bare feet, facing each other in the sort of slippers provided by a spa or a hotel, augmented the melancholy induced by her remark. He remembered them straight and brown on the sand at Littlehampton where their grandparents had a beach hut.

'Anyway, I wouldn't know who to invite to yours,' he said, watching as the sun projected a tremulous bar of mauve light through the window, striking a prismatic star on the side of the kettle.

'I think I chose all the wrong music for Mum's funeral,' said Beryl. 'Do you suppose we could do it again, and say the first one was a rehearsal? Only, it's a bit late now – most of the original audience will be gone.'

'I guess that's where a memorial service comes in handy; you have more time to get it right. If you're the sort of people who have memorial services.'

They had become, Beryl particularly, the sort of people who were invited to memorial services, but such events were unknown in their own family.

'I'm sorry I wasn't more help to you when your mum, when Aunty Ivy, was ill,' he said.

'Never mind.'

'I saw you once,' he said. 'It was in a wine bar, off the Strand. You were with some bloke.'

'When? I didn't see you. Why didn't you say hello?'

'I didn't want to intrude. And anyway I had a train to catch.'

The wine bar was down a flight of steps and dimly lit; it seemed the sort of place where illicit lovers met before taking their trains home, or perhaps going on to a hotel. Beryl and the man were sitting at a little table with a bottle of wine. The man was holding her hand in both of his. He'd hung his jacket on the back of his chair, loosened his tie, and looked beefy in a shirt with a broad blue stripe and red braces.

Neville watched her force down the plunger of the coffee pot. He knew so little of her life. She had come to his daughters' weddings, taller and more elegant than the mother of the bride, with a different man on each occasion, and she'd brought some woman friend to his first grandchild's christening, and come alone to the second one. They had no chance to talk much then, and this weekend, whenever he'd tried to draw her out, off she went back down Memory Lane, always to the time before the fire, and into the hinterland of their ancestors.

'I wonder if the beach hut's still there. It would be worth half a million now,' she said, pouring coffee and bringing into the kitchen a whiff of the blue salty smell of the spirit stove, with its coronet of flames invisible in the sun. 'I wonder where so many things went. We've let so much slip between our fingers.'

'Yes, but we're still here, we're still going on, living our lives, there's the present and the future. It doesn't have to be sepia to be real. If the past is all that matters, that too becomes devalued, if former happiness only makes us sad . . .'

He had picked up a small white card from the toast rack Beryl used to keep letters and bills, and was playing with it as he spoke.

Neville had boarded the homeward train at Waterloo and sat down in one of a pair of seats, with his back to the engine. When he took off his coat, he folded the smoky green fragrance of their parting embrace into the cloth, and the Dusty song began playing in his mind. Strange how Beryl's cigarettes never smelled unpleasant. He had helped himself to one after dinner last night, even though he had not smoked for years. He put his coat in the rack and gave Faith a quick ring to tell her when to pick him up at the station.

Outside the sealed capsule, the sky was black with an inflor-escence of lights here and there as they picked up speed on the frosty rails after Clapham Junction. Apart from the recorded secur-ity announcements requesting passengers to keep their belongings with them and alert staff to anything suspicious, and the headlines in the discarded newspapers on the seat beside him, there was nothing to suggest that the country was at war. Neville was thinking that it would soon be the anniversary of the Falklands War, and recalled, as he often did when travelling this route, an incident which happened one summer a quarter of a century ago, on a hot Saturday after-noon when he was on his way to visit his parents.

Then he'd been sitting in the compartment next to the buffet car. The train was crowded but he became aware, over the general chattering, of a loud monologue coming from the bar, a voice haranguing somebody, followed by an explosion of shouts and curses. People looked up in alarm as a huge man burst through the door. He was so drunk he could hardly stand, and went lurching between the seats, swinging enormous fists and roaring obscenities and accusations at the cringing passengers, spraying ugly, shocking words in spittle and sweat. He bellowed in anguish something about mates being burned alive, men on fire throwing themselves into the sea. His face and tattooed shoulders in a sleeveless vest were a scalded pink, either from the disaster he had escaped, or from sunburn, alcohol and rage. Nobody dared to meet his red eyes, or tell him to watch his language because there were ladies and children present, for all were shamed by him, and ashamed for him, and terrified. Then he picked on a girl sitting with her boyfriend, both of them skinny and small, telling her it was the fault of people like her that his mates had died, and the youth sat there in silence, because her assailant could have lifted him from his seat with one hand and dashed his brains out.

The man was almost incoherent but Neville guessed that he had been a member of the Task Force, a sailor or one of the Welsh Guardsmen aboard the *Sir Galahad* when she was bombed, or the *Sir Tristram*, as the soldiers waited in broad daylight for landing craft to take them ashore, sitting ducks for the Argentine bombs, which they knew would come. Fifty-one men were killed. Many of the troops had sailed from Southampton on the *QE2*, seen off by bands and cheering crowds waving flags – Welsh flags, Falklands flags and Union Jacks hoisted on all the boats in the harbour. Neville and Faith, living nearby with their three small children, had watched it on television, still not quite able to believe it was actually happening.

How had the episode with the drunk man ended, Neville wondered. He could not remember. Had somebody, and it would have taken several men to overpower him, intervened at last, did somebody wise and sympathetic calm him down, or was it just that he, Neville, had sat there, an insignificant, invisible little man, as he was sitting now, until the guy roared into the next compartment, unstoppable as an Exocet? Perhaps, when the guy's back was turned, he'd sneaked away in his mild civilian shoes and hidden in the toilet. Whatever, Neville had got off relatively unscathed, but what of the youngsters setting off in their provincial finery to enjoy an evening in town; could their relationship survive the boy's humiliation? Neville had been aware of himself becoming less of a man, in the recognition that the other was twice the man he was, and not just physically – but he had just himself to face, as the only witness to his own cowardice, his weakling's mixture of fear, hatred and pity. His father had served in the Merchant Navy in the Second World War, and since his death Neville wished profoundly that he had shown more interest, and admiration. He wondered now how many of the other people who had been on that train were still haunted by their summer afternoon's encounter with the emissary from the South Atlantic.

Tonight, twenty-five years on, Neville was impatient to be home, looking forward to a quiet supper with Faith. Beryl had invited Faith for the weekend too but she'd refused, saying truthfully that she was demented with work. From the start, though, she'd been slightly sniffy about their project, and Neville suspected that she considered her own family to be effortlessly more distinguished than his.

'All this digging up the past on the internet, all those millions of virtual messages in bottles whirling round cyberspace – what's the point of it?'

The conversation took place in Faith's studio where she stood, a Luddite at her loom, shuttling charcoal grey through silver threads as they talked. Abstract works in rich emotional colours throbbed on the walls, among embroideries of seedheads, pods and berries. Neville stroked a hank of sheep's wool on the spindle of her spinning wheel.

'For the girls. The grandchildren. You might find it boring but they'll thank us for it in the future.'

'What future?' said Faith. 'Anyway, we'll all meet up in Heaven, DV, and then all will be revealed. Or not.'

'Beryl thinks she might write a book — about the Florence Graham I was telling you about. And her chap, Archie, the one who worked on the Atmospheric Railway.'

'Mmm.'

'Well, she does have publishing connections.'

'Possibly. In her heyday. You know how fickle those people are.'

Beryl had been the doyenne of an old established publishing house, in charge of the switchboard, answering the telephone with her characteristic and much imitated smoky 'Chalice and Chalice', with its dying fall which so intimidated nervous callers. She was a legendary dragon whom tyros mistook for a mere employee at their peril, for Beryl was an inspired editor to whose judgement the three Chalice brothers deferred, and she had been a fixture on the guest lists of all important literary occasions. Ten years ago, the firm had been swallowed up and the imprint Chalice and Chalice was no more, although its books could be found in second-hand bookshops such as the one in Charing Cross Road where Beryl worked after she was fired by the new management. She found that too painful, and switched to Haberdashery at Peter Jones, and thence, following in her mother's footsteps, took a job in the shoe department of Morleys of Brixton. Faith was right; the smart invitations had stopped coming but it was only some-times in the white bitterness of the early morning that Beryl minded, before resolutely immersing herself in her *Life* of Florence Graham. Also, she had rediscovered the pleasure of being a random reader at the library, and not having to bother with the book reviews in the papers.

Lately she had become more intrigued by Archie Erskine and admiring of the little she knew about him. She tried to superim-pose his qualities on men she saw working in the street or builders gentrifying the neighbourhood houses, but they seemed more like regressive gangs of serfs and villeins than gentle craftsmen such as Archie, who was a woodcarver and painted landscapes, all lost as far as she knew, and played the flute in his spare time. Yet Archie, as a navvie, must have experienced squalor and dissoluteness in Norwood New Town, where he had come to live while working at the Crystal Palace and the experimental railways. Beryl shuddered at descriptions of the hordes of rats who invaded the tracks nightly to devour the tallow-coated leather seals and valve-flaps which were intrinsic to the design of the trains, and contributed to their abandonment. The leather dried out and, when the tallow and wax used to lubricate them melted, it proved irresistible to the local population of rats. Hundreds of them were sucked through the pipes in the pumping stations every morning when the pumps started up. Beryl wondered if Archie was one of the men in the engine room who put sacks over the inlets to catch them as they poured in. What they did with the squirming sacks didn't bear thinking about. Poor rats. Poor Archie, flautist and Pied Piper. Beryl searched the local junk shops and car boot sales for a painting with his signature, without success.

Beryl and Faith were distantly affectionate, without understanding each other's lives. Faith had always been happiest in the country, she never got the point of south of the river and she hated London now, believing its grand houses to be owned by foreign criminals and its mean streets populated by human traffickers and slaves, drug dealers and teenage gangsters with knives and guns. Most of her friends had wings and tails, which was another reason for not going away; she ran a sort of almshouse and hospice for her poultry pensioners, two retired greyhounds and a donkey, several cats, and an assortment of wildlife in rehab, including on occasion one of the ponies which grazed the common land beyond their garden. It is often said that people grow to resemble their pets, but in Faith's case there were too many for that to be possible. Instead, she was slowly turning into a replica of their house, *Coltsfoots*; her once-golden hair was getting thatchier by the year, and her glasses glinted like windowpanes under time-bleached eaves. They had lived in *Coltsfoots*, bought with help from Faith's family when Neville's firm had relocated to Southampton, for some thirty years now. Faith taught needlework, embroidery and tapestry, spinning and weaving, and when her services became surplus to the requirements, and beyond the budget, of the college which employed her, she started a private class, which was greatly oversubscribed because her work was much sought after and exhibited. Her art, her animals and her family were all that concerned her; Neville was bad at remembering dates, anniversaries and birthdays, but the threads and skeins of her children's and grand-children's lives were always neatly sorted in Faith's heart.

Out of doors, in her gumboots and Burberry faded to the non-colour of wintry tussocks, Faith was part of the landscape. Beneath her coat she wore forest-coloured garments of her own weaving, according to the seasons; at present her clothes were putting on the pink tinge at the tips of twigs which precedes the green haze of early spring. A few weeks ago she had set aside her current project, *The Midsummer Cushion*, which was based on the poems of John Clare, in order to work on a commission for the village church. She had been asked to make a wall-hanging in commem-oration of two young regimental medics, a local boy and girl, killed by a roadside bomb in Afghanistan. The honour invested in her by the commission, the tragedy of its subject, the weight of respon-sibility to the bereaved families, were giving her sleepless nights. She got up, from muddled dreams, before dawn, defeated already by the task of creating something contemporary with these young people's lives which would embrace the universality of doomed youth, and yet be celebratory, emphasising idealism and heroism rather than futility. From the start, she had conceived a nest at the heart of the canvas, John Clare's 'The Pettichap's Nest', that scrappy, risky, warbler's nursery which was 'lined with feathers warm as silken stole/And soft as seats of down for painless ease/And full of eggs scarce bigger e'en then peas/Here's one most delicate with spots as small/As dust — and of a faint and pinky red — we'll, let them be and safety guard them well . . .' but, as Faith stitched, over the borders of the picture there came tramping, swarming, stumping on crutches and wooden pegs, a Bruegelesque army of the blind-folded blind leading the blind.

Cousin Beryl lived in an area of Dulwich transformed from the quiet suburb of their childhood into a place of cookware shops, cafés, organic butchers, fishmongers and delicatessens, with a number of junk and antiques shops, where the new affluent population could buy the amusing old furniture and kitchenware which had belonged to the previous owners of their houses, and put it back. Neville and Beryl, instead of going to the chippie as once they might have, had their pick of several restaurants for dinner on

Friday and Saturday night. Neville could hardly bear to look at his old family home, which he had sold after his parents died. It had been converted into flats long ago, and now all the windows were draped with heavy curtains, as they had been in the blackout. The front garden was concreted over and accommodated several wheelie bins and a dead fridge.

'It's probably a cannabis factory,' said Beryl, hurrying him past. 'At least it's not a crack house any more.'

Beryl's own parents' house, Uncle Frank's and Aunty Ivy's, which she had inherited, was still what her mother had once termed a little palace, if much modernised. And Mr and Mrs Kinsella still lived next door, behind ancient net curtains, with their three green Sylvac rabbits on the windowsill, a miniature fairyland of gnomes and toadstools in the front garden, and cascades of plastic flowers in their window boxes and hanging baskets defying the circling estate agents. 'Is that them? The Kinsellas?' said Neville, pointing at the two largest gnomes, all their paint gone and their features crumbling. Round the corner, on the site of the Frank L. Graham Photographic Gallery, a shop named Whirligig sold brightly coloured children's clothes and wooden toys. Faith would not have resisted buying something for the grandchildren but Neville found himself nostalgic for the Sunday inertia of his youth, the aching afternoons of waiting for something to happen.

The fire changed everything. It was as if the tainted black ash from the photographic gallery had got into them all. Beryl and Neville avoided each other. Uncle Frank took a job in a photo-processing laboratory, to which he cycled every day, and Aunty Ivy went to work in the shoe department of Morleys of Brixton. Beryl left school and took a secretarial course, instead of applying to an art school as she'd always wanted. Her first job was as office junior on a women's magazine. She started going around with a much older man, a Polish wheeler-dealer named Ziggy. Beryl said he was a war hero, from a noble family. Neville's father called him Comrade Ossipon, and Uncle Frank called him Count Poncakoff. Ziggy wore a flying jacket, and Neville thought now that he probably had been a hero, one of those pilots badly treated after the war. But that was no excuse for seducing a young girl. As a father and grandfather Neville cursed him and all his kind, who prey on the lovely and susceptible romantic girls who long for something beyond their sphere. But, whatever she'd done, Uncle Frank and Aunty Ivy should have taken better care of Beryl. After all, she was their jewel.

Beryl and Neville had grown up with a vague awareness of their distant aunt Florence Graham, one of whose journals, for the years 1863–1867, had somehow survived in a box of their grandparents' books. Florence had been a teacher at a private academy for young ladies on Beulah Hill. At the age of twenty-six, when she had decided that it was unlikely that she would marry, she received a legacy from the grandparents of a pupil she had befriended, a girl who had died from tuberculosis at the age of fifteen. Florence used her inheritance to establish a free school for sickly children, which she named The Garden School. She bought a house with an adjoining plot of land where the school was constructed to her own design; a single-storey brick building consisting of a narrow hall with pegs for the children to hang their things on, one airy classroom with large windows, informally arranged tables and chairs, a stove and a piano, a kitchen, and a cloakroom with little pedestal lavatories and washbasins. Whenever it was possible, lessons took place out of doors, for Florence's pupils were frail etiolated seedlings that needed to be carried into the light if they were to thrive. As Beryl remarked to Neville, it is quite possible that there are people living now, maybe distinguished people or just those whose lives have been enriched, descendants of the original scholars, who owe their love of nature, their education, their very existence to Florence Graham's Garden School.

'I wonder what became of The Garden School?' Neville had said. 'Florence's house, the school building, the garden itself. Do you think there's a chance it belongs to us?'

'All long gone, I guess. Even if it isn't, I don't suppose we'd have any claim. Nobody in the family ever said anything about it, did they?'

'We should find out.'

'You mean *I* should.'

Over the years since the school's closure, generations of children had made it their secret camp, a forgotten building whose roof was held on by ramblers, where ancient ivy cracked the white pedestals and basins where wrens nested. If you had pushed through the briars or tunnelled your way in, you might have sensed that it was once a happy place, where people were good, because the best was brought out of them. By the time Neville and Beryl were growing up, all that remained was a bomb crater filled with willowherb and buddleia, where children seeking treasure among the rubble might find a shard or two of porcelain, the leg of a small chair or a blackened brass coat peg clinging to a piece of rotten wood with a persistent streak of bird's-egg blue paint. At the beginning of the twenty-first century the garden was so overgrown that nobody, kids, lovers, criminals, attempted to explore it or use it for their hidden purposes. There had been some talk among conservationists of making the land into a little wildlife reserve but its potential as real estate had proved too tempting for the council, and a Big Yellow self-storage depot was in process of construction on the site of the school.

Beryl had come across several references in Florence Graham's journal to Archie Erskine and she suspected that there had been a romance between them but her research had not yet taken her that far. Like many families, the Grahams, from Scottish farming stock, had had their social ups and downs. Archie, a navvie born in Greenock, was not the obvious soulmate of a Victorian school-marm, but from what Beryl knew of her, such distinctions would not have bothered Florence. When they met, Florence would not have known anything of Norwood New Town, except that it had been built to house the artisans and navvies who built the Crystal Palace. It was walled to separate them from the respectable popu-lace nearby, and its gates patrolled by police to keep the drunks inside. At that time, although there were many public houses in the vicinity, there were also grand and beautiful houses whose residents must be protected from the rough influx of workers. Archie seemed to have been a cultivated, or at least a musical man, because there was more than one mention in Florence's diary of him accompanying the Garden School children's singing on the flute and the piano. Beryl imagined Archie as a gentle giant, an autodidact and radical who read widely, and studied in the evenings at Working Men's Institutes. Neville's interest in Archie Erskine sprang from the information that he had worked on the experimental Atmospheric Railway which ran for just a few months, in 1864–1865, between the Sydenham and Penge entrances of the Crystal Palace Gardens.

The Atmospheric Railway. Its name had enchanted Neville since first he heard it as a schoolboy. At once he'd seen a silver superstructure – the Atmospheric Railway arching across the sky on a series of viaducts supported by immensely tall pylon-like legs – and high, high up, a silver train streaming its own vapour through the clouds. What disillusion to discover that the train had actually been driven along the ground by the atmospheric pressure from earthbound pumping stations.

It was rather like the constructions he envisaged building with his Meccano; they never lived up to his imagination either. Neville and Beryl, and Faith too, had grown up at a time when children, except the poorest, were expected to have hobbies. Beryl had dozens of them, all faultlessly executed, from pompom golliwogs, French knitting, felt brooches, pokerwork, matchboxes, cheese labels and beyond; she collected film stars' autographs and had penfriends galore, and she had conducted a correspondence with Big Chief I-Spy himself, the author of the *I-Spy* books. She had badges up both sleeves of her Girl Guide uniform. Neville would not admit it, but she was actually better with fretwork, balsawood and Airfix kits than he was.

After leaving school without much idea of what he wanted to do, rather than pursue some more glamorous aspect of engineering, Neville took an apprenticeship in the firm where his father worked, a company which made central heating boilers and radiators. Neville, looking back, saw the sixties as a party to which he hadn't been invited. But he'd been happy. He progressed from the shop floor to the drawing office, met Faith in the National Gallery, fell in love at first sight, and pursued and married her. Meanwhile, Beryl's life had become a mystery, and Neville prospered, invested wisely, and was now enjoying his comfortable retirement as a grandfather, stalwart of a reading group and leading member of the Music Society, which was preparing to celebrate Elgar's 150th birthday.

Over the years, in a desultory hobby-ish way, Neville had done a bit of research into some of the other experimental atmospheric or pneumatic railways of the nineteenth century. The idea of travel by atmospheric pressure had caught the public imagination, and the trains were commended for their ability to climb steep gradients, the fact that they did not emit sparks which set fire to the railway banks, and did not frighten cattle and sheep into stampeding. He had read about the Dalkey and Kingston Railway, and Brunel's South Devon Railway, which cynics referred to as his 'Atmospheric Caper'. That was the most extensive of the atmospheric railways built, but only part of the fifty-two-mile section between Exeter and Plymouth was completed before Brunel, or the directors of the South Devon Railway, had to admit defeat. The railway proved devastatingly expensive and ran only between September 1847 and September 1848. There were frequent breakdowns, when third-class passengers had to disembark and push, but the chief problem again was the leather sealing valve, which deteriorated, and was eaten by rats. Constant replacement would have proved too costly.

Neville realised that he was just a dilettante and that there existed a cyber-community of troglodytes who were experts in the lost tunnels and rivers of England, subterranean trolls and elves inhabiting the ghostly pumping stations and engine houses of south London. Once there had been a railway flyover at South Norwood which carried the atmospheric line over the steam line to Brighton, and William Cubitt, engineer of the London and Croydon Railway, was such an advocate of the atmospheric principle that a railway was installed on a special experimental track from Forest Hill to West Croydon. How these names caught Neville's heart; with hindsight and increasing age, they were almost his Hornby and his Barlow long ago. Pumping stations were built at Forest Hill, Norwood and West Croydon. These were constructed with aesthetic consideration for the great houses nearby, in an ecclesiastical Early English or Gothic style, with their tall chimneys which carried away the smoke and exhausted air soaring like grandiose bell towers. The engineers referred to these towers as 'stalks'. The Forest Hill stalk, whose architect was W. H. Breakspear, stood 120 feet high. It was documented that on this line too there were unfortunate occasions when the male passengers were invited to alight from the train and help push it. On several occasions the train then went on its way, leaving the passengers behind.

Neville's train was not crowded but he was aware that there were several people in the carriage, probably going home like him, a few students with backpacks returning to Southampton University. He closed his eyes and let segments of the weekend replay themselves in his mind. The angels and obelisks of West Norwood Cemetery, crunching over frosty grass and leaves, snowdrops, celandines. That dead fox at West Norwood Station, when he was saying goodbye to Beryl. He became aware, with increasing irritation, of a toddler running, shrieking with laughter, up and down the aisle between the seats.

Neville, who indulged his own grandchildren, was determined not to make eye contact with this disruptive infant, but did notice that he was dressed in a rainbow-striped jumper and jeans and baby Timberland boots, and braids bobbed on his head as he ran past. The kid was under the misapprehension that the train was a playground provided for his amusement, and seemed to expect the applause of an admiring audience. Neville marvelled dully at such energy and high spirits so late in the day, and wondered if they were natural or induced by too much sugar, fizzy drinks and crisps.

Beryl and Neville had wandered through West Norwood Cemetery where, without a plan of the burial plots, they searched the wilder slopes, looking in vain among broken masonry for the graves of Florence Graham and Archie Erskine. By the time they walked the short distance to the station, from where they would go their separate ways, it was getting dark, and the station lights sparkled on some mineral component of the grey stone steps. They were waiting for Neville's train when Beryl suddenly gasped and grabbed his arm. Stretched out beside the rails, just under the lip of the opposite platform, was a dead fox. From where they stood it looked perfect, bright russet, white, grey and black in the dusk, without any sign of injury, but indisputably dead. None of the handful of people on either platform gave any sign of noticing it.

'We should tell somebody,' said Beryl. 'They can't just leave it there.'

But of course there was nobody to tell. The booking office was closed and there were no railway personnel on the station. Neville was secretly relieved, imagining the short shrift they would have incurred. He looked away from the beast in its red prime lying among the litter on the dirty stones and said, 'Did you know that Samuel Coleridge-Taylor, composer of *Hiawatha*, collapsed on West Croydon Station?'

'I don't blame him.'

'He died soon after, of pneumonia. In 1912.'

She shivered, pulling together the tawny faux-fur lapels of her coat, reminding Neville of photographs in the albums which they had been looking at, of their grandmothers and great aunts with dead foxes clasping their paws round their necks and birds' wings on their hats. Urban foxes all. Beryl had an old camera slung round her neck, although she hadn't taken any pictures, and was wearing a gingery hat pulled over her ears. Neville thought it was probably very chic, and the word 'cloche' came, inaccurately, to him.

'Did *you* know that Fitzroy, the one who replaced Finisterre on the Shipping Forecast, took his own life in his house on Church Road? We probably passed him in the cemetery,' she said. 'Here comes your train.'

She pulled him towards her in a hug, pushing the camera into his chest and knocking her hat askew.

'You take care,' he said, straightening her hat and stepping back.

'Look at you,' said Beryl, giving him a little push towards the train. 'Standing there like Rupert Bear in your checked scarf and little boots! Off home to Nutwood with you.'

The little boy was still rampaging, unchecked by whichever adult accompanied him. Neville could not see who it might be. He opened the book Beryl had lent him, *The Phoenix Suburb: A South London Social History*, by Alan Warwick. It was a second edition, published ten years after the original 1972 work, with an added final chapter by John Yaxley, Chairman of the Norwood Society. Neville flicked through the photographs, unable to concentrate on the text. What a wonderful, heartbreaking in view of the area's decline, portrait of Crystal Palace and its environs in its heyday. He recalled Faith's disparaging reference to Beryl's heyday, and erased it. But 'heyday' didn't come close to describing the beauty and inventiveness of those glory days of the nineteenth century, the great houses, woods, hills and meadows full of flowers and butterflies, the springs and wells, rivers, fountains and canals, all gone, and the people taking to the skies in enormous, fragile air balloons and aeroplanes; intricate, inflammable structures of wood, silk, paper and glue, soaring, drifting, banking over fields of lavender. And crowning it all a palace of crystal which changed colour with the sky, blazing red in the sunset as if rehearsing its final conflagration.

How we have degenerated, he thought. So many people now don't know how to make or mend anything, can't cook, can't read and write, can't look after their children. Both pride and shame have disappeared. When Neville looked up from his book he could see a man two seats up on the opposite side, on one of the four seats facing a table, a middle-aged man in biker's leathers with a shaven head and a forked grey beard. He watched him rip open a can of lager and drink, then put the beer on the table and open a newspaper. At which point, the kid who had been cruising the aisle approached, climbed onto the seat beside him, picked up the can and put it to his mouth.

'Hey!' Forkbeard suddenly noticed his new companion, and took the lager from him quite gently, but his whole head flushed scarlet, as if he was embarrassed at being mugged by such a tiny assailant. Neville laughed, and was ready to exchange a grin, but Forkbeard hid behind his paper. Soon Neville's amusement at the fearless innocent turned to dislike again as the child kept running, squealing, between the doors at either end of the compartment. Couldn't whoever was in charge exert some control, teach the kid some consideration for others? Of course not. Nobody had any respect for anybody else's space these days. As the smell of a noisomely digesting burger drifted towards him, he wrapped his scarf round his mouth and nose, inhaling the last traces of Beryl's scent. This happened every time he was on a train nowadays. Had nobody any self-control any more? Thumpety thump, here came those little boots again. And he could see a student's great plates of meat, in filthy trainers, on a seat. This lout had annoyed him earlier by going into the loo just as the train drew into Woking. He had that smell of unchanged polyester sheets. Neville felt his blood pressure rise at the thought of this generation stalking the earth, who know nothing, who don't know that you don't use the toilet while the train is standing at the station. Neville almost stuck out his foot to trip up the little boy as he came running past.

Beryl had told him that there was a reference in Florence's diary to an excursion with her pupils on the Atmospheric Railway. It cost sixpence a ride and she must have paid from her own pocket, Beryl said. Neville had not read it yet but was looking forward to Beryl's photocopied version. The railway, propelled by a steam engine coupled to a fan 22 feet in diameter, ran through a tunnel 600 yards in length and 10 feet in diameter. The tunnel gradient was 1 in 15 inches, with a sharp curve. He closed his eyes and pictured Florence, graceful in white muslin, shepherding her little flock through the sliding doors into the coach. It must have been a magical day for those children, dressed in their Sunday best, the girls in starched aprons, the jostling boys with polished boots. Or were they ragged and barefoot? He could remember kids at his primary school with holes in the seats of their trousers, no underpants, and the toes cut out of their plimsolls when they outgrew them, the ones in the Free Dinners queue. Nobody wanted to sit next to them on the Sunday School Treat, the annual visit to the seaside. There were thirty-five seats in the Atmospheric Railway's coach; perhaps respectable ladies had drawn their skirts away from Florence's school party, a top-hatted gentleman sniffed, and plump well-dressed children stared and sniggered.

No, it hadn't been like that, Neville decided. All the passengers must have shared the excitement, united in a democracy of novelty as they travelled into the scientific future. The children clung together as the coach took the curve, and when they emerged from the tunnel, the smiling top-hatted gentleman gave Florence half a crown to buy ice creams. Or perhaps Archie Erskine had accompanied them, explaining the mysteries of the ride. Neville saw him swing a pale, tubercular child onto his shoulders with one great hand, while pushing the invalid carriage of a boy too frail to walk with the other. And then Florence and Archie took the children to see the dinosaurs.

Neville remembered racing to the lakes of Crystal Palace Park with Beryl and their friends, the moment when suddenly the antlers of a giant elk loomed through the branches of the trees, and then a massive iguanadon hulked in the thickets, and the necks of marine reptiles reared out of the lagoons. They had returned to the park this afternoon, with its sad remains of balustered promenades and crumbling sphinxes, for a brief visit to the museum, housed in the old engineering school where John Logie Baird had established his television company. Of the Atmospheric Railway they could find no trace, although Neville had read that remnants of the tunnel had been unearthed in 1992.

Down the aisle the child, exhausted now, whimpered loudly, grizzled and began to yell. Why didn't somebody soothe him into sleep, or give him a drink, some sweets, a comic, crayons, anything? Neville had seen stone-faced mothers on buses, staring into space as if they had no connection with a hysterical child who was driving everybody else mad. This child's distress brought back to Neville the feeling of holding one of his own children when she was demented by tiredness, trying to contain the writhing body thrashing about in his arms, and her hard head splitting his lip. Surely this one must cry himself out soon. But the screams went on, the little boy would not be consoled or placated; his throat must be raw. There was something in the timbre of his voice which impacted on Neville's nervous system like an electric saw. Each relentless 'aah aaah waaah' drilled through his chest, giving him actual physical pain. There was darkness outside and bright lights within and this terrible noise was forcing him into a corner. Forkbeard had lain his head on the table, with his arms clasped round it. Neville felt like crying. He thought about Faith, who was programmed to burst into tears whenever she heard a baby's first cry, in however schlocky a film or TV play it might occur.

'Shut up, shut up, can't you make it shut up?' Neville shouted silently.

He knew he should move seats, further up the train, but sat there, holding his breath in the vacuum between two screams, waiting for the next one. Every time the kid drew breath, Neville pictured his lungs, painfully pink and distended. Neville sat on, hating himself for feeling murderous towards that little body, to the scream person ified that the kid had become. So much for Archie Erskine tenderly hoisting an ephemeral child onto his shoulders.

The train drew in to Eastleigh Station where it was to divide, and Neville realised that a blissful silence had fallen as the guard repeated his announcement that passengers for stations to Poole should be in the front five carriages. Forkbeard got out. When the train started again, Neville stood up to check if the child had left and saw him, all cried out, on a woman's lap. There was a man sitting next to her, presumably the dad, reading a newspaper.

Breathing a deep sigh of relief, Neville opened his book again and started to leaf through the photographs. He looked up with a stab of alarm as a big man in a bulky padded jacket rushed past, causing a wind that ruffled the pages. Then he realised that the train had stopped, and he became aware of a commotion further down the carriage. The train started going backwards. An announcement came over the intercom: 'This is your driver informing you that due to an operational incident, we will be returning to Eastleigh Station.'

Well, that's just typical of a Sunday night on South West Trains, thought Neville. He looked at his watch. About now, Faith would be plugging herself into her valiant little Honda Civic and setting off through the forest to the station car park. He was about to ring her to say that he'd been delayed, and vent his fury at this hideous journey on her, when he saw the man in the padded coat, with a fluorescent strip across the shoulders, returning down the aisle.

'Excuse me, can you tell me what's going on?'

'The train pulled out of Eastleigh, leaving the guard behind on the platform. I saw the rear doors were open and I managed to alert the driver and secure the doors. I'm an off-duty guard from up north,' he explained, towering over the seated Neville.

Neville stared at his mild, kindly face, topped with curly brown hair.

'An operational incident? Sheer bloody incompetence! How long's this going to take? My wife will be waiting for me.'

'Dunno, mate. I'm just a passenger like you.'

When, after a long, slow reverse, the train arrived back at Eastleigh, Neville saw the off-duty guard talking to a couple of uniformed figures on the platform. No doubt incident sheets and forms would have to be filled in in triplicate. A woman took advantage of the stop to alight and have a cigarette. Suddenly he was back in the restaurant with Beryl. He'd taken a cigarette from her initialled gold cigarette case – not her initials, those of some man, he supposed, or even that woman who had left a lipstick in the pocket of the bathrobe. As Beryl lit it for him, she said, 'Careful with that. I don't know if I can trust you with cigarettes.' The waiter had brought the bill and the significance of her seemingly jocular remark passed him by. Now it hit him. For all these years, Beryl had thought he was responsible for the fire which had destroyed her father's shop. She *had* been at her friend Susan's house that night.

Neville could not begin to explore the implications, because only then did it strike him that if the child had not cried himself to sleep, if he had still been charging up and down, he would have run, laughing, straight out of the open doors into a black void, and his little boots would have gone on running a few steps on nothingness, before he fell through darkness onto the track.

The train was inching forwards again. He sat frozen in shame. It was almost as if he had willed the child to disappear. As if the collective hostility and indifference of the adult passengers had conspired to punish him. But it didn't happen. It didn't happen, he told himself.

The child was still sleeping and, out of the past and into the quietness, there came to Neville the memory of another desolate noise. It was the sound of a woman howling and howling. Neville, Faith and the children were on a plane, coming back from a holiday. It was the day after the roll-on-roll-off car ferry the *Herald of Free Enterprise* sank off Zeebrugge, on the 6th of March, 1987. Nearly two hundred people drowned. Because somebody forgot to secure the bow doors on the car deck. Neville saw the off-duty guard getting ready to leave the train at Southampton Airport Parkway Station. If it were not too fanciful, he might think that this burly bloke was not merely a guard, but the little boy's guardian angel.

Neville stood up. He realised that it might not have been only the child who was in danger, but anybody aboard the train. He,

Neville, had not seen that the doors were open. He had been surly and petulant, and now he must acknowledge what the guard had done.

'Well done, mate. Good thing you were there. Thanks.'

The guard laughed. 'I can't wait to tell them about this back home,' he said cheerfully.

Faith was waiting in the car park.

'"Well, I declare, it is the pettichap!" At last,' she said, as he got into the car. 'How's Beryl? And the Atmospheric Railway?' she asked, and as she spoke, Neville remembered the little white card with which he'd been playing at Beryl's kitchen table. It had on it the name of a Spiritualist church. Who would Beryl be trying to contact? How bleak to have left her standing on West Norwood Station.

'Fine. You? How was your weekend?'

'Oh, fine,' she said eventually, braking behind two ponies which were ambling along in the middle of the road.

Nanny

London was beige, taupe, grey and dirty white, the river the colour of the cappuccino he bought at the station, when the writer and critic Campbell Forsythe left the city, in a first-class compartment of a train heading eastward. He was on his way to give a talk to a literary society in the country town of Ditcham. Campbell took off his wide-brimmed leather hat, shaking loose the shoulder-length grey hair which matched his silky beard, removed his fur-collared trench-coat and stretched out his legs, in snakeskin boots and jeans, leaning back in his seat to enjoy a hot meat pasty with his newspaper. As he read, gravy spurted onto the obituary of a former colleague. He rubbed it and licked his finger while combing the text with his eyes in a practised technique for any reference to himself. Nothing. The old fool's egocentricity persisted beyond the grave. Campbell turned to the crossword, slapping the paper into shape.

Professor Campbell Forsythe had no need to study the text of his lecture, *Metamorphosis and Metafiction*. He had delivered it many times, at home and abroad, from Palookaville to Hotzeplotz, and now Ditcham, dull as ditchwater. This gig was a piece of cake. The group's president, one Sidney Black, presuming on a slight acquaintance, had invited Campbell, who had retaliated by demanding a higher fee than the society usually paid. The lecture would be followed by an early dinner at some local hostelry, in time to catch a train back to town. Normally, Campbell would have turned down the meal but today he was glad of an excuse to stay out as things were not too good on the home front. It might have been assumed that the domestic arrangements of a man of Campbell's years would have involved a wife rather than a partner of six months' standing, but the truth was that he had had three wives and was actually still married to a fourth. So far as he knew, he had seven children and several grandchildren.

London had been dreary, but as soon as Campbell emerged from

Ditcham Station and stood on the forecourt looking for the taxi rank he felt a bit of excitement in the sky, speeding clouds and a warm damp wind flirting with his hair and beard, a frisson in the leaves as if the trees were a welcoming party, a line of frou-frou majorettes shaking green and yellow pompoms to greet him. It was a short drive to the venue, which stood at the centre of a municipal park, and Campbell noticed that neither nature nor human beings knew what season it was. A bird flew past with a beakful of twigs, some trees were shedding scarlet and gold leaves while others were green or in blossom, roses consorted with michaelmas daisies, and the tips of spring bulbs pecked through the mould where the autumn crocuses were dancing like girls, girls, girls in purple dresses. Some of the flesh-and-blood girls he passed were wearing sleeveless tops and shorts, others had gone into boots and jumpers, and the rest had opted for a mixture of both styles. Campbell had an odd sensation, as if he were entering the hall carrying a bunch of regrets like anemones.

Metamorphosis and Metafiction ran true to form; polite applause was followed by a period of question time, where his anecdotes about literary celebrities neither he nor the audience had met united everybody cosily. The light above the lectern where he stood glared onto his reading glasses, but as he spoke he raked the hall for talent, somebody attractive whom he would invite along to combat the dullness of dinner, using the expertise with which he had combed the obituary for his own name. Again as he had expected, he was addressing an assortment of cauliflowers, whiskery mangel-wurzels and hard-boiled eggs; in short, his contemporaries.

His eye found a bespectacled woman on the end of the front row, crossing one leg over the other so that it projected into the aisle. The folds of her skirt fell back, revealing her shin. Campbell blinked, he faltered, and broke off in mid-sentence. The last time he had seen a leg like that was in Borough Market where, disembodied, it pointed up from the centre of a display of charcuterie and cheeses. The leg was slender and elegant and covered in dense hair, and it terminated in a polished cloven hoof.

'I . . . I . . . I . . . ' he stuttered, 'I'm sorry, I've lost my thread. Could you repeat the question please? Have I ever met a were-wolf in real life? Not to my knowledge, no.'

The woman in the front row shifted in her seat and her skirt fell back again, so that all he could see was what could only be the pointed toe of a boot.

'We have time for just one more question,' said Sidney. 'You, sir, in the beige windcheater.'

'Would you contend, Professor Forsythe, in view of recent scientific developments, such as GM crops and the cloning of animals and cross-species embryonic experimentation, that truth is still stranger than fiction, or, in this instance, metafiction?' The speaker sat down, looking pleased with himself.

'Ah, but what is truth?' parried Campbell, bringing the proceedings to a close.

Volunteers were setting out coffee cups and glasses, and not a moment too soon the wine was opened. An egghead was offering a silver foil tray of warm cocktail sausages and Campbell grabbed a handful, cramming them into his mouth, so that grease ran into his beard, as he signed a copy of one of his books with the hand which held his glass. 'I can see that you're well-practised at this signing lark,' said the book's owner. 'I was so lucky to pick it up in the PDSA shop this morning. Quite a coincidence, really. Makes you think.'

Somebody else had brought along her copy of *The Golden Bough* for Campbell to sign. He left a grease stain on its flyleaf.

'Hello, Campbell. Have a napkin.'

The woman from the front row was holding out a bunch of paper napkins. Campbell wiped his chin, trying to get a look at her legs, but short of lying on the floor, there was nothing he could do.

'Do you two know each other?' asked Sidney.

'I don't think we've met,' Campbell was replying as the woman said, 'It's Nancy.'

'Nancy? The name rings a bell, but I'm sorry . . .'

'A bell on a child's tricycle?' she suggested. 'Church bells pealing for a wedding, perhaps?'

'Nancy's one of our poets,' explained Sidney.

'You used to call me Nancy with the Laughing Face,' she prompted Campbell.

'Oh, surely not . . .'

Campbell stared. She had a long face, her teeth were not good, and her grizzled hair was caught back in a clasp and fanned onto the collar of her grey coat. He could not read the expression in her eyes because they were shaded by the tinted lenses of her rectangular-framed spectacles.

'Or nanny with the laughing face . . .'

Then it came to him. The woman had been a nanny to some of his children, but from which family, he couldn't remember. They'd had to get rid of her. He thought he recalled a tedious aspiration to poetry.

'Nancy!' he exclaimed, switching on a smile. 'What brings *you* to Ditcham?'

'Oh, I've lived here in poverty and obscurity for some years.'

Presumably she had not been so hirsute in the past. Hadn't she been all milk and roses then? He tasted vanilla and heard, through the high windows of a nursery, the chimes of an ice-cream van in a summer street, on an afternoon when he had found himself alone in the house with Nancy.

'We should be making a move if we're going to eat,' said Sidney. 'I'll just round up a few folk – I'm afraid it'll be a bit of a crush in the car but . . .'

'Oh, I'll take Campbell in mine,' said Nancy. 'The Capricorn Bistro in the Shambles. We'll see you there.'

'Well, actually, I rather think I ought to get straight back after all. It's getting late and . . .'

But almost without knowing what was happening, Campbell found himself outside, in his hat and coat, Nancy leading him firmly by the arm through the moonlit park.

'I'm in a side street, it's not far,' she told him.

After walking for some ten minutes in her grasp, Campbell complained, 'Just where *is* your car? Have you forgotten where you parked it?'

'It's really quicker to walk. Through this gate now.'

'But this looks like some sort of track. We seem to be getting farther and farther from the town. My boots are getting ruined.'

'Trust me,' said Nancy, dragging him along.

'No, this is getting ridiculous. We're in a field. Let go of me!'

'Let go of you? Like you let go of me?'

'What do you mean? You're insane.'

'You sacrificed me to save your marriage to Jill, then a year later you left her for somebody else. You broke your children's hearts as well as mine when you threw me out.'

Her grip was cold and hard; he couldn't shake her off. 'But Nancy,' he bleated, 'it was so long ago. We were so young – just a couple of crazy kids!'

'I was,' she said. 'And when I published my book of verse, you trashed it in *Poetry Now. I* was ruined, and you come here in your fur and cashmere and snakeskin and tell me your boots are ruined!'

They struggled, and Nancy's glasses were knocked to the ground. In the moonlight, he saw with terror that the pupils of her yellow eyes were rectangular, as she clamped a hoof either side of his head. 'Nancy, who *are* you? What have you done to yourself? No, no, please, Nancy!' he cried, as her rough cheek grazed his and her mouth approached. Then she lifted her upper lip and sank long yellow teeth into his lower lip. Campbell howled as she sprang back, bunched up all four of her legs, leaped sideways onto a hillock, and was gone, leaving a baaa-ing laugh trailing across the night sky.

Campbell tried to stumble back the way they had come, holding his handkerchief to his throbbing lip, but the moon had disappeared behind clouds. At the same moment he realised that not only was he utterly lost but that he had lost his hat, his mobile, his wallet and his lecture. He was aware that the rankness in his nostrils was coming from his own mouth, and that Nancy's breath had smelled of sweet milk and roses. On he went, tripping and falling over tussocks and thistles, towards a block of buildings on the flat horizon. He thought it must be some structure housing immigrant agro-business workers. Surely somebody there would be able to help him.

Was that sound the throbbing of a generator, or the blessed hum of the motorway? Skirting an encampment of pigs in corrugated-iron Anderson shelters, for he was very afraid of pigs, he approached the buildings. He could hear music. Somebody was having a party inside. There were no windows but a beam of light blazed through a crack in one wall, and he choked on the vilest stench he had ever encountered, from heaps of chicken manure mixed with burned feathers and rotting carcases.

Campbell ran, as a chained dog gave voice, and ran until he sank onto a bale of straw, and huddled there, a dank billy goat at the end of his tether. Nancy, he sobbed, but it came out as a desolate whimper of 'Nanny'. He wanted his old nanny now. He needed Nanny Gomershall to soothe him, 'There, there, little one, go back to sleep, you've just been having a bad dream.' Chekhov was right, Campbell thought through his tears, Chekhov understood that however eminent a man might be, however towering his intellect, at the end of the day, the only person who would do was his old nurse.

Radio Gannet

There were two sisters, Norma and Dolly, christened Dorothy, who lived in a seaside town. Norma and her husband, Eric, resided in a large detached house in Cliftonville Crescent, while Dolly's caravan was berthed at the Ocean View Mobile Home Park, on the wrong side of the tracks of the miniature steam railway. Norma and Dolly's elder brother, Walter, was the curator of the small Sponge Museum founded by their grandfather.

Eastcliff-on-Sea was a town divided. The prizewinning municipal gardens overlooked Sandy Bay where all the beach huts had been bought up by Londoners wanting traditional bucket-and-spade holidays, and as their offspring watched the Punch and Judy show while eating their organic ice cream, or played a sedate game of crazy golf, they could see the lights of the funfair winking across the tracks, and hear the shouts of less privileged children on the rides and smell their burgers, doughnuts and candyfloss drifting on the breeze from the ramshackle plaza that was Ocean View.

Norma had five children and fourteen grandchildren, thus ensuring that she had somebody to worry about at any given moment. One particularly hot summer night, she lay awake fretting at the news that a giant asteroid was on course to hit the earth sometime in the future. She groped for her bedside radio and switched it on low so as not to disturb Eric. Her finger slipped on the dial and out of the radio came the squawk of a gull, followed by a voice singing 'All you hear is Radio Gannet, Radio gaga, Radio Gannet. Greetings, all you night owls, this is Radio Gannet taking you through the wee small hours with Joanne and The Streamliners and their ever-lovin' "Frankfurter Sandwiches".'

At the female DJ's voice, Norma sat bolt upright, hyperventilating. Over the music came the spluttering of fat in a pan, and a muffled expletive. It was the indisputable sound of her sister Dolly having a fry-up. 'Whatever happened to the good old British banger?' grumbled Dolly. 'Answers on a postcard, please.'

Norma sat transfixed, picturing Dolly at the Baby Belling with her tail of grey-blonde hair hanging over her dressing gown, slipshod in downtrodden espadrilles, in that terrible caravan with its tangle of dead plants in rotting macramé potholders, Peruvian dream-catchers, etiolated things growing out of old margarine tubs, the encrusted saucers left out for hedgehogs by the door, the plastic gnomes bleached white by time. The budgie. The cat. The slugs.

She hadn't seen her sister since their father's funeral, when Dolly had grabbed the microphone from the vicar and launched into 'Wind Beneath My Wings'. Dolly was dressed in frayed denim, cowgirl boots and a kiss-me-quick cowgirl hat.

In the morning Norma dismissed the radio programme as a bad dream. She was taking a brace of grandchildren to buy their new school shoes for the autumn term. It was one of those days when people tell each other that 'it's not the heat, it's the *humidity*'. In the shoeshop they were served by an apathetic girl with a film of sweat on her upper lip who showed little enthusiasm for measuring the children's feet, gazing ahead as if watching a procession of Odor-Eaters marching into eternity. Music played in the background; a common family was creating havoc with the Barbie and Star Wars trainers. Norma looked fondly at her grandchildren. Their legs were the colour of downy, sun-kissed apricots in the sensible shoes she was insisting on. Suddenly, there it was again, the squawking gull, that idiotic jingle.

'This is Radio Gannet coming to you on – some kilohertz or other, I can never remember. Kilohertz – what's that in old money, anyway? I blame the boffins in Brussels, myself. This one's specially for you, all you metric martyrs out there: "Pennies from Heaven" – hang on, a road traffic report's just coming in. It's Mr Wilf Arnold ringing from the call box on the corner of Martello Street where a wheelie bin has overturned, shedding its load . . .'

As soon as she had paid for the shoes Norma hurried the children round to the Sponge Museum to consult her brother. Walter's nose had grown porous with the passing years; it was an occupational hazard.

'Great Uncle Walter, have you ever thought of making the museum a bit more interactive? You need a hands-on approach if you're going to compete in the modern world,' said Matilda.

'Yeah, like Sea World. With octopuses and killer whales and sharks. Everything in here's dead,' agreed Sam.

'There's far too much of this touchy-feely nonsense nowadays in my opinion,' said Walter. Norma nodded agreement, imagining herself in the wet embrace of an octopus.

'Go and improve your minds,' Walter told them. 'And if you behave yourselves, you can choose a souvenir from the shop. How about a nice packet of Grow-Your-Own Loofah seeds?'

When they had slouched away, sniggering, Norma told Walter what she'd heard, recounting how Dolly had signed off, saying, 'Keep those calls and e-mails coming, and as always, my thanks to Mr Tibbs, my producer.'

'Mr Tibbs? Isn't that her cat?' said Walter.

'Exactly. She's totally bonkers – remember the spectacle she made of herself at the funeral? *I* wouldn't have said that Daddy was the wind beneath Dolly's wings, would you, Walter?'

He considered. 'Well, he did sponsor her for that bungee jump off the pier, *and* he made her that fairy dress with glittery wings for her birthday.'

'It was *my* birthday,' said Norma.

'Yes, I'm afraid our father always indulged Dolly,' admitted Walter.

'Well, look where it's got him. I hardly think even Daddy would approve of her latest venture. We can only trust that nobody we know will tune into Radio Gannet.'

Walter's Rotarian connections and Norma's aspiration to serve as Eastcliff's Lady Mayoress hung unspoken between them.

'Radio Gannet, eh? How appropriate.'

Walter remembered a plump little fairy flitting about the table at a children's party, touching cakes and jellies with the silver star at the tip of her magic wand. Norma thought about her sister's three helpings of tiramisu at her youngest son's wedding. She'd turned that into a karaoke too. Then the sound that she and Walter had been half-listening out for, that of a display cabinet toppling, recalled them to the present.

'Where is this so-called radio station to be found?' asked Walter.

'Oh, at the wrong end of the dial. Where you get all those foreign and religious programmes.'

'But is she legal? I mean, do you think she's got a licence to broadcast? It could well be that our dear sister is a pirate, in which case something can be done to put a stop to her little game. Leave Dolly Daydream to me, Norma.'

It was time for a weather check at Radio Gannet. 'Let's see what Joey the weather girl has in store for us this afternoon. Over to you at the Weather Centre, Joey.'

The Weather Centre was the budgerigar's cage which hung in the open doorway with strips of seaweed trailing from its bars. Dry seaweed denoted a fine spell, while when it turned plump and moist, rain was in the offing.

'Pretty boy, pretty boy,' said Joey.

'Pretty dry – good news for all you holidaymakers, then. Uh oh,' Dolly stretched out to touch a ribbon of kelp and found it dripping. The caravan park was shrouded in grey drizzle. 'Joey says better pop the brolly in the old beach bag, just in case.'

Joey was popular with the listeners. A recent beak problem had brought sackloads of cuttle-fish and millet from well-wishers, many of them students. 'I'm only sending this ironically,' one of them had written. Dolly was flattered; she knew that students do everything ironically nowadays; watch kids' TV, eat Pot Noodles; they even iron their jeans ironically. She placed her 78 of 'Any Umbrellas' on the turntable, put her feet up and reached for the biscuit barrel.

Dolly was truly happy, having found her niche at last in public service broadcasting. Her *Send a Pet to Lourdes* campaign was coming along nicely and the coffers were swelling with milk-bottle tops and unused Green Shield stamps; the jigsaw swapshop was up and running, and the day care centre had asked her to put out an announcement that they had exceeded their quota of multi-coloured blankets. That *Unravel Your Unwanted Woolies and Make Something Useful* wheeze had been a triumph; the charity shops were full of its results. But fame, Dolly knew, came with a price. Like every celebrity, she had attracted a stalker. Hers had staring yellow eyes and a maniacal laugh. He tracked her through the plaza on pink webbed feet, he snatched ice lollies from her hand in the street, and chips from her polystyrene tray, tossing them aside if she hadn't put on enough vinegar. He brought a whole new meaning to 'take-away' food.

Radio Gannet went off the airwaves altogether when Dolly had to go down the shops; at other times listeners heard only the gentle snoring of the presenter and her producer Mr Tibbs.

'Coming up – six things to do on a rainy day in Eastcliff, but now it's paper and pencils at the ready, for *Dolly's Dish of the Day*. And it's a scrummy Jammie Dodger coffee cheesecake recipe sent in by Mrs Elsie Majors of Spindrift, Ocean View Plaza. For this, you'll need four tablespoons of Camp Coffee, a large tin of condensed milk, a handful of peanuts for the garnish, and a packet of Jammie Dodgers, crushed. And here's a Dolly Tip for crushing the biscuits: place them in a plastic bag, tie securely, and bash them with a rolling pin. If you haven't got a plastic bag handy, the foot cut off an old pair of tights will do just as well . . .

'Thanking you kindly, Elsie,' she concluded. 'Your pipkin of Radio Gannet hedgerow jam is winging its way to you even as we speak.'

Or will be, as soon as Dolly has soaked the label off that jar of Spar Mixed Berry and replaced the lid with one of her crochet covers.

In Cliftonville Crescent Norma and Eric were listening in horror as the programme continued.

'This one's for all you asylum seekers out there – "They're Coming to Take Me Away Ha Ha". That ought to get the politically correct brigade's knickers in a twist. Which reminds me, don't forget to text your entries for the Radio Gannet Political Correctness Gone Mad competition. "Fly's in the sugar bowl, shoo fly shoo,"' she sang. '"Hey hey, skip to my loo . . ."' and Radio Gannet went temporarily off the air.

'Dolly inhabits a parallel universe,' said Norma, scarlet with shame.

How it rained. Pennies from heaven. Stair rods. Cats and dogs. In the museum the sponges trembled and swelled in their glass cases, great sensitive blooms and castles and honeycombs saturated with the moisture in the air. Walter listened glumly to 'Seasons in the Sun' on Radio Gannet. He'd been in touch with the authorities. Yet, like the man in the song, the stars that he'd reached were just starfish on the beach. His only visitors had been a couple of Canadian tourists on the Heritage Trail. Apparently they'd been misled by something they'd picked up on their hotel radio and were expecting an exhibition of sponge cakes through the ages. From King Alfred to Mr Kipling.

Dolly's voice broke into his thoughts.

'Joey at the Weather Centre has handed me a severe weather warning. "How high's the water, Mamma? Six feet high and risin' . . .'''

Walter rushed out to check his sandbags.

That night a tremendous crash brought Norma and Eric leaping from their bed to the window. Norma had lain awake worrying about an asteroid hitting the earth. Now she was about to experience the collision of two worlds. Cresting a tsunami was her sister's caravan and then the whole parallel universe was deposited in Cliftonville Crescent. It was like a scene from a Stanley Spencer Resurrection; the entire population of Ocean View Mobile Home Park were struggling out of their caravans in their night clothes, clutching plastic bags doubtless filled with old Green Shield stamps and unwashed milk-bottle tops, and there was Dolly splashing through the debris with her producer Mr Tibbs, Joey the Weather Girl, and a herring gull perched on her head.

The Lower Loxley Effect

Everybody said it was easy to get hold of a gun in this part of town. So far she'd drawn a blank. Not that she'd consulted anyone of course, but the newspapers and radio and television were full of reports of weapons changing hands for comparatively small sums of money. Although Linda Carpenter had only one victim in mind, increasingly nowadays there was murder in her heart. Almost every aspect of modern life had her trigger finger itching and her fantasy hit-list was long and growing. It was just as well, she thought, that she had not been armed on the bus she had taken to get here.

At dawn she had stood at her back door watching a flock of parakeets wheeling and skirling in the white sky and they had lifted her heart and taken it over the treetops; her neighbour Mr Errol emerged to enjoy his first cigarette of the day on the bench beside his pumpkin patch; the coils of his smoke lay on the frosty air. He never smoked in the house. Miss Carpenter and Mr Errol had slept side by side for thirty years, separated by a thin barrier of brick and plaster. They were familiar with each other's nightwear, for both liked to take the air early and beneath the stars. On torrid nights when nobody could sleep their formal greetings flew like pale night birds. In the summer they exchanged gifts of pumpkins, beans, tomatoes and jam over the garden wall and every Christmas they swapped a bottle of over-proofed rum for a festive tin of shortbread. Neither knew whether the choice of present was appreciated, as they had never crossed one another's thresholds, yet Miss Carpenter counted Mr Errol as a friend.

The day had come gift-wrapped in white tissue and sparkling tinsel but now, several hours later, Linda was elbowing through slow-moving herds of mothers with buggies, crowds who blocked the pavement at bus stops, failing to form orderly queues, and battling along past traffic at a standstill with horns blaring and belching out exhaust fumes and music, for want of a better word, and flinching

35

from the yelping of a trapped police car. There was not a smile to be seen on that long road except among the bunch of teenagers tormenting a companion. One note of sweetness came from the paper bag of guavas she was carrying; seduced by their pink-flushed fragrance, she had bought them from a shop which boasted, on the blackboard outside, parrot fish, octopus, shark's fin and cowheel. She held the bag to her face like a nosegay to counteract the smell of cooking meat from a kebab shop.

Passing the nightclub, so tawdry by day with its unlit coloured bulbs, sealed up since the latest shooting, she felt a pang of envy for her brothers, Maurice in the English countryside, Jim in rural France, where he and his wife Jill were living their retirement dream of running an organic snail farm. The rope of their home-grown garlic hanging in her kitchen was a pungent reminder that she had still not yet read the manuscript of *Precious Escargot*, the account of their adventures which they were confident would be a bestseller and possibly a television series. Jim and Jill assumed that Linda, as a former English teacher with time on her hands, would enjoy knocking it into shape, but her days of marking homework were over, thank you very much. The garlic might have warded off vampires for all she knew, but it had failed singularly to deter her mortal enemy from his nocturnal predations. Herding gastropods was not her idea of bliss but oh, she was sick of this bad-tempered city where everything was dirty and broken.

There was a place where she would love to be, a village called Ambridge, the jewel of Borsetshire. How happy she and her cat Tybalt could be in that rural community; in fact she wished heartily that she had put in an offer for Nightingale Farm when game old Marjorie Antrobus had to move into The Laurels retirement home. Brian Aldridge's wistful words, as he agonised over whether to flee to Germany with Siobhan and baby Ruairi, haunted her. 'Borsetshire is such a beautiful county,' he'd sighed. And she knew it to be true for her brother Maurice had sent her the *Archers* calendar for Christmas, as she had posted one to him. Maurice, a retired Classics master, shared her addiction to the long-running radio soap opera, which meant that they were never at a loss for something to say on the telephone. 'Well, I'm just off to a blind beef-tasting in Jolene's restaurant,' he had signed off their last conversation.

'And I must take my lemon drizzle cake out of the oven,' she countered. 'Don't shoot any badgers.'

To get out of the noise of the street she pushed through the bedspreads and assorted shopping trolleys hanging either side of the doorway of a shop. At first it seemed an Aladdin's cave full of sparkling treasures, fluorescent flashes, spotted and striped animal pelts, phosphorescent spinules, lava lamps and the gleam of gold and silver threads on velvet cushions, then she realised there was nothing on the shelves one could possibly want. The emporium, once some grander establishment, was spacious, with crammed shelves running round the walls and central banks displaying bedlinen and towels and baskets of goods, underwear, socks and scented candles on the floor. She caught sight of herself in a gilt-framed mirror which reflected a stout pixie in a quilted jerkin over a polo neck, trousers and pointed red boots. Her bobble-hat, being acrylic, had risen to perch on the top of her head and electrified her silver-grey helmet of hair. Her cheeks were as scarlet as little Cox's apples which had been left for too long in the fruit bowl. Nobody would guess that beneath that neat exterior beat the heart of a ten-year-old tomboy, living in fear of a neighbour's violent knocking on the door, to accuse about a broken pane in a conservatory. She had always been a duffer at games, and her aim had fallen far short of its target in a crash of breaking glass as her enemy's eyes glittered and disappeared in the darkness.

It occurred to her that she might find what she was after here. To the left of the entrance, on a sort of dais behind the till, from where he could observe thieves, stood the proprietor talking vehemently on his mobile. Then she saw, half concealed by a posse of fake Barbies, exactly the weapon she'd been looking for. Double barrelled, dual-triggered, it looked as if it would have a long enough range. Delighted, she waved it at the man.

'This is just what I want. I've looked everywhere, Woolworths, those newsagents that sell tacky toys. How much?'

'£3.99.'

'£3.99? That's a bit steep.'

He must have seen her coming.

'Yes, cheap.'

'Anyway, I can't be bothered to haggle. I'll take it.'

So, with a blue and yellow two-cylinder water pistol tucked into her jerkin pocket, Linda set off for home to load it in anticipation of a visit from her enemy. She couldn't wait. For the first time she hoped rather than dreaded that she would find him in her house. Twin jets of freezing water would show him what's what. Linda lived alone with her cat, Tybalt, a slender mackerel tabby, named after Tibert the cat in *Reynard the Fox*, whose name was the equivalent of Tybalt. It had more gravitas than 'Tibbles', which had been her colleague Amaryllis's suggestion. For many years they had shared the house amicably until one day, out of the blue, Amaryllis had purchased a camper van and set off for New Zealand. Truth to tell, Amaryllis was a doleful soul, but her going enabled Linda to empathise with a friend whose beloved basset-hound had passed on.

'It's coming home to an empty house . . . ' her friend mourned. 'He was always there to greet me, to give me a welcome whatever. I find myself with a trolleyful of tins in Sainsbury's, and then I have to put them all back . . .'

'I know.'

'You are such a pessimist,' Linda had told Amaryllis during one of their dull dinners, 'while I'm always the optimist. My glass is half full, whereas yours is half empty.'

'My glass is half empty because you've been drinking my wine,' Amaryllis pointed out.

Still, Linda had always been on the side of life. But now life had shrunk, while she herself had not. With Amaryllis gone Linda found herself eating twice as much because she could not get out of the habit of shopping for two. However, over-catering was not Linda's only, or her most pressing, problem.

In Amaryllis's absence somebody else had muscled in on her patch. Flatface was a white and brindled bull-headed tomcat who, sensing Linda's vulnerability, took every opportunity to invade. Linda had begun to dread going out for the evening. She had spent a quiet Christmas at home, refusing invitations because it was not worth returning to the evidence of a visit from Flatface. The place stank where he had marked out what was in actuality Tybalt's territory, but, alas, Tybalt, Good King of Cats, was a wimp, a wuss, who would hide under a chair while Flatface licked his food bowl clean. Flatface sported a new Christmas collar which no doubt claimed him as somebody's darling pet, but she could never catch him to read his disc, and so protest to his owners that he was ruining her life.

Recently she had returned from her god-daughter's wedding and, still in her nuptial coat and hat, had to snap on her Marigolds, of matching pink, and get down on her knees with a J-Cloth and disinfectant, trying to sniff out the scene of the crime. She had spent a small fortune on air-fresheners and fabric deodorants. Flatface had sprayed her clean washing with noxious liquid more than once, and slept on her bed. Worse even than that, she was now obliged to lock the cat flap at night and her sleep was disturbed by Tybalt's demands to come in and out of her bedroom window. Worst of all, one night he had jumped onto her pillow with something dangling from his mouth. Linda blamed Flatface's influence; Tybalt, despite his name, had never done that sort of thing until he came on the scene.

While Linda was shopping for her gun, her brother Maurice sat in his study deflecting the verbal blows of Mrs Furzell who came in to clean once a week.

'Family down this weekend, Professor?'

'Oh yes, they'll all be descending,' he replied weakly.

Now he would have to drag out the cardboard cut-outs to avert the no-visitor Sunday disgrace. A few years ago Maurice had hit on the idea of making facsimiles of his family and propping them in various attitudes around the sitting room so that passers-by, Mrs Furzell in particular, would see them through the window. On the occasion of their last outing he'd noticed how shabby they had become, and his son Richard's head was wobbling; he would have to reinforce his neck with parcel tape. Then, their lack of a car was a constant worry. It was only a matter of time before Mrs Furzell would notice there was no car; she was always upgrading her own. It was only just past Twelfth Night and he'd spent Christmas with Richard, daughter-in-law Suzie and his grandsons, Lawrence and Sammy, although unfortunately he'd left behind a new cashmere scarf, and now

Mrs Furzell was already starting on the weekend thing again. Was she never satisfied?

'Well, enjoy!' Mrs Furzell gave a smirking little laugh.

He suspected she'd discredited him all over the village. She insisted on bringing him leftovers from her family feasts to point up his neglected state and on some Sundays he forwent his walk to the village shop for the papers in case he met her and had to endure her 'All on your own, Professor?'

Maurice's relationship with his family suited them all, and without Mrs Furzell forever pointing out its supposed shortcomings, he would have been quite content, doing his crosswords and reading. Books were much better mannered than people; they never telephoned during *The Archers* or just as you'd put a slice of bread in the toaster. Come to think of it, the two boys had grown so much that he'd have to extend their legs or make new cut-outs altogether. He might put Sammy in a football strip, if he could remember his team. Lawrence had just passed his driving test and got a girlfriend. She and Lawrence had spent Christmas luncheon texting each other under the table and giggling. They continued during the Queen's Speech, which Maurice had insisted they all watch. He supposed he'd have to make an effigy of her as well. Lawrence mustn't lose face with Mrs Furzell, whose children led the most extraordinary social lives. It was about time Suzie's hair was hennaed again too. Damn and blast! These family weekends were getting too much for him. He could do without them flopping about all over the place while he waited on them hand and foot.

Linda decided she could not face standing all the way in the aggression of a packed bus and walked home, past the Common where the rooks were going noisily to roost against a sky streaked pink and green like the flock of parakeets which had colonised the outskirts of the city. Daylight was almost gone by the time she reached her own street. A spicy scent of cooking drifted from Mr Errol's house and from behind the closed orange curtains came the sound of voices and laughter. How snug it looked, cosy and bright as a pumpkin. Her own house was in darkness. There was nobody to put on the lights or draw the curtains.

A familiar odour greeted her. What was that on the living room floor? An unmistakable shape. Grey and dead. Furiously, Linda went to find her burying gloves and trowel. Tybalt was pretending to be asleep on the sofa. What a welcome home.

'"Tybalt, you rat-catcher!" How could you?'

As she levered the trowel under the corpse in order to carry it into the garden she saw that it was actually Tybalt's catnip mouse from his Christmas stocking, all slathered in saliva and spilling its catnip guts.

'Oh, really! That's the last straw!'

She didn't need Forensics to identify Flatface's DNA. She dropped the revolting object in the bin. The telephone rang. It was her friend who had lost her basset-hound, saying that she'd adopted a pair of retired greyhounds. Her good news left Linda feeling very lonely. It has come to this, she thought, that the highlight of my day is *The Archers* and I live my life at the mercy of a bull-headed tom. I wish I was sitting in the Bull at Ambridge saying, 'A pint of Shires please, Sid.' Or joining Elizabeth and Nigel Pargetter in sipping a glass of Lower Loxley Premier Cru.

But there was one member of the community she loved above all others, the one-time parvenue, her namesake, Lynda. Lynda Snell. Who could not applaud the heroism of Lynda Snell, tittupping through the lanes of Ambridge with a brace of high-stepping llamas on a lead? Lynda, who is constantly knocked down like an Aunt Sally for her cultural aspirations by the everyday countryfolk whose idea of a good time is de-budding calves and stuffing weaners into sausage skins, only to rise again undaunted with some new scheme for a community website or mystery play, a Christingle with a satsuma representing the baby Jesus or a village pantomime. Oh, Lynda Snell, bring on the wassail bowl!

What was that noise? Yes. Flatface's sly flicking of the cat flap. She grabbed her pistol and ran through, only to see the tip of his tail disappear. Pulling open the back door she let loose a double stream of cold water into the night. A woman screamed. Mr Errol and a companion leapt up from the bench.

Linda tried to apologise but Mr Errol's back door slammed.

Shaking, she sat on the sofa with Tybalt in her arms. This was what Flatface had driven her to. She had broken one neighbour's conservatory and destroyed her friendship with Mr Errol. It was time to get out.

The telephone rang again. It was her nephew Richard's wife, Suzie, ringing for a dutiful chat. Linda heard herself telling Suzie that she had decided to spend some time with Maurice in the country.

'Lawrence will drive you,' said Suzie. 'Maurice left his scarf here and it'll save the postage.'

'Oh, but . . .'

Suzie was a forceful woman and brooked no argument.

So it was that Linda found herself in the passenger seat beside a surly teenager at the wheel, with Tybalt shrieking in his basket on the back seat.

'It's so kind of you to drive me, Lawrence.'

'Sa punishment, innit.'

She did not ask him more and they drove on in silence punctuated by Tybalt's now plaintive mews. To drown his cries Lawrence put on a rap tape exhorting murder and revenge. Linda recalled gloomily her own exploits with a gun. She realised that in her haste of packing and locking up, and slipping a cringing note through Mr Errol's door, she had forgotten to ring Maurice. She began to wonder about that woman in Mr Errol's garden under the stars; just a fellow smoker, or something more? She almost felt betrayed. The first snowflakes of the year fluttered like moths on the windscreen but neither Lawrence nor Linda remarked on them.

'Surprise!'

Maurice, on his doorstep, looked at them in dismay. He had a roll of parcel tape in his hand.

'Couldn't you have staggered your visits?'

'Let us in, it's freezing. I've brought you some lovely guavas.'

If they were going to descend on him, why couldn't they have let him know or arrived when Mrs Furzell was here?

Linda was barging into the sitting room with her cat basket.

'Why, Maurice. I'd no idea you'd taken up art. You are a dark horse.'

What a fool. He should have ushered them into the kitchen while he hid the cut-outs. Richard, Suzie, Lawrence and Sammy, spreadeagled on the carpet, stared up at them, to shame him.

'They're jolly lifelike,' commented Linda. 'Are they based on anybody in particular?'

Maurice bundled the figures into the bin bag where they lived until it was time for one of their visits.

'I'll make some coffee,' he said, adding bleakly, 'there's one of Mrs Furzell's Death by Chocolate cakes.'

As he said her name, an idea struck him.

'Lawrence, while I rustle up the coffee, I wonder if you could just pop round to Mrs Furzell's. I forgot to give her her money. It's not far.'

He had not forgotten to pay Mrs Furzell. She would never have let him get away with that. But at all costs she must see his grandson, even if she would put it round the village that he was losing his marbles. He put some notes into an envelope and handed it to Lawrence. He prayed that Mrs Furzell would be at home, in the bosom of her family.

Linda carried the cat basket into the garden. Fortunately it was walled and Tybalt would be too timid to try to escape its confines. He stepped out to sniff the snow. The air was like crystal, dancing billions of minute sparkling crystals, melting in her lungs.

'Well, was she in?' Maurice greeted Lawrence on his return. 'What did she say?'

'Thanks.'

'Ah.'

He felt a rush of tenderness for the boy slouching in his grey, snow-specked hoodie, with a pimple at the corner of his mouth and reeking of a surreptitious cigarette.

'Good lad.' He clapped him awkwardly on the shoulder.

'Linda, coffee's ready! Linda? What are you doing out there?'

Linda was leaning over the gate, gazing into Christmas Yet To Come. She saw a white sledge, heaped with presents, drawn by two high-stepping white llamas, speeding along snowy lanes, driven through the starry darkness by a merry little driver in a scarlet fur-trimmed cloak. Brookfield Farm, Grey Gables, Lower Loxley, here we come!

That Innocent Bird

On summer days it was a pretty sight to see the white-haired land-lord of the Walrus Inn sitting outside with his little daughter on his knee, the Bible from which he was teaching her the scriptures laid aside for a moment on the bench while he let the child look out to sea, his big gentle fingers covering the small brown ones on the heavy brass telescope.

'What do you see, Jem, lass?'

'Only the seals' heads bobbing, Faither, and the gulls and the fishing boats far off at anchor.'

Jock MacSiller, the tall, soft-spoken landlord, had been a seafaring man before the loss of his left leg had made a landlubber out of him and he had kept the habit of scanning the horizon in all weathers, training the lens on the bay and sweeping it round to survey the road that led to the village. That telescope and the two green parrots swinging on their silver perch in the doorway of the inn were relics of Jock's voyaging days.

At six years old Jemima was a bonny child, with her big eyes and curls tumbling over the collar of her muslin sailor dress, and smart as paint, a chip off the old block, her proud father would boast. She was as dark as Jock was fair, for her mother Desirée was born on the island of Martinique. Jemima had inherited her mother's features, fortunately, for her father's intelligent face was as pale and large as a ham. Jock's own father had been a minister in Edinburgh and Jock had intended to follow him into the Church but when the Reverend Mr MacSiller died leaving a widow with four younger children to feed, Jock, the eldest, had put aside his scholarly ambitions and joined his uncle's ship. These two, Jock and Desirée, made as devoted a pair of lovebirds as you could wish to meet, and little Jem was all the more treasured for being their belated only chick.

★　★　★

45

As for their exotic pets, it was droll to watch those two green parrots waiting outside the kirk on the sabbath, meek as Christians, heads bowed among the grey stones, for the family to emerge, when one would fly up and perch on Jock's shoulder, and the other would flutter onto the little girl's head and nibble her ear and untie the ribbon in her hair as they walked. Jock, leaning on his crutch, was as nimble over the cobbles as any man with two good legs. He was not to be drawn on how he had come by his misfortune but Desirée had confided in Mistress Agnew, the butcher's wife, that a deed of heroism had cost Jock his limb, when pirates had boarded his ship, and folk respected him for his modesty on that score. Even so, it became common knowledge that the captain whose life Jock had saved had rewarded him generously and it was from the proceeds of that recompense that Jock had purchased the lease of the Walrus Inn in this little fishing village on the west coast of Scotland. The MacSillers had been accepted by the tightly-knit community and the Walrus Inn was a model establishment, its white paint and gleaming brass all shipshape and Bristol fashion, and a barrel of apples outside for passers-by to help themselves. Desirée's hot mutton pies, spiced to her secret recipe, were a byword and Jock himself was not averse to lending a hand in the galley, as he called the inn's kitchen. He had learned to knit while becalmed at sea and made little woollen caps and mittens for the orphans of sailors.

One heavy overcast day, a midgy, edgy day when the milk curdled and the parrots drooped on their perch, emerald green against a coppery sky, little Jemima came crying home from school. Another child had broken her slate and Jemima had been blamed. Weeping tears of rage and humiliation, she poured out her tale of how the master, Mr McMurdo, had threatened her with the tawse and made her stand in the corner all afternoon. Jock's face turned as dark as a thundercloud and he clenched his fists. The parrots screeched in sympathy. When she was told, Desirée stroked her daughter's head and observed, 'Per'aps if you have not kicked ze dour-face dominie so 'ard in ze shins, *ma petite*, 'e would not 'ave punish you so. *Toujours la politesse!* Tomorrow you apologise and you will be friends again, no?'

★   ★   ★

There were few customers in the Walrus that night. The storm had broken and thick raindrops blurred the windowpanes, making it steamy within.

'Minds me of the tropics,' said Jock.

Desirée stared wistfully into a lush distance only she could see.

'They papingos havenae much tae say for thirsels the night, Jockie,' observed wee Geordie Troon. 'Who's a pretty boy then, Billy? Come on, Poll, "pieces of eight!"'

'Pieces of – och . . .' Polly lapsed into a bored sqwawk in the cage on the bar where the parrots spent the night.

'What age did ye say they were?' asked Geordie.

'Billy I brought up by hand, egg and squab, but Polly his mother, who kens? They say a parrot can live for ever. She might be more than two hundred years old although to look at her, you'd think she was a babby. That parrot's been at Madagascar and at Malabar, the Surinam, Providence and Portobello. She was at the fishing up of the wrecked Plate ships. It's there she learned "pieces of eight", eh Polly?' Jock winked.

Geordie held out his glass to the bird to encourage her to drink through the bars. Quick as a flash Jock threw his handkerchief over the cage.

'Nae sperrits!' he cried, his pale face reddening. 'Polly can come out with some devilish sayings she picked up in bad company and, as a God-fearing landlord, I shouldn't like my old shipmate to offend. That innocent bird can swear blue fire when the grog's on her.'

Naturally, the drinkers wanted to put Polly to the test to hear what profanities a bird might utter, but the handkerchief stayed firmly in place.

'If only she could talk,' said one, 'converse proper-like, like you and me, what tales she could tell!'

From beneath the handkerchief came a low muffled murmur, drowned by the chorus of the old sea shanty that Jock had struck up. 'If only I could talk, me hearties? Deny an old seadog a nip of grog would you, you swab? Afeared it might loosen my beak? "Pieces of eight" be damned! Fifteen men on the dead man's chest – yo-ho-ho and a bottle of rum! Wee Jemima kens fine that I can talk – I've told her many a fine tale, but she never lets on. Jock

47

MacSiller? I've as good a Scots tongue in my head as he has and if he's a Scotsman, I'm a Dutchman. Son of the manse be damned for a lie! Mine genial host is none other than the infamous Long John Silver, beached here in this dead-and-alive hole with his ill-gotten gains, until he thinks it safe to return to his native England. And I am Cap'n Flint, the pirate parrot, scourge of the Spanish Main! I'll tell you a tale, me hearties . . .'

'Haud yer wheesht, Mither,' said Billy. 'Naebody's listening and *I've* heard it all before.'

'Some of you,' continued Cap'n Flint, 'might recall, from reading that young busybody Jim Hawkins' account of the affair, how when the *Hispaniola* with her much depleted crew sailed away at last from Treasure Island, she left behind a sizeable quantity of bar silver, not to mention a cache of arms. And you might even think that, after all his efforts, it was only just that the said silver should end up lining the pockets of one whose name is Silver. You might say that Long John and I fought shoulder to shoulder for our share of the booty, for I spent most of that wretched adventure perched on his.

'What Hawkins never knew was that after we fled the *Hispaniola* with the connivance of that cheesy old reprobate Ben Gunn, we laid low for a while then got together a crew to return to Treasure Island for the silver. The three fellows marooned there were half-dead from fever and dysentery, despite the supplies Dr Livesey had provided them with, and we took them along when we sailed away. They was grateful of course; it was "Cap'n Silver, sir" this, and "Cap'n Silver, sir" that and "Beggin' your leave, Cap'n Silver, sir". Until we give them the slip when we touched port. That's why Long John sleeps with a loaded pistol under his pillow and is forever peering through his telescope; he's mortal afeared that one of them will come looking for him to tip him the black spot that declares a buccaneer's fate. Should have stowed them safely in Davey Jones's locker, say I.

'The silver were worth nothing compared to the gold that Livesey, Trelawney, Smollett and Hawkins made off with but it still amounted to a tidy sum. Bristol being too hot for Long John and me, we cast anchor here and Desirée joined us as soon as she got word. She were a trifle dark-complected for that mealy-wigged buffer Squire Trelawney's taste, but young Jim Hawkins wished the couple well. In this world at least. "Barbecue", they called Long John when he was ship's cook on the *Hispaniola*, and Jim reckoned he was in for a roasting himself in the next. Hero, says them as don't know, who lost his leg in the course of his dooty. Says I, you never saw that crutch go whizzing through the air point-first to catch a man full in the back and fell him to the ground!

'You might argue that Squire and Co. had no more claim on that there treasure than the rest of us, or even that it rightly belonged to old Ben Gunn who ended up as a lackey in uniform mopping and mowing to the gentry. Be that as it may, all I got out of that particular adventure was a perch fashioned from a bar of beaten silver. No, not quite all. For while we were on that accursed island I met up with a retired seafarer who had settled there, an Amazon like myself. His eyes were yellow topaz and the flashes on his green wings were scarlet as hibiscus flowers. By the time we left Treasure Island behind for the last time, I knew I was with egg. When my chick hatched, Long John named him Billy, after Billy Bones the buccaneer, but his true name is Emerald.'

The parrot fell silent as the last customer left the inn and Long John reached for the bottle of rum and poured out a glass for Desirée and himself. Desirée took a clay pipe from the pocket of her skirt and tamped in a wad of tobacco with a practised thumb.

The following morning dawned bright and fair. Jemima opened the parrots' cage and Polly perched on her shoulder, nuzzling into her ear, and then clinging on with her neat grey feet when the little girl ran upstairs to her bedroom.

'*Dépêche-toi*,' called her mother. 'You will be late for school.'

When Jemima came down again, Desirée said, 'Why don't you take a rosy apple for Mr McMurdo?'

'No, I've made him something myself.'

'*Au' voir* then, *ma petite, sois sage*.'

'I'm always *sage*,' said Jemima.

When she came skipping home from school her father was lifting a batch of scones from the griddle.

'Did you make your peace with Mr McMurdo?'

'Aye.'

'And was he sorry he made my wee girl cry?'

Jemima slipped a lump of sugar from her pocket into Polly's beak. 'Not as sorry as he will be, eh Polly?'

'How's that, Jem lass?' said Jock.

'I tipped him the black spot.'

The Heart of Saturday Night

Over the years Alex had developed his innate talent for being in the wrong place, so he felt no surprise when a balmy Saturday evening found him astride an ostrich on a stationary carousel on a deserted campus lawn. It was almost the end of the academic year, and for the past week or so the streets had been alive with students trooping around in gowns, and parents taking photographs. Fairground music drifted in with the smell of crushed grass, hot dogs and popcorn through his window. Half-heartedly, Alex tried to spur his ostrich into motion but its gilded barley-sugar pole was locked; soon the carousel would be gone, like the dismantled marquees and the boys in tuxedos and the girls in their ballgowns with flowers in their hair and cleavages. Girls whose skin made Alex, who at thirty-eight had thought of himself as young until he met his students, feel old and sallow and stubbly. Alex had not been to university himself but, on the strength of his two volumes of poetry, he had been given a residency in the English department here to teach a course of creative writing. The university buildings, geometric constructions of mirrored glass, stood high above the city and the docks beyond, reflecting sky, water and trees, and now a flock of parakeets flying shrilly to roost.

While Alex, a large man in badly-fitting shorts, sat hunched on the merry-go-round, a circus was getting under way in the municipal park. He had two tickets for the performance in his pocket and he should have been sitting in the big top now, beside his sometime girlfriend Rosella, but she had let him down once again, with a summer cold this time. Unable to bear another evening in by himself, he had wandered along the paths which intersected the grounds and come upon this carousel left over from other people's celebrations. He had been looking forward to showing Rosella the parakeets, her namesakes, which nested in the high trees. Rosella was a crime writer whose feathered hair, when they first met, was dyed green and pink and yellow.

Alex was living in the apartment reserved for visiting professors. His residency was over but he had agreed to run a couple of workshops at the university's poetry summer school, in order to prolong his stay. One of the reasons Alex was reluctant to leave was the visitors' book on the hall table of his apartment, in which occupants were required to write something witty or profound. A haiku was the very least that would be expected of him, but he could think of nothing which would delight or impress, and so vindicate his tenure. Alex was disappointed in himself and guessed that the university was disappointed in him. He had hoped that this sojourn in a strange city would inspire something remarkable, but he had failed. Neither he nor his polyglot students had produced anything of merit and he had spent a lot of time helping them to fill in forms and write letters to landlords. Every night Alex leafed through the visitors' book, looked at the ideographs, cartoons, sketches, the fulsome limericks, bars of music and incomprehensible mathematical, scientific, Arabic, Greek and Latin entries, inscribed by his erudite chuckling predecessors in various coloured inks, and every night he closed it in despair.

The main reason, however, that he didn't want to go away was a woman named Blythe Beaumaris Gridley, the American wife of Professor Mort Gridley, a philosopher and television pundit, characterised by his towering pompadour of strawberry-blond hair. How, wondered Alex, could you trust a moral philosopher with such self-regarding hair? The Gridleys' son, Atticus, was a pupil at the *lycée* in the city here and they were waiting until his school term finished before flying to New York and thence to their house in the Hamptons. Since Alex had been introduced to Blythe by his head of department he had often seen her cycling about the campus with her bicycle basket full of books or fresh-baked cookies, and on one occasion, a speckled hen she was taking to the vet. Sometimes she braked and spoke to him, or waved, calling out some greeting such as 'Are you coming to the bunfight at the museum?' or 'Will we see you at the shindig in the music faculty later?' The answer, had she paused to hear it, was almost invariably 'no'.

What an exciting life she leads, he thought bitterly, with all those wingdings and shindigs and bunfights, but Blythe was so like her name, so vital and interested in everything, including, it seemed, him, that Alex could not really sneer at her in his dull English way. Smart as a whip, she was, rangy, with what he thought of as taffy-coloured hair, and silver bracelets riding up and down her freckled arms. There was old money in the background, he imagined, and blue blood powering those strong slender legs and sandalled feet on the pedals. She was doing a doctorate in either Quilter or quilting, he wasn't sure which one she'd said, and couldn't ask now, but he liked the idea of Blythe among a heap of big, soft multicoloured quilts.

When Alex had received a rare invitation, to a reception for a delegation from Taipei, he found it a dreary occasion, marked by an absence of flying buns, where people nursed paper cups of wine and bored on about departmental affairs. Like Alex, the visitors were left pretty much to their own devices and they were obliged to talk animatedly among themselves. Blythe, he noted, was almost alone in making a social effort. She had on a sea-green dress and a necklace of silver mussel shells. Blythe saw him studying the spines of textbooks on an aluminium shelf and came over. Alex took a gulp of tepid red wine and heard himself blurt out, 'What's that smell?'

She looked alarmed. 'Smell?'

'I mean that perfume you're wearing. It's nice.'

'Oh, it's just my old Florida Water. I always stock up at Bigelow's. Do you go to New York?'

'Sometimes,' he mumbled. 'Coney Island, that's my favourite place.'

Blythe laughed. 'You know what they say, if you come from Coney Island you always have sand in your shoes.'

Professor Gridley came over and steered her away. 'Time to go, honey?' she said and, turning to Alex, asked, 'Are you coming on to the dinner?'

'I don't think so,' he replied, hoping it sounded as if he had a choice. Gridley blanked him. He was wearing his academic's summer garb of a cream linen suit and a silk scarf knotted like an overblown rose, matching the pink rosebud in his buttonhole.

Alex felt desolate as he watched them follow the vivid Taipei contingent through the glass doors. Had there been a hint of cruelty in Mort Gridley's thin, red-lipped smile at his wife? Was his grip on her elbow unnecessarily hard? Perhaps Blythe's own smile was a tad too tight, her eyes over-bright. Was she compliant through fear, or was she a willing partner in secret marital games? Alex sublimated a shameful frisson into a picture of himself landing a punch on Gridley's supercilious beak.

Melancholy set in as he helped himself to another drink, ignoring the disapproving student bartender. The unspoken rule was one cup of wine per person. He had, as usual, presented himself to Blythe as a klutz. Blythe was the only person at the university who had been friendly to him, but did she really like him, or was it just her Waspish good manners which made him feel that she was interested in him and his work? She had said once that he must sign his books for her, but nothing had come of it, and he had never been invited to any shindigs or wingdings at the Beaumaris Gridley place. He looked down at his huge trainers; klutzy clown shoes, and what did a mothballed tuxedo found hanging in his bedroom cupboard and worn over a T-shirt and jeans say about his own aesthetic? The sleeves didn't reach his wrists and he hadn't shaved. He was, as his sister once pointed out, shambolic. Although women did sometimes tell him he had nice dark eyelashes and his eyes were a lovely deep blue, even though they were small. Like cornflowers, Rosella had said a long time ago.

The truth was, Alex felt that if he made an effort with his clothes people might sneer, thinking he didn't realise how ugly he was. Coney Island? She must have guessed he had never been there. It was the first place that had come into his head. Besides, obviously Blythe Beaumaris would only go to Coney Island ironically; she was hardly a boardwalk and Luna Park sort of person. Then, out of his childhood, from a favourite LP of his mother's, came romantic violins and guitars and the voices of The Drifters harmonising that they still had some sand in their shoes, and a Ferris wheel drew a circle against the stars.

On the evening when Blythe and Mort were at the dinner to which he had not been invited, Alex had walked over to their rented house. He had looked up the address a while ago, although he still fantasised Blythe in a white antebellum mansion standing among live oaks veiled with Spanish moss. He stood at the gate of an undistinguished brick house and saw, through the front room window, a cello and three music stands in graduated sizes. The Three Bears String Trio. Then a light came on and somebody, a babysitter perhaps, drew the curtains. That night he telephoned Rosella and they arranged that she would come and stay for a weekend. And she had cancelled on the morning she was supposed to arrive.

So here he is, sitting on this flightless bird, with the Tom Waits song about looking for the heart of Saturday night playing in his head. Where was the heart of Saturday night? Certainly not in the student union bar. Or, he suspected, in the city's clubs; he had seen herds of half-naked hoydens stomping along the pavements in stilettos, tugging at slipping boob tubes and crop tops, bare arms swinging, thighs pumping; he had watched the other participants in this primitive mating ritual, the gangs of swaggering boys in their comfortable shoes, wearing T-shirts or open shirts over their jeans, and the black-uniformed bouncers at the glittering thresholds to which he would not have been admitted, and he thought that some of those vulgar, vulnerable girls would always miss the heart of Saturday night.

He had never found it. Or the bohemian quarter of this city. Could it be that he had washed up in the only port in the world without a bohemian quarter? Where were those raffish establishments down by the docks, spiced with danger, where artists, gangsters and sailors drank down the moon and the talk flowed like rum or wine while somebody banged out sentimental tunes from a battered piano and poets had their pick of the wild aristocratic girls and golden-hearted ladies of the night? The grass around the carousel is dry and slippery from lack of rain. The sharp leaves of bushes rustle and in the dusk the painted eyes and nostrils of the horses widen and their lips flare over bared teeth. Then, from the heart of somebody's Saturday night, comes a burst of music, notes that blaze for a moment in the sky before dissolving like a starburst from a firework. He remembers the time when he was backpacking in Italy. He arrived in Genoa, where he had a rendezvous with Rosella, expecting it to be like Flecker's poem 'The Old Ships', and got lost, finding himself, as night fell, at a derelict fairground set in industrial wasteland. There was a waltzer which appeared to be made up of cheeky smiling faces, but when he approached he saw that the seats were enormous pink shellacked bare bottoms. He climbed inside one of them and fell asleep. Later he discovered that Rosella had decided to go to Rome.

It had crossed Alex's mind when he bought the circus tickets that he and Rosella might run into Blythe and Mort there with little Atticus. A bittersweet scenario. Alex had grown up with the scent of sawdust; if Coney Island people had sand in their shoes, he had sawdust in his. His first castles were built from sawdust not sand, and his earliest memories were of showmanship, sequins and coloured lights – as his parents' butcher's shop underwent a magical transformation every Christmas, with claret-faced master-butcher Dad like a ringmaster in his sparkling topper directing the extravaganza, and Mum his glamorous blonde assistant. The tree was hung with scarlet baubles, the walls festooned with pink garlands of sausages, chops and cutlets nestled in beds of excelsior, and even the turkeys wore paper hats. On Christmas Eve, Dad, dressed as Santa Claus, would zip his two assistants into a pantomime reindeer suit and harness them to a cart, to deliver any unsold birds to the local hospitals and children's home. They were accompanied by Alex and his older sister, Barbara, dressed in the elf costumes Mum had made them. Barb, after sowing a patch of wild oats, grew up to be a surgeon, and Alex became a vegan. This did not exempt him from being sent to barbecue slices of fatted calf when Barb came to visit with her deadbeat boyfriends, and later, her psychoanalyst fiancé. They had twin boys now. 'Which one do you like best?' Alex had asked on his introduction to the identical white bundles.

Alex had arrived late for the twins' fourth birthday party; he hadn't seen them for a couple of years. He was ambushed by a crowd of little boys grabbing his knees and pelting him with a volley of toy juggling balls, and he was drenched by a fusillade of water pistols. When he managed to beat them off, the twins sobbed, 'But Uncle Alex, Daddy *said* you were a clown!' Alex thought about that incident now, and of the time a wasp got into his shorts at a school sports day. How we laughed, he thought grimly.

Suddenly he felt a draining certainty that the Gridleys had left for America, as if all hope was sluiced from him. Blythe had gone without saying goodbye, and he would never see her again. He bashed his forehead repeatedly on the ostrich's metal neck, then in tears of pain and fury rang Rosella on his mobile. He saw that he had two missed calls – probably his mother. He got Rosella's machine. The lying – she wasn't ill at all, she had obviously had a better offer. The only point of her visit would have been to show Blythe he had a girlfriend. Thank God she wasn't coming. Rosella was an appalling house guest. He remembered dank towels, grey bubbles on the new soap he had put out for display, and finding used cotton buds and make-up remover pads in the bathroom bin long after she had departed. He never used it himself. Privately, he'd always thought her books misogynistic; creepy forensic stuff, where the victims were always women and little girls, parasitically close to real-life atrocities. What a blowfly she was. Rosella had stolen a working day from him, making him shop and clean and buy towels, flowers and wine for her; a day when he might have been inspired to write the visitors' book poem.

Worse, and he hadn't acknowledged how wounded he felt until now, she had stolen his profession and his past. Turning her hand to poetry while between novels, she had published a volume of verse. Whereas Alex's poems about his childhood had made little impression, particularly on his family, Rosella's *Turkeys in Tinsel* was a Poetry Book Society Choice. His parents were thrilled. Then it came to him with a jolt that he had drunk most of the wine before leaving the apartment, and he *had* written in the book. He had written *When you come from Coney Island you always have sand in your shoes*. A secret tribute to Blythe, which should be enigmatic and beautiful enough for anybody, he'd thought.

The moon, which had been hanging about palely for hours, was now low, full and orange. Alex heard dogs barking and looked up to see two university security guards in fluorescent jackets half-running towards him across the grass, pulled along by alsatians straining at their leashes. To his right, on one of the paths which criss-crossed the campus, a humpbacked figure was waving; he recognised Rosella weighed down by her enormous rucksack. Then, out of left field, Blythe's bicycle breasted the slope and cruised down towards the carousel. In her streamlined cycle helmet and yellow jersey she looked like the winner of the Tour de France. Alex sat on his ostrich and waited for them all to arrive.

Jumbo Takes a Bath

The oil was a beautiful deep purple in its glass bottle, like the liquid in the apothecaries' jars in old-fashioned chemists' windows, but when Eloise poured it into the bath it lay on the surface in disappointingly grey circles. She looked in vain for a tinge of mauve. The bottle was labelled *Mood For Romance* and promised sensuous bliss. Foolish to have thought you could buy romance in Superdrug, two for the price of one, particularly as she saw now that it had been manufactured on an industrial estate in her home town, a place not noted for its sensuality. That was one of the reasons she had moved to London. The circles of bath oil were spreading out now into amoebic forms with greasy pseudopodia and grey nuclei. 'Because I'm worth it,' those models and actresses smirked on the television ads. Because I'm worth it? Eloise wondered as she stepped into a bathtub swimming with amoeba.

She turned on the hot tap and inverted the bottle under its flow. Should have done that in the first place to get some bubbles. Naturally, she hadn't read the instructions. As in bath, so in life. That would probably be her epitaph: She Didn't Read the Instructions. 'Sally Slapdash,' her headmistress had called her. Writing enthusiastic reams in answer to the wrong questions in exams, passing the baton to the opposing team in relay races, Eloise had not distinguished herself academically or sportingly. Then there was the science lab incident. 'I could countenance a conflagration in the chemistry laboratory,' Miss Cracknell shook her bandaged head, 'but in a biology lesson . . . !' Eloise had dreamed of some heroic deed, a rescue from a blaze that she had not started herself, to show the world her true colours. She was still waiting for the one person who would recognise her soul and walk through the world with her, bringing out the best in her, as she would in him.

She had no hopes of this blind date tonight with the friend of a friend. James had been working in Brussels, was out of touch and lonely, and Eloise was only meeting him as a favour. James Tate. Laddish and infantile, fixated on sport, smut and lager and those TV programmes where hirsute and beer-bellied men sit in a row braying with smug laughter, or the sort of smoothie who would wrongfoot her and make her spill her drink and come back from the Ladies with a paper towel stuck to her shoe? Snob, yob or a brussels sprout with a green leafy head? She examined her thigh and saw that the burn from the aromatherapy candle she had knocked into the bath last week was fading, and might leave only a tiny scar.

Eloise lay back, reading the ingredients of *Mood For Romance*. 'Ylang-ylang'. It always reminded her of the records her father played. 'Doolang doolang. I met him at the candy store.' How sweet and simple life was in those songs of candy stores, juke-joints, soda fountains and high school hops, and butterscotch-fudge-flavoured heartbreak. 'Mysterious patchouli'. Its scent wafted from her mother's every gauzy garment; no mystery there. But what to wear tonight? Just when you've relaxed into Boho chic, the fascistic fashionistas inform you that tailoring's back, and that your baguette bag's as stale as yesterday's sandwich and everybody's carrying bowling bags. Not me, thought Eloise, whose finger would always be crooked after her first and last unlucky strike. She reached for the nail clippers, and winced as a fragment of nail flew into her eye.

In a moment she would have to face the boredom of drying herself. How many thousand times in a lifetime could a person bear to do that? And there was too much of her to dry. Last night she couldn't stop eating, trying to fill a gap that food could not satisfy. A picture of an elephant, from a childhood book, came into her mind. Its title was *Jumbo Takes a Bath*. There was a zookeeper with bristling moustache and broom, and a mountain of food. 'Every day Jumbo eats her way through 20 pounds of bananas, 30 oranges, 6 buckets of porridge, 10 loaves, a hundredweight of potatoes, 15 pints of milk.' Greedy Jumbo. Poor Jumbo. Eloise wallowed, imagining Jumbo hoovering up a trunkful of water to squirt playfully at her keeper. Or with malice aforethought. Jumbo trampled her heap of brussels sprouts contemptuously to a mush.

No time now to agonise. She grabbed a dress from a hanger,

tore off the polythene and bit through the plastic tag on the dry-cleaner's label. Then, just as she discovered the remains of a bar of whole-nut chocolate melted at the bottom of her bag, the discarded polythene which had been lying in wait struck, and she slithered, slipped and fell. Her friends had sensible skiing accidents; she crashed down on a piste of polythene. Bruised and despairing, she embarked on the evening, an irredeemable klutz limping towards a pointless date, under a threatening sky.

A man was standing outside the wine bar, hair spiked by the rain, holding together the lapels of his jacket. His tie was wrapped in a clumsy bandage round the bleeding fingers of his right hand. 'I think you're waiting for me,' said Eloise.

His face lit up. It was a comical, kind face, but it fell into a tragic mask as he held out his injured hand.

'I'm terribly sorry – you'll never believe it – the most bizarre thing – this squirrel got on the tube at Green Park and . . .'

Two pairs of apprehensive hazel eyes regarded her, as a squirrel's head squirmed out of his jacket.

'Right,' said Eloise. 'First we get the squirrel back to Green Park – pop him in my bag, James, fortunately I've brought along a few nuts – and then it's straight to Casualty.'

She stepped into the road, and there was a taxi with its light on, speeding towards her, slowing down at her command, braking sharply to receive them.

Shalimar

There goes Mrs de Vere, towed across the Low Green like a water-skier by that crazy yellow dog of hers, over the road and up onto the sea wall. The two of them struggle for a minute and the skirt of her raincoat billows into a spinnaker as she fights to unclip the lead before the wind takes her and deposits her on the crest of a breaker. Released, the dog scrambles down onto the sand, tail and ears flying, and Mrs de Vere negotiates the slope to the shore. It's impossible to tell if it's the wind blowing tears from her eyes or if she's crying. The Heads of Ayr, Ailsa Craig and the Isle of Arran have all disappeared in the haar and spume, drowned or blown away. You'd have to be mad to be out on a day like this. The fishing boats are huddled in the harbour and only Mrs de Vere, the dog and raucous birds are abroad. The dog jumps and curvets, advances and retreats, with the wind snatching its bark and flinging it into the cries of the herring gulls. Mrs de Vere's hair whips out from her hood, her fine complexion is abraded by flying sand, dune grasses lash her legs, as she stumbles along above the ridge of seaweed, driftwood, razor shells and whatever the tide has flung up, and flickers out of sight like a patch of St Elmo's fire.

Ten minutes' walk behind her, the house waits. From the outside Shalimar is like a thousand others; red sandstone, lace curtains, a square of garden; nothing to suggest that there was ever a whiff of scandal about it. Inside, the walls are hung with framed posters and signed photographs of theatricals in their heyday, and the bookshelves crammed with memorabilia and programmes from the Gaiety Theatre and Green's Playhouse; mementoes of the spangled days when Mrs de Vere served porridge and kippers to the stars, and brought them down gently after triumph or disaster with libations of whisky or cocoa.

Nothing in the house recalls the mysterious disappearance of that foreign magician many years ago, the illusionist who wore an embroidered bolero and silk pantaloons with an ornamental dagger in his belt, who was so madly in love with Mrs de Vere. One morning he was gone. His bed unslept in. All that remained were the tricks of his trade. Some folk concluded that he had been practising an Indian rope trick that worked too well, but be that as it may, he was never seen again.

A portrait of Mrs de Vere with a lipsticked smile and her hair swept up in a pompadour like an ice-cream wafer hangs above the gas fire and trembles gently in its heat. A violin lies on a little table beside an empty birdcage; her last lyric tenor is dead, her last maestro has lain down his baton.

So the world has moved on, discarding glamour and gaiety like outworn costumes; it's apparently *nil carborundum* as far as Mrs de Vere is concerned. Let her portrait be slowly kippered, let her neighbours suspect her name is but a courtesy title; Mrs de Vere is never without a companion now. So Shalimar smells a bit doggy, and the dog will eat only the finest cuts, and snarls at anybody who speaks to her and won't let anybody else over the threshold; at least it gets her out of the house.

Effie de Vere no longer lets out rooms but last summer she had a great-great-nephew to stay. Alec, a peelie-wally eight year old from Paisley with a stud in his ear, whose mother was out at work all day. One rainy afternoon Great Aunt Effie gave Alec her mother's old photograph album to look at. Back in the days of those tiny photographs with deckle edges there had been family pets, prosperous-looking cats with furry plus fours, dogs with the air of pillars of the community. Alec showed more interest in the animals than in any of his ancestors and stroked them with a grimy-nailed finger, saying, 'I wish I could have a cat or a dog but they're not allowed in our flats. I'd even settle for a stick insect. We had some at school and the teacher asked people to take them home for the holidays but my mum wouldn't let me have one. *You've* got a privet hedge already, Aunty Effie, which is what stick insects live on ... and you'd save on the clipping ...'

In her mind's eye Effie saw a jar filled with green leafy twigs, topped with a pinpricked jampot cover secured firmly with a rubber band, housing an insect camouflaged to the point of invisibility. What harm could there be in that? Then her heart hardened as she looked at Alec slumped in her favourite armchair, scrunching up the antimacassar, with a kicked-over can of Irn Bru dribbling onto the carpet. A stick insect would doubtless proliferate. And escape. Then there'd be a plague of them to deal with. Twiggy, brittle things, frazzling in the lampshades and getting into her hair and the bath.

'Sorry, son. No Insects has been a house rule ever since I had Mamzelle Pucelle and Her Remarkable Performing Fleas for a summer season. A stick insect would be the thin end of the wedge,' she said severely.

Alec lunged the remote at the TV, and the screen almost cracked in an explosion of sound and colour. He slumped back, putting the head of his plastic Power Ranger into his mouth.

'Look at you, a great big boy sucking on that thing like a baby's dummy!' said Effie.

'It wasn't *my* idea to come here,' he retorted. '*You* invited me!'

'That I did *not*!' she snapped back, but silently. She had learned to control her fiery temper, and she didn't want Alec crying to his mother on the telephone. She went into the kitchen to put the kettle on, wondering why people harp on about childhood being so short. Another two weeks with this one seemed like an eternity. He'd done something to the clock, making its hands turn more slowly and its tick louder, and she'd had to cancel her regular date to play bridge.

Her great-niece had practically begged Effie to take him in. Leckie couldn't be left home alone, and the sea air would do him good. Effie wouldn't have wanted the boy's exposure to drugs, amusement arcades and paedophiles laid at her door, but weren't there summer camps where inconvenient children could be sent? Adventure Camps and Fat Camps? Although it would have to be Thin Camp in Alec's case. You couldn't even turn kids out to play these days, send them off to the skating rink or the pictures; you had to take them everywhere.

Effie was exhausted. She didn't sleep well, and sometimes at night she fancied she heard policemen's feet clumping up the stairs, or woke from a dream of brown eyes and a silken neck wearing a gold chain with an emblem of clasped hands, and heard a voice in her head saying, 'You'll never escape me, Effie, in this world or the next. I am your destiny.' But in the clear light of day she didn't believe in predestination or reincarnation or any of that nonsense. She'd cooked breakfast for too many fortune-tellers and charlatans to have any credence in the supernatural.

'I think the rain's slackening off,' she said. 'We'll take a walk and maybe see if the shows are on.'

'The shows?' said Alec.

'The big funfair that always used to be along the front. I haven't been that way for years, but you never know.'

'Can we go to the harbour too?' he asked.

Effie hesitated. 'There's nothing there.'

Then, seeing his face settling into a sulk, she said, 'I suppose we can. If you must. But only for a minute, mind.'

They walked down to the Low Green in silence, two hooded figures, Alec hunched in his parka and Effie in her raincoat that changed through shades of green and blue in the watery light and short blue wellingtons. There was a smell of chips in the air and the sky was like the inside of a mussel shell above the ribbed sand squiggled with wormcasts and the flat silver sea. Alec brightened when she bought him a snake ring with a ruby eye and a lurid ice lolly from one of the kiosks, and a postcard for his mother. She treated herself to a twist of pink candyfloss.

There was nobody about at the harbour. Fishscales underfoot, gulls on bollards, rigging, a great dredger rusting on the far side. An iron ladder with vivid hanks of weed on the rungs leading down into dark, oily water. Effie shivered.

'Is that a seal? Look, there!' cried Alec. 'It's got to be a seal!'

'Oh, yes. I think I see a head but I can't really tell without my glasses. You do sometimes get seals out at sea, but I've not seen one in the harbour before. Careful now, Alec, not too near the edge.'

'I thought seals were supposed to be black or grey, but that one's yellow,' said Alec. 'It's got a weird face.'

Effie thought of Silkies, half-human, half-seal. 'Come on,' she said. 'Let's go to the shows. I think I can hear music.'

She sensed danger. Pictured a corpse bobbing towards them.

'Alec! Will you get away from the edge, I've told you! Come here at once!'

She grabbed at him but he twisted away, skidding on a fish tail, tripping over a heavy chain. Falling, screaming, arms and legs extended, into the black water.

Effie shrieked and hurled a plastic crate after him like a lifebuoy and then she was tearing off her coat, kicking off her boots, going down the iron ladder, her hands and feet slipping on green beards of weed, yelling, 'Catch hold of the crate, Alec, I'm coming, hang on, don't let go!'

At the shock of icy water she kicked free of the ladder and struck out towards Alec through muck and oil. He'd caught the crate but was dragging it down, his weight in his sodden parka pulling it under the surface. He disappeared and re-emerged several feet away. A current was carrying him towards the mouth of the harbour, out to sea. A wave slapped over her head, engulfing her last thought – let me drown if I can't save Alec – as she felt herself being sucked down, down, with a roaring in her ears and her heart and lungs bursting.

Then she was carried up, up into the light and air, nudged along through the water, and found herself clinging, gulping and spluttering, to the ladder, with Alec's streaming face looking down into her own. A heavy head bumped her up the rungs; a sharp nip to the calf spurred her on.

'Steady, Missis.'

Strong arms reached out to haul her onto hard ground, where she collapsed, spewing out harbour water.

'N–not a s–seal, a d–dog,' Alec was gibbering through blue lips. 'S–saved our lives. T–take him home.'

Somebody had wrapped Alec in a jacket and sat him on an upturned box. Effie crawled over and hugged him as hard as her weak arms could, until they both choked. She heard an ambulance and only then did she put out a hand to their rescuer. She felt a scar in the dog's wet chest fur. Her fingers fastened on a chain round its neck, on an emblem with clasped hands, and she looked into fathomless brown eyes.

A voice in her head was repeating, 'You'll never escape me, Effie, in this world or the next.' There had been a secret assignation, after midnight, while the guests in Shalimar slept. A walk along the shore to the rocks. She relived the quarrel at the harbour's edge when she told him she didn't love him. The struggle. Snatching the dagger from its scabbard, its jewels glittering in the moonlight. Who'd have thought that it was real and would tear through cloth and flesh in that sickening way? The resounding splash that filled the night. The rushing silence.

The body was never washed up. Over the years Effie had almost managed to convince herself that the whole event had been staged by a master of illusion and that the magician was alive and well, practising his art in some foreign country with a beautiful woman waiting in the wings. But when the heroic dog scrabbled into the ambulance just before they closed the doors, it found Effie hysterical, in the throes of a hideous conversion to belief in reincarnation.

That was last summer, and here comes Mrs de Vere again, in the teeth of a howling gale, trudging home to Shalimar behind that famous yellow dog of hers.

Nay, Ivy, Nay

Once upon a time there lived a professor in a house which was so old that a forest of concrete had grown up around it. Holly House had withstood and weathered centuries before the first paving stones were ever planted there. Its solitary inhabitant was a professor of botany and his head was so full of ferns and fungi that he was quite impervious to the preoccupations of the rest of the populace. In the short dark days and long nights of December, while some folk wrapped presents and others lagged themselves in polythene against the blast, when revellers, barrow boys and beggars took to the streets in novelty Santa Claus hats, and turkeys and conifers counted the cost, the professor's mind ran on the furtive inflorescence of dank and secret places. The eminent mycologist was tall and thin, with a voice as dry as sawdust and you might imagine that he dined like a worm on the crumbled detritus of dead foliage or bored like a beetle through the ancient volumes on his bookshelves. He proposed to spend Christmas Day working on a paper he was to deliver at the South London Botanical Institute, a treatise titled *Some Mutations of Crusted Fungi in Metropolitan Cemeteries*.

Sharp and smooth-leaved hollies, glossy, dark and variegated hollies with berries of every shade of red and yellow, surrounded the house and two gnarled trees had twined into a thicket over the gate, where they clutched the professor's few visitors in their prickly fingers. The high walls of the garden at the back were thick with ivy and globes of mistletoe hung in the apple boughs. A lead sundial marked the hours, there was a birdbath with a trickling fountain and here and there the silhouette of a bird clipped from laurel, privet, box and yew. It was this walled garden that held the professor's greatest treasure; a slender holly tree with a crown of waxen leaves and, threaded on milky stalks, clusters of berries whiter than snow. He loved the white holly more than

anybody in this world; he had cherished her since her first tentative, astonishing, leaf had pierced the mould, protected her until
she was strong enough to dance in the winter wind; she was his
pale darling decked in pearls.

Now, although the professor cared not a candied fig for the
Christmas conventions, he was not averse to certain archaic carols
and, when the fancy took him, he would creak out 'The Holly
and the Ivy' in counterpoint to the garden birds' chorale or declaim
in his sawdusty, sing-song voice a version of the ballad for which
he had a particular fancy:

> Nay, Ivy, nay,
> It shall not be, I wys;
> Let Holly have the mastery
> As the manner is.

Not far from the professor's house, in the heart of the concrete
forest, stood a tall tower where there lived a poor woodcutter and
his wife. Her name was Ivy, his was John, and they were contented,
honest and hardworking, he in pruning and felling the borough's
trees and she on the bakery counter of Simmington's Supermart.
But late one evening, Ivy stood at her high window in the tower
looking out with a heavy heart. Her sister Blanche, whom she had
not seen for many years, was arriving soon from Australia with
her family and, on the telephone, Blanche had instructed her,
'Don't forget now, Ivy, we're all looking forward to a white
Christmas. We insist on it. We're counting on you, so don't let us
down!'

There was a hard frost that night but, alas, the forecast for
Christmas was damp and mild. Then, as Ivy gazed sadly down,
she saw the white tree glittering in the professor's garden far
below, so sharp and clear in the moonlight that it seemed as if
a breath of wind would set icy music tinkling through its branches.
A frozen plume rose from the birdbath and, among the statuary
and topiary, was a frosted bush as round as a perfect Christmas
pudding.

'If I cannot order a white Christmas out of doors,' Ivy told
her husband, 'I will create one here in our flat on the eleventh

floor, a miniature world as magical as the scene inside the glass snowstorm ball that Blanche and I loved when we were children.'

'Go for it, girl,' said he.

On a foggy evening not long afterwards, the professor was enraged by a knocking at his door. He opened it to find a woman standing in his porch. Her hair was like a raven's wing, a single bead of blood as red as a berry stood out on her ivory cheek where a holly had scratched her. She carried a pair of secateurs and a white box.

'If you've come to demand figgy pudding,' said the professor, 'you've come to the wrong house. I've just seen off a couple of young scoundrels who had the effrontery to interrupt my work with their caterwauling for figgy pudding. "Good tidings we bring to you and your *king*", indeed! I'll guarantee they won't make that mistake again!'

'It's a traditional carol,' said Ivy, 'and it's traditional for children to get the words wrong, but I haven't come for figgy pudding.'

She shivered in the draught from inside the house that was colder than the air outside, and noticed a tracery of lichen on the professor's teeth.

'Who *are* you then, and what do you want? Why do you have those secateurs in your hand?'

'My name is Ivy and I have come to ask for a single spray of your white holly, which I can see from my window on the estate,' she said. 'I borrowed the secateurs from my husband who is employed by the council. My sister Blanche who is flying from Australia has set her heart on a white Christmas and as I cannot bear to disappoint her, I have transformed my flat into a fairy-tale grotto with a silver Christmas tree and perspex icicles and frosted baubles and a kissing bough of artificial mistletoe. I have hung silver paper chains, sprayed snow on the windows and made a round pudding from white sugar and spices, pale sultanas and blanched almonds. A sprig of white berries would be its crowning glory.'

'How dare you!' shouted the professor. 'Have you any idea what desecration, what violation you have the temerity to suggest? You have the impertinence, *Hedera helix vulgaris*, to presume to stick my precious holly in your pallid pudding, to shrivel and blacken in the blue flames of your cheap cooking brandy! Leave my property at once, return to your vandal husband and the common, ignorant hooligans of your estate and never darken my door again!'

'I may be common, but I am not ignorant,' said Ivy. 'I have brought you a box of our luxury cognac mince pies. Deep-filled, with latticed lids and suitable for vegetarians. I work at Simmington's Supermart where the baking is done in-store and I can vouch for all the ingredients.'

'Pah!' said the professor. 'What sort of exchange is that? My holly is beyond price and No Frills mince pies are two a penny at Kwik Save. It is apparent that you look upon the festive season as an excuse for intemperance and gluttony. You would do well to heed the sorry example of a family by the name of Cratchit who, I recollect, gorged themselves silly on a super-fattened fowl. It did for the youngest, a peevish and sickly lad, and serve him right!'

'That is a wicked lie. Everybody knows that Tiny Tim did not die. You are as cruel as dead King Herod in your hatred for little children.'

The professor laughed. It sounded like holly leaves rasping in an icy wind.

'What makes you think King Herod is dead? Do you never watch your television or open a newspaper?'

'I only wanted to make Christmas magical,' Ivy whispered.

'To make Christmas magical?' he repeated. 'You confuse the secular with the sacred, my good woman.'

'I am not your good woman, nor am I of the Druid persuasion, but my philosophy can accommodate mistletoe and miracle, Magi and magic, faith and Father Christmas. I acknowledge that I was wrong to ask for your white berries, but even as we speak, my sister Blanche is homing through the clouds in the anticipation of snow.'

The professor took the box from Ivy and, biting into a pie, spoke through a mouthful of mincemeat.

'In opting for the Antipodes your sister Blanche has forfeited her claim to snow and deserves no more than sand in her Christmas pudding. However, if you insist on humouring her, I suggest that you apply to the Clerk of the Weather.'

'I had no idea that such a person existed outside the pages of the *Rupert* Annual,' said Ivy, adding, 'It is evident that you never had a sister.'

'I had a sister once,' the professor told her, 'Gladdon by name, a scholar like myself, but fleet of foot and skilful at spinning yarn. She was put under a spell by an enchanter who turned her into a dancing bear, and now she has been sold to a travelling circus.'

'Bears are not born to dance,' said Ivy. 'Why do you not enlist the services of an animal welfare agency, or force the enchanter to lift the spell?'

'That I cannot do, for the enchanter is Time himself, but I believe she is quite happy, although it is hard to tell,' the professor replied. 'She shambles and her fur is rather shabby but everybody says how kind her master is; he feeds her titbits from his own plate and the people love to see her dance in the circus ring and toss coins into her paper cup when she leads the parade.'

'I do not believe you,' said Ivy. 'I am going home now and I wish you joy of your white holly!' So saying, she turned and walked down the path to the professor's sing-song refrain:

> Nay, Ivy, nay,
> It shall not be, I wys,
> Let Holly have the mastery,
> As the manner is.
>
> Holly stands in the hall,
> Fayre to behold;
> Ivy stands without the door,
> She is full sore a-cold.

Ivy did not look back as the mocking verses pursued her.

> Holly and his merry men,
> They dance and they sing;
> Ivy and her maidens,
> They weep and they wring.

73

Ivy hath a chilblain,
She caught it with the cold,
So might they all have one
That with Ivy hold.

When Ivy reached the gate prickly fingers held her captive while the professor's cawing, sawing voice came carolling through the gloom.

Holly hath berries,
Red as any rose,
The forester, the hunter
Keep them from the does.

Ivy hath berries
As black as any sloe,
There comes the owl,
And eats them as she goes.

Holly hath birds,
A full fayre flock,
The nightingale, the poppinjay,
The gentle laverock.

Good Ivy, tell me,
What birds hast thou?
Only the owlet
That cries how, how!

As Ivy freed herself from the thicket, she could not imagine the professor dancing and singing with any merry men, unless they were a company of ghosts. The professor may have the mastery, she thought, or perchance the mystery, but I shall not weep and wring my chilblained hands like a poor maid consigned to the ice and muck of a medieval midden. Ivy's berries, black and green, are as lovely as any, her sweet-scented flowers are full of bees, and passionate shepherds weave belts of straw and ivy buds with coral clasps and amber studs. Besides, I have always been rather partial to owls.

★   ★   ★

By midnight on Christmas Eve the professor had consumed all but two of the luxury pies.

'This mincemeat is rather rich for my digestion,' he decided, laying aside his pen. 'I shall scatter the remains where my feathered friends may find it more to their taste,' and he went out into his garden, heedless of the falling rain.

High in the nearby tower, John the woodcutter, his brother-in-law and nephews and nieces were all asleep, but Ivy and her sister Blanche still sat up talking.

'Midnight,' said Blanche. 'Let us pull up the blind and listen for sleigh bells as we used to long ago.'

The sisters stood at the window looking down. They heard church bells pealing out and from deep in the concrete forest came the first cry of a newborn child, that breaks and heals the heart in the same instant.

'Look, Ivy! Look at the magical tree!' Blanche exclaimed. 'How luminously it shines, with moonstones glimmering among its leaves! But how weird – it may be jet lag or the white port we have been drinking – but that garden below appears to be full of flying birds, dipping in and out of the rising cascades of the fountain and surely that's a topiaried bush but it's fluttering down from its pedestal, and there's a peacock spreading its tail! That long-legged striding figure, look, it seems to be growing taller and taller! Ivy, is it a man or a walking tree?'

'I cannot tell,' said Ivy.

And as she watched the great dark shape moving down the garden, reaching out branching arms to embrace the white holly tree, a white owl detached itself from the flock and circled upwards, soaring over black treetops and hazy street lights, beating through the rain towards the tower on dipping snowy wings.

Wasps' Nest

Wasps' nests are architectural marvels. Paper lanterns that contain cities and societies. The first wasps' nest I saw was brought into school by a boy in my infant class. The wasps were all gone. Miss Edwards, our teacher, had on a blue smock printed with red and yellow flowers. She put the nest on the nature table and children from the other classes came in to look at it, and we infants felt very proud. Years later, I saw a wasps' nest hanging from a bush in a garden, like one of those paper moon lampshades, so light it seemed as if the wind would take it. So, I have always loved wasps' nests.

One night last week I was woken from a deep sleep by the telephone. When I found the phone and the light switch, I saw that it was three o'clock. As if in a bad dream, I heard my father's voice droning on about an invasion of wasps in his bedroom.

'I could hear them scratching on the light bulb,' he was saying. His voice scratched my consciousness like wasps' wings on glass. I felt invaded myself.

'How many?' I asked.

'Four or five,' he said.

I remembered his next-door neighbour pointing out to me wasps flying in and out of an airbrick near my father's roof. 'Live and let live' has always been my philosophy, so I said nothing to my father at the time. Also I disliked this neighbour, who played loud music late into the night. Now retribution had come. At ninety years old Father was fit as a flea, and I didn't want him stung to death by wasps. In a straight choice between Father and the wasps, what could I do?

Still groggy from being woken at three, I spent a day of frustration and anxiety on the office telephone. Calls to and from my father, the housing association which owns his flat, Pest Control.

Being kept on hold by electronic music, people promising to call back, and leaving me in limbo. Now, according to my father, there were thirty or forty wasps buzzing round. At last the wasps' fate was sealed: a pest control officer would visit in the morning.

So he did. But he arrived without his ladders, and the execution was deferred. My father had shut his bedroom door and the rest of the flat seemed wasp-free. He often slept in the front room anyway because of the neighbours' noise, so that was no problem.

At nine o'clock the following morning the phone rang. It was Father telling me the deed had been done. I said I would call in after work. One of my colleagues told me about a wasps' nest he'd found in his attic. 'It was taller than you,' he said. He sketched it with his hands and I saw this huge domed edifice, an elongated palace, frailer than balsawood, chewed into being by a million tiny mandibles.

The bedroom door was closed when I arrived at Father's. I opened it and saw a dozen or so dead wasps on the bed and on the floor.

'I'll deal with them,' said Father.

'No, I might as well do it,' I said.

I couldn't find the brush and dustpan. Eventually I located them outside the back door, the bristles soggy and the red pan half-full of dirty water. From the corner of my eye, I saw something moving. In an old flowerpot filled with rainwater, a wasp was struggling. Bright gold and black. Bigger than any of the wasps in the bedroom.

I went inside and swept them up. Their bodies were brittle and crumbled into the dustpan, glittery detached wings caught in the fibres of the carpet.

'Just throw them in the garden,' Father said.

Neither of us wanted to put them in the bin. They deserved at least to become part of the natural world.

I carried the dustpan outside. The large, black-banded gold wasp was still moving faintly in the water. I saw the dragged-down wings, the antennae. So much larger and stronger than the others, so determined to survive, banded in regal gold. She could only be the Queen.

I dipped the edge of the dustpan into the water and scooped her out. I couldn't look. I didn't want to know if she was dead

or alive. I carried the dustpan to the bottom of the garden and
tipped it gently onto the earth. The Queen among her broken
warriors. I went in and shut the door.

'That's done,' I said.

But outside in the garden there was a Queen, who surely had
a royal destiny to fulfil.

Windfalls

It was Martinmas, the eleventh of November, and in the front room of the house called Fernybank the morning sun of a St Martin's summer – the halcyon days which sometimes occur at this time of year – was diffused with shadows of leaves through the three green panes at the top of the window. A *Fatsia japonica* grew close to the house, always unclenching new green hands to knock on the window, and a rockery, thickly embedded with plants, among them the eponymous ferns, and divided by a crazy-paving path, sloped down to a low wall. The play of light on the foliage outside and the houseplants gave the room the aspect of a botanical glasshouse; it was a green faded room with bookshelves either side of the tiled fireplace, racks of LPs, tapes and CDs, a music stand and a clarinet. On the mantelpiece stood a mahogany-cased clock and a Newton's cradle tick-tocking from a recent encounter with a duster. Martin Elgin, sixty-three-year-old orphan, widower and housewife, had lived in Fernybank, one of a pair of semi-detached villas, for several years without redecorating anywhere. He had never heard of Martinmas until his wife Shirley told him about it, or a St Martin's summer.

After Shirley died, Martin had sold his share in their electrical repair business to his partner and moved from London to this town some twenty miles away, to be nearer their married son, Danny, and his family. His retirement freed him to not practise his clarinet, to not do up the house or redesign the garden or play any of the language tapes he had been given as presents, or join any clubs or make new friends, or do any of the things expected of him. It had, however, given him endless leisure to brood on his parents' last years and his wife's last months and conclude that he had made a botched job of every emotional emergency call-out. He knew that he could not go on like this indefinitely, and filed inside the latest Robert Goddard novel from the library was an application form from B&Q, who were taking on older staff.

This morning he was pleased he wasn't at work and he was getting ready to go out, because his daughter-in-law had asked him to collect his grandson, Noah, from school. Noah, who was not five yet, was in his first term in the Infants, mornings only, and it was difficult sometimes for Megan, a trainee IT consultant, to pick him up. Danny commuted to London where he worked as a systems analyst.

Martin was wearing a black waistcoat unbuttoned over a dark grey flannel shirt with a yellow tie, graphite-coloured cords and black suede boots. He looked what he was, an amateur jazz musician. Martin took the train to London once a month to play with his old mates, staying the night with his brother and visiting his wife's grave in Norwood Cemetery the following day. He put on his jacket, with the two poppies intertwined in the buttonhole; a white peace poppy in protest at the illegal war in Iraq and the red poppy he would not renounce. The white poppy, bought in a local bookshop, reminded him of a little white-haired lady who used to stand outside the tube station in all weathers when he was young, calling out in a whispery voice, 'Pacifist papers, pacifist papers.' Martin never bought one. And he would never have expected to join the beard-and-sandals brigade, yet he had boarded the coach to London with a local contingent to swell the massive anti-war march of 2003. He had always been Mr In-Between, too busy with his work and music to get involved in anything else. Which was possibly why he would never be a first-rate musician.

Shirley, a CND veteran, was the political one. She had cried with joy when Labour won the 1997 election. Sometimes he thought it was good that she didn't know what was happening to their country, the bus and tube bombings, accusations of witchcraft, more guns and knives on the streets, the police shooting of an innocent 'terror suspect', all the loony legislation and nonsense about ID cards, the list went on and on. Don't even get him started on Transport for London or South West Trains. Thing was though, Shirley would have tried to do something about it.

To be fair, there were no sandals among his lot on the march but loads of trainers, several beards, and fleeces, woolly hats and gilets galore. Danny had cried off at the last minute. Megan had a migraine. The shouting and banging drums and shrilling whistles as they marched through the streets deafened and embarrassed Martin until he could bear it no longer and slipped down a side street where he spotted a pub. Fortified, he made his own way to Hyde Park. His contingent was lost for ever and he found himself entering the park in a phalanx of black-clad Muslim women holding banners in a language he couldn't understand. The freezing mud of Hyde Park, penetrating his boots as he listened to Shirley's hero, Tony Benn, gave Martin his first attack of rheumatism. And what had the march achieved, apart from Martin's brief experience of being at one with a crowd and satisfaction that for once he'd spoken out?

Martin, born towards the end of the Second World War, had grown up despising the ordinary Germans who knew what was going on and did nothing. He lived lately in a constant state of unease about atrocities and injustices about which he did nothing. He had never questioned the fundamental decency and innate sense of fair play of the British, but now information was coming to light about an abomination known as the London Cage where prisoners of war had been tortured, and secret interrogation camps in Germany after the war. Holocaust deniers were springing up all over the place and every time you turned on the radio you heard about Guantánamo Bay and Abu Ghraib prison, you heard the word 'torture' bandied about, and discussions as to whether its use could ever be justified. If Martin were to count, he must have lived through, and hardly paid attention to, almost as many conflicts as there were pages in his boyhood stamp album. His grand-daughter, Lily, had shown only a brief polite interest in his prized collection of flimsy, magical oblongs, squares and triangles – stamps, like cigarette cards, played no part in her world.

Armistice Day was affecting him more this year than he remembered it having done before, perhaps because he had more time to watch the local news. He had woken to the early morning news on the radio announcing that four soldiers from his father's old regiment had been killed in Basra and a dozen police recruits had been blown up in a separate suicide attack. Somebody's boys. The old cliché would never lose its power to hurt. Both his grandfathers had been in the first war but he couldn't remember them talking about it, and Martin's father had never spoken about his time in the army. Martin and his brother had wondered lately if that was because Dad had not 'had a good war'. National Service had been abolished by the time the Elgin boys reached conscription age and so military matters had never impinged on their family, beyond the Forces' requests on *Two-Way Family Favourites* at Sunday lunchtimes. Martin would have preferred to observe the two minutes' silence alone with his radio but now he would have to do his shopping before picking up Noah, and the eleventh hour of the eleventh day of the eleventh month would find him on the hoof.

It was too warm for an overcoat and Martin wound a scarf round his neck before going through to the kitchen to lock the back door. He was distracted by the window; the leaves were late in falling this year, but the chestnut was almost bare and the sun turned its bellied trunk and branches to a brass chandelier. Elsewhere in his garden and beyond the trees were hung with green, yellow and russet flounces. Martin had come to enjoy, as much as he felt entitled to enjoy anything Shirley could not share, this house and garden with its visitors, the night people, the moths and rats, badgers, foxes and hedgehogs; he tolerated the slugs and snails who always left a little mesh of glitter in the space between the back door and skirting board, and most of all he enjoyed observing the sky and tree people whom he was privileged to have as neighbours. He kept a pair of binoculars on the draining board to catch their performances.

There was a sunny smell of toast in the kitchen and a counter-tenor singing like a fallen angel on the radio as two squirrels chased each other through the branches of the oak tree; first one, followed by the other, leapt in an arc the seemingly impossible distance through the empty air to a hazel tree, just catching a bunch of twigs almost too frail for their weight, swinging wildly before dashing onto a bough of bleached, ivy-girdled dead tree slanting across a tall willow. The squirrels sat side by side on a branch, in silver jackets opening onto white shirt fronts, and one of them appeared to put an arm around the other. Then, sensing that somebody was trying to capture that tender gesture in the twin round

84

eyes of binoculars through a kitchen window, the marvellous acrobats were gone.

When Martin was a boy there had been a WANTED poster of a grey squirrel in the post office. The reward offered was 'A Shilling a Tail'. Squirrels, like pigeons and any other wildlife to which mankind took a dislike, had become 'fair game' again. Martin had read about restaurants putting roast squirrel on the menu. In the prevailing climate of cruelty people had become shameless in their gluttony, while the more hypocritical claimed that by eating these long-established immigrants they were helping the cause of the red squirrel and our little native songbirds. For his part Martin decided that what the birds and animals did to get by was none of his business and he forgave the squirrels in advance for the bulbs they would dig up before the spring. He had watched one of them, it was grey with a reddish stripe running from the back of its head to the tip of its plumed tail, sitting on the stone step holding a dug-up crocus, green and white, and nibbling it as we might eat a spring onion. The thing about squirrels, they really seemed to enjoy life.

Although Martinmas was such a benign, blue-skied, scarlet-berried day as Martin set out, there had been high winds and rain during the night. Remembrance Sunday a few days earlier had been characteristically grey with a bitter wind stirring the medals and cockades, buffeting the flags and banners and the poppy wreaths pooling on the granite steps of the war memorial, watering the eyes and hanging dewdrops on the noses of some participants, the heroes in black and camel overcoats and anoraks who had survived ordeals that Martin had never been called upon to face. Martin had watched the measured tread of the wreath-layers, white gulls wheeling above the bugler sounding the Last Post, bareheaded men weeping and the marching girls and boys in the uniforms of youth organisations. Although he always bought a poppy, he had not attended any such ceremony since he was a boy, but when he went out for his newspaper, he found himself walking from the newsagents to join the gathering in the civic park, to be caught up in the melancholy grace of the occasion. What, he wondered, was passing through the mind of the lone survivor of the First

World War, huddled under a blanket in a wheelchair, paying his respects perhaps for the last time to his fallen comrades, boys dead for almost ninety years? And of course Martin had to ask himself, not for the first time, how would I have measured up, would I have had a good war? He became aware of a smell of old face flannels and fried chicken coming from someone standing near him and stepped away.

When he got home his heart was so heavy he didn't know what to do with himself. He went into the garden to plant, belatedly, the snowdrop bulbs Megan had given him for his birthday. Each thrust of the trowel into the cold wet clay hurt his hand. It was a duty discharged; he didn't give a monkey's if the little blighters came up or not.

As he walked to the shops Martin noticed that the road and the pavement were strewn with smashed rowan berries, crab-apples, split conker cases, all sorts of red, yellow and purple ornamental fruits; winged seeds and nut shells cracked beneath his boots. Nature's bounty. They must have been brought down in the night. His way took him past drives and front gardens where drifts of leaves and apples lay under the trees. A wealth of fruit that people couldn't be bothered to harvest.

At the small shopping precinct, Martin's heartbeat quickened at the thought of looking through the window of Gemini, Unisex Hair Salon, and the possibility of seeing the proprietor, Valerie, at her work. He had encountered Valerie twice, when he had taken Lily to have her hair cut. Lily was ten and walked the short distance home from school with a friend. Martin would look after her and Noah until Megan got back. He had thought a lot about Valerie, whether he could, or should, try to get to know her better. He was half disappointed, half relieved, when Megan had taken Lily herself last time; it was Megan, the old hand, who explained that Gemini was one of the 'air signs. Although Gemini was unisex, Martin felt he could not go there on his own account. He always went to Jimmy's, the barber where Danny and Noah had their hair cut, to maintain his neat grey fuzz. He wondered if he had the energy to even begin a friendship with another woman. Too much baggage, as they say. Valerie was somewhere in her forties;

she would either be married, or divorced with problem children and dependent parents, or living with an abusive partner – there she was, with her great legs in sheer tights and kitten heels, wielding a hairdryer, dressed in a white blouse, with a discreetly deep cleavage, cinched into her black pencil skirt with a broad patent leather belt, and over it an unbuttoned black gown with the sleeves rolled to the elbow, making her look a devastating combination of academic and factory girl. Her blonde hair was swept up and held at the back in a big shiny black clip.

The thing about Valerie was, she had the quality of kindness. Valerie was one of those women who, as they go about their daily business, do more good in the world than many who set themselves up as professionals or charge around emblazoned with charitable logos, wearing their hearts on their T-shirts. The first time Martin had taken Lily to Gemini he had sat intrigued, watching the stylists, all in black and white, and the black-gowned customers reflected in the bevelled deco mirrors which could reproduce somebody to infinity or capture passers-by outside and make them walk the wrong way until they disappeared into the looking glass. The silver and black and white choreography of this salon of mirrors was like a gelatin print and deserved, he thought, a Busby Berkeley soundtrack, rather than the local radio station banging on in the background. He watched Lily's wet rats' tails blooming into soft curls under the drier and falling in snippets round her chair, and he watched Valerie, presiding over her kingdom. An old lady had come in to have her hair done for her husband's funeral, and when it was time to pay, she found she'd forgotten her purse. 'It's on the house, my love,' Valerie said, putting her arm round her. The whole salon was in tears.

Martin gave Valerie a smile and wave as he walked on. Her face lit up and she acknowledged him with a pair of scissors, but he wasn't entirely sure that she knew who he was. Then he remembered with a jolt of shame a dreadful thing which had almost happened to him. Something he had been just saved from. It had happened the week before, in Haggerty's, the town's remaining department store. Martin had been travelling up the escalator to the second floor when he saw the naked polystyrene torso of a woman on a pedestal just within reach. He gave a sort of groan, a sigh,

87

yearning towards her, stretching out to embrace her – and snatched his hands back in horror when he realised what he was doing. He looked round. Nobody had seen him. But the disgrace if they had. How could he have done such a thing? Suppose some woman had screamed. He saw himself escorted from the premises by a security guard. And that would have been getting off lightly. How could he have faced the family ever again? It was a spontaneous gesture of tenderness, but what an inexplicable, seedy, shabby assault it would have seemed to them. Did the figure even have a face? He couldn't remember now. It was a sort of caryatid, waiting to display some garment.

He had to go to Woolworths for light bulbs, and while there decided to buy some sweets for the children. He was by the confectionary, noting gloomily that the shelves were full of Christmas chocolates already, when he thought to check his watch. One minute past eleven. When it seemed as though the two minutes' silence must have elapsed, the music from the CD counter stopped and loud giggling came through a PA speaker; a girl's voice could be heard saying, 'Get off me! No *way* am I doing it! You'll have to. It aint *my* job.' Martin caught the affronted eye of a woman standing to attention near him. She hurried towards the doors with her head bowed as, over the dull clang of something falling in a scuffle, a young man's voice, bursting with suppressed laughter, announced that as a mark of respect the staff and customers of Woolworths would now observe a two minutes' silence. Martin focused on the Pic'n'Mix, the multicoloured assortments of sweets in perspex cages, pastels and stripes and shiny jellified shapes which carried the warning that they contained pork and bovine gelatine. He was struck by the inherent loneliness of the Pic'n'Mix. It reminded him of lying in bed in the dark with too many radio stations to choose from and the display of his DAB radio shining like one of those blue fluorescent insect killers in a butcher's shop. Spoilt for choice, he left without sweets or light bulbs. This meant that he had to go to Robilliard and Daughters General Stores.

The light bulbs were to be found between the petfood, obscure brands with foreign labels, and sacks of biscuits and bird food and a pungent box of dried pigs' ears, and the knitting wool. Martin found what he needed and took them to the counter, where a pile of rodent glue traps lay beside an animal charity collection tin. One of the Robilliard daughters was in conversation with a customer. She almost spat the words, 'Do you know what I think they ought to do? They should build prisons under the sea! That would solve the problem for good and all.'

On Martin went, past Slots-Of-Fun, a cosy-looking little techni-coloured gambling den, and the charity shop where the bloke he knew as Jeff was standing in the doorway chowing on a Ginster, and past Tanya Hyde Sunbeds and Nail Parlour to the newsagents where, as was his habit, he adjusted a couple of the worst redtops, turning their faces, and the rest, to the wall. What sort of message were newspapers and top-shelf magazines giving to his grand-children and all the other kids who came into this shop? A headline flashed into his mind: GRANDAD ON MANNEQUIN GROPE CHARGE. He bought his paper and a packet of liquorice Rizlas, a couple of samosas and two Crunchies.

He reached the school with minutes to spare and stood in the infants' playground with a handful of mums accompanied by babies and crazy toddlers careering about, uttering shrieks that their mothers seemed quite impervious to as they chatted. Noah was released at last, carrying an awful lot of stuff for a little boy who was only part-time at school, and flung himself into Martin's arms, dropping half of it. Martin sorted him out and they walked the short distance to Noah's house hand in hand.

'How was your morning?'

'Foine.'

Noah looked worn out, white faced, and his hair, which was no particular colour until the sun highlighted all sorts of subtle tones in it, was sticky with some sort of yogurt or glue, which had also globbed onto his blue school sweatshirt.

'What shall we play, Grandad?'

'It's such a lovely day I think we'll just muck about in the garden after we've had some lunch.'

'I'll show you my latest tricks on the trampoline.'

The garden, with its double swing and trampoline, had a cidery smell, from the large misshapen cooking apples lying on the grass. Martin rolled a cigarette as Noah bounced, trying to invent tricks to impress his grandad, delighted to have him to himself.

His sweatshirt and T-shirt rode up exposing his white tummy and as he turned a somersault Martin experienced with such clarity a memory of his son Danny as a boy that he choked on his cigarette. It was Danny, in his last year at primary school, playing the lead in *The Shirt of a Happy Man*. Danny, his bare chest white above baggy black trousers, his dark eyes shining, somersaulting and handspringing across the stage. He had loved doing it, the audience had loved him, Martin and Shirley had wept through their laughter. It was as though a camera trans-fixed him mid-leap from his childhood into the future, and a black-and-white photograph was imprinted on Martin's heart while time moved on.

'Noah, did your daddy ever tell you the story of the king who wanted to wear the shirt of a happy man?'

'No.'

'Well, once upon a time there was a king who had everything his heart could desire, a beautiful queen, a palace, servants, jewels, but still he was not happy. He grew ill with sadness and nothing could make him laugh. People came from far and wide to try to cheer him up but the king grew sadder and sadder until one day a wise man told him that he would only be happy if he could wear the shirt of a happy man. So he sent his servants all over the kingdom to find a happy man and bring the king his shirt, but they all came back to say that they couldn't find anybody who was perfectly happy. The king grew sadder still until he almost died of sadness until at last . . .'

'I'm bored of this king.'

'Anyway the point is, the only man in the whole kingdom who was happy was this man who had no shirt, and the king laughed and laughed and they all lived happily ever after.'

'Why didn't the king have any children?' Noah was slashing the air with a plastic sword.

'Mind that sword. Why don't you play in the sandpit for a bit?'

'It's not a sword, it's a Lightsabre, only it doesn't flash any more.'

Martin lifted the lid off the sandpit to find that the greyish sand was full of half-buried toys. He pulled out a dead football, buckets and spades, various dinosaurs and grotesque humanoid robotic figures.

'"I shall find him, never fear. I shall find my grenadier,"' he said, holding up a soldier from no recognisable regiment.

'He's a baddie. He's Hitler.'

'Hitler?'

'Da guy what made World War One!'

'Two, and I wouldn't exactly call him a guy. It wasn't like *Star Wars*, you know! Hitler . . . look at all these apples going to waste.' He flicked one with the toe of his boot.

'They've got maggots.'

'Yeah, they might have *now* but they didn't always have. Come on, help me to pick them up. They're called windfalls.'

'I don't like the brown bits.'

'We can cut those out. How would you like to make an apple pie?'

Some apples were beyond use, turned to mush or stippled with circular patterns of white mildew. Noah unearthed a doll's head, which he brought to his grandad like little Peterkin presenting old Kaspar with the skull in the poem, thought Martin, feeling as defeated by attempting to explain Hitler to Noah as old Kaspar had been by the Battle of Blenheim. And should he try? Kids today had enough on their plates already, with wars and famine, climate change and endangered species thrust down their throats, as it were, before they could even speak. When he was a boy, aliens and mutants dressed in weird robes or aluminium foil, with goldfish bowls on their heads, were always intercepting our spacecraft, pleading 'Our planet is dying. You must save us!', but now the boot was on the other foot. What kind of useless punctured football of a world would Noah's children inherit?

By the time the apples were peeled and cored, Lily had arrived home and wanted to help make the pastry.

'Fine breadcrumbs, mind,' said Martin. 'Make it like the sand in your sandpit.'

As he watched the children working, Martin suddenly thought, I'm happy. I'm as happy as a sandboy. As happy as Larry. And a little dog, a bright-eyed, grinning fox terrier sort of dog, jumped into his mind.

'Hey, supposing Grandad got a dog? A little dog called Larry?'

Can you see me, Shirley? I'm making this pie with the grandchildren, with Noah who you never got to meet.

They heard Megan's key in the lock just as the pie, golden,
glazed with egg and decorated with pastry leaves, was lifted out
of the oven. Perfect timing. The children ran to meet her. Megan
stood in the kitchen doorway with her black laptop case, in her
grey suit and pink shirt, staring at the state of the kitchen. Mud,
sand, flour, scraps of pastry and apple peel on the floor.

'We were just going to clear up, weren't we, kids? Only we got
a bit sidetracked,' said Martin.

'No, that's fine. Lily, why haven't you changed out of your school
uniform? Come on, Noah. Into the bath with you, I think.'

'But Mummy, we made you a pie! Out of the apples from the
garden!'

'So I see. It looks lovely. I'll put it in the freezer as soon as it
cools down.'

'Why can't we eat it?' said Lily.

'We will. One day. I've already planned tonight's dessert.'

Noah burst into tears. Lily ran out into the garden. Martin could
see her through the window on the swing pushing herself higher
and higher.

'Look, Megan, I'm sorry.'

'No, I'm sorry. It's just that I'm utterly, totally, exhausted. It's
just that some of us don't have the time to go grubbing about for
rotten apples in the garden!'

'I'd better be going then. I'll go out the back way and say
goodbye to Lily.'

'Aren't you staying for supper?'

Two samosas and a can of beans at Fernybank, or waiting here
till Danny gets home?

'I don't think I will. I've already planned my supper. Where's
my shopping bag? Oh, here's a couple of Crunchies for a rainy
day. Noah, have you got a kiss for grandad? Give my love to Daddy,
and ask him if he remembers *The Shirt of a Happy Man*.'

Swansong

'The Hertford Hotel, please,' Louisa Grayling told the taxi driver at the station.

'The Hertford? You sure that's where you want?'

Across the dual carriageway towered various corporate hotels and beyond them a shopping mall, and then the hills. A sleety wind was trying to turn her umbrella inside out.

'The Hertford on Longley Road,' she said, getting into the cab, although she might have asked him to drop her at the end of Lonely Street, because the similarity of the names set 'Heartbreak Hotel' playing insistently in her head.

'You're the boss,' he shrugged.

'Yes,' Louisa agreed, crossing one knee over the other and inspecting her elegant boot for slush damage as they began to negotiate the town she hadn't visited for some forty years. Well, she thought, her baby had left her, as in the song, but although she missed her son now that he was at university, she was by no means heartbroken. She had it half in mind to look up her first love, Jeff Toland. He could buy her dinner for old times' sake.

Louisa had chosen the Hertford rather than one of the hotels which had sprung up in her absence, because of its proximity to the little French church where her old schoolfriend Monique's funeral was to be held. The service was at ten o'clock the following morning. Louisa was wearing a black coat and hat, though not in mourning for Monique, with whom she had maintained only a Christmas card relationship. She had come, as she put it to her husband, to pay her respects.

The Hertford, Louisa knew, would be nothing like as ritzy as Heartbreak Hotel, which she had always pictured as a deluxe fifties establishment. Its lobby was a symphony in black and chrome presided over by the desk clerk dressed in black, while the lachrymose bellhop wore tight black livery with silver buttons and a pillbox cap on the side of his head. Beyond the lobby were dark velvet-padded recesses where broken-hearted lovers tried to cry away their gloom. The first time Louise heard Elvis singing 'Heartbreak Hotel' it had electrified her heart, but with a simultaneous jolt of recognition that one day she would be checking into Heartbreak Hotel; somewhere down the line there was a room reserved in her name.

Out of the town centre, the taxi turned down a wide avenue. Balmoral Road. She stared out of the window. Yes, it was still there, Balmoral Court, the 1920s block of flats where Jeff had lived with his parents, no doubt dead now, like hers. But two letters had fallen from the building's façade. If Jeff did still live here, his address would be number 13, A MORAL COURT. Then the taxi passed St Etienne's church, and they were in Longley Road. The Hertford Hotel, dingy brick with a small spire and turret and Gothic windows, stood incongruously in the residential street.

There was nobody behind the desk in the hall. Louisa dinged the bell on the counter. The walls were hung with celebrity photographs signed with love and kisses. To her amazement, a hundred stars of stage, screen and radio – Dusty Springfield, Buddy Holly and the Crickets, the Everly Brothers and even Elvis – had stayed at the Hertford. It must have been quite a place in its heyday. She peered to read what Elvis had written and confronted a bloated impersonator in a white jumpsuit. The sort of guy you'd find working in a chip shop. Feeling foolish, she realised that she was looking at a gallery of tribute acts.

'Mrs Grayling. We've been expecting you.'

A tired-looking woman in a black dress, with a platinum blonde chignon spiked by a plastic gardenia, had come up behind her. The greeting sounded so like a line from a horror film that Louisa almost laughed, but really it didn't say much for her to be expected in this lounge with an out-of-order cigarette machine and a dead fibre-optic orchid on the desk.

'Your room's all ready. Number five, the Turret Room.'

As she opened the door of the Turret Room, a chambermaid, clutching a Hoover and duster, was giving a squirt of air freshener to the potpourri in a ceramic swan on the dressing table, before backing out. Louisa noticed that the chambermaid was

94

wearing school uniform. She had written 'dust' with her finger on the mirror and forgotten to wipe it off. The Turret Room looked out over the street where nothing was happening except a January afternoon. Two identical prints of the town in bygone days hung above the bed, and the minibar contained a miniature of Malibu. Instead of a Gideon Bible, there was a kirby grip in the bedside drawer. The rattle of wire coathangers in a wardrobe and a single rusty kirby grip in a drawer can make you feel so lonely you could die.

Louisa stretched out on the candlewick bedspread and concentrated her thoughts on Monique, recalling the school assembly when the headmistress had itemised various activities to raise funds for the new swimming pool; Miss Harker read out notices of events such as a cake sale, a plimsoll-whitening service, and then she announced that the sixth form were to hold a lunchtime dance session where the records of – here she squinted at the paper with disdain – the records of Elvin Priestley would be played. The hall erupted. Monique and Louisa hugged each other in bliss at Miss Harker's ignorance, and in pity for the black-gowned staff stranded on the platform across the gulf of hysterical girls.

Jeff Toland's phone number had always stayed in her memory. Her heart started beating too quickly as she rang it on her mobile, substituting the old code with the new. They had met when they both worked at the publishers Cockleshell Press, specialists in local history. Long gone, she supposed. For Louisa it was a holiday job; Jeff had been there since he left school. He loved history but she was bored to sobs by smug sepia people whose lives were so much harder and more heroic and worthy than one's own. It broke Jeff's heart when her family moved to London. Louisa was so elated that she forgot to give him her new address.

The phone rang in Amoral Court but no one answered. Pity. Louisa had imagined taking his hand across a restaurant table and saying, 'Remember how we used to make fun of those old fogeys at Cockleshell, Mr Abinger and Miss Ellingham? Well, time has had the laugh on us, Jeff – we are old Abinger and Evelyn Ellingham now!' And Jeff's incredulous laughter that she could think such a thing of herself.

In her tiny ensuite bathroom the shower curtain hung perilously from a rusting rail, reminding her of the Bates Motel. She had to get out, and walked into a terrifying provincial sunset, a conflagration of reds and pinks and golds blazing in the window of St Etienne's church and threatening a freeze when darkness fell.

Jeff Toland *was* still a resident of Amoral Court but today he was at work. Jeff was now the manager of the Greenfields Association charity shop, which raised money for disadvantaged children. Jeff Toland, popular with his customers, always hungry, always sad, forever suppressing the desire to look up his two old friends cannabis and alcohol, had once known the Hertford Hotel too well. In one of its metamorphoses the Hertford had been the House of the Rising Sun, and had caused the ruin of many a poor boy. He never went near it now, even though his estranged daughter lived there with her mother.

It was a slow afternoon, no drunks or deranged people, the vultures eager for the weekend's pickings had flown, Jeff's volunteer was in the back steaming a rack of clothes, while a couple of students mooched around to music from the local radio station and a mum killing time jiggled a twin buggy holding three infants whose mouths were plugged with dummies, and an obvious dealer covertly examined the marks on a tea set. Jeff was shelving a consignment of books, including some old Cockleshell Press titles, while keeping an eye on one of his regulars, whose mobility scooter, which took up half the floorspace, was customised with shoplifting panniers, a Union Jack and a *World's Best Nan* sticker. Jeff suspected that it was a vehicle of choice rather than of necessity.

'Here, lovey,' she wheedled to one of the students, 'pass us down that little windmill, if you'll be so kind. My poor old arms won't stretch that far. And that Dutch clog, if you don't mind.'

Jeff knew he would not see the blue and white delft planters, complete with wizened corms, again but they were of little value compared with some of his stock, which he had recognised on a daytime TV auction show. His strategy of placing things out of her reach had failed. He put a couple of pasties in the microwave and set about sorting a bin liner full of unwanted Christmas gifts.

★ ★ ★

The nearest parade of shops, Louisa discovered, consisted almost entirely of charity shops. Then, crossing the road, she was a victim of a hit-and-run. She was struck from behind and sent sprawling into a pile of slush at the kerb. The murderous vehicle had no numberplate, only a sticker saying *The World's Best Nan*. The driver was shrouded by a plastic raincover. None of the moon-faced witnesses moved to help Louisa so, shaking, she limped into a charity shop to recover. The palms of her gloves were badly grazed but although her knees felt bruised, her tights were intact. The shop radio was playing 'Dream a Little Dream of Me' and on a shelf was the twin of the pearly swan on her hotel dressing table. Still in shock, she bought a cashmere jumper for £2.59.

In the second shop there were two white swans, lustrous with gilded beaks and rose-tipped wings, and the yearning sound of Gerry Rafferty's 'Baker Street'. Now she embarked on a swan quest. Swan-upping. In the third shop was a single enormous swan with uplifted wings. Where did they come from, all these white swans a-swimming to the hits of yesteryear? They were like the white swans at Golders Green Crematorium, placed there by loyal fans of Marc Bolan, in memory of his song 'Ride a White Swan'. They were the sort of swans old people had on their windowsills; they had plastic ones too, sprouting crocuses among the gnomes in their gardens. This was the swansong of a generation.

The next shop triumphed. In the window, on an oval mirror, three swans floated on their reflections in a glass lake. Louisa went in. Then she saw Jeff. Her heart pounded. She hid her burning face in a box of broken jewellery. From the back Jeff looked almost unchanged, with long legs in skinny jeans, except that his hair matched his grey jumper. He turned round. A massive tangle of grey beard streaked with white cascaded over the paunch distending his sweater, and it was flecked with pastry crumbs. Louisa pulled down her hat brim and made for the door, but stayed, transfixed.

'Daydream Believer' had segued into David Bowie singing 'There's a starman waiting in the sky' and Jeff and all the browsers were humming or singing under their breath, with a far away look in their eyes. Outside the steamed-up windows the world was going to hell in a handcart but within, these disparate souls whose treasures were tomorrow's bric-à-brac were practically waltzing with the cast-off clothes amidst the smell of microwaved pasties; citizens of the democracy of dreams united in the hope of a stellar ambassador from a better world.

Louisa almost ran along the street back to the hotel. There was nothing more sinister about the Hertford than the Gothic of everyday failure. Tomorrow, she would get through the funeral, and take the first train home. Everything was OK. If only her stupid boots wouldn't keep beating out the chorus of 'Heartbreak Hotel'.

Ennui

Domestic interior, Granby Street. Near number 247 Hampstead Road. Sometime in 1913 or 1914. A man is sitting at a circular table smoking a cigar. If he were to reach out, he could grasp the woman standing behind him by the waist or hip, and pull her onto his knee. But he's immobilised, and she has her back to him and is gazing in a reverie at the glass dome of stuffed birds on the chest of drawers.

What time of day is it? An hour when the corner of the heavy marble mantelpiece casts a deep shadow, motes of inertia settle like dust on the furniture, when ash crumbles at the tip of the cigar. The time of day when a man and a woman wonder why fate has cast them together in these lodgings, where the solidity of the rented objects augments their feelings of impermanence. Let us call them Hubert and Milly. Hubert is some years older than Milly, his thick hair silvered while hers is still dark.

Did she settle for him perhaps? *Faute de mieux*, after several disappointments, when the bloom of youth was fading? Maybe he saved her from some intolerable situation, from a brute of a man, or destitution. It might have even been true love. Traces of the charm that seduced many women linger in his features, coarsened by time and drink. In his brown suit, he looks the sort who'd be at home in a public house or on the racecourse. In fact, he has on occasion been mistaken for a publican. He has the air of a heavy loser, and his melancholy face suggests losses on the horses not yet admitted to her.

The tumbler on the table holds a clear liquid. Water with gin, a mixture of both. Or water with a splash of white rum, in memory of his days at sea. A Jack ashore, he calls himself, an adventurer who sailed under several flags, now washed up in London, marooned in Camden Town. With his luck it's probably water in the glass.

Milly wears a neat, short-sleeved blouse tucked into her long skirt, with a belt whose leather catches the light. Although the fabric's gone limp, a faint whiff of starch comes off her blouse, fresh in the mingling odours of old cigar and some other lodger's grilled mutton chops. Milly taps idly on the glass dome that holds the display of stuffed birds. Shimmering jewels, with eyes like jet beads. They've travelled with her from lodging to lodging, giving respectability and an illusion of home to dwellings shabbier than this, glowing in dusty corners when there was no fire in the grate. Emerald, jet, ruby and gold, they perch in eternity, with wings poised for flight.

The light quivers in the lustre of their feathers, making tiny pulses beat in glittering throats, their beaks about to open in liquid song. Sometimes, catching sight of them, startled by colour, her heart lifts and she wants to prise off the glass and stroke them with her fingertip. Today, they are dull-eyed sad dead little things who ought to be flying under sunny skies. Their dome is a cruel contrivance; she could carry them to the window and tip them into the sky, fling them onto the air, to go chirruping and fluting, into the skies of Camden Town, to soar over the buildings and tramlines to the trees of Regent's Park or Primrose Hill. But no doubt they'd be mobbed by the native birds.

It crosses her mind that among them there might be a bird of ill-omen, a bird whose feathers you shouldn't bring into the house. Something had to account for her rotten luck. Some people say peacock feathers bring misfortune, even death. But maybe it's just the way their eyes watch you.

Milly's an expert in feathers and beads, working as she did in the back room of Madame Vertue, Milliner by Appointment. She was happy there, among the pretty silks and plumes. Shaping and stitching and gluing. Joking with the other girls. Until Hubert turned up drunk once too often and got her the sack. Cards. Dice. Feathers. Things that make your luck. Walking under ladders, a black cat, or a chimney sweep crossing your path. Hubert's employer, the artist, who keeps asking her to pose for him, he had peacock feathers in a copper vase in his studio last time she was there, doing a bit of cleaning. As well as great jugfuls of lilac and may, flowers she would never take indoors. Talk about provoking Providence. She's done it before, sat for an artist, never minded, but she doesn't fancy taking her clothes off now, for all the world to gawp at in some gallery. A friend of hers did it recently, only to have the critics condemn her as a 'hideous middle-aged woman in sordid surroundings'. She wouldn't have minded quite so much, only she wasn't even middle-aged, let alone hideous. But whoever cares about the feelings of the model? Well, not to mention the artist, however much of a gentleman he might be. Staring at you with his head on one side, screwing up his eyes. Measuring you with his brush at arm's length the way they do. Scrutinising you while you sit there like a lemon, with all the life going on in the street outside, as it is now.

Milly shivers in the blouse she ironed last night while Hubert was out at the music hall. Down at the New Bedford, the Bedford Palace of Varieties, with the artist and his cronies. Sneaking out and shaming her in front of her mother, who'd come round for a bit of supper with them.

But her resolve would weaken, she could get talked round again, desperate for a few shillings for the rent. The thin end of the wedge there. One minute you'd be sitting there respectably, dressed up as a coster girl, or something picturesque in a hat, and before you knew it you'd be sprawled naked on the bed with your throat cut. Posing as that poor girl in what the newspapers called the Camden Town Murder.

Hubert sat for the artist several times in various costumes. But naturally he'd never been required to remove more than his jacket. Who'd want to buy a picture called *Nude with Bowler Hat and Cigar*?

She was a prostitute, the girl who died, but she wasn't expecting anybody that night. Her golden hair was done up in curling pins. It was said at the trial that her throat was cut as she slept. Milly hopes it was. The thought of those curling pins makes her feel sad. The girl was only twenty-two. They arrested a commercial artist for the murder, but the evidence didn't stand up in court. He was defended by the great Marshall Hall himself. Hubert's been behind bars, and she suspects he keeps up with his criminal associates.

A painting of a woman hangs on the wall, against the mottled grey-green wallpaper. The woman, partly draped in puce material, lies on a couch, resting on her bare arms, leaning out of the picture and looking past the couple in the room. Her bright glance suggests that it is she who is alive, and they but components of a *nature morte*: *Still life with figures, stuffed birds, glass and box of matches.*

Nevertheless, Hubert's heart is thudding and his brain racing, but like a horse whose wind is broken it stumbles and stalls at every fence. He thinks he might take a ride on a tram to clear his head but he cannot move, and then there's the matter of the tram fare, and the price of a drink at the other end. He drums his finger on the table, notices the sound of Milly's fingers tap-tapping on the glass, and reaches for a match to relight his cigar. Coughs as the pungent smoke fills his mouth, and wipes his moustache. His stomach growls, complaining of too many oysters over the years, too much beer and champagne, eels and pies and liquor and mash and tobacco. He's pickled and smoked and kippered himself. He's a flitch of bacon. An old salt cod. If only Milly would go out of the room he could take a nip of what's left of the port in the decanter on the mantelpiece to settle his stomach. He wills her to move but she lounges there moping. If she put out her hand to ruffle his hair everything would be all right. If he could think of anything to say to put himself in a better light about last night. If he could put his hand in his pocket and pull out a handful of money. But he's done that, and knows his fingers will encounter nothing but fluff and shreds of tobacco, a shrimp's tail and a crumpled betting slip. He's done all the pockets in the house, furtively, and Milly's purse, and looked under the mattress in hope of a miracle. He's searched the tea caddy where she used to hide her savings. She's grown very sly. He sees her as she was when they first met, in her white dress. All in white but the boots, the boots were black. It's sad how women's true colours come out once they've got a ring on their finger. A noose round a fellow's neck.

He couldn't remember much of the day, before the evening. It was now a blur of plush and chandeliers, cupids and caryatids. But he recalled the old charlady, Milly's mother, sitting there in her plumed hat that Milly had given her before she'd lost her job at the milliners. The old girl had said nothing. In fact, she said, 'I'm saying nothing', but the feathers on her hat were positively trembling with disapproval. It wasn't his fault he had to go along to the Bedford with the artist, who wanted to sketch the boys in the gallery for a painting he'd been commissioned to do by one of his wealthy patronesses. Some people have all the luck. Take two innocent little lads in a school playground. Years down the road, one of them goes swanning off to Brighton and Paris and Dieppe at the drop of a hat, hobnobbing in society, while the other ends up as his super-annuated odd-job boy, in the soup and on his uppers.

Sunk in his thoughts, unaware of what he's doing, Hubert runs his finger down the side of his chair, between the wood and the upholstery. A jolt goes through him. An electric shock from hand to heart. His fingers close on paper and metal. The crinkle of notes and the hardness of coins. He exhales a silent prayer of thanks.

At last he turns, and pulls Milly onto his knees, where she sits, stiff as a statue, refusing to look at him, tossing her head when he tickles her under her chin.

'How do you fancy a night out?' he says. 'What say the first house at the Bedford and a slap-up supper?'

'Oh yeah, I fancy it all right,' she replies heavily, 'and then what shall we do for the rent?'

'Oh ye of little faith,' says Hubert, all a-twinkle now, 'trust your old Hubie, when has he ever let you down? How about a little kiss?'

The names of the man and woman could well be Hubert and Milly, or they might be Hubby, full name unknown, and Marie Hayes, who was possibly his wife. Hubby acted as a general factotum of the painter Walter Sickert and, singly and together, he and Marie were the models for many of his pictures. Hubby and Marie, in a painter's studio, posed in a tableau of their own life. Hubby was an old schoolfellow of Sickert's, who fell on hard times and was taken into the painter's household, and dismissed more than once for his drinking. At the outbreak of war, Hubby, deeming himself not too old to serve his king and country, set off for Aldershot to enlist. Perhaps he was grateful to the Kaiser for getting him out of his latest scrape.

It's thought that Marie stayed on in the painter's employ. This is the last we know of them, Hubby and Marie, who were immortalised on canvas as the embodiments of ennui. But they are all of us, any of a thousand couples trapped by time, in the hour when the shadow of the marble mantelpiece falls like the gnomon of a sundial.

Bananas

'Gin? You want cheap gin?'

In vain had she oiled her basket on wheels. The dreadful young man leaped from his doorway and was standing on the opposite pavement shouting at her.

Imogen Lemon's face swelled into one of the gross, foreign, beefsteak tomatoes sunning themselves outside his shop and such a headache hit her brow that she felt her skin would split and spill hot seeds onto her white sundress. She hurried to the safety of the supermarket, thirsting for one of the discreet little English tomatoes which had graced the shop before it fell into the hirsute hands of its present owner. The wicker basket followed at her heels like a faithful stiff old Airedale.

Two tiny veiled women in black passed in a cloud of patchouli. Imogen Lemon was a tall, slender divorcée with long hands and feet which had been much admired. Once her boss, coming upon her unexpectedly, typing in the gloaming, had momentarily mistaken her for a young girl seated at the virginals. Now she felt suddenly huge and white and freakish and half-naked in her summer frock against these scented bolts of black silk, and resented it.

On these warm evenings, after her supper and the nine o'clock news, Imogen would pour a tiny amount of gin into a tall glass and carry it, with slimline tonic brimming big rocks of ice, onto her balcony where she smoked two slow cigarettes and read the paper, the noise of the traffic blurred by the darkening leaves, and would sit in her iron garden in the sky until the leaves were black and the roses white and the glass an insubstantial rind floating at her foot.

Now, with him shouting out to the street like that about cheap gin, she felt as though his prickly face had thrust through the perfumed air, dirtying the roses.

She should never have bought gin in his shop.

The trouble was, she reflected gloomily as she trailed round the supermarket, his shop was so handy. She would often pop in after work for something quick for supper or, when Claud, her cat, declared that his breakfast was smelly and unfit for feline consumption, she could dash through the traffic for a packet of frozen fish and be back in five minutes. Lately, however, the young man's stock seemed to have deteriorated. Of course it was not his fault that they were demolishing the buildings opposite and brick dust drifted through the open door and settled in a reddish haze on everything, although she supposed that he could employ one of his mothy feather dusters to remove it, instead of lounging about exchanging gibberish with his cronies in the back of the shop. And, of course, if she should need a card of rusty hair grips or a dented tin of chick peas, a pair of tights with one leg shorter than the other, or a tub of gangrenous yogurt at midnight, a Christmas pudding in July or Easter eggs at Christmas, it was nice to know that he was there.

She would not touch his meat, however; and always avoided looking at the strange red glossy animals, peeled heads and foreshortened limbs that hinted at barbarism under their sweaty perspex cover. She left the supermarket and went into the butcher's, shouldering the English beasts of honest yeoman stock which hung in the doorway.

As she emerged, a troupe of goblins flurried round her, banging her knees, and one trod heavily on her toe. As she gasped and disengaged herself, clutching at the wall with one hand and her spinning basket on wheels with the other, she realised it was only the little girls from the preparatory school, in their distinctive red caps and lethal sandals, on their way to the swimming baths. She limped home.

That evening a storm broke on West Kensington and Imogen was quite pleased to give in to her headache and sore toe and retire early, conjuring up, as usual, an angel, in a long white nightdress not dissimilar to her own, at each corner of her bed.

In the morning, as she passed on her way to the tube, he was outside the shop unpacking a crate of bananas. He straightened and stood grinning at her through the very small white pointed teeth that glittered in his stubbly muzzle. The sun struck a gold medallion lying in the black curls that gushed from his chest and eddied round his throat, and turned the stiff fans of hair at the armholes of his blue singlet to a rusty coral. He thrust a bunch of bananas in her face.

'You want bananas? Very good today.'

'No, thank you. I'm on my way to work. Perhaps later.'

She forgot about him but on her way home she saw him, from the corner of her eye, on the other side of the road waving a banana at her. She steadfastly, if painfully, walked on. She did not know his name, so Bananas was what she came to call him to herself.

Later that evening she slipped out in sunglasses and plastic mac to the Victoria Wine for a bottle of tonic. Her toe was still swollen, so as well as enjoying the comfort of them, she felt that her pink slippers added the finishing touch to her disguise. On her return Claud leaped at her as if congratulating her on her cunning, and she was laughing into his fur when the telephone rang.

'Mum?'

'Hello, Jenny darling.'

'You sound very cheerful.'

'Yes, well . . .'

'We thought we might come to see you on Sunday . . .'

As she shook hands with Father Smillie on the church path and shook the scent of incense and a drifting lime flower from her hair, it came to Imogen that she should buy some limes for the family's pre-luncheon drinks. Fortified by the rites of the Holy Church, she decided to brave Bananas. By a small miracle he was in the back of the shop with a chum and an exquisite little boy in a long white nightshirt was standing by the fruit display outside.

'Two limes, please.'

What a tragedy that Time would turn him into another Bananas . . .

He reached for two greenish warty lemons.

'No, dear. I said limes. Those are lemons,' she told him firmly. 'Two limes.'

'No. Those are lemons. I asked for limes,' she said very slowly and clearly. 'Those small green things are limes. Could you give me two, please, I'm in rather a hurry?'

She was about to reach for them herself when Bananas hurtled into the doorway, snatched the lemons from the boy, dropped them into a paper bag and handed them to her.

'No! I don't want them. I want limes!'

'You don't want?'

'I want two limes!'

'Ah!'

He reached up, took two limes and dropped them into the bag.

'Seventy-four pence. Anything else for you today? Bananas, gin, cigarettes?'

Half-blinded and deafened by a wash of tears, she saw his little teeth moving as she put down the money and, blundering through the door, collided with a woman in black, whose beaked mask gave her cheek a sharp peck.

'You see, I was beginning to think the whole thing was an elaborate joke at my expense. An absurd pun on my name. That he had somehow found out my name – silly, really . . .' Her voice trailed off. Obviously they found her story completely incomprehensible.

They were sitting on the balcony, the slices of lime stranded on melted ice in the bottoms of their glasses, Imogen, Jennifer and her husband Tony and Toby the baby who had a clownish red circle on each cheek and who was grizzling and banging his head on his mother's chest.

'You mean this woman deliberately attacked you with her beak?' asked Jennifer, warding off another blow from the hard head.

'No, of course not. Shall we go in and eat?'

'I'm awfully sorry, Mum,' Jennifer said as she surveyed the goodies spread out on the table, 'Toby won't eat anything when he's teething. Could he just have a banana?'

'A banana?' Imogen looked desperately at the blue grapes and oranges in the fruit bowl. 'I suppose I could pop across the road . . .'

'I'd go, only he screams if I put him down.'

Imogen looked at Tony, but he had buried his face in the *Sunday Times*. No hope there.

The baby flung out a fist and pointed at the door.

'Of course,' Imogen said weakly, picking up her purse.

Two elderly men in white robes with red and white checked tea towels on their heads pushed past her as she went into the shop with her bunch of bananas, got into a limousine parked outside, and were driven away. She joined the queue at the checkout and a black robe fell in behind her. Bananas seemed gloomy, even morose, she was pleased to notice. Perhaps his visitors had upset him. He grabbed the bananas and bashed them, bruisingly, into the scales.

'You got no need to go to Victoria Wine for gin,' he accused her, 'I got cheap gin. You want any today? Any cigarettes?'

To her horror she saw that it was not a black-robed woman behind her, but Father Smillie in his soutane. And Bananas was waving a bottle of gin.

The luncheon party was not a success. The children went early, using Toby's teeth as an excuse, and Imogen was left trying to drown Bananas' voice in the washing-up water, but Father Smillie wouldn't go down the drain.

On the following Sunday she was too ashamed to face him at Mass and had to take a bus to the Brompton Oratory. When she returned she saw the limousine parked again outside the shop and the sound of angry voices came across the road.

She had resolved never to enter his shop again and to ignore him if he spoke to her, but several days later Bananas caught her as she passed with her basket on wheels.

'Good morning. What can I get you today?'

'Nothing, thank you. I'm on my way to the library,' she lied.

'You like books. I got lots of books.'

Imogen looked past him, at his dubious stock of literature.

'I only read the classics,' she lied again.

'I got classics. You want *Lady Chatterley*, *The Thorn Birds*, *Third Term at Malory Towers*?'

Thus it happened that she was standing, a lurid-covered paperback in her hand, and Bananas calling from within, 'Any gin today?', as Father Smillie passed her with a curt nod, his soutane flapped with brick dust, hurrying from some errand of mercy on the demolition site.

'Cheap gin and cigarettes. Cheap gin and cigarettes,' the little girls were chanting as they skipped in the playground as she passed. Imogen tried to convince herself that they were saying something quite different, but that did it. She arranged to take a week of her holiday at once, organised a neighbour to look after Claud, and fled to a friend's cottage in Ilfracombe.

As she lay on the beach, healed by the waves and sand, she saw how absurd the whole thing had become.

On her return she strode on tanned legs into the shop to buy some special fish as a homecoming present for Claud, determined to restore Bananas to his right proportions – a foolish, over-friendly, small, foreign shopkeeper who must be politely but firmly shown his place.

A strange man, trim of beard and neat of collar and tie, stood behind the till.

'The other man, the one who used to be here, is he away?' she asked.

'He's gone.'

'Gone? Isn't he coming back?'

'No.'

'Why not?'

'He was losing money. He bad man. He won't be back.'

'Oh.'

Imogen felt a strange disappointment as she turned away. 'Oh,' she said again and her eye for once lingered on the meat display where a fly sat up on the perspex lid and rubbed its hands. Between two writhing heaps of mince was the boiled head of some animal, and set in its glistening jaws were two rows of tiny, very white, pointed teeth.

Evening Surgery

A Chopin prelude was strained through the speaker on a little
shelf on the surgery wall, above a garish oil painting shining in
the cruel neon striplight that picked out the lines and blemishes
and red-hawed eyes of the patients on the black vinyl benches.
Mavis Blizzard, senior receptionist, was proud of the picture; it had
been painted by one of 'her' old ladies, a purblind resident of
Peacehaven House for the Elderly. Mavis visited regularly, cheering
up the old girls, surreptitiously putting right the great holes and
loops that shaky fingers made in bits of knitting and jollying
them along when they grew tearful over old snapshots that she
had persuaded them to show. No matter that the picture was upside
down, the artist had now lost her sight completely; it would hang
as a testament to their friendship.

From time to time the name of one of the four doctors flashed
on a board, a buzzer sounded and a patient departed; the telephone rang, Mavis answered it, and greeted favoured customers
by name when they came through the door; her two minions
busied themselves among files and coffee cups; although they
wore blue overalls like Mavis's own, they seemed interchange-
able, merged into one subdued lady in glasses, for she was the
star of the surgery. Sounds of passing cars came through the glittering black panes of the window, people coughed, pages turned.
The music stopped abruptly, then an orchestral selection from
South Pacific washed softly over the surgery.

'That's better!' announced Mavis Blizzard brightly. 'We'd all have
been asleep in a minute. Dr Frazer's choice. Much too highbrow
for my taste.'

She was leaning out of the hatch behind which she operated
and enveloped her audience in a conspiratorial wink. As she opened
her eye she couldn't believe that the young woman in the corner
was almost glaring at her. She had a quick read of her notes before

sending them into Doctor. An invisible hand had placed a cup of coffee at her elbow; she clattered the pink cup with a red waxy smear on its rim onto the saucer.

'Well, I won't be sorry to get home tonight. I've been on my feet since six o'clock this morning and my poor hubby will have to get his own tea tonight. It's his Church Lads' Band night. They're practising some carols to entertain the old folks at my senior citizens' party, bless them,' she announced to one of her sidekicks or to the surgery at large.

If there were any who thought that her husband had had a lucky reprieve, they were rifling through the *Reader's Digest* or *Woman and Home* and registered nothing.

The telephone rang.

'Hello, you're through to Surgery Appointments.'

Her voice grew louder.

'Of course, Mr Jackson. Is it urgent, only Doctor's very booked up tomorrow? What seems to be the trouble? Pardon? Oh, your waterworks, Mr Jackson.'

Someone sniggered behind *Tatler*, others squirmed on the squeaky vinyl at this public shaming. It was enough to send two girls into fits; they snorted through their noses. The old man beside them moved an inch or two away from their cropped, hennaed heads, their ear-rings, their dark red mouths.

'You'll be old yourselves someday and it won't seem so funny then,' he said. The comic they hid behind shook in disbelief. Mavis Blizzard rolled her eyes; her own daughter was a Queen's Guide.

'– well,' she went on, 'Doctor's got a late surgery on Thursday. We could squeeze you in then at eleven forty-five. That's eleven forty-five on Thursday then. Not at all. See you Thursday then. Byee' – by which time the unfortunate man might have burst.

'Deaf as a post, bless him,' she explained.

'Next Patient for Dr Frazer' flashed up on the board. The woman in the corner jumped up, tossing her magazine onto the table, upsetting the neat pile. Mavis watched her disappearing jeans disapprovingly. She prided herself on getting on with all sorts, you had to in this job, but this one she definitely did not trust.

★　★　★

The woman walked into the consulting room. The doctor rose.

'Cathy! How've you been?'

'Bloody awful. You?'

'The same.'

She sat down. He took her hand across the desk.

'It's good to see you.'

'Yes.'

She was staring at the desk, twisting a paperclip with her other hand. There was so much to say, and nothing. They sat in silence. Then, as if suddenly aware of the briefness of their time together, he came round to her side of the desk.

When Mrs Blizzard had to come in to fetch a file the patient was buttoning her shirt. Dr Frazer stood beside her. Nothing unusual about that. So why did she feel as if she was fighting her way through an electric storm? The stethoscope lay on the desk.

'Come and see me again if the pain persists,' said Dr Frazer.

'OK,' she replied casually, without so much as a thank you or goodbye. Mavis rolled her eyes at the doctor, expecting a confirmatory twinkle at this rudeness, but he was grinning like a fool at the closing door.

'Well, really!' she said.

He pressed the buzzer as she went out. Nobody appeared. He was just going to buzz again when Mavis led in a frail old lady and helped her onto the chair.

'Let's make you comfy. I'll just pop this cushion behind your back.'

What a kind soul she is, the doctor thought. He realised that he hated her.

'Well, Miss Weatherby, let's have a look at you.' What's left of you, he almost said.

She struck the cushion to the floor with a tiny, surprisingly strong, gloved hand.

'I want you to give me a certificate, Doctor.'

'What kind of certificate?'

'A certificate to confirm that I am unfit; not well enough to attend her senior citizens' party!'

He had to fumble in his desk drawer, but she had seen his face.

'You can laugh, you don't have to go!'

She was laughing too, but tears glittered in her eyes.

'Neither do you, surely?'

'She's threatening to collect me in her car. I'll have to wear a paper hat and sing carols to the accompaniment of her husband's appalling boys' band, and then her daughter will hide behind the door and shake a bell and she will say, "Hark! What's that I hear? Can it be sleighbells?" and her husband will leap into the room in a red plastic suit and give us gift-wrapped bathcubes.'

'Couldn't you pretend a prior engagement?'

'She's managed to ferret out that I have no family or friends. She wants me to move into Peacehaven as soon as there's a coffin, I mean a bed.'

'I'm afraid I can't really give you a certificate, but I'll have a word if you like, about the party . . .', wondering how he could.

'It wouldn't do any good. I'll just have to turn out the lights and lie in bed until she's gone.'

'No you won't. Come and spend the evening with us. I can't promise any paper hats or bathcubes, but it would be nice if you did. OK?'

'OK,' she managed.

As she left he saw that her legs had shrunk to two sticks around which her stockings hung like pale, deflated balloons. Time unravels us, he thought, like old, colourless silk flags in churches, which have outlasted their cause.

At home, Mary's eyes, which lately a vague unhappiness had turned a darker blue, dimmed and were brighter, like mussels washed by a little wave, when he told her of Miss Weatherby's plight.

'Of course she must come. But why does she hate Mavis? She's so kind.'

'She's a ghoul. She feeds on illness and disease and death!' he burst out.

'But . . .' Mary closed her mouth. She went to the sideboard and poured him a drink. As she gave it to him he took her hand and kissed it. 'Thank you,' he said.

When Catherine opened the gate of the little terraced house she shared with her daughter and son she saw the room as a stranger might, through the unpulled curtains, lit from within like a candle whose wick has burned down below its rim; the paper moon suspended from the ceiling, the bowl of satsumas, the old chairs, the television glowing softly like a tank of tropical fish; the familiar tenderised and made strange by the darkness.

At seven o'clock in the morning a soapy fragment of moon was dissolving in the damp sky; birds assembled in the trees to wait for their breakfast, black shapes against the blue that slowly suffused the cloud. Catherine sat on the back step. She was glad that he could not see her in the old summer dress she was wearing as a nightdress, Lucy's clogs and her ex-husband's ropey bathrobe; her eyes stung as she looked along the length of her cigarette, such a lot to get through, her mouth felt thick and dry; behind her in the kitchen the washing machine threw a last convulsion and gave a little sob, like a child who has fallen asleep crying. Paul would be back from his paper round in a minute. She went in and ran a bath. As she lay in the water, left disagreeably tepid by the washing machine's excesses, she saw how she had failed with her husband, whose robe huddled in a heap on the floor; she had never let him see that she needed him. Because she had known that he would fail her. But if she had. She recalled Hardy's poem 'Had you but wept'. Such watery half-thoughts as float past when people are alone and naked vanished with the bubbles down the plughole.

She put the kettle on, switched on the radio, woke Lucy, made tea, made toast, made two packed lunches, flung the washing over the line, a jumble of socks and jeans and shirts that would not dry in the damp air, tested Lucy on her Latin while she combed her hair and coaxed some moribund mascara onto her lashes; the phone rang — for Lucy; wrote a note for Paul who had been absent the day before; the phone rang again; Paul, eating the remains of yesterday's pudding from the fridge, dropped the bowl on the floor, Lucy ironed a PE shirt and the pop music on the radio crackled like an electric drill so she turned it up. No doubt, Catherine thought sourly, the Frazers are sitting down to muesli and motets. Someone called; the children left.

She found a splinter of glass on the floor near the sink and held it up to the light from the window. If one just stared at pretty glass fragments or soap bubbles or the sediment round the taps or studied the patterns left by spilled pudding on the tiles. Is that what it's like to be mad; or sane? But if everyone did there would be no glass, no iridescent bubbles in the washing-up bowl. Even as these thoughts drifted through her mind the glass splinter was in the pedal bin, a cloth was attacking the bleary taps. As she attempted to leave the house a plant pulled her back with a pale parched reproachful frond. 'I'll water you tonight,' she promised, but had to run back for the watering can and then run down the road, as usual, to the bookshop where she worked.

Her legs ached. With every book token, every cookery book, every DIY handbook, every copy of *Old Surrey in Pictures*, *Bygone Surrey*, *Views of Old Guildford*, *Views of Old Reigate*, *Views of Old Dorking*, every *Wine Bibber's Guide* that she sold she felt less Christmassy. How stupid and greedy the customers were, flapping cheque books at her and Pat, the other assistant, slapping fivers down on the counter so that they had to pick them up, taking all the change so that she had to go to the bank twice for more.

'Isn't Christmas shopping murder? Isn't it hell?' the customers said. 'I'll be glad when it's all over!'

Greetings flew from throats that sounded as if they were already engorged with mincemeat. No doubt several books were slipped into shopping bags.

'It must be lovely working here – all these lovely books!' people told them. 'I could browse for hours!'

'Oh, yes!' Pat agreed mistily, not seeing the floor which muddy feet had reduced to a football pitch and which she would not clean. She was twenty-nine and wore little girl shoes, and dresses which she made herself; Cathy thought that she must be too embarrassed to take her own measurements, because they never fitted very well. She spent her lunch hours in the stockroom eating packets of pale meat sandwiches and drinking tisanes, reading children's books and lives of the saints. Mr Hermitage, the shop's owner, who was bowing and gesticulating like a puppet in his velvet suit in the back of the shop, and who was too mean to employ a cleaner, did not like to ask Pat to wash the floor so Catherine's less spiritual hands were calloused by the mop.

When she got the chance Catherine went into the little kitchen behind the stockroom and put on the kettle and lit a cigarette. There was nowhere to sit so she leaned on the sink.

'I won't go to the surgery tonight,' she told herself, 'I mustn't. I know it's wrong. It's stealing. I'm not going to go.'

Mr Hermitage came in rubbing his hands.

'Coffee! That's good!'

His body contrived to brush against hers, as it always did.

'Sorry,' he said, patting her as if it had been an accident, as he always did.

She carried her coffee and a cup of cowslip tea for Pat into the shop, taking a gulp on the way to drown the smell of nicotine. Six or seven people stood at the counter, impatient at the speed of the two robots behind it. Pat rolled panic-stricken eyes at her; she was up to her ankles in spoiled wrapping paper. The sellotape sneered and snarled. As Catherine reached into the till Pat pressed the cash total button and the drawer slammed on her fingers. She yelled and swore. The customers looked offended; shop assistants' fingers don't have feelings, especially at Christmas time. Catherine waited for her nails to turn black. Now she would have to go to the surgery. Alas, her fingers remained red and painful, but could not justify medical treatment. Her hopes abated with the swelling.

She arrived home late that evening and dumped her heavy carrier bag. It had taken ages to do the money; it had been twelve pounds short. Pat had been flustered into making several over-rings; customers had asked for books and then changed their minds after they had been rung up, there was an unsigned cheque. Catherine's face ached with smiling at browsers and buyers; she had eaten nothing all day. There was a warm smell of cooking.

'Dinner's almost ready,' said Lucy.

'I've made you a cup of tea, Mum,' said Paul.

She did not let herself notice the potato peelings in the sink, the spilled sugar, the teabag on the floor, which he had thrown at the pedal bin, and missed, the muddy rugby boots on the draining board.

'You're dear, kind children,' she said. She unbent her cold fingers one by one.

'Mum? . . . Are you all right? I mean, you're not ill or anything, are you?'

'Of course I'm not. Why?'

'It's just that you look so sad. You never smile. And you went to the doctor's.'

'It's just the Christmas rush in the shop. You've no idea what hell it is.'

Catherine felt ashamed. She saw that she was dragging them into her own abyss.

'Nobody's going out tonight, are they? And nobody's coming round? Good.'

She wanted to draw them to her, to spend the sort of family evening they had enjoyed before this madness had overtaken her; the curtains closed, the gas fire blooming like a bed of lupins, the telly on; the sort of evening you thought nothing of.

Halfway through *Top of the Pops* the phone rang. 'I'll get it!' Catherine grabbed the receiver with crossed fingers.

'Hello, could I speak to Lucy, please?'

Dumbly she handed it over. They had agreed that he should not ring or come to the house. And yet . . .

Later the doorbell rang; Catherine clamped herself to her chair. 'Door, Paul.'

A male voice at the door. She stopped herself from running to the mirror and glued her eyes to her book, looking up slowly as Paul slouched back, behind him John Frazer metamorphosed into a tall boy, through a sort of grey drizzle.

'Hi. I've come to copy Paul's maths.'

'Oh. How about some coffee, Paul?' Or a quadruple gin. Or a cup of hemlock.

As the boys went to the kitchen Catherine said to Lucy, 'Actually I don't feel very well. I keep getting headaches. The doctor gave me something for them, but it doesn't seem to work. I think I'd better go back tomorrow . . . so don't worry if I'm a bit late . . . Well, I suppose I'd better get on with the ironing.'

'Would you like me to do it?'

'Of course, but I'd rather you did your homework.'

Anyway it would kill an hour or so.

The case of a certain Dr Randal and a Mrs Peacock had, natur-ally, aroused much interest among the receptionists in the surgery.

Mr Peacock had brought an action against the doctor, accusing him of the seduction of his wife, and it had become a minor *cause célèbre*, partly because there were those who thought that the rules should be changed, partly because there had been no meaty scandal of late, no politicians floundering in the soup. Dressed like their namesakes, he in flashy tie and cufflinks, she in drab brown tweed plumage, an invisible blanket of shame over her bowed head, the Peacocks strutted and scurried across evening television screens and stared greyly from the newspaper in Mavis Blizzard's hand.

'Of course, it's the woman I blame in a case like this; a doctor's in such a vulnerable position . . . It's the children I feel sorry for. And his poor wife! What she must be going through.'

Mrs Peacock must be pecked to pieces by the rest of the flock; her brown feathers, torn by Mavis's sharp bill, drifted about the surgery.

'And she's not even pretty!'

'Must have hidden charms,' came with a timid snort from behind Mavis.

'Ssh.'

If their words were not, as she suspected, directed at Catherine, they none the less pierced the magazine she was using as a shield and managed to wound.

Mavis slotted in a cassette of Christmas carols and hummed along with it. A sickly fragrance of bathcubes emanated from her sanctum; she was wrapping them for her senior citizens' party, in between answering the phone and all her other tasks. Her daughter, Julie, who had come in to give her a hand, nudged her.

'That's Paul Richards's mother. He goes to our school. He's really horrible. This afternoon he and his friends turned on all the taps in the cloakroom and flooded it. They were having a fight with the paper towels. You never saw such a mess! Water all over the place, other people's belongings getting soaked! I wouldn't like to be them tomorrow morning!' she concluded with satisfaction.

A little boy, about two years old, was running round the table, bumping into people's knees, falling over their feet. His mother grew tired of apologising and held him captive. He screamed and would not be pacified. She had to let him go.

'What's all this then? What's all the noise about?'

Mavis Blizzard had emerged and was advancing in a sort of crouch in her blue overall on the startled child who backed into his mother's knees.

'We can't have you disturbing all my ladies and gentlemen, can we? Let's see if I've got anything in my pockets for good little boys, shall we?'

He clenched his hands behind his back. Mavis winked at his mother and dangled a sweet. The child gave a sob and flung himself on his mother banging his hard, hot head on her lip. A red weal sprang up immediately and the glassy eyes spilled over. The child joined a loud grizzling to her silent tears.

'I think we'd better let this little fellow see Doctor next, don't you?' Mavis looked round, 'That is, if nobody objects?'

Nobody objected. The mother jerked to her feet a silent girl in glasses who had kept her head bent over a comic throughout, and ran the gauntlet with her and the crying boy and a heavy shopping bag.

'Poor kid,' remarked Mavis as she returned to her hatch. 'She does find it hard to cope, bless her. My heart bleeds for these one-parent families. Not that I'm one to make judgements, live and let live, and lend a helping hand where you can, that's my motto.'

For a moment they were all bathed in her tolerance.

'Drat that phone! Blessed thing never stops, does it?' Evidently she forgot that most of her audience had been guilty . . .

'Hello, you're through to the surgery, can I help you? Of course. I'll drop the prescription in myself on my way home. No, it's no trouble at all. Save you turning out on your poor old legs in this nasty weather. No, it's hardly out of my way at all, and I shall be late home anyway. We've got a full house tonight!' She uttered the noise which served her for a laugh.

Catherine looked at her watch; the appointments were running ten minutes late. She reached for another magazine and saw a jar of carnations on the windowsill, slender stems in the beaded water, like cranes' green delicate legs. As the bubbles streamed to the surface and clustered round the birds' knees she wished she had not come; she wished she was at home cooking the evening meal. It was absurd; it was making neither of them happy.

'You said to come back if the pain persists. It persists.'

'Thank you for coming tonight. I've missed you so much.'

To her dismay she was crying. He scorned the box of pink tissues provided by Mavis for patients who wept and gave her his own white handkerchief. Even as she dried her eyes she realised that it had been laundered by his wife; it didn't help.

'It's not enough,' she said. 'At first it was enough just to know that you were on the same planet. Then I thought, if only we could be alone for five minutes, then it was an hour, then an evening . . . it's almost worse than nothing.'

The door handle squeaked. Instinctively she leaped from his arms to the couch and turned her face to the wall as Mavis came in.

'Mrs Blizzard! I wish you wouldn't barge in when I'm with a patient!'

'You forget that I'm a trained nurse,' she bridled. 'Dr Macbeth always asks me to be present when he's examining a female patient. I'm sorry to have disturbed you!'

She slammed the door behind her.

'I know it's not enough,' he said quickly. 'Can you get out one evening? Meet me somewhere?'

'Yes.' So that was that. How easily principles, resolutions not to hurt anybody, died.

He leaned over the couch and kissed her; she felt the silky hair on the back of his neck, his ear; she felt his hand run gently down her body, on her thigh.

'Don't, don't,' she said, but she didn't take his hand away.

'An urgent call for you, Dr Frazer,' squawked Mavis through the intercom.

Catherine slid off the couch and found the floor with trembling legs. Her face was burning.

'Just a minute,' he put his hand over the receiver. 'I love you. See you tomorrow morning? About eleven? We'll arrange something.'

Outside in the street she found his handkerchief in her hand and buried her face in it and, looking up, saw the stars over its white edge. As she lay in bed that night she put her hand where his hand had been.

★   ★   ★

He was late. She pushed her trolley up and down the aisles of Safeway's, putting in something from time to time for appearance's sake, waiting, loitering, buffeted, causing obstructions.

'I'm sorry.'

She whirled round. The smile withered on her face. A little girl was seated in his trolley. He rolled his eyes towards his wife's back, at the deli counter. As Mary turned to them he said, 'How are you?'

'As well as can be expected.'

She blundered to the checkout with her almost empty trolley. '. . . a patient,' she heard him explain, betray.

After crying for a while in the precinct she had to go to Sainsbury's to finish her shopping and trudge home to transform herself from lovesick fool into mother. Loud music hit her as she opened the front door. An open biscuit tin stood on the kitchen table, seven or eight coffee cups had been placed thoughtfully in the sink; she had to wash them before she could start on the potatoes. Several pairs of muddy shoes lay about the floor. Teenage laughter came from the bedrooms. Not jealousy. Not bitterness. Just pain. Like the dull knife blade stabbing a potato. The telephone rang. Feet thudded towards it.

'She's not in.'

'I am in!' she shouted and ran to the telephone.

'Cathy?' Her ex-husband.

'Oh, it's you.'

She had to stop herself from hurling the receiver at the wall.

'Cathy, I was wondering about Christmas . . .'

'Yes?'

'Well, I just . . . I mean, what are you doing?'

'Oh, this and that. One or two parties. The children have lots of things on. We're going to my parents' on Boxing Day, all the family will be there. I suppose we'll go to church on Christmas Day. Why?'

She longed to be beyond the tinsel and crackers, in the greyness of January where melancholy was the norm.

'Well, I just wondered. I mean, it's a bit of a bleak prospect – the kids and all . . .'

'You mean you want to come here. You might as well. It makes no difference to me. Why not? It will make everything just about perfect.'

She replaced the receiver, not wanting to wonder about whatever desperation had driven him to call, unable to contemplate any hurt but her own.

At last the three of them sat down to lunch.

'Mum?'

'What?'

'We are going to get a tree, aren't we?'

She looked at her children, her babies; Lucy's long hair glittering in the electric light, Paul's pretty spikes. She determined to stop being such a pain.

'Of course we are. We always do, don't we? I thought we might go this afternoon.'

'Great.'

'You'll come, won't you, Paul?'

'Well, you'll need me to carry it, if we get a big one, won't you?'

At nine o'clock that night John was called to Miss Weatherby's house. A neighbour, taking his dog for a stroll, had been alarmed by her milk-bottle on the step, her newspaper jutting from the door, and had found the old lady very ill. Had she had any family, John might have comforted them: she died in my arms; but she had none. He drove away feeling infinitely sad. There was only one person he wanted to tell about it; to lie in her arms and be comforted, to have wiped away the memory of the one card on Miss Weatherby's mantelpiece which said, 'A Merry Xmas From Your Unigate Milkman'. He stopped at an off-licence and bought a bottle of whisky. What a shabby figure he had cut, with furtive meetings in the surgery and Safeway's. Why hadn't he telephoned her this morning after the fiasco in Safeway's? OK, so he hadn't been alone for a minute, but he could have made some excuse to get out to a call-box, couldn't he? Why on earth did she put up with him? There could be only one reason. She loved him. He switched on the radio. Music flooded the car. He was singing as he drove into her road. Soft pink and green and yellow stars, Christmas tree lights, glowed against black windows. He was touched by these talismans in little human habitations. But when he reached her house he couldn't park. A line of cars stretched along each side of the street. He caught the poignant sparkle of her Christmas tree in a gap in the curtains. He found a space in the next road and walked back. The terraced house seemed to be jumping up and down between its neighbours, blazing with loud music. A volley of laughter hit him. He turned and walked away. He dumped the bottle in its fragile tissue paper in a litter-bin.

As Catherine cleared away the remains of last night's impromptu party from the carpet the telephone rang faintly through the Hoover's noise. She switched off. Only the radio. She switched on again. The phone rang again. Nothing. At last she decided that the ringing was conjured up by her own longing or was some electrical malevolence. The phantom telephone drilled out a shameful memory; last night, among her friends, as the party wore on, alcohol sharpened her loneliness until she dialled his number. Even as she did so she told herself that she would hate herself in the morning. She did. A woman's sleepy voice had answered. She hung up. Boring into their bedroom. Disturbing pink sheets; dreams.

She couldn't read, couldn't watch television, couldn't listen to the radio. She had to admit relief when the children went out that afternoon; when you are a mother, you can't scream that you are dying of loneliness and boredom, that your soul is rotting within you. Let his shadow fall across the glass in the door. Let the telephone ring. She stood at the window for a long time staring at sodden leaves and apples, then she grabbed her coat and went to borrow a dog from a neighbour, a patchy-skinned mongrel called Blue.

Ducks pulled melancholy trails across the dingy lake. It was no better here. When she had first met John, people's faces, pavements, skies were irradiated, familiar buildings blossomed with pretty cornices and swags of flowers. Now how ugly and pointless everybody seemed, the whole of Creation a dreary mistake. Damp seeped into her boots, her coat hung open in the cold wind, her bare hands were purple and scratched from the sticks that the fawning Blue laid at her feet to be flung. She glared at the parents trundling past with their prams and tricycles, forgetting that she had been happy once doing that. She found a bench out of the wind and huddled in the corner; the wind whipped the flame from her lighter as she tried to light a cigarette. Ignited, it tasted dirty, the smoke blew into her hair. Without realising it she was rocking slowly back and forth on the bench, head hunched between her shoulders. If only she had never gone to that party in the summer.

'Do you know Dr Frazer?' someone had asked.

'Actually, I'm one of your patients.'

'Oh, I'm sorry . . . I should have recognised you . . .'

'It's all right, we've never met. I'm never ill.'

'That's a pity.'

She had not met his wife, who was at the far end of the room in a group round the fire, but now, Oh God, wasn't that them coming round the corner? There was no escape.

'Hello.'

The family surrounded her bench. Blue jumped up at John; she saw him wince as the claws raked his thigh. He threw a stick; Blue bolted after it.

'I'm sorry. Your trousers. They're all muddy.'

'Don't worry about those old things! I'm always trying to get him to throw them out, but somehow he always retrieves them!'

Mary gave her a wifely smile; it might as well have been a dead leaf falling or the crisp bag bowling down the path. Mary shivered.

Blue was back with the stick, grinning through frilled red gums.

'I didn't know you had a dog.'

'It's not mine. He belongs to a friend.'

The three children in knitted hats, and Mary, grew impatient. Catherine stood up.

'Goodbye then. Come on, Blue.'

John bent over the dog, stroking it inordinately. 'Goodbye, Beautiful.' Fondling its ears.

As Catherine walked away she heard a child's voice say, 'Dad, can we have a dog?'

'Don't you think your mother has enough to do?' his voice snapped, as she had never heard it. Good. I hope your bloody afternoon's ruined. Intruding on her in her ratty fake fur coat, jeans frayed with mud, smoking a cigarette on a park bench, with a borrowed dog; flaunting his family, his wife in her neat tweed coat and matching blue woolly hat. Well, that's that then. It's over.

Good. Him in that anorak of horrifying orange. They were welcome to each other. To complete the afternoon's entertainment Mavis Blizzard was bearing down the path pushing part of an old man, wrapped in a tartan rug, in a wheelchair.

When John arrived at the surgery on Monday morning Julie Blizzard was there with her mother.

'Morning, Doctor,' said Mavis.

'Morning, Doctor,' parroted the clone.

He searched his frosty brain for a pleasantry.

'I suppose you'll be leaving school soon, Julie? Any idea of what you want to do?'

'I'm going to work with underprivileged children.'

'They will be,' he muttered as he went through. Then he turned back. 'By the way, Miss Weatherby died on Saturday night.' Or escaped, he might have added.

'Oh dear, the poor soul,' said Mavis absentmindedly. Miss Weatherby merited a small sigh then Mavis added, 'It's the weather, I expect. You know what they say, a green December fills the churchyard. I've got to go over to the hospital myself this afternoon to visit an old boy, that is if he's lasted the night, I'd better check with Sister first. He's blind and his wife's . . .'

'Doctor,' called Julie after him as he turned away rudely, 'you'll get a surprise when you go into your consulting room!'

Grey, rainy light filtered through white paper cut-out Santas and snowflakes pasted on the window. He punched the black couch where soon a procession of flesh in various stages of decay would stretch out for his inspection, and none of it that which he wanted to see.

Catherine ducked down behind the counter as Mavis Blizzard entered the shop with much jangling of the bell and shook sleety pearls from her plastic hood. When she emerged it was to confront Mary, who gave her a vague smile, as if she thought she ought to know her, and went distractedly from one row of books to another. A pair of wet gloves was placed over Mary's eyes. She gave a little scream. Mavis uncurled her black playful fingers.

'Oh, Mavis! You made me jump!'

As she served people and found and wrapped books Catherine managed to catch snatches of conversation.

'. . . peaky. Down in the dumps.'

'. . . Nothing really . . .'

'I always start my Christmas shopping in the January sales. Just a few last-minute things.'

'. . . he's just tired, I suppose . . . so bad-tempered . . . I can't seem to do anything right . . .'

You poor little fool, thought Catherine, confiding in that old harridan.

She stared icily at Mavis as she paid for her book, a reduced volume of freezer recipes, putting the change down on the counter rather than into her hand, but could not kill the thought; I first liked him because he was so kind and now he is less kind because of me.

It was way past the end of Pat's lunch hour. Catherine went into the kitchen and found her, sandwich drooping in her hand, enthralled by the life of a modern saint. She lifted her eyes from the page.

'Do you know,' she said dreamily, 'she drank the water in which the lepers had washed their feet!'

'I think I'm going to throw up,' said Catherine.

She saw that the sink was clogged with cowslip flowers. Then, at a brawling sound from the street, they both ran back into the shop. A gang of teenagers was rampaging down the pavement, school blazers inside out, garlands of tinsel round their necks and in their hair, which some of them had daubed pink or green. Catherine's eyes blurred at their youth, their faces pink with cold, the flying tinsel. One detached himself and banged on the window.

'Hello, Mum!'

She managed a weak salute.

'Disgusting! No better than animals!' said a customer's voice.

'At least they're alive!' Catherine retorted, because for the moment they *were* young animals, and not fossicking among freezer recipes and jokey books about golf and fishing.

'I thought she was such a nice girl,' the customer complained to another as they went out.

'It's the other one who's a nice girl,' her friend explained.

★　　★　　★

'If Blizzard answers, I'll hang up,' Catherine decided as she dialled Surgery Appointments. One of the underlings took the call. Hers was the last appointment of the evening. She couldn't believe the little scene that was being enacted in the waiting room. Mavis evidently had caught a woman in the act of tearing a recipe from one of the magazines.

'But it is dated 1978 . . . ' the culprit was quavering in her own defence.

'That's not the point. It's the principle of the thing!'

Mavis thrust a pen and a sheet torn from a notepad at her.

'Here, you can copy it out, if you like. If everybody did that . . .'

It was impossible to see from the woman's bent head if she was writing ground almonds or ground glass, but when her turn to go in came her face was stained a deep red.

Mavis had only Catherine with whom to exchange a triumphant glance; their eyes met for an instant before she retreated to her sanctum, which, Catherine was amazed to see, was decked with Christmas cards.

'Next Patient for Dr Frazer.'

Catherine went in.

'I knew it! I knew it! I knew something was going on! What do you think I am? Stupid?'

John and Catherine were frozen together as in a freak snow-storm.

'It's disgusting! It's smutty! It's . . .'

'I realise that's how it must seem to you, but really, I assure you . . .'

Catherine felt his fingers slide from her breast.

'That's how it appears to me and that's how it is. What do you take me for? I'm not stupid you know.' She turned on Catherine.

'You come here night after night and yet there's never anything written on your card, never any prescription. How do you explain that? Just because you couldn't hold on to your own husband you try to pinch someone else's! Well, you're not so clever as you think you are, or you, Dr Frazer! Perhaps you'd care to read this?'

She flung an evening paper on the desk. The verdict in the Randal and Peacock case. The condemned pair would not look.

'Guilty, of course. It's his wife I feel sorry for. And the children. What they must be going through! I'd hate Mary to suffer what that poor woman's –'

'You wouldn't!'

'I –' She had to duck as a paperweight flew past her head and crashed into the door, then Catherine was struggling into her coat.

'Don't go,' he said, but she was gone, blundering through the empty surgery in tears.

A trombone belched outside the window.

'Oh my Gawd, the mince pies!'

Mavis ran from the room as the broken notes of 'Silent Night' brayed. Les Blizzard and his Church Lads' Band had mustered outside to give the doctors a carol.

Someone had rescued Mavis's mince pies, her annual surprise to the doctors, from the little oven she had installed in the office; they were only slightly blackened. The festivities took place in Dr Macbeth's, the senior partner's, room. John looked round: the three receptionists in their blue overalls, Johnson sucking burnt sugar from a painful tooth and trying to smile, Baines eyeing the bottle, Macbeth, eyes moist with sweet sherry, mincemeat in his white moustache, giving a convincing performance as a lovable old family practitioner, which of course he was. The window, like his own, was decorated with white paper cut-outs. Macbeth raised his glass to Mavis.

> 'I have heard the Mavis singing.
> His love song to the morn.
> I have –'

'*Her* love song, surely,' corrected Mavis, reducing his song to a gulp of sherry.

John drained his glass.

'Well, Happy Christmas, everybody. I must be off.'

'But Doctor, you haven't pulled your cracker! You can't break up the party yet!'

Mavis was waving the coloured goad in his face. He grasped the end and pulled. 'What is it?' scrabbling among their feet. 'Oh, it's a lucky charm. There, put on your hat!'

She crammed a purple crown on his head; it slipped over his eyes. As he pushed it up, to his horror, he saw a sprig of mistletoe revolving on a thread from the light.

'Ho ho ho,' rumbled Macbeth.

Under cover of the crackers' explosions John muttered, 'Do you think you could remove those bits of paper from my window? They block the light.'

She gave no sign of having heard.

'Oh, I almost forgot! Pressies! You first, Dr Frazer, as you've got to rush off.'

She crammed his weak arms with parcels.

'Just a little something for the children. You'll love little Katy's present! It's a doll that gets nappy rash when it wets itself! Isn't that a hoot? Whatever will they think of next?'

The minions duly hooted.

Catherine watched her ex-husband's feet tangle and tear wrapping paper. He sat down heavily beside her on the floor, pushing parcels out of his way and pulled her to him. His shirt, an obvious Christmas present, perhaps from someone who wished he was with her now, burst open at the neck.

'I still fancy you, you know.'

The whisky smell was like a metal gate across his mouth. She wanted to howl and weep and, failing John's, any old shirt would do, even this one, smelling so new, with a frill down the front.

'Your shirt. I'm sorry.'

'It doesn't matter. I didn't like it anyway,' pressing a button into her eye.

The bookshop. Mr Hermitage. Pat. Christmas. I'll get through this one, she thought, then the next one and the next. But this will be the worst. The years ahead. Each day that she would not go to the surgery, would not pick up the phone. She saw a series of bleak victories, a lone soldier capturing pointless hills when there was no one to see.

'Do you want to watch the children opening their stockings?'

John realised that she had never had to ask this before; the Christmas tree wavered into a green glass triangle shot with lights;

Mary's face, above her pink dressing gown, was pale and wary; she had sensed his absence beside her in bed and come to find him, and now excited sounds were coming from the children's rooms.

'I love you,' he said.

For a moment, before he followed her upstairs, the doctor placed his hand over the pain in his heart.

Pink Cigarettes

As the cab dawdled down Pimlico Road Simon slithered and fretted on the polished seat. The shops, which had so recently enchanted him with glimpses of turquoise and mother-of-pearl and chandeliers spouting jets of crystal lustres against dark glass, now threatened him with a recurrence of his old complaint, boredom. He looked neither to the left nor the right lest he see again a certain limbless torso, a gilded dodo or a headless stone lion holding out a truncated paw. Surely it would be kinder to put it out of its misery? He saw himself administering the *coup de grâce* with a mallet and sighed, and closed his eyes but was too late to escape the sight of two Chelsea Pensioners lurking like wind-bitten unseasonal tulips among the grey graves of the Royal Hospital. He pulled off his red tie and stuffed it into his pocket. His misery was complete as they crossed the King's Road and he turned from the fortunates on the pavement in their pretty clothes to his own reflection in a small mirror; nobody, he feared, could call him yesterday's gardenia, more like yesterday's beefburger in a school blazer. He had been forced to leave the house in his uniform, and he had a cold. He had poisoned his ear with a cheap ear-ring and it throbbed with the taxi's motor.

He thought that this was the most unpleasant cab in which he had ever ridden – a regular little home-from-home with a strip of freshly hoovered carpet on the floor, a photograph, dangling from the driver's mirror, of two cute kids daring him to violate the *Thank you for not smoking* sign, and a nosegay of plastic flowers in a little chrome vase exuding wafts of Harpic. He remembered with envy a taxi ride he had once taken with his mother; she had had no time to look out of the window or be bored. She had replenished lipstick and mascara and combed her hair and then she had taken from her bag a bottle of pungent pink liquid and a tissue and rubbed the varnish from her nails, decided against repainting them, and lit a cigarette and when she had stubbed it out on the discarded tissue, the ashtray had gone up in flames. It had been lovely.

He was thrown forward when the cab braked suddenly as the car in front pulled into a parking space.

'Woman driver!' said the cab driver.

'Or a transvestite,' said Simon.

The driver did not reply, but added ten pence to the clock after he had stopped. Simon ran down the steps, hoping to avoid being spotted by the housekeeper, who had taken an unaccountable dislike to the slender blond, amanuensis of the tenant of the basement flat.

'Don't kiss me, I've got a cold,' he greeted the old poet who opened the door. The cocktail cabinet was closed; that was always a bad sign. He wondered if he dared risk opening it while the old man was pottering about in the kitchen, dunking a sachet of peppermint tea in a cup of boiling water.

'Simon?'

He lounged in the doorway wasting a winning smile on his host.

'Would you like a tisane?'

'Wouldn't mind something a bit stronger . . .'

'There's some Earl Grey in that tin,' said the cruel old buzzard who was dressed today in shades of cream, with a natty pair of sugared almonds on his feet and a dandified swirl of clotted cream loosely knotted at his throat and a circlet of gold-rimmed glass pinned with a milky ribbon to his wide lapel. Simon became conscious again of his own drab garb.

'Sorry about the clothes,' he said sulkily, 'my mother was around when I left so I . . .'

'I've told you before, dear boy, it doesn't matter in the least what you wear.'

Simon was not mollified. He watched him lower his accipitrine head appreciatively into the efflorescence from his cup, complacently ignoring as usual the risks Simon took on his behalf, and risks for what? He stared out of the window at a few thin early snowflakes melting on the black railings.

'Snow in the suburbs,' he said.

'I should hardly call this the suburbs.'

'It was a literary allusion.'

'Not a very apt one, as anyway it has stopped snowing. Now, are you going to have some tea, or shall we get straight down to work? We've got a lot to get through today.'

'*We*,' echoed Simon bitterly and sneezed.

'I expect that lake of yours is frozen this morning?' added the poet.

'Not quite.' Simon proffered a stained shoe.

'I've got an old pair of skates somewhere. I must disinter them for you.'

Simon, who thought that they were already on thin ice, drummed his nails on the windowpane. The scent that had intrigued him early in their acquaintance he knew now to be mothballs and it was coming strongly off the white suit.

'You're very edgy this morning. For goodness sake stop fidgeting and pour yourself some absinthe, as you insist on calling it.'

With three boyish bounds Simon was at the cocktail cabinet smiling at himself in its mirrored back as he poured Pernod into a green glass. It was amazing how good he looked, when he had felt so ugly before. Was he really beautiful or was there a distortion in the glass, or did the poet's thinking him beautiful make him so? He could have stood for an indefinite length of time reflecting, sipping his drink, a cocktail Sobranie completing the picture, but the old man came into the room casting his image over the boy's. Simon turned gracefully from the waist.

'Got any pistachios, Vivian?'

'No.'

'You always used to buy me pistachios,' he whined.

'It would take my entire annual income, which, as you know, is not inexhaustible, to keep you in pistachio nuts, my dear. Now, to work.'

Simon gazed in despair at the round table under the window spilling the memorabilia of more than eighty years; diaries, khaki and sepia photographs, yellow reviews that broke at a touch, letters from hands all dead, all dead, with here and there a flattened spider or a fly's wing between the brittle pages, or the ghost of a flower staining the spectral ink, into boxes and files and pools

135

of paper on the floor. Simon shuddered. His task was to help to put them into chronological order so that the poet might complete his memoirs, while the little gold clock that struck each quarter made it ever more unlikely that he would. He plunged his hand into a box and pulled out a photograph of a baby in a white frock riding on a crumpled knee, which, if it could be identified, would no doubt belong to someone very famous. He tried to smooth it with his hand.

'Do be careful, Simon! These things are very precious!'

'It's not my fault!' Simon burst out. 'I don't really know what I'm supposed to be looking for, and when I do manage to put anything in order, you snatch it away from me and mess it all up again!'

'What? Listen, Simon, I want to read something to you. Go and sit down. Have a cigarette. Are you old enough to smoke, by the way? There are some by your chair. Light one for me.'

Simon gloomed over the cigarettes, like pretty gold-tipped pastels in their black box, not knowing which to choose. He had expected tea at the Ritz and hock and seltzer at the Cadogan Hotel, and here he was day after day grubbing through musty old papers for a book that would never be finished, that no one would publish if it was finished, and that no one would read if it was published . . .

'Of course it never occurs to some people that some other people are going to fail all their "O" Levels,' he muttered.

'No, we didn't have "O" Levels when I was at school,' agreed Vivian. 'Listen, Simon, this will interest you . . .' The words spilled like mothballs from his mouth and rolled around the room, '"and so I set foot for the first time on Andalusian soil, a song in my heart, a change of clothing in my knapsack, a few pesetas in my pocket, travelling light, for the youthful hopes and ideals that made up the rest of my baggage weighed but little" – you might at least pretend to be awake . . .'

'I am. Please go on, that last bit was really poignant.'

'Oh, do you think so, Simon, I'm so glad. I rather hoped it was.'

Simon selected a pink cigarette and, wondering if it was possible to pretend to be awake, fell fast asleep. He woke with a little cry as the cigarette blistered his fingers.

'I thought that would startle you,' chuckled the poet, 'you didn't expect that of me, did you?'

'I don't know . . .'

What deed it had been, of valour or romance, he would never know, but his reply pleased the old man.

'Come on, I'll take you out for a drink, and then we'll have some lunch.'

Simon attracted some attention in his school blazer in the Coleherne.

'This is a really nice pub,' he told Vivian, 'do you know, three people offered to buy me a drink while you were in the Gents?'

The poet stalked out, the black wings of his cloak flapping and smiting people, and Simon had to scramble up from the dark corner where he had been seated and follow him.

Much later, as he ran across the concourse at Victoria and lunged at the barrier he collided with a friend of his mother, on her way to her husband's firm's annual dinner dance in a long dress and fur coat, a dab of Home Counties mud on her heels.

There was nobody in. That is to say, his parents were out. Simon made himself a sandwich and took it upstairs. His room was as he had left it; the exploded crisp bags, the used mugs and glasses, the empty can of Evo-Stik, the clothes and comics, records and cassettes on the floor untouched by human foot, for no one entered it but he. He looked out of the window, and the pond in the garden below, glittering dully in the light from the kitchen, provoked an image of himself curvetting round its brackish eighteen-inch perimeter on a pair of archaic silver skates. He shivered and pulled the curtain, vowing feebly once again to extricate himself as he flopped down on the bed. When he had met the poet, not expecting the acquaintance to last more than an afternoon, he had constructed grandiose lies about his antecedents and house and garden, and had sunk a lake in its rolling lawns. He became aware of the sound of lapping wavelets; somebody next door was taking a bath, and he felt loneliness and boredom wash over him.

★　　★　　★

137

It was boredom that had led to his first timid ring on the poet's bell. One afternoon, in Latin, deserting from the Gallic Wars and tired of the view from the window, the distant waterworks like a grey fairground where seagulls queued for rides on its melancholy roundabouts, he had taken from his desk a book; an anthology whose faded violet covers opened on names as mysterious as dried flowers pressed by an unknown hand. Walter Savage Landot, Thomas Lovell Beddoes and Lascelles Abercrombie, whom some wit, in memory or anticipation of school dinner, had altered to Brussels Applecrumble. Vivian Violett – Simon selected him as the purplest, and turned the pages to his poem.

'What's that you're reading, Simon?'

'It's only an old book I found in the lost property cupboard.' Simon lifted tear-drenched eyes to the spectacles of the master who had oozed silently to his side.

'Let me see. My goodness, Vivian Violett! That takes me back . . .'

'Is he good, sir?'

'I think that this is, er, what's known as a good bad poem . . .'

He wove mistily away, adjusting his headlights, shaking his head as if to dislodge the voices of nightingales from his ears.

'Is he dead, sir?' Simon called after him.

'Oh, undoubtedly, undoubtedly. Isn't everyone? You could check in *Who's Who*, I suppose.'

'You are a creep, Si,' whispered the girl sitting next to him, 'I got a detention for reading in class.'

'Of course,' said Simon.

'Poseur,' she hissed.

'Moi?'

Simon, for whom the word *decadence* was rivalled in beauty only by *fin-de-siècle*, found that, at the last count, Vivian Violett was alive and living in London.

The next day he climbed the steps of an immense baroque biscuit hung with perilous balconies and blobs of crumbling icing, to present himself in the role of young admirer. His disappointment at being redirected to the basement by a large weevil or housekeeper in an overall was tempered when Vivian Violett opened his door, an eminently poetic Kashmir shawl slung round his velvet shoulders, and scrutinised him through a gold-rimmed monocle clamped to the side of his beak and a cloud of smoke and some other exotic perfume. The poet was charmed by his guest.

'I do enjoy the company of young people,' he sighed, 'especially when they're as pretty as you . . .'

Simon reclined on faded silk, fêted with goodies, not yet knowing that he was not only the only *young* person, but almost the *only* person to have crossed the threshold for many years.

'You must tell me all about yourself,' Vivian said, at once swooping and darting into his own past to peck out tarnished triumphs and ancient insults, shuffling names like dusty playing cards; a mechanical bird whose rusty key had been turned and who could not stop singing. From time to time he cocked his head politely at Simon's poor attempts, over a rising mound of pistachio shells, to attribute a little grandeur to himself before flying again at the bookcase to pull down some fluttering album of photographs or inscribed volume of verse to lay them at Simon's feet. It was then that the idea of Simon helping with the memoirs was born. A faint murmur about having to go to school was brushed aside like a moth.

'Nonsense, dear boy. You will learn so much more with me than those dullards could ever teach you. Besides, I have so little time . . .'

Simon was struck with sadness; the figure dwindling to a skeleton in its embroidered shawl had been, by its own account, the prettiest boy in London. Already he had noticed in himself a tendency to grow a little older each year.

'You will come and see me again soon, won't you?' the poet pleaded.

'Very soon,' promised Simon over the ruins of a walnut cake.

'Such a pity one can't get Fuller's walnut cake any more,' mourned Vivian for the third time.

'Mmm,' agreed Simon again, without knowing in the least what he was talking about.

'I hope you don't find this too cloying, Simon,' resorting to a tiny ivory toothpick, a splinter of some long-departed elephant.

Simon was dribbling the last drops from his glass onto some dry crumbs on his plate and licking them off his finger; the effect was agreeable, like trifle.

'Do you know that poem of mine "Sops in Wine"? Of course

you must, it's in the *Collected Works*,' – a volume which Simon had claimed to possess and which he had glimpsed only on a shelf of one of the tottering bookcases which lined the room – 'I'll say it to you.' And he laid back his lips like an old albino mule and brayed out the verse, sing-song in a spray of crumbs.

Simon reached for the decanter of madeira as if it might drown the sound of the last plausible train pulling out of Victoria, for he had not told his parents of his proposed visit. He need not have worried because when he telephoned home they had gone out.

That had been the first of his visits, and as he lay, weeks later, on his bed wondering how he could make the next one the last, toying with the idea of a severe illness, the telephone rang. He had difficulty at first in recognising the voice of his best friend.

'Do you want to come round to my place?' he was asking.

'OK, I'll be round in ten minutes.'

But as he was leaving the house the phone rang again.

'Oh Simon, I've just had such an unpleasant encounter with the housekeeper, complaints of playing my radio too loudly, accusations of blocking the drains with bubbles, I mean to say, have you ever heard of anything so ridiculous . . . all lies of course, you know she wants to get me out, it's all a conspiracy with the landlord so that he can re-let at a grossly inflated price. Bubbles! What would you do with such people, Simon? I know what I'd do, you must come and see me tomorrow, Simon, I'm so upset and lonely and blue . . .'

'I really can't. I've really got to go to school.'

'Well have dinner with me then at least.'

'I haven't got the fare,' said Simon weakly, 'my building society account's all . . .'

'Of course I shall give you some more money tomorrow, you should have reminded me.'

'I've got to go. The phone's ringing. I mean, there's someone at the door!'

On his way to school the following morning Simon was over-taken by his friend Paul.

'What happened to you last night? I thought you were coming round?'

'I was, only I got depressed . . .'

'Old Leatherbarrow's been asking about you, you know. Why haven't you been at school? Are you ill or something? You don't look too good.'

Suddenly school was an impossible prospect.

'I don't think I'll come in today after all.'

'Well, what shall I tell him? He keeps on at me! He'll be phoning your parents soon!' Paul's voice rose among the traffic.

'That's all right, they're never in. Tell him I'm suffering from suspected hyperaesthesia. I'm waiting the results of tests. Don't worry, I'll sort it out.'

He turned and left Paul standing on the pavement exhaling clouds of worried steam.

'Simon, it was sweet of you to come!'

Simon was shocked to see him still in his dressing gown, albeit one of mauve silk with a dragon writhing up its back, and a pair of unglamorous old men's pajamas. The flat smelled stale, like a hothouse where the orchids have rotted.

'Aren't you going to get dressed?' he asked disapprovingly, being young enough to think that if a person was old or ill it was because he wanted to be so.

'I will, now that you're here,' said Vivian meekly. 'I wasn't feeling very bright this morning.' His hand shook and a purple drop spilled to the carpet as he handed Simon a conical glass of *parfait amour*.

'Ah, meths,' said Simon, 'my favourite.'

'What are you grinning at?'

'Old Leatherbarrow. The St Lawrence Seaway . . .' replied Simon enigmatically. The forced daffodils which he had brought on an earlier visit hung in dirty yellow tags of crêpe paper against a small grisaille.

'Why have you been so ratty lately?'

'Have I? I'm so sorry, Simon, if I should have appeared to be ratty towards you, of all people, the person in the world to whom I should least like to be ratty when I am so grateful to have your friendship and your help. I suppose I have been worried. A thousand small unpleasantnesses with the housekeeper, and most of all about this . . .' he waved a hand at the tower of papers on the table. '"Time's winged chariot . . ." and Christmas . . .'

'Christmas?' said Simon. 'Christmas is OK –' and stopped.

'I shall go and dress now. Can you amuse yourself for a few minutes? Then perhaps we could do a little work on the memoirs. Where did we leave them?'

'You had just enlisted in the 'nth Dragoons,' he said as Vivian disappeared into the bedroom. Simon entered with a drink as he was impaling a cravat with a nacreous pin.

'Ah, my little Ganymede,' said the poet, smiling palely, 'what should I do without you?'

It was raining when they set out that evening for the Indian restaurant round the corner.

'Oh dear, oh dear, where's my umbrella? Simon, haven't you got a hat?'

'Of course not.'

'We don't want you to catch another cold. You'd better wear this.' He placed a large soft fedora on Simon's head. 'Yes, it suits you very well.'

Simon smiled at himself in the glass. He wondered if Vivian minded that the hat looked so much better on him.

A fake blue Christmas tree had been set in the restaurant window and cast a bluish light on the heavy white tablecloth and imparted a spurious holiness to the bowls of spoons and the candle holder by staining them the rich deep blue of church glass. Two pink cigarettes were smoking themselves in the ashtray. In an upstairs room across the street, behind a sheet looped across the window, an ayatollah or mullah was leading a congregation of men in prayer; their heads rose and fell. Simon felt suddenly the sharp happiness of knowing that, for a moment, he was perfectly happy. He smiled over his wine at Vivian. The old man gripped the handles of his blue spoon and fork.

'I don't think I can bear,' he said, 'to spend another Christmas alone in that flat.'

'But it's a lovely flat,' answered Simon inadequately and then there was silence while the waiter brought the food.

'I can't face any more unpleasantness. Days and days of not seeing you . . .'

'Mushroom bhaji?'

'No. No. You help yourself.'

Simon looked with embarrassment at his own heaped plate but was too hungry not to spear a surreptitious forkful and tried not to look as if he was chewing. He crumbled a poppadum while he tried to think of something to say.

'Do you know what I have been thinking?'

The poppadum turned to ashes in Simon's mouth.

'Why don't I spend Christmas with you?'

Simon choked on unimaginable horrors; carols round the telly, stockings suspended from a storage heater, a mournful quartet in paper hats silently pulling crackers, Vivian crushed like a leaf between his parents, in bulky, quilted body-warmers, asking for *parfait amour* at the bar of the local; their sheer incomprehension . . .

'What do you think, Simon?'

When he could speak he muttered desperately, 'I'm not sure that you'd get on with my parents.'

'We have one thing in common anyway, so that's a good start.'

'They're really boring. We never do anything much. You'd be bored out of your mind.'

'I'm never bored when we're together. Besides a quiet family Christmas is just what I need, what I've missed all these years. We could do some work on the memoirs. I'm sure your parents would be interested. We could go for long walks, that would be very good for me, and you could introduce me to your friends. What do you say?'

'I –'

'It's a large house, as you've told me, so I shouldn't be in the way.'

Simon had to stop him before he actually begged. Maybe his train would crash tonight, maybe his parents would have run away . . .

'I think it's a great idea,' he said, raising his glass, 'I'll tell them tomorrow.'

Vivian had to apply his napkin to his eye. He reached for Simon's hand and pressed it, then fell with a sudden appetite on the cold food in the silvery blue dishes.

'I wonder where those skates have got to?' he mused. 'Must be in a box somewhere, on top of a bookcase or under the bed. Ring me tomorrow when you've spoken to your parents, won't you?'

He put Simon in a taxi, and he was driven away with a despairing flourish of the black fedora through the window.

Simon could not ring him the next day, which was Saturday, because of course he had not spoken to his parents. On Sunday he woke late from a nightmare of Pickwickian revelry on the garden pond to the realisation that he had left the hat on the train. He went downstairs to find a message in his mother's hand on the pad by the telephone: 'Violet Somebody rang. Can you call her back?'

'They're delighted,' he told Vivian on the telephone, tenderly fingering the lump on his head where he had banged it on the wall. 'I can't talk now, but I'll come to see you tomorrow.'

He arrived hatless, sick with guilt, a dozen excuses fighting in his brain, clutching a paper cone of freezing violets, at Vivian's house. Before he could descend the steps the housekeeper flung open the front door.

'If you want to see Mr Violett, you're too late. They've taken him away.'

'What?'

'Last night. It seems he was climbing up on some steps to get something off the bookcase. Pulled the whole lot down on top of himself. There was an almighty crash, I dashed downstairs with my pass-key, in my nightie, but there was nothing I could do. It seems the actual cause of death was a blow to the head from an ice skate.'

A stout woman, wearing if not actual, then spiritual jodphurs, appeared on the step beside her. 'This is Mr Violett's great-niece. She's taken charge of everything.'

As Simon turned and ran he thought he heard the great-niece boom, 'Of course he was always a third-rater,' and the housekeeper reply, 'Oh, quite.'

He hailed a passing cab, and as he sat, still holding his violets, he saw that the windscreen carried the Christmas lights of Sloane

Square in a little coloured wreath all the way to Eaton Square. 'There must be a good bad poem somewhere in that,' he said to himself.

'The Headmaster would like to interview you, Simon, about your frequent absences.'

Simon knocked dully on the door, stuffing his handkerchief into his trouser pocket, his heart and thoughts miles away.

'Don't kiss me, I've got a cold,' he said, then saw in the mirror behind the astonished pedagogue the reflection of a red-eyed schoolboy in a blazer, whose crying had brought out spots on his nose, and as he pulled out his handkerchief again, saw a broken pink cigarette fall to the floor, and an irrecoverable past diminishing in the glass, when he had been Ganymede for a little while.

Babies in Rhinestones

The Alfred Ellis School of Fine Art and the Araidne Elliot School of Dance and Drama stood semi-detached from one another behind a small tearful shrubbery of mahonia and hypericum, snowberries, bitter blue currants, spotted laurel and pink watery globes of berberis spiked on their own thorns. A crooked hedge of yellow-berried holly divided the two gardens. The artist's was distinguished by a rusting iron sculpture, while Miss Elliot's, or Madame as she was addressed by her pupils, held a grey polystyrene cupidon bearing a shell of muddy water.

In the green gloom of his hall Alfred Ellis held up a letter to the light to see if it contained any money. It was in fact addressed to Araidne Elliot and had come through the wrong door. As he crumpled it into his pocket he wondered again if she knew that her name should be Ariadne. He fancied, as he passed the half open door of his front room, or atelier, that something moved, but when he went in all the easels were posing woodenly in their places. In the kitchen he poured boiling water onto an old teabag and was sitting down to read the paper when a round striped ginger face appeared at the window.

'Good morning, Ginger,' he said as he let in the cat.

'I suppose you want your breakfast. I was about to read the Deaths, to see if I had died recently. Now I shall never know.' He brushed at the bouquets of smudgy paw marks on the black words and poured out a bowl of milk.

Dead or alive, half an hour later he set off for the shops. Ginger ran down the path before him. At the same time his neighbour emerged from her gate, struggling with a green umbrella. Araidne Elliot seemed more at the mercy of the elements than other people; the mild late autumn rain had, on her walk down the garden path, reduced her piled-up hair to a spangled ruin sliding from its combs. A scarlet mahonia leaf was slicked to the toe of her boot. A cluster of red glass berries dangled from each ear.

'Miss Elliot, you look the very spirit of autumn . . .'

She did not reply, being unsure, as so often, if he was being unpleasant, and looked down at Ginger who was rolling on his back on the pavement at their feet, displaying his belly where the stripes dissolved into a pool of milky fur.

'Home, Rufus!' she said sharply. 'You can't come to the library with me.'

'Rufus?'

She blushed. 'I call him that. I don't know his real name – he's not really mine, I'm afraid. He just walked in one day and made himself at home. He always comes for his breakfast and sometimes he stays the night. He sleeps on my bed.' She blushed again. 'I wish I could keep him, but he's obviously got a home . . .'

'His breakfast?' repeated Alfred Ellis. 'That's impossible!'

'Oh yes, every day, but the funny thing is, he won't touch milk!'

'You little tart, Ginger,' he said softly, inserting a not very gentle toe into the cat's wanton chest. Ginger gathered up his legs and departed, tail worn low, between two branches of a spiraea.

'What a very unpleasant shrub that is,' said Alfred Ellis.

'How can you say that,' she cried. 'All flowers are lovely.'

Her doubts about him as an artist tumbled through her head; a rat's skull on the windowsill, a drain blocked with dead leaves, his profile like a battered boxer's, the sculpture like a rusting vegetable rack in his garden. They walked on.

'This is yours, I think.' He fished in the pocket of his stained corduroy trousers and handed her the letter.

'Not bad news, I trust?' He capered at her side, squinting over her shoulder.

'Not at all. Just a bill,' she said coldly, putting it in her bag.

'Manage to spell your name right, did they?'

'I don't know, I didn't look. Why?'

He could hardly tell her that every time he saw the board outside her house he had to suppress an urge to seize a paint-brush and alter it.

Those grey trousers with bald knees make him look like an old elephant who has been in the zoo too long, she was thinking as they crossed the railway tracks at the level crossing. Alfred Ellis suddenly stopped and waved an arm at a large bronze ballerina pirouetting in the wind.

'Ah, Dame Margot!' he cried. 'An inspiration to us all, eh Miss Elliot? Born plain Alice Marks in this very borough and still dancing away in all weathers . . .'

She strode away, her feet almost at right angles, a dancer in dudgeon. He laughed. He was often bored and it amused him to provoke his neighbour. He was often lonely too, and was disproportionately hurt by the news that his friend Ginger was so free with his favours.

He crossed the road and forced to return his greeting an ex-pupil who was obviously about to cut him.

'I thought of you on Saturday,' she admitted. 'Yes, I was helping with the school Autumn Fayre and one of your pictures turned up on the bric-à-brac stall. I almost bought it, but the frame was in such poor condition . . .'

The artist turned away with what might have been a laugh.

He thought about her as he walked; one of too many ladies striding about the town with shopping trolleys, whose skin, from years of smiling at the antics of dogs and children and husbands, creased into fans of angst at the eyes, whose arms were muscled from turning over the pages of *Which?* and cookery books borrowed from the library; they never had time to read fiction; whose faces were still faintly tanned from their camping holiday in France where they had sat in the passenger seat of the car with maps and Blue Guides and Red Guides on their laps, reflecting that if they had gone to Cornwall they would not be boiling along between endless fields of sweetcorn and poplars; who had once suggested that they might stop and look at a cathedral, but had been hooted down by the rest of the family – and anyway the 'O' Level results hung in a thundercloud on the horizon; who sometimes came to his art classes to draw dead grasses and bunches of dried honesty.

He was struck by a house garlanded with a green climbing plant and stood watching the wind lifting the leaves so that the house looked airy and insubstantial, as if it might take wing, and remembered a birthday cake that his grandmother had sent him when he was a boy, white icing and green maidenhair fern, and marvelled that someone should once have thought him worth such a cake. A twist of smoke from his thin cigarette burned his eye. The pure white icing attacked his stained teeth as he went into the greengrocer's to buy the still life for his morning class. He was crossing the car park on his way home when he passed a stall selling fresh fish, cockles and mussels. He retraced his steps. So, banging his shin on the metal rim of a bucket of briny shells, he began his campaign of seduction.

'Oysters,' he said, his teeth glistening in his beard.

'We haven't any.'

He looked over white fluted shells holding tremulous raw eggs.

'Give me a mackerel. The bluest you have.'

In his mind's eye he saw the mackerel with a lemon on a plate.

He was painting it that afternoon, the blue fish curved on the white oval plate, the lemon with the faintest blush of green, beside the darkening window when he saw a figure slinking through the black grass under the holly hedge. He flung open the window and, wrecking his still life, waved the fish at the cat. Ginger stopped, sniffed, laid back his ears, lifted a loyal paw in the direction of Araidne's house, then leaped through the window.

'Gotcha!' Alfred slammed it shut. Soon heavy swirls of fishy steam mingled with the smell of linseed oil and paint and Ginger was arching his back, walking up and down the kitchen table, purring in anticipation. Half an hour later he lay replete and Alfred Ellis smirked and wiped his greasy fingers on his trousers as the sound of 'Puss, Puss, Puss' came through the rain. Ginger raised an ear, shook his head and stuck out a hind leg to wash. A cloudy eye watched from the draining board.

In the morning Araidne Elliot had to plug in the electric fire to take the chill off the air before the Tinies' Tap Class.

'Bit chilly in here, isn't it?' said a mother, pulling her fur coat around herself.

'We'll soon warm up,' replied Araidne listlessly. Rufus. She supposed he was the only person who loved her.

'Yes, well. Tara's only just got over a shocking cough. I was in two minds whether to bring her. She was barking all night.'

Araidne's ears, on either side of her hairnet, strained to hear a miaow. She looked in despair at her class. The cold was marbling the Tinies' thighs pink and blue to match their leotards and head-bands. They seemed to troop incessantly to the toilet, returning with their leotards hiked up over their knickers. She feared that most of them had not washed their hands.

"'I'm putting on my top hat . . .'"

If she were to fit a lock on the bathroom door, she thought as she danced, that took two-pence pieces . . . her cane flashed dangerously.

"'. . . polishing my nails.'"

In a dusty corner lay an unperformed revue: *Babies in Rhinestones*, written and choreographed by Araidne Elliot, in which strings of sparkling babes, shimmering in precision, crisscrossed a vast stage under a spinning prismatic globe, scattered like broken jewellery, and grouped and regrouped in endless stars, rings, necklaces, bangles, tiaras of rainbow glass.

On the other side of the wall Alfred Ellis elicited some disapproval from his students as he executed a bit of inelegant hoofing through the easels to the tap, tap, tap of forty little shoes and one clacking big pair.

'Really, Mr Ellis, that music is most distracting!'

'Lovely chiaroscuro on that teasel, Mrs Wyndham Lewis,' he attempted to placate her. 'If I might suggest . . . the onions . . .'

He added a few strokes of charcoal.

'I think I preferred it as it was,' she said, recoiling from his fishy breath.

'What I object to,' murmured one to another, 'is the fact that one can never finish anything. One embarks on a *nature morte* one lesson, only to find that he's eaten it by the next . . . most unprofessional.'

Araidne could hardly close the front door quickly enough; it clipped the heels of the last mummy, and forced herself to wait until the last car had pulled away before rushing out to check the gutters for a furry body.

She wondered if she would be able to pick it up. Her hair escaped like a catch of eels from its net as she stooped.

'Looking for something, Miss Elliot?'

The loathsome artist was grinning over his gate. She strode on, blushing. Rufus could be presumed alive so far, at least. She thought of his white-tipped paws, his meticulously striped tail, its white tip. She told herself that she was being absurd; he had simply been kept indoors; the people with whom he lived, or condescended to lodge, showing some sense of responsibility at last. Nevertheless she scanned every garden that she passed and encountered some striped and tabby persons, but not the face of the beloved. She wandered for some time and at just after one o'clock arrived, or found herself, in a little road near the station. The few small shops were shut. There was nobody about; the terraced houses looked empty. She heard her heels on the pavement and suddenly felt dispossessed, as if she were in a Tennessee Williams movie. *The Fugitive Kind*. She hesitated in front of a phone box; there was no one to call. It was a relief to arrive in the High Street. She purchased prematurely a bottle of pallid rosé and a stiff slice of Camembert to take to the end-of-term party of her French class, an event to which she looked forward with some gloom. Experience had taught her to avoid the Evening Institute on the first evening of the spring term, when, new aftershave failing to mask the scent of loneliness, people would be required to give details of their sad Christmases in French.

'On m'a donné beaucoup de cadeaux – er – le smoker's candle, le déodorant, le très petit pudding de Noel de Madame Peek . . .'

It was as she came out of the delicatessen that she saw, slouching along with a baby buggy, cigarette in hand, her one-time star pupil, the one for whom she had had the highest hopes. Could it be three years ago that she had brought down the house with her rendition of 'Send in the Clowns'?

'Karen!'

'Madame!' She dropped her cigarette.

'What's his name?' She peered into the buggy.

'Neil.'

'I suppose we'll be seeing Neil in the Tinies' Class soon?' She chucked him awkwardly under the wet chin. 'I could do with a nice boy . . .'

'Couldn't we all?' replied her ex-pupil.

Araidne's eyes filled with tears. She couldn't resist calling after her in a slightly wavery voice,

'Shoulders back, Karen, and do tuck your tail in!'

★   ★   ★

While the riches of the sea, sardines painted in silver leaf, shrimps like pink corals, saucy pilchards, fins and tails, poured out in the artist's kitchen and Ginger waxed fat and indolent, his whiskers standing out from his round head in glossy quills, Araidne Elliot grew as bony and twitchy as a hooked hake. Alfred Ellis expected her daily to ask if he had seen the cat, but she did not come.

One morning, while picking a branch of snowberries from the front garden, he saw, further up the road, on the opposite side, a yellow removal van. He went to investigate and saw carried into the van a wicker basket whose lid was pushed open by a ginger face; it flapped shut, and then a striped tail flicked out in farewell.

'Mr Ellis!' Araidne was at her open window with a letter in her hand. 'I'm afraid the postman has muddled our mail again.'

He took it and, seeing the postmark, almost ran to his own house, without a word of thanks or a word about Ginger's departure. It was from a man who owned a small gallery in Gravesend, who had seen some of Ellis's paintings in the Salon de Refusés of the South Surrey Arts Society exhibition and proposed to visit him with a view to mounting a one-man show of his work. Alfred gobbled gleefully at what would have been Ginger's supper as he read and re-read the letter until it was creased and oily.

That evening he took down a large prepared canvas which had stood empty for months and would now receive his masterwork, the heart of his exhibition, the flowering of his genius; but his brush kept dancing to a faint beat coming through the wall – 'From the top again please, Mrs Taylor' – and the image of Araidne's old accompanist's resigned shoulders at the keyboard superimposed itself on the canvas, so eventually he had to admit defeat and switch on *Dallas*. Later he went for a walk. It had rained, but now the air was frosty, the ivy all diamanté, the hedges cold and hard like marcasite.

'Rufus . . . Rufus,' came palely through the starlight.

The Muse was still recalcitrant the next morning, so he thought that he might seduce her with a pint or two in convivial company. He saw Araidne in the High Street; she saw him too and turned, but too late; he was performing a grotesque dance at her on the pavement, and whistling.

'I'm sorry if my music disturbed you,' she said stiffly. 'I do have a living to make . . .'

'Please don't apologise. The clog dance from *La Fille Mal Gardée* just happens to be my very, very, all-time favourite – especially when I'm trying to work.'

'Excuse me.'

He followed her at a distance and entered a shop behind her. She placed her basket on the counter and took out a packet.

'These tights aren't at all what I wanted.'

'What do you want then?'

She burst into tears, grabbed her basket, and ran out of the shop.

Alfred Ellis winked at the astonished assistant, but he could have wept too. Before Araidne had fled he had looked into her basket: a packet of Fishy Treats, two frozen cod steaks and a library book, *Some Tame Gazelle* by Barbara Pym.

In the pub he muttered into his beer, attracting a fishy glance from the landlord who knew him of old. The shop assistant had asked her what she wanted and the book had replied for her: '"Something to love, oh, something to love."'

'"Some tame gazelle, or some gentle dove" . . . give me a whisky, George. Better make it a double.'

The seduction of Ginger seemed less amusing now.

'"Something to love, oh, something to love,"' he murmured to the fruit machine as it turned up two lemons and a raspberry. He put a coin in the jukebox to drown the rusty voice of shame, but he had to go and look for her.

'Miss Elliot, please. Will you come and have a drink with me? Don't run away. I've got something to tell you. It's most important. It's about Rufus.'

He saw her turn as white as the snowberries in his garden, as red as their twigs, and blanch again.

Two hours later two slightly tear-stained dishevelled people with foolish smiles, clutching a cardboard cat-carrier, a wicker basket, a sack of cat litter, a plastic tray and a carrier bag of tins, struggled down the High Street.

'I think Beulah for the little black one, what do you think?' Alfred Ellis was saying.

Araidne caught sight of their reflection in a shop window.

Goodness, we almost look like a couple, she thought. She said, 'We want to give them nice names, sensible names, that won't embarrass them when they go to school – grow up, I mean. Names are so important, don't you think?'

'I hated mine when I was a boy. Did you like yours?'

'I chose it,' she admitted. 'My real name's Gwen. I saw the name Araidne in a book and I thought it was so beautiful and romantic. So when I opened the dancing school I changed it to Araidne.'

'Ah,' he said.

'What about Tom for the boy? Can we put these down for a minute? My arms are breaking. Oh, I can hear a little voice! Oh, we'll soon be home, darlings.'

Outside their houses he turned to go into his, she into hers. The cat-carrier was almost torn in two. Instant sobriety, hangover, realisation of what they had done. They stood on the pavement staring at one another. A cold wind blew up; the miaows from the box grew wilder.

'Whose dumb idea was this anyway?'

'Yours, I think. But don't worry, I'm taking them.'

'Oh no, you don't!'

'I refuse to stand here brawling in the street. Give me those kittens!'

She tried to snatch them, but he broke free and bolted down his path with them and she grabbed the rest of the stuff and hurried after him lest she be locked out and lose them altogether.

In his kitchen he set the box on the floor and opened it and they knelt on either side gazing at the two tiny faces, one black, one marked like a pansy, looking up, pink and black mouths opening on teeth as sharp as pins. Then, gently, with his big stained fingers, he lifted the kittens out, and on little rickety-looking legs they entered into their kingdom. Alfred Ellis capitalised on Araidne's softened look by opening a bottle of wine; she opened a tin of evaporated milk.

'Let's go into the other room, where it's more comfortable,' he said, 'and try and think of some solution. Perhaps they should stay here tonight, anyway, as they seem to be making themselves at home . . .'

Some hours later, two empty bottles and a pile of dirty plates stood on the table. Blue cigarette smoke lay flat across the air like branches of a cedar tree. Araidne was lying heavy-eyed on the sofa with the kittens asleep in her lap. A gentle purring could be heard.

'Perhaps you should all stay the night,' said Alfred Ellis, putting a balloon of brandy to his lips. 'It would be upsetting for the kittens if you should go now . . .'

Araidne slunk up her path in the morning, feeling very ill, just in time to pre-empt her morning class.

'From the top, Mrs Taylor. But pianissimo, please.'

She was obviously not in a good mood when she returned.

'Switch that thing off! I've got the most appalling headache in the history of the world. What on earth are you doing?' she shouted, wrenching the plug of his Black and Decker from the socket.

'It's the perfect solution,' he said, his hair white with plaster dust. 'I'm drilling a passage from my house to yours so that the kittens can come and go as they please. There's half a Disprin left, if you want it,' he added.

As he spoke a crack zig-zagged through the plaster, then another.

'Oh dear. Perhaps we'd better take the whole wall down?'

The man from the gallery at Gravesend rang and rang the door-bell, and at last walked round the side of the house and looked through the window. The hindquarters of a man, covered in plaster and brick dust, were wriggling through a hole in the wall, while a woman, with a savage look on her face, stood in a lumpy sea of broken plaster, with two kittens running about her shoulders and biting her distracted hair. She was gulping a glass of water and grasping an electric drill as if she might plunge it into her companion's disappearing leg. He was a timid man, and he crept away.

The kittens proved to be bad wild infants who tore up canvases and danced away with the ribbons of ballet shoes in their mouths. Araidne lost a pair of twins from her beginners' ballet class due to alleged cat-scratch fever; a major disaster as they had three younger sisters. She started to choreograph a ballet based on the kittens, but when Alfred opined that the adult human impersonating a feline was the most embarrassing sight in the universe, and the infant human doing so was only marginally better, she lost heart. Alfred received a deep scratch on his thumb while disentangling Tom from a curtain, infected it with paint, and had to wear a clumsy bandage, which made painting impossible. They hardly spoke, addressing most of their remarks to the kittens.

Then one grey day, while the taped carols of the Rotarians pierced the woolly hat he had pulled down over his ears to muffle them, sidestepping a plastic-suited Santa shaking a tin, Alfred Ellis entered the Craft Market, a portfolio in his good hand, shame-facedly and without hope, and found himself appreciated as an artist at last.

He sold several rough studies, executed sinisterly, of the kittens; posing under an umbrella, gazing up expectantly from a pair of old boots, entangled in a ball of knitting wool and needles, Tom asleep with his arms flung out behind his head and Beulah curled into him with her paws crossed. He was commissioned by a local gift shop to supply it with more, and was approached by three golden retrievers who wanted portraits of their owners, or vice versa.

It was almost midnight. The kittens lay in one another's arms; their new jewelled collars sending reflections of firelight and the broken baubles they had torn from the tree, which stood in a huge jagged hole in the wall, sparkling round the room as the last bong of Big Ben rang in the future; babies in rhinestones. And the parents? They stayed together for the sake of the children.

The Most Beautiful Dress in the World

There are houses which exhale unhappiness. The honesty rattling its shabby discs and dominating the weedy flower bed, the carelessly rinsed bottle still veiled in milk on the step from which a tile is missing, the crisp bag, sequinned with dewdrops, which will not rot and will not be removed, clinging to the straggly hedge, are as much manifestations of the misery within as are the grey neglected nets, respectability's ghosts, clouding the windows like ectoplasmic emanations of despair.

The woman in the back garden of such a house, although with her uncombed hair falling onto the shoulders of an old pink dressing gown belted with a twisted striped tie, she looked very much in keeping with her habitat, was not, that morning, unhappy. She was lifting a mass of honeysuckle that sprawled over the grass, trying to disengage the brittle red stems without breaking them and winding them through the almost fragile zigzags of trellis that topped the fence. The bed beneath the honeysuckle had been a herb garden and its last survivors trapping and trapped by the serpentine stems with their little ophidian heads of furled leaves, released the scent of chives. Harriet's movements were slow, with the hesitancy of one weakened by a series of blows and wounds both delivered and self-inflicted, but now, although the healing sun bathing her dressing gown and the smell of the chives on her hands could provoke weak invalidish tears, she felt convalescent, as if she had taken her first shaky steps from an asylum gate, leaving pills and bottles in a locked cabinet in a dark corridor behind her.

Other people's gardens were refulgent with sunflowers, and dahlias riddled with earwigs; the glutted trugs of Surrey bulged with late and woody runner beans. Harriet had found, at dawn, a green and yellow striped torpedo on her own step, with so hard a carapace that she knew in advance how the breadknife would break as she tried to cut it and the blade would remain embedded in its shiny shell. The early October sunshine had an elegiac quality that reminded her of the slow movement of a cello concerto, still golden but foretelling full-blown autumn melancholy, the tomatoes that would never ripen, the last yellow fluted flower of the barren marrow, the falling of the leaves. The narrow lapis lazuli bracelet that rolled up and down her wrist as she worked had lost some of its stones. She had worn it for so many years that she had ceased to see it but on the rare occasions on which it had been lost, caught in a sleeve or sloughed into a shopping bag, she had been aware at once of its absence circling her arm like a bangle of air. Her daughter had played with it as a baby, had cut her teeth on it, and it had become a sort of talisman to them both.

On the underside of a curled-over leaf, cocooned so that she could not tell if it were alive or dead, lay a caterpillar. 'The caterpillar on the leaf/Repeats to thee thy mother's grief,' she thought as she placed the leaf gently against the trellis. As she reached up the bracelet slid down to rest above her elbow and a fly, with a bravado that suggested that it knew its days were numbered anyway, alighted on the knob of her wrist bone as if it would await its quietus grazing there among the fair down. A movement of the hand sent it flying heavily onto the silvered leaf of a blighted rose. As the glassy facets of the fly's wings sparkled she felt one of those painful flashes of joy, engendered by the natural world, which have no foundation in circumstances or power to change the lives which they illumine so briefly and which give a momentary vision, too fleeting to analyse, of the universe as benign. A long arm of honeysuckle encircled her neck in a gentle green-leaved garotte. She thought she had never known an October so golden, and that if she had not emerged from so black a pit of horrors that still writhed half-forgotten in her soul she would not have been able to appreciate the gold of the day.

As she went into the house Auden's prayer that his sleeping love might find the natural world enough came into her head. That wish, that the beloved might face the light with eyes unshielded by spectacles of alcohol or dope, seemed the best that one could ask. There was only one person for whom she would ask such a gift, and that was her daughter, Miranda. She had unconsciously adapted the quotation, as she discovered when she looked up the poem in the blue book whose spine had faded to dun in the dusty bookcase: it was the mortal world which the poet hoped that his love would find enough. That would do, she thought, smiling as she replaced the book, running her finger along the shelf. Today even dust did not look like an enemy.

She felt the brush of a warm coat on her bare legs as Bruno lifted his head from his bowl and trotted past her to fling himself in a pool of sun on one of the beds. Her apparel and the state of the kitchen, strewn with breakfast debris, belied the fact that Harriet had been busy since seven o'clock that morning but the black rims of her nails, as she rinsed Bruno's bowl, and piled dishes into the sink, testified to the fact that she had repotted some house-plants; the loaf and margarine and smeary knives suggested she had made sandwiches for somebody; in fact for Miranda, who had caught an early train for the college where she was starting, that morning, her career as a fashion student. The sandwiches, though scorned, would, Harriet hoped, be welcome if they could be consumed in secret, out of the sight of fellow students posing as day-trippers and professors masquerading as ticket collectors and secretaries.

This was the first whole day that Harriet had had to herself for a long time and she determined not to waste it. She was going to paint, which was not only now the only activity which gave her any pleasure – and there was an enchanting tangle of flowers and leaves and berries hanging over an old wall down the road that she wanted to preserve on paper before it was desolated by winter – but was also the occupation which engendered the sluggish trickle of income which kept them afloat in the poverty to which they had become accustomed, of which Miranda did not always hide her resentment. The summer had been filled with Miranda's friends and alternately with Miranda's boredom and excitement, neither of which Harriet found conducive to working even on those rare occasions when the kitchen was empty; and she found that, as those who work at home know, the anticipation of arrivals and departures creates an enervating limbo peppered with frustration and irritability, and the failure of an awaited letter to arrive, or the telephone to ring, can sour the day as hope curdles to despair.

She decided to wash the curtains before she started work and as she gathered the smoky clouds of net in her arms to place them in the machine she was reminded of Miranda's dress.

'Don't you think it's the most beautiful dress you've ever seen?' Miranda had said, pulling handfuls of grey tulle from the plastic carrier bag, a radiant conjuror about to produce her most brilliant trick. 'Isn't it the most beautiful dress in the world?'

Harriet had stared at the crumpled greenish roses mouldering on the boned bodice, with yellow stains under the arms, that rose from vapours of mothy gauze hanging over a skirt of grey tulle that time had turned to perforated zinc.

'You might be a bit more enthusiastic . . .'

'It's perfect for the party. It'll be lovely when it's had a wash.'

'I'm not going to wash it!'

Miranda beat the air from its folds and shovelled it back into the bag, and the thud of her feet on the stairs told Harriet that she had deflated and disappointed – why could she not have dredged up some spurious enthusiasm instead of flinging her own fear like a handful of grey dust over that grey dress?

The truth was, she hated the dress. It had dangled like a spectre, a mocking *memento mori* against her daughter's young face; the whisk of its skirt brought a whiff of the grave, of black lips of earth and churning worms.

It was the sort of dress that Harriet had fled from in her youth, hurtling herself down the path that had led through the years to the defeated house; but in Miranda's eyes it had the charm of an antique. Later Harriet had tried to repair the damage by praising the dress exorbitantly and asking too many questions about the party for which it had been bought.

'I probably won't go,' said Miranda.

Now it came to Harriet that she would wash the dress while Miranda was away, redeeming it as well as herself, and surprise her with its restored beauty when she came home. It was so delicate that it would have to be washed by hand, and she imagined a million trapped glittering bubbles irradiating its mesh as she lifted it white and virginal from the dirty water, the stains of another dancer's sweat of ecstasy or panic dissolving from the boned bodice, the mildewed roses unfurling plump petals as it waltzed with the October wind.

Whether it was her fault or not, Harriet was not a practical person. So much of the energy that might have been expended in kisses and fun had been frittered away in the foothills of mountains that other people took in their stride. She would have been perfectly happy painting, or lying in bed or in the garden all day smoking and reading detective stories, but love must be expressed in practical, financial and nutritional terms. She had never quite come to terms with the fact that a wall once painted, a room swept or dusted would not remain in that state. She regarded Hoovers and mops and dusters not as helpmeets but as enemies and symbols of her servitude; she was cruel to her household implements; their duties were not onerous or even very regular, but when they were called upon to perform they were often kicked and beaten. Sometimes in calm moments she had meant to observe herself to see if there was perhaps a pattern to her savagery, but she had never been sufficiently organised to correlate the evidence, and instead wept baffled tears as she clutched a bruised hand or toe and surveyed the broken plug or splintered handle that would add shame and self-inflicted pain to her resentment the next time she performed some hated chore.

As she turned to wash the breakfast dishes, in order to clear the sink for Miranda's dress, her eye caught the cream-coloured telephone clinging like a flung vanilla blancmange to the kitchen wall.

There is not one person in the whole world who wants to speak to me, she thought.

She was wrong. At that moment the telephone rang. It was her elderly neighbour asking, or commanding, her to go across to the shop to buy a large tin of prunes and two flat packs of soft toilet tissue. After having learned more than she wished to know about the state of the widower's intestines, and having promised to do the shopping later in the morning, she put down the phone. It rang again.

'It's only me. This is the third time I've rung. You were engaged,' the voice accused.

'Oh, hi, Mo. I'm sorry, it was my neighbour – he tends to go on a bit,' Harriet heard herself apologise.

'Never mind. What are you doing? I've got the car and I thought we could go out somewhere, it's such a lovely day. Are you still there?'

'Yes, it's just that I'm a bit tied up – there's something I want to do – some painting –'

'Oh well, if you don't want to – it was just a thought, as I've got the car . . .'

'I'd love to, really, it's just that today's the first day I've had to myself for weeks so I thought I could really get down to some work.'

'Couldn't you do it this evening? We needn't be back late.'

'Miranda will be back. It's her first day today, and I don't want to be preoccupied . . . you know how it is . . .'

'OK. It doesn't matter. I'll give you a ring later in the week. Happy painting!'

As Harriet stood with the dialling tone buzzing in the receiver in her hand, a young dustman passing the window, in a sleeveless vest, an empty bin on his shoulder, the hair under his raised arm flowering like the sooty stamens of an anemone against his white flesh, called something inaudible to her. She interpreted his greeting as condemnation of her slatternly state. Mo's disappointed voice had reduced her need to work to a selfish, self-important whim.

A small envelope, with a rustling and clatter inappropriate to its size, came through the letterbox and landed on the mat. Harriet picked it up and saw a photograph of a little girl dressed in white, captioned 'The Party Dress She'll Never See', and was at once blinded herself by trite tears and muttered, 'That's all I need,' as she hid it behind a stack of letters. Reminded of Miranda's party dress she finished the dishes, and was called down from halfway up the stairs by the front-door bell. The milkman, another witness to her mid-morning disarray, lounged in the doorway watching her as she wrote the cheque. His cheekbones were embroidered with tiny amber pustules and his nails rasped on his scalp as he pushed back his cap to scratch in his hair; she winced at the thought of those nails on the silver-foil milk-bottle tops.

When he had gone she determined not to let the impulse to work dissipate and wiped the kitchen table, which was the only surface big enough, and set out paper, paints and brushes and a jam jar of water and tried to dissolve her guilt at Mo's disappointed voice in the clear water that held the faintest turquoise tinge reflected from the walls of glass that confined it and spawned spiralling strings of minuscule bubbles like glass beads. I'll put Miranda's dress to soak, she thought, have a quick bath and get dressed, go to the shop and have another look at the plants on that wall and then start work. I don't believe it!

The phone was ringing again.

The voice that came through was furred-up, like an old waste pipe, with whisky.

'Dad.'

'I thought you might have rung yesterday to see how I got on at the hospital.'

Oh God. She had forgotten all about it.

'I did ring. All the lines to Rottingdean were busy. How did you get on?'

Her heart was banging about in the old painful way. She drummed her fingers on the marrow which lay on the table radiating vegetable calm from its green and yellow stripes.

'I didn't go!'

His triumphant crow was splattered against her ear in an eruption of wet coughing. She held the receiver at arm's length.

'Why didn't you? Did they change your appointment?'

'I was dressed and waiting for that sodding ambulance at eight o'clock. Do you know what time they turned up? Gone eleven. I told them what they could do with their bloody appointment.'

'I bet that showed the bastards,' said Harriet wearily, realising that she would have to apologise, make a new appointment and accompany him.

'What? Showed the bastards, didn't I? Who do they think they are?'

'I expect some of them think they're people who are trying to do a very unpleasant job with very little money, or resources.'

It didn't matter what she said, he would neither hear nor remember.

'Bloody hospitals.'

'You chose not to know when I was in hospital.'

'How would you know, you've never been in hospital. Except when Miranda was born, I suppose. Anyway, I just thought you'd be interested to hear how I got on.'

'Fascinated.'

'Has she gone back to school? You said she was coming to see me in the holidays. When's she coming?'

'I'm not sure. Soon . . .'

'What?'

'I don't know, Dad. She's a big girl now, I can't force —'

'What do you mean, force?' – he had heard that all right. 'You're just jealous of Miranda and me. Just because I'm old and ill. You'll find out one day, when you're old and ill and nobody wants to know . . .'

'It's not *just* because you're old and ill, Dad, it's because you're also boring and disgusting and totally selfish.'

Her words were lost in his coughing.

'Listen, Dad. I'll come to see you tomorrow. Can you hear me, Dad? SEE YOU TOMORROW. I'LL BRING SOME LUNCH.'

'Nobody bloody cares if I go to the hospital or not. The nurses don't care, the doctors don't care, you don't care . . .'

'If you ever looked at me, if you had the slightest interest in, or conception of what my life has been like, you would see that I had nothing left to care *with*. Why should I care? For a moment's carelessness on your part and a few miserable years I have to pay in blood for the rest of my life.'

'Harriet, are you still there? Harry?'

'I said, I'LL SEE YOU TOMORROW. GOODBYE, DAD, I'VE GOT TO GO, THERE'S SOMEONE AT THE DOOR.'

She went to answer it with an image in her mind of herself and her father, writhing in their separate torment, joined across the miles by an inseverable twisted plastic cord.

'Ms James?'

A young woman in jeans and a short overall bearing the logo of a local flower shop was holding out a huge cellophane cone of flowers rosetted with yellow ribbon.

'No. I mean, I'll take them for her,' Harriet lied, realising that it would be inconceivable to the girl that anyone should send flowers to a person such as herself. But he had, and she knew who he was without reading the card – the husband of one of her friends.

'The last bloody straw.'

She propped up the sheaf of flowers in the kitchen, lit a cigarette – the first one of the day, as she congratulated herself – and ran upstairs to Miranda's room. The dress hung from a wire hanger and Harriet was caught by a rush of love for the body that would fill it, the bony shoulders that would rise from the stained bodice, the downy arms. 'Let her be happy,' she prayed, and was assaulted by the memory of a very small girl saying with such vehemence, 'Mummy, when you go to Heaven, I'm going to *cling* on to you and fly up with you,' that she could still feel those fingers digging into her flesh.

She gathered the dress to her, as she would have liked to embrace her daughter, and the tip of her cigarette caught a fold and a tongue of flame leaped up the gauze, and died, leaving a hideous black valley up the centre of the skirt.

Her carelessness. Her carelessness that amounted to cruelty – her stupidity that might be misinterpreted as spite – she pulled the folds together as if the damage would disappear, and opened them to display the blackened horror. The burn might come out when she washed it and perhaps she could mend – there was no white or grey thread – get some when she went for the prunes and toilet paper. If only she hadn't interfered, had let well alone – Miranda hadn't wanted it washed – if she hadn't lit that stupid cigarette – it was all to prove her love – all for herself. She stood in the smell of scorched dust cradling the corpse of her attempt at redemption.

In the kitchen, the net curtains, which had not been burned, tumbled careless gouts of foam through the black outlet hose into the sink. Harriet laid the dress in the washing-up bowl and turned on the taps gently and scattered detergent like someone dropping earth on a coffin. As she watched, the stems of the roses unwound in slimy slow motion and the petals disengaged one by one as the glue dissolved, and floated separately on the surface of the water.

The door bell rang.

'Go away,' she screamed.

It rang again.

'Who is it?'

'Gas meter.'

'Can't you come back later?'

'No.'

'In a few minutes –' she pleaded, tearing at her hair with sudsy hands.

'I've got to –' The rest of his words were lost as she wrenched the door open. He stepped into the kitchen and smiled around at the disorder, the sun striking brassy notes in his cadmium-yellow hair.

'Caught you on the hop, did I?'

Harriet stared at him, thinking that the black tufts in his nose, contrasting so blatantly with his hair, effectively cancelled out the charm that he so obviously thought he possessed, and caused the cheeky grin to lose its confidence. How could anyone be so mistaken about himself? At least she was aware of every aspect of her unkempt looks and dowdy *déshabillé*.

'Who's a lucky girl then?' He indicated the flowers.

'Someone's birthday today?' She glared at him as if distaste would turn the bunches of hair into iron filings and choke him. She saw the stems of the flowers protruding from his mouth, his throat jammed with cellophane. She slammed on the radio.

'Mind if I use your toilet?'

She pointed silently upwards, then pushed past him and ran upstairs but had time only to claw a heap of Miranda's night things from the floor, drape a wet towel over the rail and glimpse a nail-brush and sponge stranded in the bubbles dying in the bath and retrieve a pair of espadrilles from the basin before he was standing at the lavatory, waiting for her to leave. Bruno padded in and sniffed at his ankles; Harriet shooed him away.

Downstairs, shreds of gauze came away in her hands, and as she acknowledged that the dress was disintegrating, the young man returned. He squatted down in front of the cupboard, shining his torch into the cluttered interior, then started scrabbling objects out on to the floor.

'Bit of a glory hole, innit?' he remarked, cheerfully piling up cobwebbed cake tins, a broken cup and saucer, the split plastic bag of Christmas cake decorations which scattered around him. Then, whistling along with the radio, he raked out empty bottles and stood them in a semicircle around his haunches. Harriet could have explained that they were the accumulation of past months of drinking, waiting to be taken to the bottle bank in a friend's car, that she had not in fact had a drink for weeks, but the bottles stood in a silent green hostile crowd and any defence that she offered would be contradicted by these glass perjurers. One, she saw, bore a label that said Goldener Oktober, like the golden October day that had been wrecked.

All I wanted to do today was paint a bloody little picture, she thought. She looked at the twin shiny patches on the seat of his grey trousers. How dare he force his way in here and rake through my life?

All her self-hatred was directed at the slight figure in the inglorious uniform. She grabbed the marrow, lifted it high with both hands, and he received the full weight of the ruined dress, the empty bottles and the years of failure and despair on the back of his head.

She stepped back as he sprawled slowly sideways and the bottles fell like skittles around him. One rolled to her feet, almost full, splashing purple onto the floor as a bright red sticky gout dyed his yellow hair. His hand closed on a plastic reindeer. Harriet picked up the bottle and, as she gulped, the purple vinegar sprayed her face and dressing gown and the shiny grey jacket. She forced the wine down her throat against the rising nausea. She knew she must obscure with a purple haze the enormity of what she had done; the widow and orphans and bereaved parents and siblings she had created with one mad blow. The room became darker as if the alcohol had created its own twilight. Her resistance was low and her ears were filling with purple cotton wool. A fly, like the one which had grazed on her wrist in the garden, settled on the fallen man's head as if on a luscious yellow flower oozing red nectar, and that final violation of the innocent violater was more than she could bear. She rushed from room to room getting ready to leave for ever, finally grabbing her purse and tying the first thing that came to hand to Bruno's collar, finished the wine and leaving the radio buzzing away on low batteries, the washing machine throbbing in its final spin, the sheathed flowers a cone of blurred colour lying across a heap of bottles, the man sprawled on the floor among the Christmas cake decorations and Miranda's dress in the washing-up bowl, slammed the front door behind her.

On her way to the station she lurched unbelievingly against the old brick wall that she had meant to paint, long ago, that morning, in an irrecoverable guiltlessness. Only yesterday it had been hung with hearts, a tangle of convolvulus, nightshade, elderberries, snow-berries and ivy. Now all the white bells and berries and green hearts were gone and she traced with her fingers the fuzzy scars that laced the wall where the ivy had been ripped from the brick. At the end of the wall, through the rolled-up door, she saw a man with silver hair standing on a stepladder, whistling as he painted the interior of his garage. A rage possessed her at the sight of the neatly stacked tools and tins on his shelves, that someone's life should be so well ordered that he had to fill his time by painting the inside of a garage. The garden wall which had been so beautiful had been desecrated as she, who had once been beautiful, was ruined. She walked into the garage and kicked away the steps, hearing a scream as he fell to the concrete floor.

Bruno was dragging at his lead and she had to pick him up and carry him. As they crossed the road they passed one of Miranda's friends, a girl with long fair hair falling about her shoulders. Harriet was transfixed by the knowledge that the girl must grow old and die. "'All her bright golden hair/Tarnished with rust,/She that was young and fair/Fallen to dust,'" she told her as a milk float screeched at her, frightening Bruno and fluttering her skirt. She couldn't remember where she was supposed to be going, only that it must be somewhere very peaceful, a haven out of the swing of the sea. "'I have asked to be where no storms come . . .'" She couldn't remember. 'Not Rottingdean,' she said, 'definitely not Rottingdean.'

She swayed into the station. There were two station staff who looked so alike that they might have been brothers: one was friendly and cheerful and the other sullen. Harriet encountered one of them in the booking hall.

'Are you the nice one, or the other one?'

He did not reply.

'I want a ticket to Innisfree, to the Lake Isle. I shall find some peace there.'

She wandered down the platform and sat on a bench. She was aware that her bracelet was missing and was conscious at the time of a blacker grief but it was like trying to fit together the pieces of a grotesque jigsaw whose edges are slippery with blood, and then the darkness became absolute as she closed her eyes.

When a dream becomes unbearable the sleeper awakes. Harriet struggled through blackness, with the alarm clock shrilling like a siren in her ears, to the blessed realisation that the monstrous epic which she had lived through had been only a nightmare.

'Thank God,' she said as she pushed Bruno from her chest and sat up in the disoriented dawn, shaking her head to dislodge three uniformed figures on the edge of her headache, blinking away the last remnant of the dream.

They made straight for her. After all it was not difficult to spot, on a station platform, a woman in a pink towelling dressing gown splashed with wine, clutching a cat on the end of a string of bloody tinsel.

'It was an accident,' she mumbled as the policewoman pulled her to her feet.

'One man is dead and another in hospital, and you're saying it was an accident?'

Harriet blinked at them in bleary bewilderment.

'The dress – it was an accident.'

Cardboard City

'We could always pick the dog hairs off each other's coats . . .'

The thought of grooming each other like monkeys looking for fleas sent them into giggles – anything would have.

'I used half a roll of sellotape on mine,' said Stella indignantly then, although she wasn't really offended.

'It better not have been my sellotape or I'll kill you,'Vanessa responded, without threat.

'It was His.'

'Good. *He'll* kill you then,' she said matter-of-factly.

The sisters, having flung themselves onto the train with no time to buy a comic, were wondering how to pass the long minutes until it reached central London with nothing to read. They could hardly believe that at the last moment He had not contrived to spoil their plan to go Christmas shopping. For the moment it didn't matter that their coats were unfashionable and the cuffs of their acrylic sweaters protruded lumpishly from the outgrown sleeves or that their frozen feet were beginning to smart, in the anticipation of chilblains, in their scuffed shoes in reaction to the heater under the seat. They were alone in the compartment except for a youth with a personal stereo leaking a tinny rhythm through the headphones.

With their heavy greenish-blonde hair cut straight across their foreheads and lying flat as lasagne over the hoods and shoulders of their school duffels, and their green eyes set wide apart in the flat planes of their pale faces, despite Stella's borrowed fishnet stockings which were causing her much *angst*, they looked younger than their fourteen and twelve years. It would not have occurred to either of them that anybody staring at them might have been struck by anything other than their horrible clothes. Their desire, thwarted by Him and by lack of money of their own, was to look like everybody else. The dog hairs that adhered so stubbornly to the navy-blue cloth and bristled starkly in the harsh and electric light of the winter morning were from Barney, the black and white border collie, grown fat and snappish in his old age, who bared his teeth at his new master, the usurper, and slunk into a corner at his homecoming, as the girls slunk into their bedroom.

'It's cruel to keep that animal alive,' He would say. 'What's it got to live for? Smelly old hearthrug.'

And while He discoursed on the Quality of Life, running a finger down Mummy's spine or throat, Barney's legs would splay out worse than they usually did and his claws click louder on the floor, or a malodorous cloud of stagnant pond water emanate from his coat. It was a sign of His power that Barney was thus diminished.

'We'll know when the Time has come. And the Time has not yet come,' said Mummy with more energy than she summoned to champion her elder daughters, while Barney rolled a filmy blue eye in her direction. The dog, despite his shedding coat, was beyond reproach as far as the girls were concerned; his rough back and neck had been salted with many tears, and he was their one link with their old life, before their father had disappeared and before their mother had defected to the enemy.

'What are you going to buy Him?' Vanessa asked.

'Nothing. I'm making His present.'

'What?' Vanessa was incredulous, fearing treachery afoot.

'I'm knitting Him a pair of socks. Out of stinging nettles.'

'I wish I could knit.'

After a wistful pause she started to say, 'I wonder what He would . . .'

'I'm placing a total embargo on His name today,' Stella cut her off. 'Don't speak of Him. Don't even think about Him. Right, Regan?'

'Right, Goneril. Why does He call us those names?'

'They're the Ugly Sisters in *Cinderella* of course.'

'I thought they were called Anastasia and . . . and . . .'

'Embargo,' said Stella firmly.

'It's not Cordelia who needs a fairy godmother, it's us. Wouldn't it be lovely if one day . . .'

'Grow up.'

So that was how He saw them, bewigged and garishly rouged, two pantomime dames with grotesque beauty spots and fishnet tights stretched over their bandy men's calves, capering jealously around Cordelia's highchair. Cordelia herself, like Barney, was adored unreservedly, but after her birth, with one hand rocking the transparent hospital cot in which she lay, as a joke which they could not share, He had addressed her half-sisters as Goneril and Regan. Their mother had protested then, but now sometimes she used the names. Under His rule, comfortable familiar objects vanished and routines were abolished. Exposed to His mockery, they became ludicrous. One example was the Bunnykins china they ate from sometimes, not in a wish to prolong their babyhood but because it was there. All the pretty mismatched bits and pieces of crockery were superseded by a stark white service from Habitat and there were new forks with vicious prongs and knives which cut. Besotted with Cordelia's dimples and black curls, He lost all patience with his step-daughters, with their tendency to melancholy and easily provoked tears which their pink eyelids and noses could not conceal, and like a vivisector with an electric prod tormenting two albino mice, he discovered all their most vulnerable places.

Gypsies had travelled up in the train earlier, making their button-holes and nosegays, and had left the seats and floor strewn with a litter of twigs and petals and scraps of silver foil like confetti.

'We might see Princess Di or Fergie,' Vanessa said, scuffing the debris with her foot. 'They do their Christmas shopping in Harrods.'

'The Duchess of York to you. Oh yes, we're sure to run into them. Anyway, Princess Diana does her shopping in Covent Garden.'

'Well then!' concluded Vanessa triumphantly. She noticed the intimation of a cold sore on her sister's superior lip and was for a second glad. Harrods and Covent Garden were where they had decided, last night, after lengthy discussions, to go, their excited voices rising from guarded whispers to a normal pitch, until He had roared upstairs at them to shut up. Vanessa's desire to go to Hamleys had been overruled. She had cherished a secret craving for a tube of plastic stuff with which you blew bubbles and whose petroleum smell she found as addictive as the smell of a new

Elastoplast. Now she took out her purse and checked her ticket and counted her money yet again. Even with the change she had filched fearfully from the trousers He had left sprawled across the bedroom chair, it didn't amount to much. Stella was rich, as the result of her paper round and the tips she had received in return for the cards she had put through her customers' doors wishing them a 'Merry Christmas from your Newsboy/Newsgirl', with a space for her to sign her name. She would have been even wealthier had He not demanded the money for the repair of the iron whose flex had burst into flames in her hand while she was ironing His shirt. She could not see how it had been her fault but supposed it must have been. The compartment filled up at each stop and the girls stared out of the window rather than speak in public, or look at each other and see mirrored in her sister her own unsatisfactory self.

The concourse at Victoria was scented with sweet and sickening melted chocolate from a booth that sold fresh-baked cookies, and crowded with people criss-crossing each other with loaded trolleys, running to hurl themselves at the barriers, dragging luggage and children; queuing helplessly for tickets while the minutes to departure ticked away, swirling around the bright scarves outside Tie Rack, panic-buying festive socks and glittery bow ties, slurping coffee and beer and champing croissants and pizzas and jacket potatoes and trying on ear-rings. It had changed so much from the last time they had seen it that only the late arrival of their train and the notice of cancellation and delay on the indicator board reassured them that they were at the right Victoria Station.

'I've got to go to the Ladies.'

'OK.'

Vanessa attempted to join the dismayingly long queue trailing down the stairs but Stella had other plans.

'Stell-a! Where are you going?' She dragged Vanessa into the side entrance of the Grosvenor Hotel.

'Stella, we can't! It's a HOTEL! We'll be ARRESTED . . .' she wailed as Stella's fingers pinched through her coat sleeves, propelling her up the steps and through the glass doors.

'Shut up. Look as though we're meeting somebody.'

Vanessa could scarcely breathe as they crossed the foyer, expecting at any moment a heavy hand to descend on her shoulder, a liveried body to challenge them, a peaked cap to thrust into their faces. The thick carpet accused their feet. Safely inside the Ladies, she collapsed against a basin.

'Well? Isn't this better than queuing for hours? And it's free.'

'Supposing someone comes?'

'Oh stop bleating. It's perfectly all right. Daddy brought me here once – no one takes any notice of you.'

The door opened and the girls fled into cubicles and locked the doors. After what seemed like half an hour Vanessa slid back the bolt and peeped around the door. There was Stella, bold as brass, standing at the mirror between the sleek backs of two women in stolen fur coats, applying a stub of lipstick to her mouth. She washed and dried her hands and joined Stella, meeting a changed face in the glass: Stella's eyelids were smudged with green and purple, her lashes longer and darker, her skin matt with powder.

'Where did you get it?' she whispered hoarsely as the two women moved away.

'Tracy' – the friend who had lent her the stockings, with whom Vanessa, until they were safely on the train, had feared Stella would choose to go Christmas shopping, instead of with her.

Women came and went and Vanessa's fear was forgotten as she applied the cosmetics to her own face.

'Now we look a bit more human,' said Stella as they surveyed themselves, Goneril and Regan, whom their own father had named Star and Butterfly.

Vanessa Cardui, Painted Lady, sucked hollows into her cheeks and said, 'We really need some blusher, but it can't be helped.'

'Just a sec.'

'But Stella, it's a BAR . . . we can't . . . !'

Her alarm flooded back as Stella marched towards Edward's Bar.

'We'll get DRUNK. What about our shopping?'

Ignoring the animated temperance tract clutching her sleeve, Stella scanned the drinkers.

'Looking for someone, Miss?' the barman asked pleasantly.

'He's not here yet,' said Stella. 'Come on, Vanessa.'

She checked the coffee lounge on the way out, and as they recrossed the fearful foyer it dawned on Vanessa that Stella had planned this all along; all the way up in the train she had been expecting to find Daddy in Edward's Bar. That had been the whole point of the expedition.

She was afraid that Stella would turn like an injured dog and snap at her. She swallowed hard, her heart racing, as if there were words that would make everything all right, if only she could find them.

'What?' Stella did turn on her.

'He might be in Harrods.'

'Oh yes. Doing his Christmas shopping with Fergie and Di. Buying our presents.'

Vanessa might have retorted, 'The Duchess of York to you,' but she knew better than to risk the cold salt wave of misery between them engulfing the whole day: a gypsy woman barred their way with a sprig of foliage wrapped in silver foil.

'Lucky white heather. Bring you luck.'

'Doesn't seem to have brought you much,' snarled Stella pushing past her.

'You shouldn't have been so rude. Now she'll put a curse on us,' wailed Vanessa.

'It wasn't even real heather, dumbbell.'

'Now there's no chance we'll meet Daddy.'

Stella strode blindly past the gauntlet of people rattling tins for The Blind. Vanessa dropped in a coin and hurried after her down the steps. As they went to consult the map of the Underground they almost stumbled over a man curled up asleep on the floor, a bundle of grey rags and hair and beard tied up with string. His feet, black with dirt and disease, protruded shockingly bare into the path of the Christmas shoppers. The sisters stared, their faces chalky under their makeup.

Then a burst of laughter and singing broke out. A group of men and women waving bottles and cans were holding a private crazed party, dancing in their disfigured clothes and plastic accoutrements; a woman with long grey hair swirling out in horizontal streamers from a circlet of tinsel was clasping a young man in a close embrace as they shuffled around singing 'All I want for Christmas is my two front teeth', and he threw back his head to pour the last drops from a bottle into a toothless black hole, while their companions beat out a percussion accompaniment on bottles and cans with a braying brass of hiccups. They were the only people in that desperate and shoving crowded place who looked happy.

Stella and Vanessa were unhappy as they travelled down the escalator. The old man's feet clawed at them with broken and corroded nails; the revellers, although quite oblivious to the citizens of the other world, had frightened them; the gypsy's curse hung over them.

Harrods was horrendous. They moved bemused through the silken scented air, buffeted by headscarves, furs and green shopping bags. Fur and feathers in the Food Hall left them stupefied in the splendour of death and beauty and money.

'This is crazy,' said Stella. 'We probably couldn't afford even one quail's egg.'

Mirrors flung their scruffy reflections back at them and they half-expected to be shown the door by one of the green and gold guards and after an hour of fingering and coveting and temptation they were out in the arctic wind of Knightsbridge with two packs of Christmas cards and a round gold box of chocolate Napoleons.

In Covent Garden they caught the tail end of a piece of street theatre as a green spotted pantomime cow curvetted at them with embarrassing udders, swiping the awkward smiles off their faces with its tail. A woman dressed as a clown bopped them on the head with a balloon and thrust a bashed-in hat at them. Close to, she looked fierce rather than funny. The girls paid up. It seemed that everybody in the city was engaged in a conspiracy to make them hand over their money. Two hot chocolates made another serious inroad in their finances, the size of the bill souring the floating islands of cream as they sat on white wrought-iron chairs sipping from long spoons to the accompaniment of a young man busking on a violin backed by a stereo system.

'You should've brought your cello,' said Vanessa and choked on her chocolate as she realised she could hardly have said anything more tactless. It was He who had caused Stella's impromptu resignation from the school orchestra, leaving them in the lurch. His repetition, in front of two of His friends, of an attributed reprimand by Sir Thomas Beecham to a lady cellist, had made it impossible for her to practise at home and unthinkable that she should perform on a public platform to an audience sniggering like Him, debasing her and the music.

'It's – it's not my kind of music,' she had lied miserably to Miss Philips, the music teacher.

'Well, Stella, I must say I had never thought of *you* as a disco queen,' Miss Philips had said bitterly.

Her hurt eyes strobed Stella's pale selfish face and falling-down socks as she wilted against the wall. Accusations of letting down her fellow musicians followed, and reminders of Miss Philips's struggle to obtain the cello from another school, her own budget and resources being so limited. She ignored Stella in the corridor thereafter and the pain of this was still with her, like the ominous ache in her lower abdomen. She wished she were at home curled up with a hot-water bottle.

'Bastard,' she said. 'Of all the gin joints in all the suburbs of southeast London, why did He have to walk into ours?' Mummy had brought Him home from a rehearsal of the amateur production of *Oklahoma!* for which she was doing the costumes, ostensibly for an emergency fitting of His Judd Fry outfit, the trousers and boots of which were presenting difficulties. The girls had almost clapped the palms off their hands after the mournful rendition of 'Poor Judd is Dead'. It would always be a show-stopper for them.

Stella wished she had had one of the cards from Harrods to put in the school postbox for Miss Philips, but she hadn't, and now it was too late. Vanessa bought a silver heart-shaped balloon for Cordelia, or, as Stella suspected, for herself. They wandered around the stalls and shops over the slippery cobblestones glazed with drizzle.

'How come, whichever way we go, we always end up in Central Avenue?' Vanessa wondered.

Stella gave up the pretence that she knew exactly where she was going. 'It'll be getting dark soon. We must buy *something*.'

They battled their way into the Covent Garden General Store and joined the wet and unhappy throng desperate to spend money they couldn't afford on presents for people who would not want what they received, to the relentless musical threat that Santa Claus was coming to town. 'If this is more fun than just shopping,' said Stella as they queued to pay for their doubtful purchases, quoting from the notice displayed over the festive and jokey goods, 'I think I prefer just shopping. Sainsbury's on Saturday morning is paradise compared to this.'

Stella was seduced by a gold mesh star and some baubles as fragile and iridescent as soap bubbles, to hang on the conifer in the corner of the bare front room, decked in scrawny tinsel too sparse for its sprawling branches and topped with the fairy with a scorch mark in her greying crêpe-paper skirt where it had once caught in a candle. The candles, with most of their old decorations, had been vetoed by Him and had been replaced by a set of fairy lights with more twisted emerald green flex than bulbs in evidence.

'I wish we hadn't got a tree,' Vanessa said.

'I know. Cordelia likes it, though.'

'I suppose so. That's all that matters really. I mean, Christmas is for kids, isn't it?'

Vanessa showed her the bubble bath disguised as a bottle of gin which she was buying for Him.

'Perhaps He'll drink it.'

'Early on Christmas morning, nursing a savage hangover, He rips open His presents and, desperate for a hair-of-the-dog, He puts the bottle to his lips. Bubbles come out of His nose and mouth, He falls to the floor –'

'Screaming in agony.'

'– screaming in agony, foaming at the mouth. The heroic efforts of his distraught step-daughters fail to revive him. An ambulance is called but it gets stuck in traffic. When they finally reach the hospital all the nurses are singing carols in the wards and no one can find the stomach pump. A doctor in a paper hat tells the sorrowing sisters – or are they laughing, who can tell? – that it's too late. He has fallen victim to His own greed. How much does it cost?'

'Two pounds seventy-nine.'

'Cheap at twice the price.'

After leaving the shop they collided with a superstructure formed by two supermarket trolleys lashed together and heaped with a perilous pyramid of old clothes and plastic bags and utensils and bits of hardware like taps and broken car exhausts and hubcaps, the handlebars of a bicycle fronting it like antlers and three plumes of pampas grass waving in dirty Prince of Wales feathers. The owner was dragging a large cardboard box from beneath a stall of skirts and blouses.

'What do you think he wants that box for?' Vanessa wondered.

'To sleep in, of course. He probably lives in Cardboard City.'

'Cardboard City?'

'It's where the homeless people live. They all sleep in cardboard boxes underneath the Arches.'

'What arches?'

'*The* Arches, of course. Shall we go home now?'

Vanessa nodded. They were wet and cold, and the rain had removed most of their makeup, saving them the trouble of doing it themselves before they encountered Him. The feet of Stella's stockings felt like muddy string in her leaking shoes.

They were huddled on the packed escalator, two drowned rats going up to Victoria, when Vanessa screamed shrilly.

'Daddy!'

She pointed to a man on the opposing escalator.

'It's Daddy, quick Stella, we've got to get off.' She would have climbed over the rail if Stella hadn't held her.

'It's not him.'

'It is. It is. *Daddy!*'

Faces turned to stare. The man turned and their eyes met as they were carried upwards and he was borne inexorably down. Vanessa tried to turn to run down against the flow of the escalator but she was wedged. The man was gone for ever.

'It wasn't him, I tell you.'

Stella fought the sobbing Vanessa at the top of the stair, they were yelling at each other in the mêlée of commuters and shoppers. She succeeded in dragging her through the barrier, still crying, 'It was him. Now we'll never see him again.'

'Daddy hasn't got a beard, you know that. And he'd never wear a balaclava. Come *on*, Vanessa, we'll miss our train.'

'It was him. Let's go back, please, please.'

'Look, stupid, that guy was a down and out. A vagrant. A wino. A meths drinker. It couldn't possibly have been Daddy.'

On the home-bound train Stella carefully opened the box of chocolate Napoleons. There were so many that nobody would notice if a couple were missing. She took out two gold coins and sealed the box again. For the rest of their lives Vanessa would be convinced that she had seen her father, and Stella would never be sure. The chocolate dissolved in their mouths as they crossed the Thames.

'Where is Cardboard City?' whispered Vanessa. 'How do you get there?'

'"Follow the Yellow Brick Road . . ."'

The silver heart-shaped balloon floated on its vertical string above the heads and newspapers of the passengers.

'"Now I know I've got a heart, because it's breaking."'

'It's just a slow puncture,' Stella said. She stuck a gift label on to the balloon's puckering silver skin. It ruined the look of it, but it was kindly meant. Vanessa looked out of the window at the moon melting like a lemon drop in the freezing sky above the chimney tops of Clapham and pictured it shining on the cold frail walls and pinnacles of Cardboard City.

'I don't want Daddy to sleep in a cardboard box,' she said.

'It's a great life,' Stella said savagely. 'Didn't you see those people singing and dancing?'

Dreams of Dead Women's Handbags

It was a black evening bag sequined with salt, open-mouthed under a rusted marcasite clasp, revealing a black moiré silk lining stained by seawater; a relic stranded in the wrack of tarry pebbles and tufts of blue and orange nylon string like garish sea anemones, crab shells and lobster legs, plastic detritus, oily feathers, condoms and rubbery weed and clouded glass, the dry white sponges of whelk egg cases, and a brittle black-horned mermaid's purse. This image, the wreckage of a dream beached on the morning, would not float away; as empty as an open shell, the black bivalve emitted a silent howl of despair; clouds passed through its mirror.

Susan Vigo was much possessed by death. Sitting on a slow train to the coast, at a table in the compartment adjacent to the buffet car, she thought about her recurring dream and about a means of murder. A book and a newspaper lay in front of her, and as she inserted the word 'limpid' in the crossword, completing the puzzle, she saw aquamarine water in a rock pool wavering limpidly over a conical white limpet shell. Her own id was rather limp that morning, she felt; the gold top of her pen tasted briny in her mouth. The colour of the water was the precise clear almost-green of spring evening skies when the city trembled with the possibility of love. She wondered dispassionately if she would ever encounter such a sky again, and as she wondered, she saw a handbag half-submerged on the bottom of the pool among the wavering weeds, green and encrusted with limpets, as though it had lain there for a long time, releasing gentle strings of bubbles like dreams and memories. A mermaid's purse, she remembered her father teaching her, as she made her way to the buffet, was the horny egg case of a skate, or ray or shark, but to whom the desolate handbag in her dreams had belonged, she had no idea, only that its owner was dead.

The buffet car steward seemed familiar, but perhaps the painful red eyes were uniform issue, along with the shiny jacket spattered by toasted sandwiches; his hair had been combed back with bacon grease and fell in curly rashers on his collar, his red tie was as slick as a dying poppy's petal. As Susan waited in the queue she told herself that he could have no possible significance in her life, and reminded herself that she made many journeys and had probably encountered him before, leering over the formica counter of another train. Nevertheless she watched him, it was her habit to stare at people, with an uneasy notion that he was Charon ferrying her across the Styx – but Charon would not be the barman, but the driver of this Inter-City train, sitting at the controls in his cab, racing them down the rails to the Elysian fields, and she was almost certain that she and her fellow passengers were still alive and their coins were for the purchase of refreshments and not the fees of the dead. The barman's years of bracing himself on the swaying floors of articulated metal snakes had given him the measure of his customers. The woman in the simulated beige mink, in front of Susan in the queue, asked for two gin and tonics, one for an imaginary friend down the corridor, and was given two little green bottles, two cans of tonic, and one plastic cup with a contemptuous fistful of ice cubes. Her eyes met the barman's and she did not demur. One of his eyes closed like a snake's in a wink at Susan as the woman fumbled her purchases from the counter. It takes one to know one, thought Susan, refusing to be drawn into complicity by the reptilian lid of his red eye as she ordered her coffee. Her face in the mirror behind the bar, her shirt, her scarf, her brooch, the cut of her jacket spoke as quietly of success as the fur-coated woman's screeched failure.

Failure. That was a word Susan Vigo hated. She saw it as a sickly plant with etiolated leaves, flourishing in dank unpleasant places, a parasite on a rotting trunk, or a pot plant on the windowsills of houses of people she despised. If she had cared to, she could have supplied a net curtain on a string as a backcloth and a plaster Alsatian, but she had a horror of rotting window frames and rented rooms, and banished the image. Susan Vigo was not the sort of woman who would order two gins for herself on a train. She was not, like some she could name, the sort of writer who would arrive to give a reading with a wine-splashed book and grains of cat litter in her trouser turnups, having fortified herself with spirits on the journey for the ordeal, who would enter in disarray and stumble into disrepute. The books in her overnight bag were glossy and immaculate with clean white strips of paper placed between the pages, to mark the passages which she would read. She did not regard it as an ordeal; she had memorised her introductory speech, and was looking forward to the evening. She had done her homework, and would have been able to relax with a book by another author, had consciousness of the delivery date of her own next crime novel not threatened like a migraine at the edge of her brain. The irony was that the title of her book was *Deadline* and for the first time in her life, she feared that she would not meet hers. Notice of it had appeared already in her publisher's catalogue and she had not even got the plot. It was set on the coast, she knew that; it involved a writer – yes, and horned poppy and sea holly and viper's bugloss, stranded sea-mice leaking rainbows into the sand, and of course her Detective Inspector Christopher Hartshorn, an investigator of the intellectual, laconic school; a body – naturally; a handbag washed up on the beach – the sort of handbag that had foxtrotted to Harry Roy, or a flaunting scarlet patent number blatant as a stiletto heel, a steel-faceted purse, a gondola basket holding a copy of *Mirabelle* or *Roxy* – she didn't even know in which period to set her murder – a drawstring leather bag which smelled of raw camel hide, a satchel with a wooden pencil box, a strap purse, containing a threepenny bit, worn across the front of a gymslip – old handbags like discarded lovers. She sifted desperately through the heap of silk and plastic, leather and wicker – it had to be black, like the handbag in her dream . . .

Susan lived in Hampstead, on a staple diet of vodka and asparagus, fresh in season, or tinned. It made life simple; she never had to think about what food to buy except when she had guests, which was not very often; she was more entertained than entertaining. She loved her flat and lived there alone. She had once been given two lovebirds but had grown jealous of their absorption in each other and had given them away. Trailing plants now entwined the bars of the cage where the pink and yellow birds had preened, kissing each other with waxy bills; she preferred their green indifference. There was not a trace of a plaster Alsatian. The man who had seduced her had introduced her to asparagus, its tender green heads swimming in butter, with baked beans – her choice. Professor Bruno Rosenblum, lecturer in poetry who although his juxtaposed names conjured up withered roses on their stems, had once strewn the bed with roses while she slept. Waking in the scent and petals, she had wept. 'Ah, as the heart grows older, it will come to such sights colder,' she thought now, in the train, remembering, as the past, like the dried petals of potpourri exhaled a slight sad scent, and 'Perhaps G.M. Hopkins got it right – it is always ourselves for whom we are grieving – enough of this' she turned from the dirty window slashed with rain that obscured the flat landscape and the dun animals in the shabby February fields, to her book. She wondered if she could, perhaps, take its central situation or *donnée*, and by changing it subtly, and substituting her own characters, manufacture a convincingly original work . . .

'"If you want to know about a woman, look in her purse."' The detective dumped the clues to the dead dame's life into a plastic bag and consigned it to Forensics. Susan's own handbag, if studied, would have told of an orderly life and mind, or of an owner who had dumped all her old makeup in the bin and dashed into an expensive chemist's on the way to the station: no sleazy clutter there, no circle of foam rubber tinged with grimy powder, no sweating stubs of lipstick and broken biros leaking into the lining, or tobacco shreds or dog-eared appointment cards for special clinics or combs with dirty teeth or minicab cards acquired on flights through dawn streets from unspeakable crises. Susan could see as clearly in her mind the contents of the handbag of the woman who had bought the two gins as she could see her black stilettos resting on the next seat, and the fall of fake fur caressing her calf. She saw her lean forward and open a compact the dark blue of a mussel shell, and peer into a mirror, and her imagination supplied a crack zigzagging across the glass, presaging doom. The man directly opposite Susan was reading a report and was of as little interest as he had been at the start of the journey; on the other side of the aisle a family, parents and two children, finished their enormous lunch and settled down to a game of three-dimensional noughts and crosses, which involved plastic tubes and marbles, clack clack clack. The marbles bounced off Susan's brain like bullets. Why can't they just use pencil and paper? she thought irritably: the extra dimensions added nothing but cost and noise to the game. She put her hands over her ears, and, resting her book on the table, tried to read, but her concentration was shot to pieces. She closed her eyes, and the handbag in her dream returned like a black shell, which if held to the ear would whisper her own mortality.

There was this handbag washed up on the beach – what next? She waited for a whole narrative to unwind and a cast of characters to come trooping out, but nothing happened. There was this crime writer travelling on a train, panicking about a deadline when suddenly . . . a single shot passed through the head of the buffet car attendant's head, shattering the glass behind him . . . Susan's fascination with firearms dated from a white double holster studded with glass jewels and two fancy guns with bluish shining barrels and decorated stocks; she had loved them more than any of her dolls, taking them to bed with her at night, loving the neat round boxes of pink caps. She could smell them now, and the scent of new sandals with crêpe soles like cheese.

Dreams of dead women's handbags: the click of a false tortoiseshell clasp, the musty smell of old perfume from the torn black moiré lining, and powder in a shell, lipstick that would look as ghastly on a skull as it did on the mouths of the little white flat fish on the seaside stall, skate smoking cigarettes through painted mouths, the glitter of saliva on a pin impaling whelks. She saw a man and a woman walking on a cliff top starred with pink thrift, a gull's white scalloped tail feathers; the woman wore a dress patterned in poppies and corn and the man had his shirt-collar open over his jacket, in holiday style. A child skipped between them on that salty afternoon when the world was their oyster.

Amberley Hall, where Susan was heading, was a small private literary foundation where students of all ages attended courses and summer

schools in music, painting and writing. She had been invited to be
the guest reader at one of their creative writing courses, and was
looking forward to seeing again the two tutors, both friends, and
renewing her acquaintance with Amberley's directors whom she had
liked very much when she met them the previous year when she
herself had been a co-tutor. The house was white and stood on a
cliff; reflections of the sea and sky met in its windows. Susan hoped
that she would be given the room in which she had slept before,
with its faded blue bedspread and shell-framed looking glass and
vase of dried flowers beside the white shells on the windowsill, sea
lavender faded by time, like a dead woman's passions and regrets.
The clatter of marbles became intolerable. Susan strode towards the
buffet car. The train seemed to be going very slowly. She began to
worry about the time and wish that she had accepted her hosts'
offer to meet her at the station.

'Going all the way?' the barman asked as he sliced a lemon with
a thin-bladed knife. The other woman had not been offered lemon.

'I beg your pardon?'

'Going all the way?'

'No. Not quite.'

'Business or pleasure?'

Susan had never seen why she should answer that question, so
often asked by strangers on a train.

'A bit of both,' she replied.

Again his eyelid flickered in a wink.

'Ice?'

'Please.' She hoped her tone matched the cubes he was dropping
into her glass with his fingers, one of which was girdled with a
frayed Elastoplast. Stubble was trying to break through the red nodules
of a rash on his neck; he looked as though he had shaved in cold
water in the basin in the blocked toilet, with his knife. The arrival
of two other customers brought their conversation to an end.

As she approached her seat with her vodka and tonic she stopped
in her tracks. That woman in the fur coat had Susan's overnight
bag down on the seat and was going through her things.

'What do you think you're doing?' She grabbed her furry arm;
her hand was shaken from it.

'I'm just looking for a tissue.'

'But that's my bag. Those are my things!'

The woman was pulling out clothes and underclothes and dumping them on the seat while the noughts and crosses clicked and clacked, tic tac toe. She scrabbled under the books at the bottom of the bag.

'Stop it, do you hear?'

'She's only looking for a tissue,' said the man opposite mildly, looking up from his report.

'I'm going to get the guard. I'm going to pull the emergency cord.'

The other woman's full lips trembled and she started to cry.

The man took a handkerchief from his breast pocket, shook it out and handed it to her.

'Have a good blow.'

She did.

'I'll give you a good blow!' said Susan punching her hard in the chest, at the top of a creased *décolletage* where a gilt pendant nestled in the shape of the letter M. The lights went out. The train almost concertinaed to a stop.

'Now look what you've done, pulling the communication cord.'

'I didn't touch it,' Susan shouted. 'What's going on? What's the matter with everybody? I didn't go near it.'

She felt the woman move away, and sat down heavily on her disarranged bag, panting with affront and rage, the unfairness of it all and the fact that nobody had stood up for her. Tears were rolling down her face as she groped for her clothes and crammed them back into the bag. Marbles rolled across the table and ricocheted off the floor. The tips of cigarettes glowed like tiny volcanoes in the gloom and someone giggled, a high nervous whinny. Susan began to sweat. Rain was drumming on the windows like her heartbeats, and she knew that she had died and was to be locked for eternity in this train in the dark with people who hated her. This was her sentence: what was her crime? Battalions of minor sins thronged her memory. Her hand hurt where she had punched the woman; she sucked her knuckle and tasted blood. The lights came on. Susan screamed.

★　★　★

The barman stood in the doorway, his knife in his hand.

'Nearly a nasty accident,' he said.'Car stalled on the level crossing.'

People started to laugh and talk.

'Could've been curtains for us all,' he said as the train brayed and the orange curtains at the black windows swayed as it started to move.

The woman in the fur coat came sashaying down the aisle, reeled on a marble, and plonked herself down beside Susan.

'Sorry about that little mistake, only I mistook it for my bag. They're quite similar. Here, let me help you put it up.'

They swung it clumsily onto the rack, next to a dirty tapestry bag edged in cracked vinyl. Susan looked into her eyes, opaque as marbles, and perceived that she was mad. She picked up her book.

'Like reading, do you?'

'When I get the chance.'

'I know what you mean. There's always something needs doing, isn't there? I expect you're like me, can't sit idle. What with my little dog, and my crochering and the telly there's always something, isn't there?'

'Crochering?' Susan heard herself ask.

'Yes, I've always got some on the go. I made this.'

She pulled open her lapels to show a deep-throated pink filigree garment.

'It was a bolero in the pattern, only I added the sleeves.'

Susan smiled and tried desperately to read, but it was too late: she saw in vivid detail the woman's sitting room, feet in pink fluffy slippers stretched out to the electric fire that was mottling her legs, the wheezy Yorkshire terrier with a growth on its neck, the crochet hook plying in a billowy sea of pink and violet squares; a bedspread for a wedding present to a niece, who would bundle it into a cupboard.

She almost said, 'I'm sorry about your little dog,' but stopped herself in time, and before she was tempted to advise her to abandon her bedspread, the guard announced that the train was approaching her station. She gathered her things together with relief and went to find an exit. As she passed the bar the steward, who had taken off his jacket and was reading a newspaper, did not raise his head. She saw how foolish she had been to fear him.

'Thank God that's over,' she said aloud on the platform as she took deep breaths of wet dark air which, although the station was miles inland, tasted salty, and the appalling train pulled away, carrying the barman and the deranged woman to their mad destinations. She came out into the forecourt in time to see the rear lights of a taxi flashing in the rain. She knew at once that it was the only one and that it would not return for a long time. She saw a telephone box across the road and, shielding with her bag her hair that the rain would reduce to a nest of snakes, hurried through the puddles. At least, being in the country, the phone would not have been vandalised. A wet chip paper wrapped itself around her ankles; the receiver dangled from a mess of wires, black with emptiness roaring through its broken mouth, like a washed-up handbag.

A pub. There must be a pub somewhere near the station that would have a telephone. Susan stepped out of the smell of rural urine and started to walk. She would not let herself panic, or let the lit and curtained windows sheltering domesticity make her feel lonely. Perhaps she could hire a car, from the pub. She imagined the sudden silence falling on the jocular company of the inn and a fearful peasant declaring, 'None of us villagers dare go up to Amberley Hall. Not after dark,' and a dark figure in a bat-winged cloak flying screeching past the moon.

Mine host was a gloomy fellow who pointed her to a pay phone. The number was engaged. Temporarily defeated, Susan ordered a drink and sat down. It was then that she realised that her overnight bag had been transformed into a grubby tapestry hold-all with splitting vinyl trim. A cold deluge of disbelief engulfed her and then hot pricking needles of anger. She drowned the words that rose to her lips; this wasn't Hampstead. How could it have happened – that madwoman – Susan was furious with herself; she would have scorned to use the device of the switched luggage in one of her own books, and here she was, lumbered, in this dire pub, with this disgusting bag, and worse, worse, all her own things, her books

– the reading . . . She was tempted to call it a day then, and order another drink, and consign herself to fate, propping up the bar until her money ran out and they dumped her in the street, but she made another attempt at the telephone, and this time got through. Someone would be there to pick her up in twenty minutes. She thought of ordering a sandwich but the knowledge of the meal, the refectory table heaped with bowls of food awaiting her, restrained her, and she sat there half listening to the jukebox, making her drink last, wishing she was at home doing something cheerful like drinking vodka and listening to Bessie Smith, or Billie Holiday singing 'Good Morning Heartache'.

She thought she had found her murder victim, a blonde woman with a soft white face and body and a pendant in the shape of the letter M and a stolen bag; she lolled in death, her black shoes stabbing skywards, on a cliff top lying in the thrift that starred the grass and was embossed on a threepenny bit, tarnished at the bottom of an old handbag. Threepence, that was the amount of pocket money she had received; a golden hexagonal coin each Saturday morning. The early 1950s: a dazzle of red, white and blue; father, mother and child silhouetted against a golden sunburst in a red sky like figures on a poster, marching into Utopia.

The dead woman's dress was splashed with poppies and corn – no, that was wrong – it must be black. Her mother had had a dress of poppies and corn, scarlet flowers and golden ears and sky-blue cornflowers on a white field; Ceres in white peep-toe shoes, the sun sparkling off a Kirbigrip in her dark gold hair. Her father's hair was bright with brilliantine and he wore his shirt-collar, white as vanilla ice cream, open over his jacket. Susan's hair was in two thin plaits of corn and gripped on either side with a white hair-slide in the shape of Brumas the famous polar bear cub. Susan sat in the pub, becoming aware that it was actually a small hotel, and staring at a red-carpeted staircase that disappeared at an angle, leading to the upper guest rooms. In a flash she realised why the barman in the train looked familiar, and blind and deaf to the music and flashing lights she sat in a waking dream.

★　　★　　★

The child woke in the hotel bedroom and found herself alone. Moonlight lay on the pillows of the double bed her parents shared. The bed was undisturbed. They had come up from the bar to tuck her in. 'You be a good girl now and go to sleep. We're just popping out for a stroll, we won't be gone more than a few minutes.' Her father's eyes were red – she turned her face away from his beery kiss. Her mother's best black taffeta dress rustled as she closed the door behind them. The child pulled a sweater over her nightdress and buckled on her holster and her new white sandals and tiptoed to the door. A gust of piano playing and singing and beer and cigarette smoke bellied into the bedroom. She closed the door quietly behind her and slid slowly down the banister, so as not to make any noise. She was angry with them for leaving her alone. She bet they were eating ice creams and chips without her. She crept to the back door and let herself out into the street. Although she had never been out so late alone, she found that it was almost light – girls and boys come out to play, the moon doth shine as bright as day – she would burst into the café and shoot them dead – Susan saw her in the moonlight, a small figure in a white nightdress in the empty street with a gun in each hand. The café was closed.

She turned onto the path that led to the cliffs. Rough grass spiked her bare legs and sand filled her new sandals and rubbed on her heels. She holstered her guns because she had to use her hands to scramble up the steep slope, uttering little sobs of fear and rage. She reached the top and flung herself panting onto the turf. At the edge of the cliff sat two figures, from this distance as black as two cormorants on a rock against the sky. The sea was roaring in her ears as she wriggled on her belly towards them. As she drew nearer she could see the woman's arms, white as vanilla in her black taffeta dress, and the man's shirt-collar. She stood up and drew her guns and took aim but suddenly she was frightened at herself standing there against the sky and just wanted them to hold her, and shoved the guns back in the holster and as she did the man put his arm around the woman's shoulder and kissed her. The child was running towards them, to thrust herself between their bodies shouting joyfully 'Boo!' as she thumped them on their backs, and the woman lost her balance and clutched the man and they went tumbling over and over and over and the woman's handbag fell from her wrist and went spiralling after them screaming and screaming from its open black mouth.

When the landlady, impatient at the congealing breakfast, came to rouse the family in the morning she found the child asleep, cuddling up to a holster instead of a teddy. The parents' bed was undisturbed. It seemed a shame to wake the little girl. She looked so peaceful with her fair hair spread out on the pillow. She shook her gently.

'Where are your mummy and daddy, lovey?'

The child sat up, seeing the buckle of her new sandal hanging by a thread. Mummy would have to sew it on.

'I don't know,' she answered truthfully.

'Susan. Hi.'

Tom from Amberley Hall was shaking her arm. 'You look awful. Have you had a terrible journey? You must have.'

'Perfectly bloody,' said Susan.

'I'm afraid you've missed supper,' said Tom, in the car, 'but we'll rustle up something for you after the reading. I think we'd better get straight on with it if you don't mind. Everybody's keen to meet you. Quite an interesting bunch of students this time . . .'

His voice went on. Susan wanted to bury her face in the thick cables of his sweater. As they entered the house she explained about the loss of her bag.

'Just like Professor Pnin, eh, on the wrong train with the wrong lecture?' he laughed.

Susan wished profoundly then to *be* Professor Pnin, Russian and ideally bald; to be anybody but herself in her creased clothes with her hair snaking wildly around her head and a tapestry bag in her hand containing the crocheted tangle of that woman's mad life.

'It was the right train,' she said, 'but I haven't got anything to read.'

'I did get in touch with your publishers to send some books to sell, but I'm afraid they haven't arrived. Never mind though, some of the students have brought their own copies for you to sign, so you could borrow one. Five minutes to freshen up, OK? We've put you in the same room as last time.'

★　★　★

'No bloody food. No bloody wine. Not even any bloody books,' said Susan behind the closed door of her room. She aimed a kick at the bookcase: each of those spines faded by sea air representing somebody's futile bid to hold back eternal night. Precisely five minutes later she stepped, pale, poised and professional, into the firelit room to enchant her audience.

When she had finished reading, a chill hung over the room for a moment and then someone started the clapping. As the appreciative applause flickered out, bottles of wine and glasses were brought, and the evening was given over to informal questions and discussion. A gallant in corduroys bowed as he handed her a glass.

'You're obviously very successful, Miss Vigo, or may I call you Susan? Could you tell us what made you decide on writing as a career in the first place? I mean I myself have been attempting to —'

'I wanted to be rich,' interrupted Susan quickly before he could launch on his autobiography. The firelight striking red glints on her hair, and her charming smile persuaded her listeners that she was joking. 'You see, I was always determined to succeed in whatever career I chose. I came from a very deprived background. My parents died tragically when I was young and I was brought up by relatives.' Her lip trembled slightly; a plaster Alsatian barked in corroboration.

'What was your first big breakthrough?'

'I was very lucky in that I met a professor at university, a dear old soul, who took an interest in my youthful efforts and who was very helpful to me professionally. He's dead now, alas.' She became for a moment a pretty young student paying grateful tribute to her crusty old mentor. Most of the audience were half in love with her now.

'What made you turn to crime, as it were, Susan, instead of to any other fictional genre?'

Susan's slender body rippled as she giggled, 'I don't know really — I developed a taste for murder at an early age, and I've never looked back, I suppose.'

'Can I ask where you get your ideas from?'

The frail orphan sipped her wine before replying.

'From "the foul rag-and-bone shop of the heart".'

Other People's Bathrobes

Her underwear slipped through his fingers in silky shoals of salmon and grayling; stockings slithered like a catch of rainbow eels. He moved about the bedroom like an assassin, although he was alone in the flat, as if he were watched by eyes other than his own which glanced off the mirror's surface like fish scales reflecting the rainy morning light. Several times when he and Barbara had been together, he had felt that they were not alone; over his shoulder an invisible circle of her friends was whispering, condemning him, warning her. He imagined their nights laid out on lunchtime restaurant tables shrouded in white linen, and dissected with heavy silver knives and forks. He did not know what he was looking for as he went through her things – some evidence as dangerous as a gun lying in the silken nest, that he could possess and use to destroy her when it suited him.

Last night they had come out of the cinema knock-kneed with grief, holding onto each other against the pain of someone else's tragedy. The restaurant smelled of fish and lemon, and clouds of steam banked the lower halves of the windows and evaporated in rivulets down the black glass. He was hungry throughout, and after, the meal. She had eaten almost nothing and her refusal of wine had inhibited his own intake, as the springwater bubbling glumly in its mossy green glass dampened his desire, although her stockinged foot, slipped from its shoe and stroking his leg under the table, suggested that it had refreshed hers.

'I'm sick of mangetout peas,' he had grumbled. 'I want proper peas, without pods, from a tin.'

She had smiled at him indulgently, as at a child, although his petulant mouth was in danger of becoming merely peevish. Meanwhile he salivated discontentedly in memory of the food of his brief happy childhood. A low-slung moon hung in the north

London sky as she drove them home; the golden crescent of a pendulum slicing the blackness; it would taste of melon if sucked, a wedge of honeydew. He sat beside her in silence, aware that he was, as always, in the passenger seat.

There was nothing in the bedroom to incriminate her: dresses gave evidence of nothing that he did not know, shoes were mute and jewellery jangled to no purpose, scent left false trails and no glove pointed the finger. Books that might have betrayed her were not called to witness.

'There are some robes you can use,' she had told him on the first night he had spent with her. That had been three weeks ago and he was still there, still wearing borrowed bathrobes and dressing gowns. This morning he was dressed in a blue kimono with a red and gold dragon writhing up its back and tongues of flame licking his shoulders. He went to the window and lifted the corner of the blind. The trees in the street were hung with leaves the colour of cooked swede, and mashed swede lay in heaps in the gutters; pyracantha flung bright sprays of baked beans against the houses opposite. In his twenty years he had worn too many dressing gowns belonging to other people. He sighed and pulled the sash tighter around his diminishing waist and padded into the kitchen.

He opened the fridge and the freezer compartment and then slammed them shut, sending shivers through the bottles of mineral water shuddering in the door. There wasn't even any real coffee, just that stuff that you had to muck about with filter papers, and a small jar of decaffeinated powder, and a tiny tin of sweeteners instead of sugar. He shook four or five white pellets into a cup and added coffee and a dash of skimmed milk as he waited for the kettle to boil.

'No bleeding bread of course . . .'

He microwaved the lone croissant into a blackened shell and smeared it with low-fat spread. He could have murdered a fried egg sandwich washed down with a mug of hot sweet tea. She, of course, had breakfasted on her usual fare of a tisane and half a dozen vitamin and mineral tablets. He lit a cigarette and took it and the newspaper into the main room of the flat – he never knew what to call it: front room, although it was, or lounge, were wrong – and pushed aside the white vase of black porcelain roses and white plastic tulips and put his feet up. Smoking was frowned on almost to the point of a total ban, but since that early morning when she had sensed his absence in the bed and come into the kitchen and screamed at the sight of his legs sprawled on the kitchen floor, his head wedged firmly in the obsolete cat flap, a forbidden cigarette clamped in his lips spiralling smoke helplessly into the dawn chorus, she had relaxed slightly the interdiction. She had thought he was dead. It had taken an hour, a lot of soap, and finally a screwdriver to release him.

When he had bathed he would run the Hoover over the carpets; there was little for it to vacuum up except a light frosting of the low-fat crisp crumbs which he had consumed while she got ready for bed. It was the Hoover which had brought them together: he had arrived in response to her enquiry to a cleaning agency and had stayed on to help her prepare for a dinner party, as she moved about the kitchen with a brittle energy that teetered over into panic, her pale hair crackling with electricity in the stormy light pouring through the window. When the first guests arrived it was he who opened the door, a glass of wine in his hand, and entertained them until she emerged from the bathroom where she had fled. She could hardly have arrested in mid-arc the bowl of salted pumpkin seeds he was proffering to her friends and explain that he was the cleaner, and so he had stayed. It was not until they all sat down to eat that she realised that an extra place had been set already at the table.

After the hoovering he would take her italic list and a plastic carrier bag, as well preserved and neatly folded as if it had been ironed, and wander down to the shops. He took the radio and another cup of coffee and his cigarettes into the bathroom and as he idled in the scented oil watching mingled smoke and steam being sucked through the extractor fan on the window, he could not avoid remembering the previous night.

She had wanted both of them to go to bed early because she had had a hard day before they met in the evening, and she was nervous about a sales conference the following morning. The publishing company for which she worked had been taken over recently, and anxiety about losing her job and treachery within the firm had smudged blue shadows under her eyes, and bitten nails, spoiling her gloss, betrayed her fears. By the time Adam had joined her in the bedroom she had fallen asleep; her hair frazzled out like excelsior on the pillow, the tag of a sachet of camomile tea drooping over the rim of the mug on the bedside table. He slid into bed, smelling the sweet-sour odour of the infusion on her breath as he leaned over her face and took her, all flowers and mineral water, in his arms and slowly and cynically began to make love to her.

Their hip bones clashed; the morning would see his faint bruises mirrored in milky opals on her skin. He thought that her ambition was to be the thinnest woman in London this side of anorexia, and he remembered reading of a young girl who had almost achieved sainthood by dint of never eating; people had flocked to witness this miracle and marvel at the beautiful and holy maiden pink and white as roses and angel cake, sustained on spiritual food, until one night a nun had been caught sneaking into her room with a basket of goodies. He wondered sometimes if Barbara, too, was a secret snacker but there was never any evidence.

He licked the whorls of her ear, as cold as one of her porcelain roses, with the tip of his tongue, while in imagination he piled a plate with processed peas swimming in their bluish liquor, pickled beetroot staining the fluffy edges of a white instant-mashed-potato cloud, a crispy cluster of acid yellow piccalilli; he added a daub of ketchup to his garish still life, and then he had to stifle a laugh in her shoulder as she responded, because only he knew that the rhythm they moved to was that of a song that had been running through his head since they had got home. Food, glorious food . . . dah da da da dah dah. He had forgotten some of the words he had sung as a ruby-lipped treble taking the lead in *Oliver!*; backstage, after the last performance, before the last tremulous tear had been flicked from the lashes of the departing audience, Adam had been expelled for extortion. Oh food, magical food, marvellous food, glor-i-ous food!!! Pease pudding and saveloys, what next is the question? While we're in the mood – Glenn Miller took up the baton with a flash of brass and buttons, or Joe Loss, sleek as an otter in a dapper dinner jacket or tuxedo. 'Tuxedo Junction'. And then Adam and Barbara expired together in an ecstasy of cold jelly and custard and he let her drop back onto a steaming heap of hot sausage and mustard. She traced with her finger his lips which were parted in a grin.

'Darling.'

'Best ever?' he asked.

She nodded, smiling and showering the pillow with pease pudding from her hair as he licked the dollop of mustard from her nose.

He had slept badly in an indigestion of shame. Bits of bad dreams lay on his mind, as unappetising as congealing food left overnight on a plate. He watched beneath half-closed lids as she gathered up the clothes she would assume as silken armour against her threatening day, moving quietly so as not to wake him, but each door, each opened and closed drawer, hissed her panic. He felt her hover over him for a moment after she had placed a mug of coffee on the coaster on the floor beside him, then with a jangle of keys, a revving of the car, she was gone and he was left floundering in the billows of the duvet trying to sleep away part of the long morning. He wished to spend as little time as possible in the company of someone he disliked as much as himself.

People who had encountered Adam as an angelic-looking child had assumed that he was a good little boy. He shared their estimation of himself until at the age of six years he had been surprised by impulses that were far from good. A girl in his class at the infants' school brought in, one morning, to show the teacher, a dolls' chest of drawers that she had made by gluing four matchboxes together and covering the top, back and sides with glossy red paper, the sort of paper that they made lanterns from at Christmas time. The handles of the drawers were yellow glass beads. Adam coveted and coveted this object all morning. She had allowed him to hold it at dinner play, as long as he didn't open the drawers, and had made him give it back. It was beyond the price of the Matchbox tractor which he had offered in exchange. He could not have said why he wanted the chest of drawers so much: he had no use for it beyond the pleasure of opening and closing the drawers. He could keep matches in it, he had decided, if he had had any – perhaps it was because it was so tiny and perfect and because he could not have contrived so neat an artefact with his own clumsy fingers, which behaved in craft lessons like a bunch of flies on flypaper – his Christmas lantern had been a disaster, with the slits cut the wrong way, and had ended up, shamefully, in the wastepaper basket. He brooded through the afternoon story and squinted at it through the steeple of his fingers as they sang 'Hands together, softly so, little eyes shut tight', plotting. He had hidden behind a hedge after school and jumped out on her from behind, pulling her knitted hat over her eyes, and snatched the chest of drawers and run off. The school was a very short distance from home, with no roads to cross. He was out of sight, although not out of earshot of her wails, by the time she had freed herself from her hat.

'What's this?' His mother was waiting for him at the entrance to the flats.

'I made it at school.'

'Isn't that lovely. Just like something they make on *Blue Peter*,' she had said as they went up in the lift.

'It's for you,' he had heard himself say. There was even a pink ring from a cracker in one of the drawers, which fitted her little finger, just above the second joint.

So, eating tinned spaghetti on toast in the afterglow of his mother's kiss that afternoon, he had realised that he could assault and rob and lie; arts which he had polished over the years, after his mother's death when he was ten years old, during his six years in care and throughout his sojourns in squats all over London.

'That's that,' he said to himself as he rewound the Hoover's flex. 'Now for the next item on my thrilling agenda.' As he stowed it away in what she called the 'glory hole', although a neater glory hole than this one with no cobwebs and everything stacked on shelves could not be imagined, his eye fell on a cardboard carton. He pulled it out, not knowing what he expected to find. His heart beat faster as he opened the flaps – a baby's shoe perhaps, a bottle of gin or the heads of her former lovers, as in Bluebeard's Castle, their beards dripping blood. What it contained was books: children's books, schoolgirl annuals, an illustrated *Bible Stories* whose red and blue and gold illuminated sticker stated that it had been presented for regular attendance at St Andrew's Sunday School in a year before Adam had been born, a stamp album with a map of the world on its cover, that released a shower of shiny and brittle stamp hinges like the wings of long-dead insects when Adam set it aside with the thought that it might be worth selling; the books that heap trestle tables at every jumble sale, even to the copy of *The Faraway Tree* by Enid Blyton, with the statutory request in faded and wobbly pencil that if this book should chance to roam, box its ears and send it home, to: Barbara Watson, 59 Oxford Road, Canterbury, Kent, England, Great Britain, the Northern Hemisphere, the World, etc., etc., *ad tedium*. Barbara had been crossed out and Brenda substituted; then Barbara had deleted Brenda, but in vain. The names fought each other in sisterly rivalry all down the page and it was not clear at the end who had triumphed; Adam heard slaps and tears, and the pulling of hair. *Britain's Wonderland of Nature*: a large green volume with a butterfly embossed on its cover and glossy colour plates which must have been her best book, Adam thought. It had been given to her by Uncle Wilf in 1960.

At the bottom of the box was a photograph album. He lifted it out and took it into the black and white room. Perhaps this was what he had been looking for. He lit a cigarette to heighten the experience.

The album had a faded blue cover and crumpled spider's web paper separated the leaves; the small photographs affixed to the storm-grey pages had crimped edges, like crinkle-cut chips, and there, flies in amber and butterflies in glass, was Barbara's past. It seemed that she had spent all her childhood on a beach against an unfailingly grey sky. The photographs were captioned in a loopy adult hand. Here were the infant Barbara and Brenda, the tangled strings of their sunbonnets blowing towards a sullen sea; a comical snap of Barbara in giant grown-up sunglasses, mouth open in dismay, holding an empty cornet whose unstable scoop of ice cream had evidently just fallen to the beach. Here was Uncle Wilf, with Aunty Dolly at Tankerton – he must have been a widower then, when he purchased *Britain's Wonderland of Nature*, Christmas 1960. Adam pictured him entering the glass doors of W. H. Smith, sleet, like a dandruff of sorrow, on the stooping shoulders of his black coat, to buy books for his nieces, the icy wind, or memories of the time he had rolled his trousers and Dolly tucked her skirt up around her knees and stood with the sea gushing between their toes smiling into the camera before she had vanished off the edge of photographs, bringing a tear to his eyes.

At Whitstable, Dad, whose name was Ron, Adam discerned, had for some reason come without his trunks and, presumably unable to resist the call of the sea, was wearing what looked suspiciously like his wife's bathing suit rolled to his waist. All the sad south coast resorts were represented in shades of black and white and grey; Adam sat in the room whose colour scheme echoed the childhood tints, his cigarette burning unnoticed in a cube of black onyx striated with white, turning the pages. He had the family sorted out now, grandparents, uncles, aunts and cousins, Mum or Mavis in white shoes, Dad; Brenda and Barbara so close in age as to be almost twins, and no longer bothered to read the captions.

By the age of four or so Brenda had become noticeably plump; beside her Barbara was as frail as an elf. Brenda swelled with the years like a raisin soaked in water; she grew into a quite unfortunate-looking kid. There was one shot of her that arrested him: she stood scowling, with her bare feet planted apart on the shifting pebbles, thighs braced, her solid little body eggcup-shaped and straining the rosettes of her ruched cotton bathing suit, her candyfloss hair parted at the side, and caught in an ungainly bow blowing in the wind that blurred the sails of the toy windmill in her hand, every line of her face and body expressing such defiance and discontent that Adam found himself smiling. Behind her the horses of a merry-go-round galloped in a frieze refrigerated by time. Someone had added a comment in pencil to her mother's writing. Adam took the album to the window the better to see.

'Barbara is a fat pig,' it said, and a pencilled arrow pointed undeniably to the photograph and was corroborated by the words, 'singed Brenda'. It was impossible. 'Barbara is a fat pig, singed Brenda.' So Barbara had been the fat plain one all along. Adam sat down heavily and lit another cigarette. He felt cheated, as if

Barbara had deceived him deliberately. Under that designer exterior there was a common little fat girl. It was all a sham. She was no better than he was. He snapped the album shut. Instead of feeling triumphant at finding the weapon he had sought, he felt sad, almost like crying. Then he began to feel angry with Brenda. He flicked through the pages again and noticed that Brenda in each photograph had pushed slightly in front of Barbara, and she was often dressed in organdy and flounces of artificial silk while Barbara was in cotton. Why was Brenda always wearing party dresses to the beach, and an angora bolero, while Barbara was in print with a school cardigan?

'It seems to me, Brenda, that it was you who were the pig. And you couldn't spell,' he said to the Christmas-tree fairy with her bucket and spade. He wondered how many times Barbara had been singed by Brenda. What were Mum and Dad, Mavis and Ron, doing, to have such a discrepancy between their daughters? He hoped Uncle Wilf had loved Barbara the best.

He closed the album and put it away in the carton with the other books and closed the cupboard door. He found Barbara's shopping list and shopping bag and set out for the shops. He could not rid himself of the picture of Barbara in the bathing suit with Brenda's cruel caption, and the quotation – he had played Viola in *Twelfth Night* – 'thus the whirligig of time brings in his revenges' spun around in his mind like the windmill in her hand and the merry-go-round in the distance, and above the jangle of fairground music he heard the teasing voice of Mum and Dad and all the aunts and cousins, and Brenda's taunting laughter. He had been wrong in thinking that Barbara was no better than he was: she was much better. Everything she had she had earned for herself, while he was driven through life in the passenger seats of other people's cars, and lounged in other people's bathrobes. More, she had created herself. He stopped dead in his tracks on the pavement, colliding with a woman with matted hair, draped in a shawl of black refuse sacks.

'I'm in love,' he told her.

'Piss off.'

'Yes, yes I will,' he said and gave her a five-pound note from

Barbara's purse, which was clawed into her shawl as she spat at his feet.

Something amazing had happened. He had fallen in love, for the first time, with a cross little girl holding a windmill at the end of her goosefleshed arm. If she had been singed by Brenda he would erase the burns, like scorch marks from a table. If she wanted revenge he would oblige, on the whole pack of them. If she wanted a white wedding with all the family there, including Brenda whose childhood had been entwined with hers like the strings of two sunbonnets on a windy day, that was all right with him too.

He went into the shop; for him the best part of the movie had always been when the guy arrived at the girl's apartment with a paper sack of groceries with a fifth of bourbon sticking its neck out: to him that was New York: romance. Unbeknownst to herself, Barbara bought herself a bottle of champagne. As he walked home with his love feast in a plastic carrier bag he saw that the pavement was strewn with lychee shells, broken to show their sunset pink interiors, like shells on a beach in the rain. Outlined against the hectic light everything assumed a poignancy: a bag of refuse and a broken branch of blue eucalyptus made a haiku on the wet kerb. He felt healed, as if someone had poured precious ointment from a box of alabaster over him.

He was in the kitchen when he heard her key in the lock. She stepped inside, all unawares, in her black raincoat rolling with ersatz pearls, coming home to a steaming bowl of Heinz vegetable soup, just like mother used to make.

The Thirty-first of October

It was the time of year when people stole down garden paths to lay huge woody marrows and boxes of wormy windfalls, and jars of sloppy chutney with stained paper mobcaps on each other's doorsteps, but not on hers. There would be no sparklers on November the Fifth either, although, not five hundred yards away the young men and boys of the village had been building for weeks an enormous bonfire, a superstructure of wood, branches, mattresses, tyres and junk and garden refuse, on the village green. Now it was almost complete, a sign ordered that there should be brought NO MORE RUBISH, and members of the bonfire committee were taking turns to sleep out in a little wooden shelter in its shadow to guard it from premature pyromaniacs. A spit had been erected and stood in readiness for the pig which was to be roasted; the early morning air of that day would be tainted with the smell of oozing tissues until a bruised cloud of cooked meat drizzled droplets of fat into the evening air, which would linger for days while the bonfire smouldered, mingling with the grey ash that would coat her front garden and invade the house through the ill-fitting windows. Once she had joined in the procession, but now the prospect of the burning torches of pitch, the faces in the lurid light, the Guy dragged on a rail, filled her with dread, evoking other primitive rituals, with hunts and sacrificial blood spilled on the fields. She leaned against the window, staring into the darkening afternoon, waiting for absolutely nothing at all.

After an Indian summer, the first frost had wrecked the gardens, leaving the hydrangeas in blackened ruins that hulked on either side of the gate which led onto a rutted lane. On the other side of the lane stretched fields. The house next door, one of a pair of cottages, had double-glazed aluminium-framed picture windows, and a snouty little porch of bottle glass, and sliding patio doors at the back. A slice of varnished oak beside the front door bore the

name Trevenidor. When she and Paul had moved in he had fantasised that the house had been named in sentimental tribute to a
Cornish resort where their neighbours had honeymooned, but
when they met Trevor and Enid it became apparent that they had
intertwined their own names in a true-lover's knot. Trevor and
Enid had two daughters, Kimberley and Carly; now seven and five
years old.

She had been pleased by the fact that there were children next
door; she had thought that they might alleviate the loss of her
own two daughters who were both living abroad, but she blushed
now to recollect her fantasies of little figures draped in floury
aprons, their pudgy fingers dimpling as they pressed the raisin
buttons into gingerbread men, their faces rosy in the warmth of
her spicy kitchen; of collecting wild flowers and blackberries and
nuts with two little yellow-haired companions. There *were* hazel-
nuts, and blackberries in the hedges, but they were small and bitter
and splashed with grey mud and sprayed with pesticides; and once
a year Trevor drove down the lane with a mechanical ripper that
tore the tops off the bushes, leaving the branches stripped bare;
broken and bleeding. In the first flush of neighbourliness she had
offered to baby-sit, but she had been rebuffed. On Enid's darts
night Trevor stayed at home, and on the rare occasions that they
went out together, Enid's mother, an even larger version of her
daughter, was ensconced in Trevenidor. Carly and Kimberley had
met her overtures of friendship with silent, bright blue-eyed scorn,
clinging to their mother in a parody of shyness, burying their
faces in her short skirt, pulling it around her columnar thighs
until they were slapped off like mosquitoes, and when their new
neighbour had extended a biscuit to her, Carly had burst into
tears, as if it had been a stone or a serpent; and then later she
had heard her name tossed mockingly over the hedge – 'Claw-
dee-ya, Claw-dee-ya.'

In the winter frost formed patterns on the insides of Claudia's
windows and snow drifted in, dredging the sills like icing sugar.
Last year she had steeled herself to confront Trevor over the hedge
and ask him to look at the central heating; the bottom halves of
the radiators remained cold, while the tops gave out such feeble
heat that she could see the clouds of her breath. Trevor, risking

Enid's displeasure, for she had referred pointedly to him as My Husband ever since Paul's departure, squatting on his haunches, exposing more of his lower back than Claudia would have wished to see, gave the radiator a shake, causing a tiny avalanche of plaster behind the damp wallpaper and pronounced, 'Not much I can do. I know the cowboy who installed it – your whole system's corroded.'

'I'll just have to turn it up, then . . .'

'You can turn it up as high as you like, lady; you'll always be cold.'

His words left her with the chill of the grave.

She went to the dining table which she used as a desk, picked up a book, and let it drop. It was one that she should have been reviewing, but the deadline was slipping away. 'What was your book called again, only I couldn't see it in the van?' Enid had asked early in their acquaintance. Claudia had not explained that the mobile library was unlikely to carry two books that had been out of print for years, and thereafter she had avoided the van lest she encounter Enid in its crowded interior. She had been highly praised as a miniaturist once, and in vain did she remind herself of little bits of ivory; her talent had diminished until it had dis-appeared. She depressed a key of the disused piano; damp felt struck rusty wire, and the note hung in the air. A silvery blight was stealing over the veneer, clouding the flowers that wreathed the candle holders. It was Paul's piano, and Enid had asked him not to play it in the evenings because it disturbed the children.

Soon Kimberley and Carly would be home from school, and when darkness had fallen they would come pushing and giggling up her path, pinching each other's arms in their simulated terror, for all the world as if they were Hansel and Gretel, and she was the wicked witch. Trick or treat. What could possibly be a treat to them? The hedges and ditch testified to the chocolate bars and lollies they consumed daily on the way home from school, and although it was only late October they had anticipated Christmas already by devouring the contents of two mesh stockings, filled with sweets, one of which had blown into Claudia's garden. As she had shaken a slug from its interstices and put the torn stocking in her dustbin, she had felt a pang of pity for the children for whom there was no magic. What they would like most from her was money. She had seen their money boxes; pink ceramic pigs with lipsticked snouts and flirtatious painted eyelashes and grotesque rumps, bearing little resemblance to the inmates of the asbestos and corrugated-iron stalag whose stench drifted across the fields when the wind was in the wrong direction, where Trevor worked.

Two weeks previously, by a blunder on the part of a secretary, Claudia had been sent an invitation to a party given by her erst-while publisher. Turning it over and over in her hands, she had searched it for a sign that it was a practical joke, but there was no one who would think her worth playing a joke on. Except Kimberley and Carly, who, last Hallowe'en, had emptied her dustbin on her doorstep; it hadn't been funny but she had heard Enid and Trevor laughing. She had stood the invitation on the mantelpiece, beside the jar of shrivelled rosehips, for all, that is herself, to see. She had taken the bus to the town, where she had found at last, in despair, a diaphanous dress in the Help the Aged shop, but it had been so cold on the night of the party that she had had to wear her kingfisher blue chunky cardigan, bought from Enid's catalogue in more halcyon days, bulkily uncomfortable and protruding its cuffs from the sleeves of her coat.

In the confusion of her arrival in the loud room, where the heat, after her cold walk from the tube, had turned her face to fire, she had forgotten to deposit her cardigan with her coat. Finding herself ignored and jammed up against the drinks table, there had been nothing to do but help herself to red wine. Once, she turned and met the shock of her face; eyes bloodshot with drink and smoke, and a red clownish patch on each cheek, brilliant under the electrified chandelier, above the wrongly-buttoned cardy; but by then she had been too far gone to care.

She had realised at once that she would have done better to have come in her jeans, as others had, to have pretended a casualness that she hadn't felt; her attempt at finery was so far from the chic of those women who had dressed up. For them, she supposed, this was just another evening, somewhere to stop off before going out to dinner, or home, but she, shamefully, had invested all her hopes in it, and they died among the cigarette butts and broken pretzels and rejected gherkins on the table behind her. When, as she was burrowing for her coat, a woman spoke to her, and, recognising her name, said that she admired her work, Claudia had been so grateful that she had latched onto her, and found herself one of a party billowing down the road to a restaurant. She was happy; she was back where she ought to be; she felt a sudden conviction that her talent, after all, had not deserted her.

Only the next morning, sitting on the first train home, travelling with a gang of railway workers, apart in a corner, the picture of debauchery in her laddered tights, aware of their gentle mockery, had she realised that she had not been invited to the restaurant. Her pinched cold face flooded with blood as snatches of the evening floated among the black specks in front of her eyes; she had babbled of the pig farm and conjured up Enid and Trevor and Kimberley and Carly to sit among the guests partaking of whitebait and avocado, and plonk bluish knuckles and bloodied, half-severed trotters on their plates. Now she felt as alienated from her fellow-diners as she did from her neighbours, and from the men with their sandwiches and newspapers, their camaraderie, their sense of being in the right place at the right time. It was then that she looked down and saw the tidemark of mud on her shoes, that must have been there all the time, adding the finishing touch to her garish rig; and putting her head in her hands, discovered that somewhere in the debris of the evening, lost perhaps on her gallop to the station for the last, missed, train, lay an ear-ring, one of her only valuable pair, given to her by her grandmother.

The irrecoverable loss of the ear-ring burned in an opalescent pain in her throat, as if she had swallowed it, long after the inflammation of the self-inflicted social wounds had abated. The ear-rings had been promised to her daughter, and at some time the loss must be discovered, or confessed. The end of the evening was a merciful blur, and she would never see those people again, but the ear-ring bereaved of its twin would be an everlasting token of her disgrace.

Her anger at herself turned on Trevor and Enid. She had moved her bedroom to avoid the grunts that she imagined came through the wall, but she lay sleepless in her cold bed, in the musty smell of mildew whose spores she sometimes thought pervaded her own skin, warming herself with a scenario in which Trevor had somehow mistaken his wife for a sow, and Enid lay helpless on the slatted floor, unable to speak or to turn, squeezed between the metal sides of the farrowing pen, subjected to the torments that he inflicted unthinkingly daily on his charges; and then Trevor himself, pale, bristly boar, was driven with sticks up the ramp of his own lorry, squealing with fear, en route for the abattoir.

Changing her room to escape the pork and crackling of Enid and Trevor's intimacies meant that she was woken by the dawn chorus from Kimberley and Carly, each of whom seemed to rise each morning with a renewed ambition to earn her sister a smack. She had to put her pillow over her head to blot out the sounds of their play which came through so clearly that Claudia, sick with insomnia, almost felt the hair yanked out of her own head and teeth puncturing her own skin. They had plastic kitchens and castles and typewriters and sewing machines and cassette players, vanity sets galore; Sindy dolls and Barbie dolls and Cabbage Patch dolls and Care Bears, Rainbow Brites, Emus, and My Little Ponies complete with grooming parlours for their silky pink and turquoise manes and tails; but the girls' real favourites were two life-sized baby dolls who shared a twin buggy. These two babies vied with each other in naughtiness, but being the progeny of such mothers, they weren't very good at it and their mischief was uninventive and repetitive; nevertheless, it was always severely punished. Had they had any sense they would have unbuckled themselves from their buggy and legged it over the fields in their Babygros to the NSPCC, but being mercifully senseless, they smiled their vinyl smiles and took whatever was coming to them; unlike Tiny Tears, who wept throughout the proceedings and refused to be toilet trained despite the savage penalties this incurred.

But one day the children's grandmother had brought them someone whose arrival left all the other toys in a neglected heap. Orville was an apricot poodle puppy, with overflowing eyes that left the tracks of tears down the sides of his face, giving the impression that he was always crying, which was perhaps a true one. Kimberley and Carly were beside themselves; here was a real live baby who did spectacularly rude and naughty things. He was squeezed and cuddled and was expected to obey their every command and whipped with his little lead until even Enid protested;

he was yanked by the neck until he whimpered for mercy; and plastic ear-rings were clipped to his ears and ribbons tied to his tail. When he had soiled Enid and Trevor's duvet, Claudia could only applaud silently his magnificent *coup de théâtre*, but she could not tell if it had been by intention, or simply because his stomach had been squashed too hard; and of course the consequences for him had been dire.

Claudia had thought that Orville was an uncharacteristically inventive name, until she had discovered that he had been called after an ingratiating, lime-green, fluffy duckling, a ventriloquist's dummy with a plastic beak, who wore a nappy. She had seen the puppy Orville in a makeshift nappy one day, strapped into the buggy, with one of the naughty twin's bonnets on his head; when she had remonstrated with the children, Enid had shouted at her through the open window to leave the kids alone. A few days later she had met them coming home from school.

'Where's Orville?' she said.

'He had to go to the vet's because he chewed up the wallpaper,' replied Carly.

'Will he be all right?' she had asked, stupidly, and then she had realised that she had quite misunderstood.

'And it cost £5.99 a roll,' said Kimberley.

'Come on you two!' shouted their mother, seeing them fraternising. 'You'll miss your programme!'

'We're getting two gerbils instead,' Carly shot back over her green quilted shoulder as they ran off heavily, in their white latticed knee socks.

God help them, in their cage . . . Claudia thought.

'I don't think that's a very good idea,' she called after them.

'None of your business, you old ratbag,' came faintly down the lane.

Old ratbag. Old. Ratbag. Their words hurt far more than they should have; after all, they were only children. She reminded herself that she had always got on with children. She hurried on; the thought of her own children made her feel as desolate as a scarecrow, with the freezing wind whipping the rags of her self-esteem. They had taken her name and made it ugly – Claw-dee-ya, Claw-dee-ya; they had made her ugly. What was a ratbag? She knew what it meant, but what was it? She could go and knock on their door and say, 'Sorry to bother you, Enid, but could you tell me what a ratbag is? Perhaps you could look it up in your *Pears' Cyclopedia*?' Slam.

She was trapped as surely as the gerbils in their cage. There was no work available locally and she could not afford to move. Next month she must default on the mortgage. Buying a house in the country had been, she saw now, one of the death throes of a desperate marriage. When Paul had left, by mutual consent, and the first heady inflorescence of being alone had evaporated like cow-parsley in July, she had found the freedom to gaze uninter-rupted for hours over the flat fields of rape, inhaling the odours of the pig farm; she had fields of time, acres of time, stretching as far as the eye could see, to an uncertain horizon.

A headache zigzagged at her temple like a little firecracker as she stood at the window. She had no aspirin to alleviate it, and could not borrow any from Enid, who anyway was out, collecting the girls. Each morning, after walking them to school, Enid heaved her hams on to the minibus which transported workers to the pharmaceutical research laboratories, where she was employed in the canteen, serving lunches to the animal technicians, and one of the perks of the job was that she never ran short of painkillers and cold cures and vitamin drinks.

That Hallowe'en morning Claudia had walked to the village to pick up the magazine that she had ordered. Foolishly, she had told the woman in the shop the reason that she wanted it. The woman had already checked it out. The story wasn't there.

'I was wondering if you wrote under another name . . . ?' she said.

'No. No I don't.'

The fiction editor in her glitzy office, of course, could neither have known or cared that, miles away, beyond the rim of her consciousness, stood a small woman in wellingtons in a sub-post office in her public shame, concealing under an Army surplus jacket something that resembled a breaking heart.

'Hope deferred. Hope deferred. Hope deferred maketh the heart sick,' her boots beat out on the rutted lane; her fingers numb around the rolled-up magazine, the glossy cylinder that contained someone else's story. The lost ear-ring came into her mind.

'Swings and roundabouts,' she said to herself as she passed the deserted recreation ground. It was absurd to care so much, but that story, in a magazine too prestigious to be among the shop's regular stock, had been going to vindicate her, to prove to Enid, and thence to everybody, that Claudia had some status in the outside world, and to earn her, if not friendship, at least some grudging respect; and also to reassure herself that she still existed. Next month's would be the Christmas issue, and it was unlikely that her muted autumnal tale would take its place among the glossy gift-wraps, the shimmering scarlets and greens and golds of a feast that she would not be celebrating.

It was almost dark, and as Claudia pulled the curtains for the night, at four o'clock, Kimberley and Carly passed her window, their yellow silky hair streaming under black pointed paper witches' hats, their pointed noses, red from the cold air, pecking towards each other in conspiracy, wagging their hats towards her house and laughing, before they ran indoors.

Claudia went into the kitchen and took her sharpest knife and sharpened it. As she worked, she expanded her fantasy to include Kimberley and Carly, naked, trussed and basted, glistening with fat, their crispy skin crisscrossed and stuck with cloves, oranges stuffed in their mouths. She was very hungry; she had not eaten all day. When she had finished her preparations, she sat down in the dark to wait for the children.

They were a long time coming. She sat on the edge of her chair, straining her ears for their steps, hearing only a car door slam, down the lane, the dull explosion of a far-off firework, the blood beating in her head. She put a log on the fire and lit the candles. Everything was ready; so why didn't they come? The table floated on the darkness like an altar and on its surface glittered a long knife.

The gate moaned on its hinge. There was the sound of foot-steps, a shuffling on the doorstep; then the knock. Claudia flung open the door, with a low triumphant cry of 'Trick!'

The hiss died on her lips. There was a confusion of a woman's face above a paper sack from which protruded the neck of a bottle of wine and the white jagged heads of chrysanthemums. It was the woman from the party.

'Oh dear, I can see you weren't expecting me. Have I got the wrong day? That would be typical of me – I thought you said – I brought these . . .'

'Come in.'

Claudia held back the door, and her visitor stepped in, still prattling in her nervousness, into the flickering light and smell of melting wax. 'I do apologise – I was sure – I'll just put these down – I left the car down the lane . . . oh, a real fire, how lovely. And a turnip lantern!'

'Oh that –' said Claudia, glancing at the wicked face, lit from within by a guttering candle, 'it was just a little surprise for the children . . . Here they are now. Would you give it to them?'

Her shadow swooped over the ceiling as she picked up the lantern and held it out to her *dea ex machina*, with nails that gleamed in its light like blood.

'I'll just get rid of this.'

She carried the knife into the kitchen and dumped it in a pile of peelings in the sink.

All the Pubs in Soho

The pansies were in a blue glazed bowl on the kitchen table, purple and yellow, blue and copper velvety kitten's faces freaked with black, and also in a bed by the back door where they straggled on leggy stems around the drain and the leaking water butt. There was not a trace of blood. Joe's father's words had conjured up a wreckage of broken flowers streaked and spattered with red; the scene of a gory murder. An innocent bee investigated the absence of a crime.

Joe could not understand why they had provoked his father to such rage at breakfast, making him choke on bitter marmalade, spitting a jellified gout of rind onto the newspaper. It had reminded Joe of the time a girl with a bad cold had sneezed onto her sum book, and Miss Hunt had ripped out the page and carried it at arm's length to the wastepaper basket, and he had felt sick at breakfast as he had then, when he had also burned with sympathetic shame. Beside the blue bowl of pansies a bluebottle grazed in spilled sugar and negotiated a white papery onion, which was actually garlic, but Joe, like most of the population of Filston, Kent in 1956, was unacquainted with this pungent bulb. A bunch of brushes stubbled with paint stood in a jar; there was a smell of turpentine and paint and linseed oil, the nicest smell that Joe had ever experienced.

That summer the Sharps, that is Joe, his two little brothers and their parents Peter and Wendy, he of the camel-hair coat and thin moustache and crimped waves of rusting hair, she of the Peter Pan collars and velvet hairbands, had moved into their tall white house set back from the main village street behind a black railing hung with rest-harrow, and had furnished it with blows and tears and cold cocoa and unemptied potties.

Not long afterwards two strangers had descended from the London train and had been observed taking turns to haul a heavy suitcase along the High Street and up the hill towards Old Hollow Cottage. They wore American plaid shirts and jeans, which men did not wear in Filston unless they were of the bib-and-brace working overall variety. The small dark one had slung over his shoulder a dark green corduroy jacket and the taller fair one carried a jacket of muted claret. They were reported to have been drunk on arrival, but this may have been apocryphal information, supplied by hindsight. It was a long walk, uphill on the narrow road between dry banks bulbous with the grotesque roots of the overhanging trees, while clouds of midges nibbled the heavy air and sweat ran into their eyes, as far as the crossroads where a broken signpost rusted in a little island of grass and ox-eye daisies, then downhill between fields of cows in pasture and ripening corn, to the hollow which gave the cottage its name. That night they cruised into the car park of the Duke's Head with a shrieking of dry brakes, on an old black bicycle they had found chained with cobwebs among the nettles in the shed; one working the brakes and the other perilously side-saddle on the crossbar. Their hands were stippled with nettle stings. They had not had to do anything more scandalous to become notorious.

It was his father's vituperation about 'those bloody pansies at Old Hollow' that had brought Joe to the cottage on this empty summer holiday afternoon. He had had nothing else to do. Under the table, on the wine-coloured jacket, a wild-looking black and white cat, with burrs and green knobs of goose grass in her fur, was stretched out, nuzzled by a heap of squeaking multicoloured kittens. Joe stepped over the threshold and crept towards them.

In the bedroom at the back of the one-storeyed cottage the fair-haired young man lay on his side on the bed smoking, reading and from time to time looking at the dark one who was sitting in a creaking wicker chair, wearing only a pair of jeans, drawing him; sunshine leaked around the sides of the yellow curtain pulled crookedly across the window, brushing his skin with bloom, turning his hips into a peach, blue smoke from the cigarette in his trailing hand swirling in the lemony light. There was a faint mushroomy odour of mildew in the room. Suddenly a tenderly drooping line became a gash in the paper as the artist dropped his pencil and ran from the room.

'What –?'

The fair man felt too lazy to follow. The other returned with a struggling figure clasped to him, its legs kicking at his shins. Its T-shirt, stained with elderberry juice, was pulled askew, scratched legs kicked from the khaki shorts.

'Look what I found in the kitchen.' He let go with one hand and flung a pair of jeans at the bed.

'Cover yourself up.'

The fair man pulled the bedspread cover over himself. The child was struggling and snarling in the captive arms.

'Good afternoon,' said the man on the bed as he struggled into his jeans. 'Who are you?'

The child was trying to bite now, making futile lunges with its teeth, snapping the air.

'I think it's a wild boy of the woods,' said the fair man. 'Abandoned as a baby and brought up by the wolves.'

'They aren't any wolves in England,' snarled the wild boy with distinctly middle-class scorn.

'What excuse have you, then, for breaking and entering? Have you come to spy on us? Or to steal?'

'I only came to see the bloody pansies!'

The dark man released him. Joe stood panting and rubbing his arms where they had been held. The two men looked at each other, then the fair one said in a silly voice, 'Well, here we are, duckie. Allow us to introduce ourselves. I'm Arthur and this is my friend Guido.'

The child gave an uncertain giggle, looking from one to the other.

'Don't be silly.'

He was beginning to think that they might not murder him, even the fierce dark one, Guido.

'I knew we shouldn't have come here,' said Arthur.

'Who are you then?' Guido asked the child.

'Joe.'

Arthur raised himself on an elbow and studied him.

'Are you sure it isn't Josephine?'

A blush ran down Joe's freckled face and neck and out of his sleeves and down his arms.

'If he says it's Joe, it's Joe,' said Guido sharply.

'Well Joe, what do you say to a cup of tea?'

Joe nodded, too mortified to speak. There was the air of a stray dog following the stranger who patted his head in the street about him as he followed Guido into the kitchen without looking at Arthur.

'How old are you, Joe?'

'Nearly nine.'

Guido filled the kettle and put it on the stove. The smell of gas mingled with the turps and linseed oil filled Joe's head, and mixed with his excitement at being there and having tea with two grown-ups was the odd feeling that he was completely at home.

'Are you an artist?'

'A painter. Do you like painting?'

'Well – I can draw an elephant from the back, and a star without taking the pencil off the paper. Shall I show you?'

'That's OK. I believe you. Can you carry the tray into the garden? I'll go and get Arthur.'

Joe carried the round tin tray carefully and set it in the grass. He lay on his back and watched the sky. The sound of raised voices came from the kitchen. Joe sat up at once, tensed to run. He felt sick. He came from a house where a veneer of anxiety lay on every surface like dust, where at any moment a bark might rip up comics and scatter toys, where a fist thumping the table might make cups leap in fear, vomiting their contents onto the table-cloth, just as Joe had once been sick when his father caught the side of his head with his knuckles, and where Mummy's forehead wrinkled like the skin on cocoa and her chin puckered in fear and placation. He expected every domestic discourse between two adults to degenerate into a battle in which, by being co-opted to one side, he was considered the enemy by the other, and so always ended as the loser whoever was in power when a truce was called. But then Guido and Arthur came out together to join him. Arthur was holding a whisky bottle.

'I thought we'd have a wee celebration, as Joe's our first visitor.' He poured whisky into two cups.

'To Joe.'

'Joe.'

Gradually Joe stopped shaking enough not to slop the strong red tea from the cup which Arthur handed to him; it was the most beautiful cup he had ever seen, a pearly white shell that stood on tiny china periwinkles on a flat fluted saucer – Belleek, a legacy from Arthur's Irish grandmother.

He realised that no one would have told him off if he had slopped it. The cake was dry and crumbled like sand on a plate painted with a blue fish. They were sitting under an old apple tree hung with small red apples. Joe looked up into its branches and then at Guido, for permission.

'They're very sweet,' said Guido.

Joe reached up and an apple fell into his hand. The skin was warm and the white flesh did taste sweet. They sprawled in the grass and talked; Guido and Arthur smoked, Joe ate apples and cake. They accepted what he said without once telling him not to be silly, or to stop showing off or not to interrupt or not to dip his cake in his tea and scoop out the residue of crumbs and sugar with his finger. It all went to his head like whisky. Suddenly something in the light told him it was late. He sat up abruptly, his old panicky self. 'I've got to go. I've just remembered someone's coming to tea. I'll be late. What shall I do?'

'Take the bike,' suggested Arthur.

'But –'

'You can bring it back tomorrow.'

Joe, swooping and curvetting down the hill, straddling the crossbar, standing on the pedals, clenching the screaming brakes, the heavy black handlebars bucking in his hands, heard over and over again the words, 'You can bring it back tomorrow,' and made them into a tuneless song that was snatched by the wind whistling past his ears.

He came into the room on the awful words from his mother's visitor.

'So it's to be St Faith's then?'

She disposed of Joe with sponge cake in her mandibles.

'No!' he shouted. 'I won't.'

The glory of the afternoon fell from him as he confronted the wavering tableau of his mother's shocked face above a new pale blue necklace, the best teapot garlanded with roses floating in her hand above the tablecloth, his brothers' smeared faces above the trays of their highchairs, the yellow and red wedges of cake.

'Josephine, where on earth have you been? I specially asked you not to be late for tea. I don't know what Mrs Williams will think of your hands and face, and put on a clean frock at once.'

'I'm not going to St Faith's.'

As Joe backed from the doorway, it was what Mrs Williams would think that was uppermost in his mother's mind: that she was a poor mother who could not control her plain and disobedient daughter, that the little boys were noisy and not toilet trained, that the blue outlines of the transfer still showed at the edges of the satin-stitched flowers on the tablecloth that she had just finished embroidering that morning and had not had time to wash or iron, and that already a stain was seeping through the linen onto the table beneath the cloth. A bad mother and a bad housekeeper.

'Well, it seems the best of a rather poor bunch,' she whined, referring to St Faith's as if her disparagement of the local educational establishments might attach some credit to her disappointing daughter.

Joe was not a pretty child. Now the freckles stood out on her blanched skin against the red and white gingham dress that was quite wrong for her colouring, as her mother and Mrs Williams realised simultaneously. 'You might have brushed your hair,' her mother despaired. 'She insists on having it short although it doesn't suit her,' she apologised, regretting the ringlets that might have been.

'Nice and cool for the summer, eh?'

Mrs Williams gave a conspiratorial pat to the sweaty reddish feathers glued to the mutinous forehead. Joe tossed her hand away.

'I'm not going to St Faith's, I'm going to the village school and I'm not going to wear a stupid hat, and I'm not . . .'

'Just drink your milk. She likes to play at being a boy, I'm afraid . . . I can't think why.'

'I don't.'

'Please don't keep interrupting. The grown-ups are talking. Help yourself to bread and butter.'

'I've had tea. With my friends.'

Wendy sighed and turned away.

'Another cup of tea, Mrs Williams? Oh dear, I'm afraid the pot's gone cold.'

Joe sat silent, a milk moustache framing her savage mouth, her stomach turning to scrambled egg at the thought of walking through the village in the uniform of St Faith's. Even if she crumpled the hat and hid it in her satchel, there could be no concealment. It was hopeless. If she could do something heroic, rescue one of the other children from the river or a fire, maybe they would forget the way Daddy had shouted at them and chased them from the garden. If only she could wake up tomorrow morning and be a boy and have a suit of grey shorts and a jacket with a zip and elasticated waist and cuffs – Roy Noble had a dark blue corduroy suit, that was the best, but she would settle for a threadbare grey, worn with gumboots – and he had a television. She had heard his mother call, 'Roy, it's telly time,' and he had run in leaving her alone in the rec holding onto Timothy's pushchair.

'. . . Nancy, boys . . .'

The words clattered onto her empty plate.

Mrs Williams went on, '. . . so she went up to him in the shop and said, "Mr Morelli, I'm the president of our local Artists' Circle, and I wondered if you'd like to come for coffee one morning and meet some of our members," and do you know what he replied?'

'No. What?'

Mrs Williams leaned towards her and lowered her voice.

'He said, "You know what you can do with your blankety-blank coffee!"'

'No!' Wendy gasped.

'Can you imagine? In Carter's!'

'My husband says that people like that ought to be shot. I mean to say, it makes my flesh crawl, just to think – ugh.' She shuddered, holding out an arm so that they might see the pale hairs express their horror.

'There are men who love other men, just as there are women who love other women,' said Joe.

'Leave the table at once!'

'There's nothing wrong with it. Just because someone loves somebody they get put in prison and people call them all –'

'That's enough! I don't know what's got into you this afternoon.'

An unmistakable smell that could not be ignored was staining the disastrous tea party.

'Josephine, take Timmy to the bathroom and wipe his hands and face, and bring him back and then go to your room.'

Her eyes signalled desperately that Joe should change Timothy's nappy, as if there were a chance that Mrs Williams had not noticed.

'What can a little girl like you know about such things?' Mrs Williams's voice held reproach for the whole family.

'I just know.'

'I can't think where she – neither Peter nor I would dream of discussing such matters in front of a child . . .'

Joe did just know, she thought, as she yanked Timothy from his chair. When Guido and Arthur had talked to her, it was as if she had always known, but had just been waiting for someone to say it. She had known too, without being told, that she should say nothing of her visit at home.

Love between men. Love between women, Wendy thought, as with increasing embarrassment she realised that she had told Josephine to remove the wrong child. Away from the magazines she read, in the real world inhabited by Peter and herself, in the marital bed lumpy as semolina, there wasn't even much love between men and women.

'Would you like to look at the garden?' she asked, and called, 'Oh, Joe, look after Giles, would you?'

A big old black bicycle, a heap of junk, was sprawling on the lawn.

Carter's, where Guido had ground the Artists' Circle under his heel like a cardboard disc whose triangles graduate through the shades of the spectrum, was the biggest shop in the village. There was Dawson's, which was handy for sweets, for a packet of fags on a Sunday, and a branch of the South Suburban Co-operative Society, but people like Wendy did not shop there. Carter's had a wooden floor, which sloped down to the glass-fronted biscuit containers that fronted the mahogany counter, a wire for cutting cheese, a red bacon slicer, bins of dried fruit and glass jars of sweets, and a wines and spirits licence. The back of the shop smelled of paraffin and Witch firelighters and neat bundles of chopped firewood bound with wire, and aluminium buckets and coal scuttles and clothes pegs and new rope. Fruit and vegetables were displayed at the side entrance. The emporium was owned by Mr Carter, who presided over the bacon and cheese and cold meats and wines and spirits, and was staffed by seven part-time assistants known collectively as the Carter girls. Each was mysterious in her own way, but it was Dulcie, the youngest, who conceived a passion for Arthur.

Dulcie had been engaged, and her fiancé, called up for National Service, had been killed. Her future was hacked to pieces on the mud floor of a hut in Kenya. Her fiancé's dismembered remains lay under a white marble gravestone in Filston churchyard and her dreams were split by savage painted faces and flashing knives. She had been cheated of her rights, and had had to sell her ring back to the shop at a loss to help to pay for his funeral, and had been condemned to remain with her miserly widowed father on a squalid smallholding called Phoenix Farm. It became a joke among the other Carter girls that Dulcie blushed when Arthur came into the shop. Her usually bitter mouth simpered, her offhand manner became solicitous as she packed his shopping bag.

'Mind them eggs,' she would say as she placed them carefully on top of his purchases, or, 'You ought to take somethink for that cough.'

Other customers could arrive home with dripping bags of a dozen broken eggs, or cough themselves to death for all she cared, but she worried about Arthur. She picked her way past the steaming heaps of sodden straw through the mud in her high heels, carrying over her arm an overall washed every night and starched as white as chalk in the hope that he might come in. She was disappointed if Guido was with him but it was better than nothing. She could not understand why Mr Carter was so against them and she thought it slightly peculiar that neither of them was married, but that was her good luck. Mr Carter had installed a new refrigerator, and stocked its shelves with new exciting ice creams. As usual, when they entered the shop, fine ice crystals of disapproval frosted the air around Guido and Arthur as they hovered at the throbbing fridge, unable to agree which flavour would most please Joe.

'The Neolopitan's very nice,' suggested Dulcie, her face burning in the chill.

'Eat Neolopitan and die,' said the funny foreign one.

'No, honestly, it's ever so nice,' insisted Dulcie, offended.

Anyway it would have melted by the time they got it home.

On the afternoon of her half-day Dulcie was slouched at the bus stop contemplating the prospect of plodding around the shops of the nearest town, then catching the bus home again to get her father's tea. Boredom twittered in the hedges, crawled among the flints of the wall on which she leant and grazed the green slope of the opposite hill. She threw her half-smoked cigarette into the road, just for something to do. She was twenty; she should have been coming up to her second wedding anniversary in a new house on the new estate. It wasn't fair.

Incredibly, she saw Arthur walking down the empty road towards her. She prayed that the bus would not come.

'Fancy meeting you here!' she stuck out her thin hip and put her head on one side. It did not seem a very surprising or unlikely meeting to Arthur.

'Hello.'

He didn't alter his pace.

'Coming to the dance?' she called after him. He stopped.

'What dance?'

'That one. A week Saturday.' She pointed to a poster that announced a Grand Dance, to be held in the Village Hall.

'I don't dance.'

'Oh go on, it's a good laugh. I'm going,' she added as an incentive.

Arthur hesitated, not knowing what to say, watching a string of black and white cows crossing the hill, beyond the brittle rainbows of the split ends of her hair. He had quarrelled with Guido and stalked out of the house, propelled by his anger until stopped by this girl.

'What's your name?' she was saying.

'Arthur.'

'Arthur.' She sounded disappointed. 'That's nice. You're not foreign are you, like your friend?'

'Scottish.'

'Oh. Your friend though, he's foreign, isn't he?'

'An Eye-tie. A wop. Second generation.'

'I thought he was foreign. Aren't you going to ask what my name is then?'

'No,' said Arthur, exhausted by this interchange.

'Oh, you are awful,' she slapped familiarly at him. 'It's Dulcie. Silly isn't it? I hate it.' She heard with alarm the rumble of the bus around the corner. 'You coming to the dance, then?'

'I told you, I can't dance.'

'I'll teach you. Go on, it's a laugh. Eight o'clock Saturday, I'll see you there,' she called over her shoulder as she swung onto the bus, and then she slumped into a seat enervated by her own daring.

By the time the bus had reached the town she was convinced that not only had she and Arthur a firm date for Saturday week, but that *he* had asked *her* to the dance. She bought a pair of shoes and matching handbag, and a bag of sweets which she popped rapidly and mechanically into her mouth, crunching without tasting so that when she got off the homeward bus she was surprised to find an empty bag in her hand. She stood for a moment in the field stroking the shiny patent leather of the shoes and handbag before going upstairs to hide them from her father under the floorboard, with her mother's empty blue shell of Evening in Paris, and her bottle of California Poppy.

*   *   *

Meanwhile Arthur had sat on a swing in the deserted rec behind the village hall where the Grand Dance was to be held, smoking and scuffing his feet in the dusty trough worn by the generations of children's feet. When the packet was empty and he had tossed it over his shoulder, he suddenly laughed and left the swing performing a wild parabola on its rusty chains, and was whistling when he dropped into Carter's for more cigarettes. If, like Dulcie, Mr Carter thought that Arthur looked like a movie star, it was of no film that he would care to see; his manner was within a moustache's breadth of offensive as he handed over a bottle of bad red wine and rang up the inflated price on the till. Arthur, for his part, gave not a thought to the absent Dulcie, who might have served him. He wished that he had the bike so that he could get home faster. Guido was lying asleep on the bed, open mouthed, smelling faintly and sweetly of stale white wine.

He was always Joe at the cottage. Once, Guido had got on the bus and had seen him and Wendy sitting there in Mother and Daughter polka-dot frocks, made by Wendy from a Simplicity pattern, which had proved not so simple, and Joe's polka-dot hairband had slipped around to show the elastic. He never knew if Guido had seen them or not and neither of them had referred afterwards to the encounter. Wendy would have been surprised to discover that she had become a smoker; her account at Carter's showed evidence of cigarettes and of chocolate and other delicacies which she had not consumed. Carter's was so handy, she just gave Josephine the list and she did most of the shopping. Arthur and Guido were doubtful when Joe gave them presents and hesitant about accepting them, but he was so hurt if they refused that they took the gifts.

'You don't have to bring us presents, Joe. We enjoy your company. Just bring yourself.' Joe did, as often as he could. The kittens were growing adventurous and Poppy, the mother, was quite friendly now, her coat almost glossy. Arthur had found her in a field with her neck in a snare and had brought her home and nursed her and she had rewarded him with a litter of kittens two days later. Joe played with them or talked to Guido while he painted, receiving grunts in reply, or bashed about on Arthur's typewriter or gathered mushrooms which they fried in butter until they were black. Nobody told him not to touch the matches, or not to lick his knife or not to pick the blisters of hot paint from the back door. The corn in the field next to the house was almost ready to be cut, the blackberries in the garden were flushed with red, the heavy red tomatoes were splitting their sides and breaking their stems. Guido had cleared a patch and had planted squash and zucchini, and they fried their yellow flowers, fluted like the horn of the gramophone that poured music onto the garden, in batter. In the front room there was a broken sofa and piles of books which had come from London in a van with Guido's easel. Joe looked at the pictures, turning over the thick and glossy pages heavy with damp in the mushroomy air, and read poetry which excited him even though he did not understand it; he loved the feel of the foreign books printed on thick paper with rough edges, he felt that if he could read them they would tell him everything that he wanted to know, although he did not know yet what that was. At home at night he lay in bed listening to the rise and fall of voices below, his body tensed for the modulation that was the signal for him to put his pillow over his head.

One afternoon, having escaped at last from amusing Timothy and Giles, Joe was so startled to hear a loud woman's voice over the hedge that he swerved violently on the bike, bruising himself agonisingly on the crossbar. He rolled in silent screams on the grass, buffeted by the woman's laughter and alien men's voices. He stood outraged on the edge of the garden, pierced with jealousy. Several other men and Arthur and Guido were lounging about in the grass and, on a kitchen chair, like a queen among her courtiers, was a black-haired woman. The worst thing, the thing so shocking to the child who flicked unperturbed through books of painted nudes, was that she had taken off her blouse and sat in her brassière. Joe stared in horror as a kitten crawled between those shocking white circle-stitched cones. His freckles fused in a dull red stain, but the woman was not embarrassed, and neither, it seemed, were any of the men. He had never seen Mummy in anything less than her petticoat, four thin straps slipping down her sloping shoulders as she brushed her hair, and this lady was much older than Mummy.

'Come away, Joe, and have a drink.' Arthur's voice was more Scottish than usual. 'This is Joe, everybody, the wee friend we was telling you about.'

Joe came forward, avoiding looking at the woman, but she grabbed his arm and pulled him towards her. She thrust her face into his with a clacking of ear-rings.

'Guido, where did you find this enchanting little redhead?'

She ruffled his hair. He wriggled away. The kitten leaped from her chest, puncturing a breast with a hind claw. She screamed. A tiny bead of blood rolled onto the white brassière.

'I'm bleeding, Arthur, do something –'

'It's only a little scratch,' said Joe, his voice thick with scorn. He picked up the kitten and stroked it, comforting it.

'Anyone would think that it was that creature who was wounded, not me. Doesn't anybody care that I'm bleeding to death?'

'Oh shut up, Cathleen, and have another drink.'

She squeezed the last drop of blood from the tiny wound. Arthur splashed wine into her glass. Incredibly to Joe, he did not seem to hate or despise her. Joe turned to Guido but he was talking to a horrible man with a stained moustache that curled wetly into the corners of his mouth. Joe could not believe that Arthur and Guido liked these people, but they were laughing and joking with them as if they had really missed them.

'Whatsa matter, Joe?' called Arthur, and gulped as an unripe blackberry thrown by Cathleen landed in his mouth.

'Nothing,' said Joe.

Everybody looked ugly. Arthur's eyes were bloodshot, his lips too red. He looks like a wolf, thought Joe. Pieces of wolves' dinner, chicken bones webbed with sticky skin lay in the grass, rejected by the kittens, the air was heavy with smoke and wasps attacked the carcass of a cream cake. A squashed wasp lay on the open book beside Cathleen's chair. They were all talking loudly about people Joe had never heard of. He went into the kitchen. Guido followed him.

'Look at this mess!' said Joe in his mother's voice, waving an arm at the table piled with greasy plates and smeared cutlery and glasses and crusts and dirty paper napkins. The lovely smell of paint and linseed oil was glazed with stale cooking.

'Poor Poppy, you hate them too, don't you?' said Joe picking up the cat who was cowering under the table, and received a scratch from a flashing paw, which he scorned to notice.

'Why so sulky, Joe? Come into the garden and amuse us. Tell us all the gossip.'

'Don't know any,' said Joe.

Wendy, had she been otherwise, would have found a rich source of gossip in Mrs Cheeseman who came in to clean two mornings a week, but her nervousness manifested itself in a shrill bossiness, and Joe could see that Mrs Cheeseman despised them. She was the widowed mother of two teenage daughters, Ruby and Garnet, and had four cleaning jobs as well as keeping her own house immaculate and winning most of the prizes at the Horticultural Show. Her stoicism on her widow's pension put the Sharps to shame. Joe had once seen her throw a piece of his Meccano from the bedroom window.

'Don't be jealous, Joe. It's very dull for Arthur here with only me to talk to.'

'And me.'

'And you too, of course.'

'And the cats.'

'And the pussycats.'

Joe went back outside to hide the tears in his eyes just as Cathleen pulled Arthur onto her lap, pressing him against the squashy white cones and nuzzling his ear.

'Aw, get off, Cathleen, will you.'

'Not until you give me a kiss.'

Arthur pecked at her cheek.

'Not like that. A proper kiss. What are you staring at?' She turned on Joe who stepped back from the savagery of her eyes.

'Nothing.'

'Like hell you are. I do believe it's jealous. Arthur, has our little freckled friend got a crush on you by any chance?'

'Leave him alone, Cathleen.'

233

Guido had come out into the garden, his face snouty and mean with alcohol. It wasn't clear whom he meant Cathleen to leave alone.

'Such a waste,' Cathleen said to Arthur. 'You're much too pretty.'

'I said, lay off. Arthur, you look like a clown, but you're not funny.'

Cathleen had smeared a red cupid's bow on his forehead, and another on his cheek.

'What's wrong, Guido? You're not jealous, are you? Of me, a mere woman? Stop being such a tedious old queen. Here, Freckles, stop gawping and get me another drink.'

She thrust out her clownish tumbler.

'Don't stick your fingers in the glass. Where are your manners?'

'I was trying to rescue a fly,' said the erstwhile enchanting little redhead.

'Oh for God's sake.'

Arthur had struggled free but she kept hold of his hand. He squatted beside the leg of her chair, whose feet were embedded in the grass by her weight, with her rings digging into his hand. He did not look unhappy. The man with the stained moustache began to sing; the petals of the last rose of summer blew about on a beery wind while tears ran down his cheeks.

'Guido. Guido.' Joe pulled at his arm. Guido shook him off.

'Look, why don't you go and pick some mushrooms?'

'I did.'

Joe flung a paper bag of mushrooms to the grass and burst into tears. Everything was spoiled. He blundered towards the bicycle to escape from the party of badly behaved adults. Home seemed almost a haven. Then he felt an arm around him and he was pulled to Arthur's chest.

'What's all this about? Hey, come on . . .'

He took a handkerchief and dabbed ineffectually at Joe's eyes and tweaked his nose until he had to laugh.

'That's better. Come away into the kitchen and have a cup of tea with me.'

'You still look like a clown,' said Joe.

'Well, at least I made *you* laugh.'

When they returned to the party everybody was in a good mood. Guido said that it was his birthday next week and that he

and Arthur were coming up to London to celebrate and that everybody must join them.

'We'll bring Joe,' he said. 'We'll take him to all the pubs in Soho.'

'Look at his face,' said Cathleen. 'Look at that wicked grin.
Such decadence in one so young,' but she said it nicely. And she
had put on her blouse. Joe forgave her. He was prepared to love
her. He accepted a sip from her glass and then another and let
himself be pulled on to her knee. The gramophone poured
'Euridice, Euridice' in its scratched voice over the garden.

The trees reared up crazily at him as he zigzagged down the hill,
a little drunk. 'All the pubs in Soho. All the pubs in Soho,' sang in
his ears. Soho shone over the horizon, a golden city of shimmering
spires where he would go with Guido and Arthur and be happy.

'I picked you some mushrooms.'

Joe stood in the doorway of the bathroom holding out the
crushed paper bag which he had retrieved from the grass and
forgotten to leave in the cottage kitchen.

'They're probably toadstools. Put them in the bin at once and
wash your hands.'

'No, they're definitely mushrooms. We've had them lots of times.'

'Who's had them?' she asked sharply.

'Me and my friends.'

She hauled Giles out of the bath.

'You haven't been playing with those rough children again, have
you? You know what Daddy said. I don't know what he'd say if
he knew you'd been picking toadstools. It's absolutely forbidden,
do you understand?'

She stared in exasperation at her unnatural child in the stained
khaki shorts, her lips stained with what must be blackberry juice,
clutching a bag of poisonous fungi, and turned to Giles who was
lying across her lap. Despite her ministrations his bottom was sprinkled with the sore stars of nappy rash.

'Mummy?'

'Yes.'

'What's Soho?'

'It's a place in London. A not very nice place.'

'Why not?'

'Well – pass me the baby powder please.'

'Why not very nice?'

'Will you keep still, Giles. Timothy, if you get off that pot once more, Mummy's going to be very cross.' The baby squirmed in her lap.

'Why isn't it very nice?'

'Because not very nice people go there. Now will you stop asking silly questions and make sure Timothy stays on his pottie? It's not the sort of place people like us go to.'

'Hah,' said Joe.

It was obvious that Mummy knew nothing about Soho. He saw its name in letters of gold shining through the powder and steam. It was exactly the sort of place people like himself went to.

The floor of the village hall was dusted with talc for the feet of the dancers and dusty silver twigs were stuck into green-painted tree stumps for decoration. Crates of beer, and more ladylike drinks, were carried across from the pub and stacked on the trestle table that formed the makeshift licensed bar and coloured light bulbs looped the stage where the band stood; the bare bulbs that hung from the ceiling were dressed in crêpe paper skirts, and bunches of balloons attracted ribald remarks. The Grand Dance, after a sticky start, was in full swing. Dulcie danced with the first man who asked her, Geoff Taylor, who had always fancied her, although she did not fancy him, tossing her head vivaciously, studiously not looking at the back of the hall where the summer night streamed through the double doors, so that Arthur might arrive and see her in another man's arms, dancing with the lights sparkling in her hair.

She had not seen him alone since their meeting by the bus stop and interpreted his every word as secret confirmation of their date and had read all sorts of romantic implications into his most mundane request. She pictured him lounging in a dark suit and white shirt with a red carnation in his buttonhole, a cigarette between his lips, watching her. She was a good dancer but her new shoes hurt. After four or five dances with different partners she stood by the bar sipping orangeade through a straw, watching a wrinkled balloon deflate. The band played on. Incipient blisters throbbed on her heels. She giggled hectically with a group of girls, then danced again, desperate that he should not arrive to find her wilting like a wallflower; her smile was fixed in fresh lipstick on her face, her eyes were now unable to keep off the door. Only the knowledge that she had told no one that Arthur was coming to the dance – she had been saving that triumph – saved her from bursting into tears but in the penultimate dance, the Carter girls hokey-cokeying wildly, her face dissolved and she rushed from the hall, tearing off her shoes and running blindly barefoot across the recreation ground.

Feet pounded after her and Geoff Taylor caught her arm, swinging her around to face him as the last waltz smooched out among the stars. She sobbed against his chest the story of how Arthur had asked her to the dance and stood her up.

'Him? That queer bloke?'

She nodded, not understanding the adjective.

'I'll bloody kill him.'

She blew her nose, too miserable to be ladylike.

'I've got the bike. Do you want a lift home?'

Soon she was on the back of the motorbike, her arms clasped around his waist, holding her shoes with the heels sticking into his stomach as they blasted up the village street, towards Phoenix Farm, her skirt billowing out behind her like a parachute.

As Arthur passed the Duke's Head on his way to the post office he was seduced by the smell of warm beer in the sunshine through the open cellar door. The landlord slopped down his pint on the counter with no more than the usual contempt. A tractor stopped and a young man jumped down and followed him into the bar which was empty except for two old men in caps playing dominoes and a dog-faced woman in tweeds, morosely sucking a Mackeson while a little dog died quietly at her feet. Pipe smoke was caught in the golden cones fluting through the bottle glass and turned them blue. In the morning air the polished glasses and horse-brasses among the low beams had the clarity of a hangover; a strong smell of hops came from the dusty dry garlands on the ceiling and from the clear brown beer in Arthur's glass. He felt a frothy head of well-being wash over his boredom. He looked at the young man who had followed him, taking in the faint and not unpleasant scent of old manure around the patched dungarees, the brown arms under the rolled sleeves of the faded workshirt, the scowling face under a cow's lick of Brylcreem. Incongruously, he was drinking whisky. Arthur raised his own glass and nodded to him but the young man obviously drowning his sorrows at eleven thirty on a summer morning spat a flake of tobacco from his lip and shoved his empty glass across the bar for another shot.

'Going it a bit, aren't you, Geoff?' one of the old men called out.

Geoff uttered something incomprehensible to Arthur and they all laughed, one of them choking wetly on his pipe stem, and Arthur found himself smiling too. He ordered another beer; he had no desire to leave this pleasant place. The onslaught of the second drink prompted him to conviviality. He almost ordered drinks all around, but he had only enough money left for stamps. In his inside pocket was an envelope containing poems which he was posting to a magazine in London.

Reluctantly he went out into a morning gold and blurred at the edges. The road ran like a river at his feet. Suddenly he was on his back on the asphalt with grit and blood in his hair and Geoff Taylor's fist smashing into his mouth and an iron-capped boot chipping at his legs while its owner exhorted him to stand up and fight. He tried to get up, grasping handfuls of road and was kicked back with a boot in the chest. His head caught the kerb. Bone bounced off stone. A wild blow glanced off Taylor's stomach and Arthur grabbed his shirt and pulled himself up and landed a punch on his jaw which sent him reeling back on his feet and followed it through, but missed as Taylor stepped aside. Arthur's head was a broken ball of pain; he could taste blood in his mouth. He tried to grab Taylor around the waist to throw him but his legs buckled and he collapsed on his knees. Taylor's fist crunched again into his face and withdrew bloody, then he kicked him systematically all over his body and finally stamped on his outstretched hand.

The tractor's engine sputtered away into silence. Arthur could hear a blackbird singing in the watery tones that herald rain. His whole body was in pain. He knew that his hand lay, an injured creature, in the road beside him. It's a good thing it wasn't Guido. I can write with my left hand, he thought, then red and black swirled, dissolved as he lost consciousness.

The president of the local Artists' Circle saw him lying in the gutter, and crossed the road. It was only what she would have expected of him.

Clinging onto hedges and walls, Arthur managed to stagger as far as Carter's where he leaned on the door and fell into the shop with a jingling of its bell.

'Help me.'

'Get out of my shop,' said Mr Carter who was cutting cheese with a wire. The Carter girls in their white overalls stood like monoliths behind the counter. Dulcie gave a little scream and started forward.

'Get back to your work, Dulcie.'

Dulcie looked at the bloody misshapen bruised swede that had been her idol trying to speak through lips glued to its teeth with blood.

'Yes, Mr Carter,' she said and started weighing broken biscuits.

'We don't want your sort here,' said Mr Carter. 'Get out, and mind my clean floor. Go back where you came from.'

Arthur crawled out. He made it across the road to the surgery and swayed in the little porch hung with Virginia creeper, leaning on the bell. The doctor's wife answered.

'Yes?' she asked.

'Doctor.'

'The doctor's having his lunch. I suppose you'd better come into the surgery and wait.'

She left him slumped on a fumed oak chair whose chintz cushion was tied on with tapes. He had to brace himself to stop from sliding to the floor.

'You have got yourself in a mess, haven't you?' she said as she closed the door behind her.

Eventually the doctor came, clouded in evidence that he had enjoyed a small cigar after his lunch.

'This is going to hurt,' he said with satisfaction, expecting Arthur to wince and mince, and Arthur screamed silently with the effort not to play the role expected of him as the doctor swabbed and strapped his ribs with distaste.

'You ought to have that hand X-rayed. And your head,' he concluded without telling Arthur how to go about it. 'You'll live,' he said.

Arthur tried to thank him.

'Don't thank me. You're not one of my patients, thank God, so I'll be sending you my bill. Know where you live, but what do you call yourself?'

Arthur looked at the red cloudy water in the basin and sodden lumps of cotton wool like obscene red snowballs, and fainted.

'Pull yourself together, man. How are you going to get home? Can you pay for a car if I get you one?'

Arthur nodded. He just wanted to be with Guido. He didn't know if Guido would be able to pay but he was past caring.

The local taxi service was operated by the landlord of the Duke's Head, and so it was he who dumped Arthur on the cottage doorstep and stood jiggling coins in his blazer pocket while Guido ran to find the money for his exorbitant fare.

'You should have seen his face,' he told his customers in the bar that evening, 'when he saw the state of little Miss Nancy. I thought he was going to burst into tears.'

Wendy, who was there with Peter, almost felt sorry for Guido for a minute, but the thought of two men kissing made her feel sick: she could not conceive that they might do anything but that.

'Perverts,' said Peter.

'If there weren't ladies present . . .' said the landlord.

Two ginger cats, named Gin and Lime, one smooth, one fluffy, smirked on the bar. Wendy didn't really like leaving the children alone in the house but Peter got so cross if she made a fuss, and Joe was quite capable . . .

'You're looking very pretty tonight,' said Peter. 'That sherry's brought quite a sparkle to your eyes.'

'Thank you, kind sir,' she said, with dread.

★　★　★

All the cats, Poppy and her kittens, ran at Joe when he pushed open the kitchen door.

'Guido? Arthur?'

He went into the garden. They weren't there. His heart started to race; a sick feeling came into his stomach. The silence had a quality of finality, as if the air had closed for ever on the spaces left by bodies, and voices were gone without echoes. He ran back into the kitchen ignoring the importunate cats. There were two notes on the table. One was addressed to the woman from whom they had rented the cottage, and one to him.

> Dearest Joe,
>
> I expect you've heard what happened. We are going back to London and then to the south of France where Cathleen has a house.
>
> Please look after the pussy cats.
> – Will write. In haste,
> Guido. Arthur.

Arthur's name was shaky, as if written with his left hand.

'No,' cried Joe, 'you can't, you can't,' in desperate belated entreaty. He ran out into the road and gazed at its achingly empty blue curve, the edges fretted with birds' songs and skirmishes. 'Come back! I want to come with you. What about me?' he shouted. 'What about all the pubs in Soho?' He sank sobbing onto the grass verge. 'Come back! Come back!'

A rough furry head thrust into his wet face purring loudly.

He opened a tin of pilchards and while the cats ate he read again Guido's note. What had happened? He had no idea. Why couldn't they have taken him with them? Wild thoughts of burning the letter to the landlady and living in the cottage himself rushed through his brain and were swamped by reality the colour of cold cocoa. Guido and Arthur were the only bright colour and affection he had known and they were gone, leaving him entirely alone. The thought of St Faith's inspired more tears.

He went into the bedroom. A torn and stained shirt had been thrown into a corner. Joe picked it up, screamed, and dropped it. It was stiff with dried blood. He thought Arthur had been shot.

'Please don't be dead. Please don't be dead. Please don't be shot.'

But Arthur had signed the letter so he couldn't be dead.

Joe took the shirt and lay on the bed with it in his arms, rocking from side to side as he wept.

From time to time a sob still shuddered in his chest as he gathered up Poppy and the kittens and struggled to get them all into a large cardboard box which he tied around and around with string. It took him almost an hour; as soon as he had pushed down one wild head or paw another sprang out. At last he carried the squeaking wailing box outside and left it by the bicycle at the front hedge. He went into the field and dragged a bale of straw into the kitchen. He took the bottles of turpentine and linseed oil and methylated spirit from the draining board and splashed them over the straw and around the kitchen, and went into the bedroom. Tacked to the wall was a little sketch of Arthur lying on the bed. He tore it off and put it in his pocket, and splashed methylated spirit over the bed. He took a box of matches from the kitchen table and set fire to a corner of the sheet and to the corner of the bale of straw.

The journey home wheeling the bike with the cats bumping awkwardly on the saddle was agonising. His back hurt with the effort of balancing the box and although he had draped it with the bloody shirt he had to stop every few steps to push back a terrified head. He knew that if one got out he would never get it back again. The spinning pedal hit him sharply on the ankle many times until his leg was a mess of oil and blood. The chain came off and dragged rustily in the road. His grief was overtaken by his dread of what would happen when he got them home.

He came into the kitchen. Daddy was home early.

'Look what's come for you. Isn't that a lovely surprise? It came from Peter Jones this afternoon,' said Mummy.

There was an enormous box on the table. It must be a present from Guido and Arthur. His heart leaped.

'Well open it then,' said Daddy impatiently.

Joe lifted the lid and parted the tissue paper. Inside lay the brown velour hat with a yellow striped band and the brown serge wraparound skirt and yellow blouses of St Faith's School.

'Well, you might at least try to look pleased,' said Daddy. 'This little lot cost me a small fortune. What on earth have you been doing? Your face is disgustingly filthy. Let's hope St Faith's will —'

Mummy, who had been twisting nervously at her blue poppet beads, broke them and they went pop pop pop over the kitchen floor.

'I only hope you realise how lucky you are,' Daddy's voice went on.

But at that moment Joe realised like a blow to the stomach that Guido would not be able to write. He didn't know the address. He picked up the hat and threw it on the floor and stamped on it. His father's hand caught him across his tear-stained face. Joe seized the hand and bit it.

'I hate you, Daddy, you tedious old queen,' he screamed, kicking his father in the shins.

Behind him in Old Hollow, the cottage blazed like the fires of hell. The cats burst out of their box in the shed, and the nude study of Arthur fell to the floor in his rage.

Where the Carpet Ends

The Blair Atholl Hotel was berthed like a great decaying liner on the coast at Eastbourne; if it had flown a standard from one of its stained turrets it would have been some raffish flag of convenience hoisted by its absentee owner, flapping the disreputable colours of the Republic of Malpractice and Illegality.

The front windows had a view of the Carpet Gardens and the pier, but the back of the hotel, where Miss Agnew lived, gave on to the drain pipes and portholes of another hotel and a row of dustbins where seagulls and starlings squabbled over the kitchen refuse. Miss Agnew, compelled by the vicissitudes of life to book a cabin on this voyage to nowhere, was one of the off-season tenants who occupied a room at a reduced rate at the top of the hotel, where the carpet had ended. These people of reduced circumstances were required to vacate their rooms just before Easter when the season started, or pay the inflated price required of summer holiday-makers. After the third floor, the mismatched red and black and orange carpets gave way to cracked linoleum and, in places, bare boards. A terrifying lift, a sealed cage behind a temperamental iron zigzag door, carried them up to their lodgings, separated from each other by false plywood walls which divided what had once been one room into two compartments. One floor above them, huddled precariously like gulls, perched a colony of homeless families, placed there by the council in bed and breakfast accommodation, whose misery filled the pockets of the landlord and his manager.

If, as Le Corbusier had said, a house was a machine for living in, the Blair Atholl, thought Miss Agnew, was a machine for dying in; but at least there, unlike the occupants of the many old people's rest homes in the town, they were doing it on their own terms. The residents of the fourth floor formed a little community in exile, rescuing each other when the lift stuck, knocking on a door if someone had not been seen about, purchasing small sliced loaves for the sick and Cup-a-Soup and tins of beans to be heated on the luke-warm electric rings, and braving doctors' receptionists, in the smelly telephone booth, to beg for a home visit but dreading above all an admission to hospital, from which one so seldom returned. They met in the conservatory at the back of the hotel in the evenings for a rubber of bridge or to watch a programme on the television – a reject from the lounge, whose horizontal hold had gone – and they formed a little human bulwark against the sound of the sea and the approaching night. It did not do to think too much, Miss Agnew had decided; to dwell on people and cats and dogs and houses in the past was to inspire one to board the next bus to Beachy Head, but sometimes she could not resist stopping to speak to a cat or a dog in the street, and the hard furry head and soft ears under her hand evoked lost happiness so painfully that she strode away berating herself for laying herself open to such pangs, her red mackintosh flapping like the wings of a scarlet ibis startled into flight.

She did not know why antagonism had flared up between herself and the manager, Mr Metalious. She paid the rent on time and she was surely no more bizarre than any of her fellow residents, such as the Crosbie twins, seventy-year-old identical schoolboys who dressed on alternate days in beige and blue pullovers they knitted themselves, and grey flannel trousers and blazers. She felt sure they would have affected caps with badges if they had dared; they did wear khaki shorts in the summer and long socks firmly gartered under their wrinkled knees. Or than the transvestite known as the Albanian, a smooth-haired shoe salesman who by night flitted from the hotel, a gauzy exotic moth, to sip the secret nectar of the Eastbourne night. Or than Miss Fitzgerald who left a trail of mothballs and worse in her wake and cruised the litterbins of the town and rifled the black plastic sacks her fellow tenants left outside their doors on dustbin day. Or than Mr Johnson and Mr Macfarlane who spent their days philosophising in the station buffet. Or than the Colonel whose patriotism embraced British sherry. Or than silent Mr Cable. Or Mrs MacConochie.

Miss Agnew thought that perhaps she reminded Mr Metalious of some teacher who had shamed him in front of the class, or a librarian who had berated him for defacing a book. She had followed both these professions in her time, but she was not interested very much in his psyche, and anyway videos were more in his line than books. Perhaps she had alienated him when, on moving into the hotel, she had asked him to carry her box of books to her room. He had acquiesced with a very bad grace, telling her that his duties did not include those of a hall porter: perhaps her decision that he would have been offended by a tip had been the wrong one. Whatever the cause, and even before she had overheard him refer to her as a stuck-up old cow, she knew he did not like her.

'Nothing today, Miss Agnew,' he would call out as she passed her empty pigeonhole beside his desk.

'I wasn't expecting anything,' she told him truthfully, but he was determined to regard the lack of post as a confirmation of her low status and as a triumph for himself.

Anyone less bovine than Miss Agnew would have been hard to imagine; she was more ovine, as befitted her name which she believed to derive from the French, with her long mournful face framed by a fleece of off-white curls. Now that it didn't matter any more, she was thinner than she had ever hoped to be. The most she had hoped for in this town, which she had more than once heard referred to as 'God's Waiting Room', was anonymity. She was desirous to be known only as Miss Agnew and she expected nothing more of her pigeonhole than dust or a catalogue for thermal underwear, and why he picked on her for this particular humiliation she did not know. None of the residents got much post, except the Albanian who received thin cobwebbed envelopes addressed in a spidery hand, and the Crosbie twins who corresponded copiously with each other in the course of each of their infrequent quarrels.

It was lunchtime and Miss Agnew was seated at a table in the window of Betty Boop's, a small vegetarian restaurant that suited her herbivorous taste, ruminating over a piece of leek flan. She had managed, by taking very small mouthfuls and laying down her knife and fork between each bite, to prolong her meal for twenty minutes or so, when she saw Miss Fitzgerald pass, head bowed against the wind to avoid a spume of salty vinegar being blown back into her face by the northeaster, from what was undoubtedly someone else's discarded bag of chips.

Since a recent survey had condemned Eastbourne as a town of guzzlers, Miss Agnew had become aware of the habit of the populace of snacking out of paper bags; the precinct was sugary with half-eaten doughnuts, meaty with burgers and strewn with the polystyrene shells that had held pizza and baked potatoes. The toddlers under the transparent hoods of their striped buggies clutched buns and crisps and tubes of sweets; and now there went Miss Fitzgerald conforming, for once, to a local custom.

Miss Agnew was thinking about Beachy Head; it was comforting to know that it was there. When she had walked there in the summer she had been dazzled by the colour of the sea, opal and sapphire as in Hardy's poem 'Beeny Cliff', and she had felt a melancholy empathy for the writer because for her, as for him, 'the woman was elsewhere . . .' and nor knew nor cared for Beeny or Beachy Head and would go there nevermore. Miss Agnew had felt a powerful force pulling her to the cliff's edge, and only the thought that she would probably plummet messily onto the boiling rocks, rather than curve like a shining bird through the sky into the iridescent sea, had propelled her backwards on the turf. The Crosbie twins had told her that many more bodies were recovered than were reported; the local police and press had a policy of suppressing such information, *pour décourager les autres*. She wondered how largely Beachy Head loomed in the minds of her fellow residents.

Now she gulped down her elderberry wine, paid the bill, and succumbed to an impulse to follow Miss Fitzgerald, feeling amused at herself and more than slightly ridiculous as she turned up the collar of her mac like that of the trench coat of one of the private eyes in the detective stories she used as a drug against insomnia when she lay awake in the night and felt the hotel slip from its stone moorings and nose towards oblivion. She tracked her quarry past the pier that strode on shivery legs into a sea of gunmetal silk edged with flounces of creamy lace, like the expensive lingerie she had loved once. Now she was glad of her thermal vest and her hair blew about her head as brittle and dry as the wind-bitten tamarisk and southernwood bushes.

★　★　★

Hotel gossip had it that Miss Fitzgerald, despite her rags and carrier bags, was very rich. Any discussion of her eccentricities would include, at some point, the refrain, 'She comes of a very good family, you know.' The black sheep driven from some half-ruined Anglo-Irish castle, Miss Agnew surmised, as she hurried along, merging into the wall when Miss Fitzgerald stopped to investigate a litterbin, muttering furiously as newspapers and polystyrene foam cups and boxes showered the pavement. The few people she encountered made wide curves around her, swerving into the road as she marched on, with the tail and paws of a long-deceased animal around her neck lashing the wind. Were there sheep in Ireland? Miss Agnew wondered. Pigs and chickens certainly, and grey geese in Kilnevin: perhaps St Patrick had rid the Emerald Isle of sheep along with the snakes.

She reflected that she was getting sillier and sillier every day that she spent at the Blair Atholl; it was because she had nothing to think about. Perhaps she was manifesting early symptoms of Alzheimer's disease, brought on by the gallons of tea she had poured over the years from the aluminium teapot; aluminium found in quantities in tea, she had read recently, was a contributory factor to the disease, and that friendly familiar teapot, like a battered silver ball reflecting the firelight in the facets of its dented sides, must have made her an almost inevitable candidate for premature senility. Why else would she be following Miss Fitzgerald's erratic and litter-strewn progress, playing detective in the icy wind? The teapot had belonged to Pat, the friend she had lived with for thirty-three years. The lease of the flat had been in Pat's name too, and when it had expired Miss Agnew had neither the means nor the desire to renew it. She hoped that Pat was not watching now, and feeling that her friend's purposeless life negated the years they had spent together, but the brightness and laughter and strength that had been Pat was a heap of ash in a plastic urn, so of course she couldn't see her.

Miss Fitzgerald struck up a side road and Miss Agnew followed her past the guest houses with hanging baskets and gnomes and cards in the windows advertising vacancies, whose names, the Glens and the Blairs and the Lochs and the Braes, suggested that they were passing through a settlement of Scots in exile. They emerged into the long road called Seaside and Miss Agnew found herself studying a green plaster rabbit and a set of ruby-red plastic tumblers on the deck of a broken radiogram in the window of a junk shop, while Miss Fitzgerald contracted some business with its proprietor. A sign stuck to the glass said: 'Lloyd Loom Chairs Wanted Any Condition. Good Prices Paid.' How odd, thought Miss Agnew, that those prosaic wicker chairs should have become collectors' items; if you waited long enough everything came back into fashion, but she knew that she would not. Not yet antique, and certainly unfashionable, she stepped into an adjacent shop doorway as Miss Fitzgerald emerged still talking volubly and stuffing something into one of her plastic carriers. Miss Agnew remembered that there was a creaking circle of green wicker chairs in the Blair Atholl conservatory, which she felt suddenly sure were genuine Lloyd Looms. Miss Fitzgerald crossed the road and stood at the bus stop, but Miss Agnew decided to walk on a little before retreating to the Blair Atholl, although a heavy shower had started to fall.

This part of town seemed to be called Roselands; there was a men's club of that name, and a café; the name shimmered softly in tremulous green leaves and pink blowzy petals, the name of a ballroom or dance hall in a film, where the lost and lonely waltzed away their afternoons, reflected in mirrors full of echoes and regret.

Miss Agnew opted for the Rosie Lee Café, which seemed cheerful and steamy, where memory would not draw up a chair at her table and sit down, but as she pushed open the door she saw a fellow resident of the Blair Atholl, Mr Cable, a redundant bachelor late of the now-defunct Bird's Eye factory, seated there smoothing out the creases from a very black-looking newspaper prior to applying himself to the Quizword. She retreated.

The shower had spent itself now. All the bright and garish gardens she passed, the tubs and window boxes of the terraced houses, and the flowers in the interstices of the paving stones, the shining windows and letter boxes had a desperate air, as if neatness could stave off desolation; a cold salt wind was blowing off the sea and a palm tree rattled behind a closed gate. Tall pampas grass was lashing the houses with canes, softening the blows with hanks of dirty candy-floss, and punishing again. There was too much sky in Eastbourne, Miss Agnew thought, she found its pearly vastness terrifying; gold light poured from the Downs gilding bleakly the cold glass panes of a Victorian red-brick church and blazing in puddles on the road and pavement. Mothers with prams and pushchairs on their way to collect older children from school seemed unaware of, or immune to, all this gold that rolled from the spokes of their wheels, drenched them and turned their baby carriages to chariots of gold.

Miss Agnew had to pause to snatch her breath from the wind outside a low building set back from the pavement; it was a newly refurbished home for the terminally old. A large yellow van with 'Sleepeezee' on its side was parked in the drive and a mattress was being carried in. Then, through a window, Miss Agnew saw a girl in a white uniform bounce up towards the ceiling, and as she came down a young man bounced up. Up and down they went, trampolining, bouncing up, bouncing down, laughing, until for a second they were in mid-air in each other's arms before tumbling down in an embrace on the new mattress; the living larking about on the deathbed.

Miss Agnew was at once elated and distressed. An image came into her mind of her parents, long ago tucked up in their marble double bed with a quilt of green marble chippings to keep them warm. She caught a bus back to the town centre, and as she sat on its upper deck, she decided that it was right that the young should embrace in the face of death, and closed her ears to the profanities of a bunch of smoking schoolchildren sprawling about the back of the bus; their harsh cries sounded as sad as the voices of sea birds on a deserted beach at dusk.

As she stepped out of the lift on the fourth floor she noticed a pram, belonging to one of the bed-and-breakfast families, wedged across the narrow stair that led to their quarters, and saw the disappearing draggled hem of a sari above a pair of men's socks. She shook the raindrops from her mac and hung it up and made herself a cup of soup and a piece of toast. Later that evening she went down to the conservatory to watch the nine o'clock news.

'Pull the door to, would you?' said Mrs MacConochie. 'There's a draught.' The wind was buffeting the glass panes, the television picture shivered.

'I don't want to be part of this,' Miss Agnew said to herself, looking around, at the Crosbie twins counting stitches, the defeated fan of playing cards in Mrs MacConochie's hand, Mr Cable clawing his winnings, a pile of one-pence pieces, across the baize table whose legs were crisscrossed with black insulating tape. Wicker creaked under old bones, the horizontal hold slipped and Miss Fitzgerald mumbled under a cashmere shawl. I don't want to be a drinker of Cup-a-Soup in a decaying hotel room, whose only post is a catalogue for thermal underwear, thought Miss Agnew, just as I do not want to join the respectable army of pensioners in their regimental issue beige and aqua raincoats, whose hair is teased, at a reduced rate on Wednesdays, into white sausages that reveal the vulnerable pink scalps beneath, and who are driven to luncheon clubs in church halls by cheerful volunteers. I am not nearly ready to sleep easy on a Sleepeezee mattress. Something's got to happen.

The weather forecast ended.

'Have you put on your stove?' Mrs MacConochie asked Mr Cable. He had. It was Mrs MacConochie's colonial past that made her refer thus to the dangerous little electric circles with frayed flexes, which failed to heat the residents' rooms; her own room was almost filled by a Benares brass table with folding beaded legs, and burnished peacocks with coloured inlaid tails, and a parade of black elephants with broken tusks; herds of such elephants trumpeted silently in the junk shops and jumble sales of Eastbourne.

The Albanian paused outside the conservatory, then stuck her head around the door.

'Good evening everybody.'

There was a murmur at this diversion; they glimpsed tangerine chiffon and a dusting of glitter on the blue-black plumes of her hair. She smiled, like a dutiful daughter, round the circle of her surrogate family, but there was nobody there to tell her to take care and not to be home late, and she melted away into the mysterious night.

'Pull the door to, would you?' called Mrs MacConochie, wrapping her tartan rug tighter around her knees. 'There's a draught.'

'Something must happen,' said Miss Agnew to herself again as she prepared herself for bed. 'Something will change.'

In the morning nothing had changed. A seagull laughed long and bitterly outside her window. Mr Metalious still disliked her; there was nothing in her pigeonhole. A grey rain was slashing the street. As she crossed the foyer, she passed the Albanian, a poor broken moth caught by the morning, dragging dripping wings of tangerine gauze across the dusty carpet, blue-jawed and sooty-eyed in the fluorescent light.

The only thing which was different, she noticed as she entered the conservatory, was that all the Lloyd Loom chairs had gone, and Miss Fitzgerald was standing under a paper parasol in the rain, watching a van pull away from the back entrance of the hotel.

A Pair of Spoons

Villagers passing the Old Post Office were stopped in their tracks by a naked woman dancing in the window. Not quite naked, for she wore a black straw hat dripping cherries and a string of red glass beads which made her white nudity more shocking. When they perceived that the figure behind the dusty glass was a dummy, a mannequin or shop-front model, they quickened their steps, clucking, peevish and alarmed like the pheasants that scurried down the lane and disappeared through the hedge. After a while only visitors to the village hidden in a fold of the Herefordshire hills, those who had parked their cars outside Minimarket and, seduced by the stream with its yellow irises and dragonflies, had wandered along the grassy bank that ran down one side of the lane, were struck by the nude with cherry hat and beads, frozen in mid-dance by their scandalised stares.

The Old Post Office, which used to do business from the double-fronted room jutting out into the lane, had stood empty for several years following the death of the retired postmaster. Posters advertising National Savings, warning against the invasion of the Colorado beetle, and depicting heroic postmen struggling to the outposts of the Empire still hung on the walls, curled and faded to the disappointing pinks, yellows, greens and blues of a magic painting book, while stamps and pensions were dispensed and bureaucratic rituals were enacted now through a grille of re-inforced plastic at the back of Minimarket. In that shop window was a notice board and prominent among the advertisements for puppies, firewood, machine-knitted garments and sponsored fun-runs, walks, swims and bake-ins, was a card which read in antiqued scrolly script: We buy Old Gold, Silver, Pewter, Brass and Broken Jewellery, any condition. China, Clocks, Furniture, Books, Comics, Tin Toys, Dinkies, Matchbox etc., Lead Farm Animals, Clothes, Victoriana, Edwardiana, Bijouterie. Houses Cleared. Best

Prices. Friendly Old-Established Firm. Ring us on 634 and we will call with No Obligation.

Parts of the Old Post Office house predated the fourteenth-century church whose clock and mossy graves could be seen from the kitchen window through a tangle of leggy basil plants on the sill above the stone sink. Anybody peeping in on a summer evening would have seen the Old-Established Firm, Vivien and Bonnie, sharp-featured and straight-backed, tearing bread, keeping an eye on each other's plates, taking quick mouthfuls with a predatory air as if they had poached the pasta under the gamekeeper's eye; two stoats sitting up to table. Their neat hindquarters, in narrow jeans, rested on grubby embroidered cushions set with bits of broken mirror and sequins, which overlapped the seats of the Sheraton-style fruitwood chairs; they rested their elbows on a wormy Jacobean table whose wonky leg was stabilised by a copy of *Miller's Antiques Price Guide*.

It was Vivien, with her art-school training, who had calligraphed the notice in the village shop: after meeting Bonnie, she had taken a crash course in English porcelain and glass. Bonnie relied on the instinct which had guided her when she started out as an assistant on a stall in the Portobello Road, where she had become expert in rubbing dust into the rough little flowers and fleeces and faked crazed-glaze of reproduction shepherdesses, goatherds, cupidons, lambs and spaniels, the flair which had resulted in her co-ownership of this ever-appreciating pile of bricks and beams. Vivien and Bonnie moved through Antiques Fayres like weasels in a hen house. To their fellow dealers they were known, inevitably, as Bonnie and Clyde, or the Terrible Twins.

At night they slept curved into each other in their blue sheets like a pair of spoons in a box lined with dusty blue velvet, or with stained pink silk in summer: two spoons, silver-gilt a little tarnished by time, stems a little bent, which would realise less than half of their value if sold singly rather than as a pair.

They had grown more alike through the years since they had been married in a simple ceremony at the now-defunct and much-lamented Gateways club. How to tell them apart? Vivien bore a tiny scar like a spider-crack on glass on her left cheekbone, the almost invisible legacy of the party that followed their nuptials, where Bonnie's former lover had thrown a glass of wine in her face. Or had it been Vivien's rejected girlfriend? Nobody could remember now, least of all the person who had flung the wine.

'Vivien is more vivid, and Bonnie's bonnier,' suggested a friend when the topic of their similarity was raised.

'No, it's the other way round,' another objected.

'A bit like dog owners turning into their dogs . . .'

'But who is the dog, and who the owner?'

'Now you're being bitchy.'

That conversation, which took place in London, would have struck an uneasy chord of recognition in Vivien had it been transmitted over the miles. She had become aware of an invisible lead attached to her collar and held kindly but firmly in Bonnie's hand. There were days when she seemed as insubstantial as Bonnie's shadow; she realised that she mirrored Bonnie's every action. Bonnie took off her sweater, Vivien took off hers; Bonnie reached for her green and gold tobacco tin; Vivien took out her own cigarette papers; Bonnie felt like a cup of coffee, so did Vivien and they sipped in unison; Bonnie ground pepper on to her food and Vivien held out her hand for the mill; when Bonnie, at the wheel of the van, pulled down her sun visor, Vivien's automatic hand reached up and she confronted her worried face in the vanity mirror. At night when they read in bed the pages of their books rasped in synchronicity until Bonnie's light clicked off, and then Vivien's pillow was blacked out as suddenly as a tropical sky at sunset.

'You go on reading, love, if you want to. It won't disturb me.'

'No, I'm shattered,' replied Vivien catching Bonnie's yawn, and swallowing it as the choke-chain tightened around her throat.

One morning, noticing that her Marmite soldiers had lined up in the precise formation of Bonnie's troop, she pushed her plate away.

'Do you think you could manage on your own today? I don't feel so good.'

'You do look a bit green round the gills. I hope you're not coming down with something.'

Bonnie laid one hand on Vivien's brow and with the other appropriated her toast.

'You haven't got a temperature.'

'Well I feel funny.'

'We're supposed to be going to pick up that grandmother clock from that old boy, and there's the car boot sale – oh well, I suppose I *can* go on my own . . . hope to Christ he hasn't done anything stupid like having it valued, you can't trust those old buzzards, dead crafty, some of them . . .'

Their two egg shells lay on her polished plate, hardly damaged, sucked clean by a nifty rodent.

Vivien guided the van out into the lane; Bonnie had taken off one of the gates on the rearside wing once when she was cross. Vivien waved her off and watched the dust settle. She felt an immediate surge of energy and fuelled it with a doorstep of toast spread with honey found in the cupboard of a house they had cleared, crunching on the cells of a comb rifled from the hive by the fingers of a dead woman. The bees had all buzzed off by the time Bonnie and Vivien had hacked their way through the tangled garden, and the empty wooden hives, weathered to grey silk, stood now in their cobbled yard.

Vivien left her sticky plate and knife in the sink and, sucking sweetness from her teeth, locked the door and set off down the lane with a wave to the woman dancing in the window. The vicar, passing by on the other side, ducked his head in the cold nod that was the most, in charity, that he need vouchsafe the Londoners since Bonnie had made him an offer for the paten and chalice.

'Morning, vicar. Lovely morning, isn't it? Makes you feel good to be alive,' Vivien called out uncharacteristically, surprising them both.

The incumbent was forced to look at her across the lane, a skinny lumberjack cramming into her mouth a spray of the redcurrants which hung like cheap glass beads among the fuchsias in her red and purple raggedy hedge, and caught a glitter of glass flashing crimson fire on plastic flesh, and a dangle of cherries.

'Hedge could do with a trim,' he said.

'Oh, we like it like that,' reminding him that she was half of the dubious duo. She was sucking the end of a honeysuckle trumpet. At this rate she wouldn't need the hedge trimmer he had been about to offer. She would soon have eaten the whole hedge.

'Ah well,' he concluded.

His skirt departed to the east and Vivien's jeans loped westward. She was trying to suppress the little maggot of anxiety whose mealy mouth warned that Bonnie might telephone to find out how she was. As she passed the call-box she had such a vivid image of Bonnie impotently misting up the glass panes of an identical construction standing among moon daisies on a grassy verge, while the phone rang and rang in their empty kitchen, that she could only assume that telepathy was at work. She thought, and walked on, stopping outside a garden at a box of worm-eaten windfalls with 'Please help yourselves' scrawled on a piece of cardboard. Vivien filled her pockets.

She came to a gate, placed one hand on the topmost bar and vaulted into a field of corn, and followed a natural track through the furrows, now spitting husks and crunching sweet kernels, now negotiating an apple, until she was faced with barbed wire and a ditch of nettles. She stood wavering wildly on the wire and hurled herself forward, landing, with only the softest malevolent graze of leaves on her bare ankles, in a field whose hay had been harvested, leaving its scent in the air. The field was bordered on three sides by massive trees, oak, sycamore, ash, chestnut, and although it was only July, recent rain had brought down a scattering of tiny green conkers. Like medieval fairies' weapons, thought Vivien, whose fancy, when not stamped upon by Bonnie, flew on such flights, those spiked balls on chains. Aluminium animal troughs rusted in a heap. At the far end of the field was a gate set in a high hedge and Vivien walked towards it dreamily with the sun freckling her face and her arms beneath her rolled-up sleeves.

The latch lifted but she had to force the gate against hanks of long grass, and squeeze herself through the gap. She was at the edge of a garden and now she saw a house which was not visible from the field. Old glass in the windows glittered like insects' wings. No dog barked. The house exuded emptiness, shimmering in the heat haze while housemartins flew in and out of their shells of honeycombed mud under the eaves. As she walked over the lawn she realised that the grass here had been cut not very long ago: it was springy beneath her feet, studded with purple milk-wort and daisies and buttercups that seemed to acknowledge the futility of growing too tall. Somebody, therefore, cared for the garden. The roses needed to be deadheaded, the petals were falling from the irises and peonies revealing shiny seed cases, but apart from the soggy roses and a faint mist here and there of lesser willowherb and an occasional intrusive cow parsley and weedy seedling brought up by the rain, the flowerbeds were orderly. She meant only to peep through the windows.

It was strange, she thought, as she walked on rose petals round the back ground-floor windows, pressing her face against the old dark glass, how she did not feel like a trespasser, but as though she had inadvertently locked herself out of those rooms hung with faded velvet curtains and was entitled to walk on the pale carpets and curl up in that yellow velvet chair with a blond dog at her feet. She stared at old wooden kitchen cupboards holding china and utensils behind their half-open sliding doors, the mottled enamel gas cooker, the pyramidal iron saucepan stand, the fossilised pink soap and rusty Brillo pad on the draining board, the clean tea towels, bleached and brittle as ancient flags. A movement by her foot made her look down. A toad regarded her with amber eyes. She crouched before it and reached out to pick it up. The toad leaped for the dank shadow under a flat scratchy plant. Vivien thrust her fingers after it and scrabbled in dead leaves and needles. Instead of pulsating skin, she struck metal. She drew out a key. It came as no surprise that the key fitted the lock of the scullery door, and turned, through cobwebs and flakes of rust, to admit her to the stone-flagged floor. The mangle, the stone sink, the disconnected twin-tub, had been waiting for her.

Vivien moved through the rooms, acknowledging the pile of enamel dogs' dishes in the kitchen, the Chinese umbrella stand holding walking sticks, knobkerries and a brace of Union Jacks, the wellies sealed with cobwebs, the waterproof coats and jackets on the pegs, the polished tallboys, chests of drawers, the empty vases, the glass-fronted cabinets housing miniatures and enamelled boxes, scent bottles and figurines, the groves of books, the quiet beds, the framed photographs, the high dry baths, the box spilling shoes. Everywhere she saw herself reflected, framed in elaborate gilt on the walls, elongated in tilted cheval glasses, in triplicate and thence to infinity above dressing tables, dimly in the glass of pictures. She touched nothing. At last she let herself out again, locked the scullery door, and put the key in her pocket.

★　★　★

'The state of you!' Bonnie scolded. 'Where've you *been*? I've been back for an hour. I rang to see how you were but there was no reply . . .'

'Just for a walk. I needed some air.'

'You could have got that in the garden.' Bonnie waved an arm at the sofa spewing horsehair onto the cobbles.

'It's damp and smelly,' Vivien protested. 'Did you get the clock?'

'No, I didn't.' Bonnie brushed grimly at grass seeds and burrs clinging to Vivien's clothes. 'You look as if you've been rolling in the hay. Have you?'

'Chance would be a fine thing. Ouch.'

The village maidens had a tendency to obesity and anoraks and, this summer, fluorescent shorts. Bonnie slapped at Vivien's jeans, reactivating the nettle stings. Stung into memory of her first sight of the house, and walking again in its peaceful rooms, Vivien half-heard Bonnie's voice.

'. . . decided not to part with it for sentimental reasons, lying old toad, then he let slip that he'd heard the *Antiques Roadshow* might be coming round next year . . . thought I'd really cracked it . . . who did he think he was kidding, you could practically see him rehearsing the greedy smile of wonderment that would light up his toothless old chops when they told him his crappy clock was worth a small fortune . . . I'd like to tear up his bus pass, he practically promised me . . . sell their own grandmothers, these people . . .'

'I thought that was precisely what he wouldn't do?' Vivien returned to the present.

'What?'

'Sell his grandmother. Clock.'

'*Don't* try to be clever, it doesn't suit you.'

I am clever, thought Vivien, and it might suit me very well.

'Shall we go to the pub later?' she said.

'No. What do you want to go there for? I thought we agreed that the *ambiente* was *nonsimpatico*?'

'Well, yes. I just thought you might fancy going out for a change.'

Vivien ripped the ring-pulls from two beers from the fridge and handed one to Bonnie. It was true that the pub was un-congenial. The locals were a cliquey lot. Bonnie could take off their accent brilliantly. 'Oooh-arr' she had riposted to those guys' offer to buy them a drink, and suddenly she and Vivien were on the outside of a circle of broad backs. No sense of humour. And boring – most of their conversation was limited to the agricultural; there were so many overheard references to filling in dykes that the girls could not but feel uneasy, especially as those ditches were not a feature of the local landscape. Aggression flared in wet patches in the armpits and on the bulging bellies scarcely contained in T-shirts that bobbed like balloons along the bar. The landlord, who was in the early stages of vegetabliasis – so far his nose had turned into an aubergine – snarled at them, as if he thought they would turn the beer.

'Let's go and sit in the garden,' said Vivien, leading the way. 'How was the car boot sale?'

'Like a car boot sale.'

They ate outside, sucking little bones and tossing them against the rising moon, straining their eyes in the dusk to pick out their autumn wardrobe from the L.L. Bean catalogue, and going into the house only when it grew too dark to read even by moonlight and starlight, and it was time to luxuriate with a nightcap in the pleasures of *Prisoner: Cell Block H* on the telly, propped up in bed by pillows.

Long after Bonnie had fallen asleep, whimpering slightly as if dreaming of chasing rabbits, Vivien lay awake with a glass-fronted cabinet glowing in the dark before her eyes. A slight flaw or bend in the glass gave a mocking, flirtatious twist to the rosy lips of the porcelain boy in a yellow jacket and pink breeches, ruffled in a gentle breeze the green feather in his red hat, lifted the wings of the bird in his hands, and raised an eyebrow at the little girl clutching a wriggling piglet against her low-cut laced bodice over a skirt striped with flowers. A black and gold spotted leopard with a pretty face and gold-tipped paws lounged benignly between them, and putti, half-decorously wreathed, offered baskets of flowers.

Vivien, drifting into sleep, put her hand out in the moonlight and found that the cabinet had no key. The moon hung between the open curtains like a huge battered gold coin almost within her grasp.

★　★　★

262

A week passed before Vivien could return to her house. At the wheel of the van, at the kitchen cooker, in dusty halls where people haggled over trinkets and dead people's clothes and crazed enamel hairbrushes and three-tiered cake stands, she cherished her secret. Had she asked herself why, she might have replied that it was because it was the only secret she had ever held from Bonnie; or she might have said that for the first time she wanted to look at and touch beautiful objects without putting a price on them, or even that there was something in the air of the house that stayed her hand from desecration, but she was careful not to ask herself any questions. Once or twice she caught Bonnie giving her a look. They slept uneasily, with bad dreams of each other.

It happened that Bonnie had to attend a surprise family party for her parents' Golden Wedding. The anticipation of the celebration, where she would stand as a barren fig tree among the Laura Ashley floribunda and fecundity, put her in such a black mood that Vivien expired a long sigh of relief, as if anxiety had been expelled from her by the despairing farewell toot, as the van lurched like a tumbrel into the lane. The golden present, exquisitely encased in gold foil, with gold ribbon twirled to curlicues round a pencil to disguise its essential tackiness, had been wrapped by Vivien but her name did not appear on the gold gift tag. Bonnie's Russian wedding ring and the true lover's knot, the twin of that which circled Vivien's little finger, would dissolve into invisibility when she crossed the family threshold. An uncle would prod her stomach and tell her she ought to get some meat on her bones, a man likes something he can get hold of; a sister-in-law, made bold by Malibu and cake, might enquire after Bonnie's flatmate while rearranging by a fraction of an inch her own present of a pair of gilded ovals framing studio portraits of gap-toothed grandchildren. Later, the same sister-in-law would offer on a stained paper plate the stale and indigestible news that she had once been disconcerted by the desire to kiss a schoolfriend, and on the homeward journey the memory of her confession would jolt into her stomach and the motorway verge would receive a shower of shame, and disgust for the unnatural recipient of her secret. Meanwhile, however, Bonnie was being introduced to the fiancé of a niece, who was omitting her name from his mental list of wedding guests even as they shook hands.

'You might have made the effort to put on a skirt for once,' her mother told her. In fact, Bonnie and Vivien did occasionally outrage their friends by wearing skirts. The last time had been when they turned up at the Treacle Pudding Club in a heat wave in their batiks and had been refused entry, but she didn't tell her mother this. Bonnie went into the garden and made herself a roll-up.

'You'll die if you smoke,' said a small boy in a red waistcoat with matching bow tie on elastic.

'Want a drag?' Bonnie held out the cigarette.

He shook his head so hard that his eyes rolled like blue doll's eyes, as if they would fall out, and ran in to report the death threat, and shot her with a plastic machine-gun from an upstairs window. Bonnie looked at her watch, reflecting with relief that the late-night, half-hearted discussions with Vivien about adoption, early in their marriage, had fizzled away with the morning Alka-Seltzer. If they *had* been allowed to adopt one, they would have had to have it adopted. She went in to the telephone on the public shelf above the hall radiator and dialled home, clamping the receiver to her ear to keep out the sounds of merry making, the mouthpiece poised to muffle her low desperate 'Hi babe, it's me. Just needed to hear your voice'; words that she was to be deprived of muttering. No comfort came from the shrilling 1940s handset in the Old Post Office kitchen and, blinded by a paper hat which someone had slipped over her head, she went back to join the party.

'I rang. You weren't there,' she said as she slammed the van door and strode past Vivien who had run to meet her, into the house.

'Is that my doggie bag?' Vivien pulled at the purple Liberty carrier in Bonnie's hand. 'What have you brought me?'

'Nothing. You didn't deserve anything. I ate it in the van. Where were you, when I needed you?'

Vivien might have replied, 'I was in my house, perfectly happy. I was reading, grazing among the books, and walking in the garden, and suddenly I thought of the hard little face, the mean mouth that I fell in love with, and I came running home.'

She said, 'I went for a walk, babe. I was very lonesome all by my little self, without you.'

Bonnie, half-placated, dropped the bag on to the table.

'There's a bit of cake left.'

Vivien drew it out.

'You've eaten off the icing. You pig.'

'Yes,' said Bonnie sternly.

'What's this?' Vivien scrabbled in Bonnie's shoulder bag and pulled out by the leg a mothy-looking toy.

'My old teddy. It's so threadbare I thought we could pass it off as Victorian.

'Oh Bonnie, you can't sell him, he's cute. Look at his little beady eyes.'

'Give it here. I'll pull one off, make it even cuter – nothing more poignant than a sad teddy, is there?'

'No! I won't let you. How could you be so cruel? I'm going to keep him. He's probably your oldest friend . . .'

. . . A tiny Bonnie, rosy from her bath, toddled up the wooden hill to Bedfordshire, holding a sleepy teddy by the paw . . .

'Actually she's a girl. Tedina. I used to smack her with my hairbrush.'

Vivien thought a flicker of fear passed over Tedina's tiny black eyes. She rooted in a box and found a Victorian christening robe.

'Perfect,' said Bonnie. 'Fifty quid at least.'

'There's a fatal flaw in your plan,' Vivien told her. 'Teddy bears weren't invented in Victorian times.'

'Don't be stupid. Of course they were. Albert brought one back from Germany or something one Christmas. They're called after him.'

Sensing a flaw in her argument, if not in her plan, Bonnie let the subject drop. Tedina, in her white pin-tucked robe, was carried upstairs to their bed by Vivien and the hairbrush, a section of the carapace of a dead tortoise set in silver, was put tactfully in a drawer.

It was when she picked up the local paper that she saw an unmistakable photograph, the notice that read 'House for Sale By Auction with Contents'. She stuffed the paper under a pile of back numbers of *Forum* and *Men Only* that, with a plastic Thomas the

Tank Engine, had been purchased as a job lot, with a Clarice Cliff bowl thrown in, for a tenner. 'They're not quite the sort of old comics and toys we had in mind,' she had explained backing towards the door, when her eye fell on the bowl, holding a dead busy lizzie.

Its owner, a desperate-looking woman hung about with small children, had intercepted her quick appraisal.

'What about the bowl, then? That's antique, it belonged to my grandma.'

'There's no call for that sort of Budgie-Ware,' said Bonnie, her tongue flicking over dry lips, her nose quivering. 'We've got two or three we can't shift, taking up space, gathering dust,' as she flicked the bright feathers of the two birds on a branch of ivy that curved round the pale grey bowl patterned with darker grey leaves.

'They used to give them as prizes at fairgrounds,' Vivien added, lifting the bowl to read the signature on its base. 'They were known as fairings.'

'I thought those were biscuits,' said the woman dully. 'Cornish Fairings?'

'Of course, *some* of them *were* biscuits,' Vivien conceded. 'In Cornwall.'

The deal having been struck, the woman was so grateful she made them a cup of pale tea by dunking the same teabag in two mugs. There were no biscuits. She stroked the birds surreptitiously as she wrapped them in a piece of newspaper. One of the children started to wail, 'I don't want those ladies to take our budgies.'

There was the sound of a slap as the door closed. Vivien and Bonnie went whistling to the van.

Six wooden chairs stood in a row in the backyard. Bonnie and Vivien were hard at work in the morning sun, removing the chipped white gloss paint from two of them.

'We'll need some more stripper,' Bonnie said, straightening her back painfully. 'God, how I hate this job.'

'You go and get some and I'll carry on with what's left,' Vivien suggested and Bonnie was only too willing to agree.

Fifteen minutes later, satisfied that Bonnie was too far on the road to turn back for anything she might have forgotten, Vivien took off the Cornish fisherman's smock she wore for working, pulled on a sweatshirt and, walking as quickly as possible without attracting attention, made for the house.

'This may be the last time I shall come here,' she told it as she stood inside the scullery door, which she left unlocked in case she had to make a quick getaway. The rooks she had startled into raucous proclamation of her guilt lapsed into spasms of complaint in the copper beech. Nobody had rallied to their alarm. Vivien went from room to room, resisting the desire to stroke the dust from satiny fruitwood, walnut, maple, mahogany, to lift the plates from the dresser to read the maker's name, and the marks on the dulling silver in the kitchen, to dust the dead flies from the window ledges and to light the candles in their porcelain sticks. There, on the shelves and in the faded, painted bookcases, were all the books she would never read. She longed to take one and curl up in her yellow velvet chair and read the morning away until the yellow dog prevailed upon her to follow him into the garden where a straw hat with lattices broken by time, and a trug awaited her. She admired for the last time the spilled jewels of the crystal doorknob, and stood in front of the glass cabinet committing to memory the figures therein: the man and woman riding on mild goats to meet each other, he with kids' heads peeping from his panniers, and she with hers filled with flowers and a basket of babies on her back, riding homewards in the evening in the cawing of rooks, the . . .

'Is this a private party, or can anybody join in?'

Vivien screamed, whirling round. There, filling the doorway, just like Bea Smith in the latest episode of *Prisoner: Cell Block H*, stood Bonnie, with a knobkerrie in her hand.

'So this is your little game. I've known you were up to something for days.'

'Bea – Bonnie, I can explain.'

'You'd better. You've got a lot of explaining to do – my God, are those what I think they are?'

She advanced on the cabinet.

'Don't touch!'

'Why not? You must've left your dabs all over everything. So this is what you were up to. Planned to sell the stuff behind my back and make yourself a juicy little profit, didn't you?'

Bonnie slumped into the yellow chair. 'You were going to leave me, weren't you? Run off and set up on your own.'

Her words were thick and bitter like the tears which rolled from her eyes.

'I'll kill you first.' She leaped up, brandishing the knobkerrie.

'How can you think, I don't believe I'm hearing this –'

Vivien caught her raised arm, they fought for the weapon, Bonnie trying frantically to bring it down on Vivien's head, Vivien struggling to hold the murderous arm aloft. A kick in the shins brought howling Bonnie to her knees and Vivien dragged the knobkerrie from her hand. Vivien twisted one of her arms behind her back and pushed her face downwards to the carpet.

'Babe, I love you,' she explained, punctuating her words with light blows from the knobkerrie. 'I swear I wasn't planning to run out on you. I haven't touched anything here, and I'm not going to. Understand?'

'Ouch, you bitch, get off me.' Bonnie spat out carpet fibres.

'If I let you get up, do you promise to sit quietly and listen?'

'Ouch. Thuk.' She spat.

'Very well. Go and sit over there.'

Bonnie slunk, snarling like a dog, to the sofa at which her master pointed the club. A resurgence of rage brought her half to her feet.

'Sit!'

Vivien could see, even after ten minutes of explanation, that Bonnie would never quite believe her. 'It was like being under a spell. As if I was meant to be here. It's so beautiful. So peaceful. I just wanted to be here. It was like being in another world for a little while.'

'Another world from which you excluded me.'

'I was going to tell you. I was going to bring you here later today. I swear.'

'A likely story. Are you sure there's no one else involved? You've been meeting someone here, haven't you? Where is she, hiding under the bed? Or is it a he?'

'Don't be so bloody stupid! Look, I'll show you all over the house, you can look under every bed if you like. Can't you get it into your thick skull that I just liked being alone here?'

'No I can't. I never want to be alone without you. I just don't believe you.'

Vivien led Bonnie from room to room. They found no brawny limbs in fluorescent shorts under the beds – nothing but dust, a pair of silver shoes and hanks of horsehair from a torn mattress. Dresses and suits hung empty in the cupboards, linen lay innocently in chests and clean towels were in the airing cupboard, if the spiders in the baths should want them. They pulled their sleeves over their hands to touch door knobs and handles. In a chest of drawers they found dozens of kid gloves with pearl buttons never unfastened, in a mille-feuille of virginal tissue paper.

'Satisfied?' They were back in the drawing room.

'Bonnie?'

Bonnie was standing in the centre of the room with a rapt expression on her face.

'Bonnie? It's getting to you, isn't it? The magic of the place. You understand now?'

'What I simply cannot understand, or believe, is how someone who has been in the business as long as you have could be so incredibly stupid as to let such an opportunity pass.'

'You don't understand at all . . . I hoped. Oh forget it. Let's go.'

'How could you be so *selfish*? Not telling me. Those wonderful pieces. Just sitting there. Shows how much you value our relationship.'

'It's not like that . . .'

'Isn't it?'

'No it isn't.'

Vivien knew she could not defend herself against the charge of wanting to keep the house a secret, or wanting to be alone there. She did not know if that, or her lack of professional loyalty or acumen, was the more hurtful.

'Anyway,' she said, 'this is the last time I'll be coming here. The house goes up for auction next week.'

'Does it? That doesn't give us much time then.'

'No, Bonnie. We're not taking anything.'

Vivien looked from the miniatures and figurines to Bonnie, tear-stained and tense as a whippet, poised on the edge of their marriage.

'Come on then,' she said.

They raced for the stairs. They plundered the glove drawer, forcing their fingers into the unstretched kid; a pearl button hit the floor and rolled away.

'There's a pile of plastic carriers in the kitchen. Where's the van?'

'At home. I watched you leave the house, parked the van and followed you on foot.'

'Good. Thank goodness you didn't bring it here. I should have realised someone was there when the rooks started squawking,' Vivien panted as they worked, each knowing instinctively what to take. A team. Although Bonnie would need kid-glove treatment for a while.

'How did you find the key?'

'A toad showed me the way.'

'A toad? Sure you don't mean a robin, like in *The Secret Garden*? I know how you love poring over those mildewed kids' books.'

As Bonnie spoke she jiggled a hairpin, found in a dressing-table tray, in the lock of a china cabinet.

'Brilliant,' Vivien said but she walked over to the window and looked out into the garden as Bonnie lifted out the first cupid and the pretty spotted leopard with gold-tipped paws. They left no mess, no trace of their presence. Vivien locked the door and replaced the wiped key under the plant. As they passed the drawing-room windows she saw the person she might have been, watching them go from the velvet yellow chair in the room defiled by their fight.

They met nobody on the way home but if they had it would have been apparent that those two weirdos from the Old Post Office had been doing their shopping, and not stinting themselves from the look of their bulging bags.

At home Vivien said, 'We must be mad. We'll be the obvious suspects when the stuff's missed. The only dealers for miles around . . . We could put it back . . .'

'And risk getting caught in the act, apart from the fact that this is the biggest coup of our career? No way, José. By the way, how did you know the house is going up for auction?'

'It was in the local paper.'

'Oh. Well, the plan is, we'll drive up to London first thing tomorrow. We can stay with Frankie and Flossie for a few days while we unload the stuff. And I think I know somebody who will be *very* interested . . .'

'But . . .'

'Those frigging freeloaders owe us. Think of the times they've pitched up here without so much as a bottle of Sainsbury's plonk. Besides, they're our best friends!'

The kid gloves shrivelled and blackened on the barbie, giving a peculiar taste to the burgers and green peppers that sweated and spat on the grid above them. The tiny pearl buttons glimmered among the discs of bone, horn, glass and plastic in the tall jar of assorted buttons.

'Shampoo?'

'Shampoo!'

Bonnie and Vivien had returned in high spirits from their successful stay in London. They had taken in a sale of the stock of a bankrupt theatrical costumiers on the way back. It was nine o'clock in the evening. The man on the doorstep heard music and caught a glimpse of two figures, beyond the nude in her hat and necklace, locked together in a slow dance once known as the Gateways grind, out of sync with the jaunty song.

'Good evening, ladies. Filth,' he smiled, flashing his ID at the wolf in a lime-green beaded dress who answered the door.

'Who is it?' came the bark of the fox just behind her.

'It's the Filth – I mean the police,' came the slightly muffled reply.

For a moment they stood, the wolf in green and the fox in a scarlet sheath fringed with black, staring at him with glassy eyes, then simultaneously pulled off their heads, and he felt that they had removed their sharp, sly masks to reveal features identical to the heads they held in their hands, so that he still faced a fox and wolf, but with fear in their eyes.

He touched delicately one of the tubular beads on Bonnie's dress, standing in his linen suit crumpled from a day's policing. 'Nice,' he said. 'Bugle beads, aren't they? That's Blossom Dearie, isn't it?' He sang, '*There ought to be a moonlight-saving time, so I could love that man of mine . . .'* glancing towards the uniformed constable at the wheel of the police car.

'You'd better come in,' said Vivien the Fox. The animals, on high heels, led him into the front room. He saw a bottle of champagne and two glasses.

'I don't suppose you'd like a drink? You can't when you're on duty, can you?'

'You've been watching too much television,' he replied, picking up a dusty green glass from a sideboard. 'Regular Aladdin's cave you've here, haven't you? Cheers.'

He raised his glass to the model and looked round at the piles and rails of clothes, the jumble of china and glass, silver, brass and pewter, the old books, the trivia, the ephemera that refused to die, the worthless and the valuable bits of furniture, the glass jar that held the tiny pearl buttons snipped from two pairs of burned skin gloves.

'I caught one of her shows at the Pizza on the Park,' he said. 'Blossom Dearie.'

'Oh, so did we!' Vivien exclaimed. 'Perhaps –'

'How can we help you?' Bonnie broke in.

'There's been a break-in. At an empty house down the road, the old Emerson place. Some valuable pieces taken. I've got the list here. We thought you might come across some of them in your travels, or someone might try to pass them off on you, you being the most local and obvious outlet – if our perpetrators are the bunch of amateurs we suspect they are. If that should happen, we'd be very grateful if you would let us know.'

'Of course.' Vivien took the photocopied list he held out. It shook in her hand although there was no draught that humid evening.

'Let's see.' Bonnie read aloud over Vivien's shoulder. 'Meissen Shepherdess with birdcage. Harlequin and Columbine, cupids representing four seasons. Leopard. Man and woman, riding goats, Staffordshire. Chelsea, Derby, Bow . . . pair of berry spoons, circa 1820 . . .'

She whistled. 'There's some nice stuff here. Priceless. Any idea who could have done the job?'

'We're working on it. Whoever it was did a pretty good

demolition job on the drawing room and kindly left us a few genetic fingerprints. Shouldn't be too difficult.'

The fox went as red as the cherries on the dummy's hat, as if she had been responsible for the violation.

'But those lovely things – the shepherdess, the leopard, the porcelain – what were they doing in an empty house? Wasn't there a burglar alarm at least to protect them?'

'The house and contents were due to be auctioned the following day. It was just bad luck. Old Mrs Emerson's godson, she left it to him, has no interest in the place apart from the proceeds from the sale – serves him right, really. Nasty piece of work – greedy and careless – a dangerous combination. More money than sense already. There's an old local couple who kept an eye on the place – he did a bit in the garden, kept the grass down, and she kept the dust down. It seems likely that one of them forgot to reset the alarm the last time they were there, but that's academic really. They're both in deep shock. Aged ten years overnight. Heartbroken. Keep saying they've betrayed old Mrs Emerson's trust. From the look of them they'll be apologising to her in person soon . . . Well, thank you for your co-operation. Sorry to intrude on your evening.'

'We were just pricing some new stock,' Bonnie felt obliged to explain, waving a hand at the fox and wolf heads staring at them from the floor, as he rose to leave.

'Phew!! What an incredible stroke of luck! That someone should actually break in while we were away! I can't believe it! Somebody up there must like us . . .' Bonnie sank into a chair kicking off her high-heeled shoes.

'And us prancing around like a couple of drag queens in animal heads,' she went on, 'I thought I would die. I could hear those prison gates clanging, couldn't you! Cell Block H, here we come! Let's have a look at that list again. "Silver salt spoon, convolvulus design handle"? How come we missed that?'

'I don't know.'

Vivien crossed her fingers behind her back and hoped that Tedina, who had watched her unscrew the brass knob of the bedpost and drop in a silver spoon, would keep her mouth shut.

Then the spoon with its convolvulus wreathed stem would lie safely and inaccessibly locked in the bedpost, a tiny silver secret salvaged from her house, as long as the marriage lasted. She pulled the chenille bedspread that served as a curtain across the window, refilled their glasses and turned over the record.

'Where were we, before we were so rudely interrupted?'

She held out both her hands and they resumed the dance; the Friendly Old-Established Firm, back in business.

Angelo

The long brown beans in the catalpa rattled in the wind, brittle pods dangling in bunches among the last flapping yellow leaves of the tree, so ancient and gnarled that it rested on a crutch, in the courtyard of St James's, Piccadilly. Splintered pods and big damp leaves littering the stones were slippery under the feet of the friends, enemies and those who wished to be seen at Felix Mazzotti's Memorial Service. Drizzle gave a pearly lustre to black umbrellas and brought up the velvet pelts of collars, and cashmere and cloth, moistened hats and vivified patterned shawls and scarves.

Violet Greene settled herself and her umbrella in a pew beside a stranger. The umbrella's handle was an ivory elephant's head, yellow and polished by time like a long old tooth, the grooves in its trunk smoothed by generations of gloves. The heavy white paper of the Order of Service in her black velvet fingers, thick gold-leaf braid trimming white stone, glittering brass; Violet concentrated on these, and caught the little black eye of the elephant's head, which *was* an old tooth, taken from some Victorian tusker too long ago to worry about, and carved into little replicas of its original owner. Round her neck Violet wore a string of jet beads, mourning jewellery which Felix had given her forty years before. Felix's mother had been English, his father Italian, and although he was officially a Catholic he had never felt the slightest twitch on the thread. Hence this church rather than the Brompton Oratory or Farm Street. The lapse of time between the news of his death, and the funeral which had been a private affair in Italy, and the memorial service had accustomed people to his absence from the world, and time in any case rushes in as the sea fills holes in the sand.

When someone is shot, Violet had read, they often feel no pain at first; she had waited, after the bullet's impact of the news, for the wound of loss to bleed and burn, but she had not seen Felix for five years – which was good because she had no picture of him as the really old man he had suddenly become – although they had spoken occasionally on the telephone, and it was hard to remember that he was dead. One day she had decided to believe that he was still in his terraced garden among the olive trees that gave the beautiful green oil of which he was so proud, and felt a release. It was so simple she wondered why she had not thought of it sooner. He had once told her that his olive oil gave him more pleasure and sense of achievement than all the books he had written. It had seemed such an arrogant remark, one that could have been made only by somebody as successful in the world's eye as he was, that she had felt irritated for days. Even though she refused to recognise his death, questions would persist: What were we like? What were we like together? Who was I then? She had been sixteen when they met, he a much older man of thirty. A mere boy. And was that girl herself, Violet Clements, in a silky dress printed with pansies under a cheap, black cloth coat shivering in the March wind on the steps of a house in Gordon Square? On her way to the church in a taxi this morning she had passed a bed of blue and yellow pansies, and watched the colours quivering, trembling with the taxi's motor, the dyes running together in the rivulets on the wet glass.

Her black velvet beret with its soft pleats like the gills of a large field mushroom was skewered with a black pearl clasped in two tiny silver hands, and she wore an emerald scarf of fine wool in a loose triangle across the shoulders of her black coat. Violet Greene she was now, and supposed that Greene, her fourth surname, would be her last, although she would not quite have put money on it. She rather liked it; the pre-Raphaelite purple and viridian of her name, the hectic hues of Arthur Hughes, or of bright green Devon Violets scent in a round bottle with painted flowers. Or Cornish, Welsh, Scottish or Parma violets – the cachou odour was the same, and a sniff of it would recall seaside holidays with the boys, salt-caked plimsolls and rough sandy towels bleaching on the rail of a wooden veranda. A Present for the Best Mother in the World, bought with pennies saved out of their ice-cream money. Today a delicate waft of toilet-water was all but indiscernible as she moved.

The organ was playing a medley, a melancholy fruit cocktail in heavy syrup, as the pews filled. Violet was clasping her hands, not in prayer but to restrain them from plucking a silver hair from the coat in front of her, when a finger prodded her own back. She turned.

'Hello. I like your hat. Is it what's called a Van Dyck beret?'

Violet had made a decision long ago not to dislike a girl simply because she was young and beautiful, so she smiled at the whisperer under her hooded eyes, still violet but faded, as the flowers do. Someone's daughter or granddaughter, some child in publishing or from a gallery, in PR, met at some party – she was still invited to more than she bothered with; a fixture on some guestlists after so many years on the sidelines of the arts. She couldn't remember. All black lycra and red lipstick, with long fair hair that required to be raked back from her face every few seconds; the sort of girl seen at the cinema with a giant bucket of popcorn, climbing over people's legs, drawing attention to herself.

'It's my first time at one of these,' the girl confided in her loud whisper. 'I s'pose you must've been to hundreds . . .'

'Thousands,' Violet confirmed drily.

The girl's hat lying on the pew was the kind of crushed velvet thing you would see on a stall at Camden Market between racks of discarded dresses which might have belonged to Violet long ago and she had evidently lost confidence in her ability to wear it. Violet never went out without a hat, linen and straw with a rose or cherries or a floating scarf; canvas, wool or feline print; she was known for her amusing and assured headgear in a time when so few women know how. Her ear picked up a few bars of 'What'll I do' interwoven plaintively through strands of 'Sheep May Safely Graze', 'Voi Che Sapete', 'Memories' and 'For All We Know' . . . *For all we know, this may only be a dream. We come and go like a ripple on a stream. Time like an ever-rolling stream bears all its sons away. They fly forgotten as a dream . . . Imagine there's no heaven . . .* she was aware of the girl behind her slewing round in her pew, and the velvet hat was proving useful, she saw as she turned her head a fraction, waving frantically at some young people hesitating noisily at the back of the church, flapping them into the seats bagged for them. They should have been holding

277

enormous paper cups of Coca-Cola rattling with ice-cubes, and straws to hoover it up, rather than those unfamiliar prayer books with which they had been issued.

Here we are, out of cigarettes . . . two sleepy people by dawn's early light, too much in love to say goodnight . . . Who had chosen this music? Felix's third wife, the charmless Camilla, over there in the Liberty hairband, in the first flush of middle-age but still young enough to be his granddaughter, with children from her first marriage, who took none of his references, responded to his jokes with serious replies, mirthless barks or groans, didn't smoke, and bridled at the mention of Violet's name. There were bits of bridle or snaffles or some piece of harness across her shoes, vestiges of the nurse she had become to Felix clung to her as if demanding respect for an invisible uniform of self-sacrifice. It was hideous to imagine her snouting through naive old letters, selecting the worst photographs of Violet for the authorised biography. The only redress would be to write her own memoirs, but Violet lacked the energy or inclination to do it, and although she had given up poetry many years ago, she remembered the torture of trying to recreate the truth in words, even when only trying to describe a landscape or a lampshade.

Her uncharitable thoughts about Camilla were prompted by Camilla's hostility to her, concealed today for appearance's sake. She resented being cast as a witch, an *old* witch, because Felix had loved her best. Violet Clements had been orphaned at fourteen and a year later had left her aunt's crowded house to make her own way in the world. She had got a job at a small printing press whose decorative hand-blocked volumes were collectors' items now, and at night she had filled notebooks with her own verses by the gaslight of her attic room. She had met Felix at a tea party given by one of their poets, where absinthe was offered in rose-painted cups. The poet, killed in the war and his work forgotten, had called for a toast to 'the green fairy' as he poured the romantic liquid. Violet took only a sip or two of infamous anise but she was under the green fairy's spell, in love with and in awe of the shabby glamour of the bad fairy's court.

Felix's invitation to coffee to show him her poems filled her with joy and terror for he was an established novelist and man of letters and so she was trembling with awe as much as from the March wind when she rang his bell. Shocked, for Felix wore a spotted dressing gown, she backed down the steps blushing and starting to apologise, not looking at his bare legs, thinking she had got the wrong day. He laughed. He led her into a room with an unmade bed.

'But it's the morning!'

He had laughed again.

The poems in her bag, so carefully selected, wilted like wall-flowers at a party. It was cold, painful, and above all excruciatingly embarrassing. Violet's face had blazed for hours like the gas-fire he lit afterwards, and drinking the black bitter coffee which he had made at last, she could neither look at him nor speak.

'Violet Greene has a string of lovers,' she overheard somebody say years later, and she saw herself on Primrose Hill, against a yellow sky, pulled across the horizon by the pack of dogs whose leashes cut into her hand. Four of her former lovers were in the church today, she counted, and Felix, if she were to admit to it, was scattered over the grass at Kenwood where leafless autumn crocuses shivered on their white stalks like girls gone mauve with the cold. Camilla had brought his ashes to England in a casket.

> 'Who would true valour see
> Let him come hither;
> One here will constant be,
> Come wind, come weather;
>
> 'There's no discouragement
> Shall make him once relent
> His first avowed intent
> To be a pilgrim.'

Violet's eyes blurred, and she had to control her mouth which was unable to do more than mime the words. From Kensington nursing home and Oxford, Sutton Scotney, Bloomsbury, Maida Vale, Hampstead and points south the pilgrims had come this wild morning, old playmates summoned by the cracked bell of Fitzrovia.

'Bloody Brighton train!'

Maurice Wolverson edged into the pew beside her, knocking her umbrella to the floor, in a fury about leaves on the line. 'Not a bad house,' he commented, looking around.

Mingled smells of damp wool and linseed oil came off the camel-hair coat whose velvet lapels were stippled with flake-white, and then an amber peaty aroma rose as he unscrewed the silver top of his cane. He drew out a long glass tube and offered it to Violet, who shook her head. His last part, four years ago, had been a walk-on in a television sit-com set in a seaside home for retired thespians. He had taken to daubing views of Brighton's piers to block out the sound of the swishing tide while waiting for the telephone to ring. A cluster of tarry shingle was stuck to the sole of his shoe and a red and white spotted handkerchief in his pocket made a crumpled attempt at jauntiness.

'They'll have to paper the house when my turn comes,' Maurice muttered. Violet patted his knee.

'Choirboys. On a scale of one to ten . . . ?'

Violet slapped his knee.

Looking back she was incredulous, and indignant on the behalf of all foolish young women who took themselves at a man's valu-ation, that her fear and distaste had been compounded by worry that her body might not meet Felix's high standards, for he and his circle were harsh arbiters of female pulchritude. She had been half afraid that the jaded gourmet might send back the roast spring lamb.

'Well, what did you expect,' he had asked, 'turning up on my doorstep looking like that?'

Apologies had come years later. Even now, Violet knew that she brightened in men's company, became prettier, wittier, revived like a thirsty flower, with a silver charge through her veins. She had never succumbed to sensible underwear or footwear and no give-away little pickled-onion bulge distorted her shoes.

Her eyes closed as she listened to the anthem, and she felt a pang of affection for Felix's olive oil, and let the viscous yellow-green drip slowly from the bottle with the label he had designed, until it brimmed on the spoon, sharing his pleasure in it, not arguing. She had hated him often as he pursued her down the years like Dracula in an opera cloak or a degenerate Hound of Heaven, and she had carried a bagful of grievances against him about with her, but now the drawstrings of the bag loosened and all the old withered hurts, wrongs and frustrations flew out and upwards to the rafters, unravelled and dissolved in the gold and amber voices of the choir. As they knelt to pray, she ran the jet beads through her hand like a rosary, feeling the facets through the fingers of her gloves.

A nudge in the ribs jolted her. 'Was it Beverley Nichols or Godfrey Winn who had a dog called Mr Sponge?' came in a stage whisper.

Violet squeezed her eyes shut tight: 'Oh God, please bless Felix and let him be happy and reunited with his family and –' If there were a heaven, it was a good thing for her and most of this congregation that there was no marriage or giving in marriage there. Imagine the complications.

'Which of them got Willie Maugham's desk in the end?'

'Oh God, *I* don't know.' She didn't know, didn't know if her prayer would get through the myriad, innumerable as plankton, prayers eternally sluicing the teeth of heaven's gate. A snowball's chance in hell perhaps. 'Ask them yourself – later!' Her words hissed like sizzling snow.

A teenage boy, perhaps one of Camilla's, was standing at the front of the church, clearing his throat. He read badly, as if he had never read any poetry until this public occasion; it was Francis Thompson's 'At Lord's' that the boy was murdering but could not quite kill. Violet's eyes filled again, and her unshed tears were brackish with bitterness. The poem had brought her back to Felix once when she had been on the point of leaving him. They were in a taxi, his coat was speckled with ash and she had recoiled from his tobacco-stained kiss. They must have been passing Lord's for she had mentioned the poem, that she thought was her own discovery, a manly poem that had touched her girl's heart, and Felix had at once recited it, word perfect, and she had felt an overwhelming tenderness for him. How dared Camilla know about it? He had spread himself thin like rich pâté eked out over too many slices of toast. Desolate, small and old, she would have given almost anything to be riding in that taxi through the blue London twilight now. But Felix was in Italy, she braced up, pontificating over a bottle of young wine or extra virgin oil, holding it up to the light.

She forbade the tears to spill, it would not do for people to see her – unmanned. A man's woman – yes, she had always been that. Her women friends had always taken second place to the man in her life. 'Flies round a honeypot,' Felix would snort with jealous pride after every party. Had the essence of herself been dissipated, though, and nearly all her choices made for her, by some man's or boy's need which outweighed her own?

At a splash to her right, she glanced at Maurice. Tears were rolling down his cheeks and dripping on to his Order of Service. She gave a sharp nod at the handkerchief in his top pocket. Upstaged. She swallowed an untimely giggle that threatened to turn into a sob.

As Denzil, Sir Denzil Allen, ancient ousted publisher, began his address, Violet thought, this is odd. Very odd, if you come to think of it, as she did. She referred to her Order of Service to confirm her suspicion: all the speakers and readers were men. Felix had been such a lover of women, many of his closest friends had been women and yet those women he had loved and who had known him best, herself chief among them, were to sit in their pews and have him expounded to them by these men. Well, that was the way of the world which she had made no attempt to change, and she could have been Violet Mazzotti and have organised this service herself, and made a better job of it. Women had not always been nice to her. She remembered the resentment, the thinly veiled spite of some of Felix's old friends when they were living together. Men too. Had she really expected them to say, 'Welcome, Violet Clements, lovely and gifted youthful poet. We embrace you as one of us'? She could understand them now, but she had often been hurt and she stuck to her resolve never to snub a young girl, however pretty or silly, in whom shyness might be mistaken for arrogance.

Across the church she could see Sibyl Warner, the novelist, making a rare appearance. Heavily veiled, once a great beauty, she had long been a recluse from a world which assumed the right to comment on time's alterations. 'My God, I didn't recognise you! You've changed!' That wound inflicted twenty years ago by Jill Blakiston, in an affronted tone which hinted at betrayal and suggested that the photographs on the jackets of Sibyl's books must have been forgeries. Jill sat behind Violet today, a retired editorial director, rummaging in a £1000 worth of crocodile bag, quite unaware of what she had done, but Violet had been there and seen Sibyl flinch and gulp her drink in her eagerness to leave.

Something had shocked Violet almost as much as the revelation that people could go to bed in the morning. 'Mind if I pee in your sink?' Felix had asked. It was a year after they had met and she was living in a respectable boarding house in Mornington Crescent. She most certainly had minded. There was her cake of carnation soap on the rim of the basin and her sponge and tooth-brush in a glass. 'This is intolerable,' Felix had said. 'The sooner you move in with me the better.'

Her landlady, catching Felix tiptoeing down the stairs at one in the morning, told her to pack her bags at once and so, in a cloud of disgrace and defiance, she departed to Gordon Square. Living in sin entailed, she found out, a great deal of scrubbing shirt-collars and darning socks and hours of copying out manuscripts and typing. But it had been fun too. Fun – what a funny, bizarre, orange paper-hat word. After a while afternoon drinking clubs and hangovers and cooking for Felix's drunken friends wasn't fun any more. Felix sailed to America in 1938, for which some still condemned him. Violet had refused to accompany him and when he returned she was Violet Morton, a widow with two children, the younger boy born posthu-mously after the Battle of Britain. Violet had married George Maxwell-Smith to give the boys a father, and divorced him after he had gambled away his father's furniture factory and fled with the girl in accounts. Her third husband, Bobby Greene, a painter, had succumbed to cancer after just eighteen months of happy marriage. His pictures hung on her walls and there had been intimations recently of a small renaissance of interest in his work.

> 'Hold Thou Thy Cross
> Before my closing eyes.
> Shine through the gloom
> And point me to the skies . . .'

An amethyst cross, grown huge, loomed gleaming through swirling mist, suspended above Felix's bed; Felix rising vertically ceilingward with feet pointing down. An amethyst cross on a silver chain that had belonged to her mother, pawned and never redeemed.

As always after one of these occasions Violet was left with the thought that all that really matters in this life is that we should be kind to one another.

'Imogen, there's no heaven!' she heard a boy say outside, under the Indian bean tree leaning on its crutch.

'Ha ha, very funny,' said Imogen, the girl who had been behind Violet, and blew her nose, saying, 'Has my mascara run all over the place? You know, I really quite enjoyed that.'

A group of black-coated youngish Turks was lighting cigarettes, and one of them cast a satirical eye at the knot of Violet's friends moving towards her, and made a remark at which the others laughed. Violet wondered when the power had passed to those young men with sliding smiles and snidey eyes; when had they staged their coup? She glanced around and thought: you – girl in a black dress squirming away from the poet you had thought to flatter with your charm – you have read none of his work but someone told you he is a poppet, and now he's threatening your cleavage with the dottle from his pipe. Who are all these rouged dotards, you wonder, boys and girls, these deposed old Turks who sidle up to you with swimming eyes like macerated cocktail cherries pleading for a reissue of their mildewed masterworks, a mention on the wireless, or a book to review which you will never send? Who are they, these mothballed revenants that you thought dead for years, these relics of whom you have never heard? Who? Well, my dears – they are you.

Violet was weary: wake up, Denton Welch, Djuna Barnes, Mark Gertler, Gaudier-Brzeska, Gurdieff, et al – it's time for your next brief disinterment. Angels were warming up to dance on the heads of pins. A bored miaow from Schroeder's Cat. Stale buns, duckies. It was reassuring to be kissed by old kid and chamois leather, badger bristle shaving-brushes and paintbrush beards, comfortable if elegaic to be surrounded by elegant decaying warehouses which had stored fine wines and cheeses and garlic for most of the century, some who were as stout as their sodden purple-seeping vats and others as frail as towers of round plywood boxes that might topple and be bowled along by the wind.

'Are you coming along for drinkies?'

'No, Maurice dear, my grandson's taking me out to lunch.'

He was, but on the following day. Violet had had enough. It had been gracious of Camilla to invite her today, perhaps, but enough was enough. She disengaged herself and started to walk towards Fortnum's, rather worried about Maurice. Who would pour him into the Brighton train in the frightful gloaming when the lights of shops and taxis blaze bleakly on wan faces and all souls seem lost? Would some sixth sense carry him along, a buffeted buffoonish bygone, with the cruel and censorious commuters, or might he find himself alone on the concourse but for a few vagrants, Lily Law bearing down on him, the last train gone and all bars closed, or would he wake without a passport at Gatwick Airport, or in a black siding at Hassocks or Haywards Heath? She consoled herself with the knowledge that it was the drinks afterwards which had persuaded him to make the journey to the service, and that after a certain hour everybody on the Brighton train is drunk. Deciding against Fortnum's, she turned down Duke Street into Jermyn Street, making for St James's Square. The shop windows were lovely, still dressed for autumn with coloured leaves and berries, nuts and gilded rosy pomegranates, but behind the glass of one display an aerosol forecast snow.

Violet loved the symmetry of the gardens, that square within a circle within a square within a square. She sat on a bench with a sense of being alone with the equestrian statue of Guilelmus III at its centre and the birds that fluttered in the foliage and pecked about in the fallen leaves on the paving stones. An obelisk marked each corner of the inner square, a tiny-leaved rambling rose had captured one of them and held it in its thorns, and a wren emerged from a bush, saw her and disappeared. Her eyes were still sharp enough to identify a bird; she was fortunate in that. She was fortunate in having a tall, fair-haired grandson. Had there been a touch of smugness in her tone when she had spoken of him to poor lonely Maurice? Well, she *was* proud of Tom and delighted that he should want to take her to lunch; too bad, why should she temper her feelings to Maurice's sensibilities? She did try not to condescend to those who were not the mother of sons and had only granddaughters, instead of big handsome boys who made one feel cherished and feminine and even a little deliciously dotty and roguish at times, and it was pleasant to bring out carefully selected stories from her past, as if from a drawer lined with rose and violet pot-pourri spiced with faint intriguing muskier fruitier notes. Maurice had been involved in some unpleasantness in the bad old days, she recalled, but he must have put aside all such foolishness now, as she had. The long windows of the London Library glittered, reminding her how once she would have hoped love lurked there, playing peek-a-boo round the book stacks. She toyed with the idea of a cup of coffee in the Wren, the wholesome café attached to the church, or something worthy to eat, but putting that aside in favour of her own little kitchen and bathroom, along with the unpleasant image, like a grey illustration in a book, of Maurice in a suit of broad arrows breaking stones in Reading Gaol, she decided to take the Piccadilly line to Gloucester Road.

There wasn't a seat and Violet had to stand, but just for a moment or two until a rough-looking lad heaved himself up and nodded her into his place. Violet thanked him courteously, giving a lesson in manners to any who should be watching, and a rueful, apologetic little smile to the dowdy woman left standing. It doesn't do to judge by appearances, she thought, of the boy, while acknowledging that he, naturally, had done just that. It didn't surprise her because it had always been so; men had never stopped holding doors open for her, and even when she and the boys had been marooned in that rotting thatched cottage in Suffolk after George's defection, there had been some gumbooted Galahad to dig her out of a ditch or rescue a bird from the chimney.

A startlingly beautiful boy was sitting opposite her. She couldn't take her eyes off his face. About sixteen, with loose blue-black curls, olive skin and a full, tragic mouth. He must be South American. Venezuelan, she decided, in a city far from home.

He had the face of an angel. She named him Angelo. There was a panache, a muted stylishness, about his black leather jacket, dark charcoal sweater over a white T-shirt, black jeans, silver ring and ear-ring, the black-booted ankle resting casually across the knee. Fearing that he might imagine there was something predatory in the way she drank in his beauty, she averted her attention to the ill-featured youth on Angelo's right, but she was drawn back to Angelo's almond-shaped, lustrous, long-lashed eyes. Hyde Park Corner came and went. Violet shut her eyes, abruptly suffused by a sadness she didn't know what to do with, and a statue came into her mind, a little stone saint in a wayside shrine whose lips had crumbled, kissed away by thousands of supplicants' desires. She wanted to warn the boy: Angelo, beware. People will prey on you, want to possess you, corrupt you, exploit you for your beauty until there is nothing left of you and you are destroyed; but there was a wariness about Angelo's face which said that he had learned that long ago.

She opened her eyes. A sudden instinct told her that Angelo and the youth who had given up his seat and the lout on his right were connected, and pretending not to be. A lunge of silver, her bag ripped from her hands, fingers tearing at her rings, and as he grabbed the necklace, black against a blazing yellow and grape-purple flash of anguished desire to snatch back and relive her years, she was aware of a knife at her throat and that Angelo was a girl.

The Curtain with the Knot in It

'You can see my window from here. It's the one with the curtain with the knot in it.'

Alice shivered, although the April late afternoon sun was turning the day room of Daffodil Ward into a greenhouse.

'Goose walked over your grave.' Pauline gave her abrupt laugh.

Alice looked out reluctantly across to the staff residential block, a three-storeyed cube of mottled brick, and located a dull curtain tied in a knot at a top-floor window.

Why, she wondered, had she shuddered like that? Was it the knot? Or the intimation that Pauline the Domestic had a life beyond Daffodil?

Pauline laughed again, at the antics of Jack, one of the patients, who had almost managed to slide under the tray which confined him to his chair.

'Come on, Jack Be Nimble, Jack Be Quick,' she said as she pulled him back. 'You'll be having your soup in a minute.'

If a coypu were to laugh, Alice thought, or did she mean a capybara? Something with unattractive teeth and lank fur, unpopular with visitors at the zoo. The two women were of an age and dressed similarly, but with a world of difference between Alice's visitor's tracksuit and trainers and what was visible of Pauline's; pinkish-white and greyish-white peeking from under her nylon gingham overall. Pauline's hair hung limply from a rufflette of brown and yellow gingham, while Alice's was in a longish shiny bob.

Ada had been shouting from her chair for the curtains to be pulled since the rain had stopped and the sun had appeared two hours earlier, and now Sister was exasperated into swiping out spring with a swish of the orange curtains.

Alice's father had been wheeled into the ward so that something could be done to him, so she sat on a massive vinyl chair attempting to read a Large Print book whose pages had been glued together with Complan. Pauline went about her work, tearing sheets of pale blue paper from a large roll and slapping them down at each place on the long table, and on the trays of the chairs where the immobile were propped up on lolling and slipping pillows. Supper would not be served for an hour, but those who could Zimmer themselves there or who could be yanked and hoisted were seated at the table. Children's BBC blared on the television.

Anybody familiar with the tragedies, the dramas, the macabre comedies played out daily in places such as Daffodil, and the aching, aching boredom, the cross-purpose nature of every exchange, will need no description of suppertime in this nursery of second child-hood. Suffice it to say that it was a Wednesday and the big wooden calendar read *SUNDAY*, that the two budgies, presented by a well-wisher after the goldfish's suicide, twittered unregarded, that a voice called incessantly 'help me, help me, somebody please help me'; the never-opened piano and record player were there, and the floral displays in beribboned baskets, faded to the colour and texture of Rice Krispies, and in the side ward people who had died long ago were cocooned in cots and tended as if they might, some day, hatch into something marvellous, or exude skeins of wonderful silk.

When it became apparent that Dad had been put to bed, Alice went to say goodnight to him.

'Don't know why you bother coming every day,' said Pauline. 'He doesn't know you from a bar of soap, nem-mind though, I've got a soft spot for your dad myself.'

She was pouring powdered soup into the orange plastic beakers from an aluminium jug. George was spooning out his reconsti-tuted bits of mushroom and laying them neatly on his blue paper. Mrs Rosenbaum didn't want any soup because she was dead.

'Aren't you staying for your tea tonight?' Pauline asked Alice.

'No, I'd better be going. Got a lot to do at home.'

She felt unequal to the nice milky one, two sugars, tonight. A misunderstanding early in their relationship made it impossible now for her to explain that she liked her tea black and unsweet-ened. 'I look after my *friends*,' Pauline would say darkly, with a pointed glance at Dolly's daughter who had unwittingly offended and was therefore not allowed tea. One of Alice's worst fears was that Dad would not die before Pauline's, as yet unspoken but looming, invitation to an off-duty cuppa in her flat.

Croxted Memorial, originally a cottage hospital, was built to a strange hexagonal design, with a small Outpatients and Casualty tacked on to one side, and even after a year of visiting, Alice could get lost, take a wrong turning and end up where she started or at the dead end of the permanently locked Occupational Therapy, or the kitchens with their aluminium vats and trolleys. The grey floor gleamed with little bubbles of disinfectant, a sign that read *Cleaning in Progress* half blocked her path, as it did every day although there were so few visitors or staff around that the place was like a morgue in the evenings, and there was Kevin the cleaner, leering over the handle of his heavy-duty polisher, pallid as a leek with a tangle of pale dirty roots for hair. She knew she should have taken the other exit.

'Off out somewhere nice, are we?'

She gave a smile which tried to be enigmatic, distancing and hinting at a world beyond his overalls and disinfectant.

'When you coming out with me then?'

Alice pulled out her diary and flicked through the pages, aware of him squirming with incredulous lubricity.

'Let me see, I think I'm free on the twelfth.'

'You what . . .'

'Yes. The Twelfth of Never.' She snapped the diary shut triumphantly.

That was cruel, Alice, she admonished herself as she inhaled healing nicotine and evening air after the dead atmosphere which was Pauline's and Kevin's element, standing on the asphalt marled with white blossom while a blackbird sang in a cherry tree. Still, Kevin's idea of a venue for a good night out was probably that dark place behind the boiler room, where the wheelie bins lived.

Alice had lied to Pauline about having things to do, and deceived Kevin. The pages of her diary were almost all blank. Since she had been made redundant her world had shrunk until Daffodil and the long journeys by foot and tube and bus were her whole life.

She no longer thought of herself as Alice at the Mad Hatter's tea party nearly as often as she had in the beginning. Her father, a Detective Inspector struck down and withered by illness over the years, was all the family she had and she loved him and grieved for his plight. She did not cry tonight; she had cried in so many hospital car parks over the years.

Kevin watched her from the doorway, drawing deeply on a pinched roll-up. His glance went up to a window with a knotted curtain, billowing, deflated, in the wind that had sprung up, ruffling his hair.

Inside, in Daffodil, Pauline ruffled George's white hair as she collected his dishes.

'All right, Georgie Porgie?'

Writhing in agony from the pressure sore that was devouring him like an insatiable rodent, he drew back his lips in what Pauline took to be a smile.

'Pudding and Pie,' she added.

'You haven't eaten your sandwiches,' she accused Mrs Rosenbaum, whipping away the three triangles of bread and ham. When she had been brought in, Mrs Rosenbaum had tried to explain about eating kosher, but none of the staff or agency nurses had been able to take it on board, and she had shrunk into silence under her multi-coloured crochet blanket, while her feet swelled in the foam rubber boots fastened with velcro that Physio had provided, as slow starvation took its course.

The commodes that doubled as transport up the wooden hill to Bedfordshire were rolling into the day room.

'Come on Mary, Mary Quite Contrary,' said Sister Connelly as two of the Filipinos, they all looked the same to Pauline, and they never spoke to her anyway, started loading Mary on board. Quacking away in Foreign like a load of mandarin ducks. Thank God it was nearly time to knock off. She was really cheesed off today. Ada was singing, if you could call it that, ''Ere we are again, 'Appy as can be. All good pals and JOLLY . . .' She always got stuck there.

'Change the record, Ada!' Pauline shouted as Ada started up again.

'Pack it in, Joey. I've got a headache,' she told the budgies.
'Noisy buggers!'

'What are their names?' Alice had asked her once.

'I call them Joey. Can't tell them apart,' Pauline had replied.

'One's more emerald and the other's more turquoise.'

'You don't have to clear up after them!'

It was all right for some people with nothing better to do to
go all soppy over a pair of budgies.

'I know why the caged bird sings,' Alice had said, but before
she could go on Jack had tipped his chair over. Alice had had to
sign a form as a witness, to show that there had been no negli-
gence, after the doctor had been called, but that was the last they
had heard of the matter.

Outside at last, Pauline had an impulse to take off her trainers
and walk barefoot over the daisies in the grass, but Kevin was
lurking around so she didn't. A blackbird was singing in the
cherry tree, black against the white blossom. Pauline stood still
for a moment, then, 'I've got a lot to do at home,' she said to
herself and headed for the concrete stairs that led up to her flat.
It was her thirty-seventh spring. Later that evening she went
down to the payphone and dialled a number. She knew it by
heart; it had stuck in her brain as soon as she had looked it up,
and she had rung it many times. On the third ring Alice answered.
Pauline hung up.

'Just having a chat with my mate,' she said as the dietician and
his girlfriend came through the door in white tennis clothes with
grass stains and a faint smell of sweat. They didn't look at her as
they took the stairs two at a time, laughing at something. Pauline
went slowly after them and finished off the last of the ham sandwiches from supper in Daffodil.

'She's gone, that little lady.' Pauline jerked a thumb towards the
place where Mrs Rosenbaum had sat. It was the following afternoon. Alice made her heart blank, and looked down at her book.

'Having a nice read?'

Pauline tipped the book forward. 'Janette Turner Hospital. She
must be the same as me.'

'She's Australian, I think.' Alice didn't want to be too much of a know-all.

'No, I mean, she must've been found in a hospital, like me. I was left in the toilets at Barts, that's why they give me the name. Pauline after the nurse who found me, and Bartholomew after Barts. Ee-ah, nice milky one, two sugars.'

'Thanks, Pauline, you're a pal.'

As she drank her tea, Alice realised that she had been given the central fact about Pauline. That beginning had determined her progression to this institutional job, that overall, the trolley, the table for one in Spud-U-Like, the holidays spent in shopping precincts.

'I had my picture in all the papers,' said Pauline, and Alice saw a crimson, newborn baby waving feeble arms from swaddling clothes of newsprint, on a stone floor under a porcelain pedestal.

'Your mother – did they – did she?'

Pauline's eyes filled as she shook her head, strands of hair whipping her clamped mouth. 'I've never told anybody that before. Nobody here, I mean. Not that they'd be interested anyway, toffee-nosed lot.'

Alice had noticed that the staff hardly gave Pauline a glance or a word. Poor, despised capybara, whose cage everybody walked past.

That revelation led to Alice's following Pauline up the concrete stairs after visiting time, with a sense of danger, knowing she had taken an irrevocable step. She hadn't known how to refuse the long-threatened invitation after Pauline's tears. To her horror Pauline at once took an unopened bottle of Tia Maria from a cupboard in the tiny kitchen, which was a scaled-down replica of the kitchenette at Daffodil.

'Ah, the curtain with the knot in it! At last!' Alice cried, a bit too gaily, as they carried their glasses through.

'Tell me, Pauline, why does it have a knot in it?'

'I'm a fresh-air fiend. All the cooking smells from foreign cooking get trapped in here so I leave my window open and I have to tie the curtain back or it knocks my ornaments off in the wind.'

'I'd imagined a much more sinister – I mean exotic – explanation, but I see your balloon-seller's head has been glued back on at some stage.'

Pauline topped them up.

'Mind if I smoke?' Alice asked.

'That's all right, I'll get the ashtray.'

It had been washed but Alice detected a smear of grey under its rim which indicated that Pauline had at least one other visitor, who smoked.

'It's a lovely flat, Pauline. A little palace. You've made it really homely.'

'It is home.'

'Well yes, of course.'

'You haven't seen the bedroom yet, have you?'

Alice gasped. Fifty pairs of eyes stared at her from the bed; the big eyes of pink and yellow and white and turquoise fluffy toys, and squinting eyes of trolls with long fluorescent hair.

'Meet the Cuddlies,' said Pauline. 'Sometimes I think they're more trouble than all my patients put together.'

Alice felt sudden fear, of all the goggle-eyes, the garish nylon fibres, strong enough to strangle. Pauline had lured her here to kill her. Get her drunk on Tia Maria and do away with her. In cahoots with Kevin.

'What a wonderful collection. Well, I suppose I'll have to think about going, Pauline. Long journey and all that.' Oh God. That was the mistake people always made in films; saying they were going instead of just making a run for it when the murderer was off-guard.

'Oh, I was going to do us a pizza. Won't take a minute in the microwave.' Pauline was bitterly disappointed. That was what friends did, ate pizza on the sofa in front of the telly. Then her face broke into a smile when Alice said, 'OK, great. Thanks, that would be lovely. Mind if I use your loo?'

'Help yourself.'

As Alice left the room she paused, 'Pauline, mind if I ask you something? Kevin, are you and he . . . I mean does he come here sometimes?'

'Not often.' Pauline was upset at the intrusion of Kevin into the evening. 'I let him come up once in a while. Only when I'm really browned-off.'

Cheesed-off. Browned-off. Alice had an image of Pauline's brown and yellow overall bubbling in a microwaved Welsh Rarebit.

Pauline put Kevin out of her mind and went into the kitchen as Alice closed the bathroom door behind her. She selected two pizzas from the tiny freezer and got a sharp knife from the drawer to score along the marked quarters. The door bell rang.

Alice, in the bathroom with her ear to the wall, heard the freezer door slam, and the metallic scrape of cutlery. The door bell. In total panic she wrenched open the bathroom door. Kevin stood inside the front door, blocking the way. And Pauline had a long knife in her hand.

Alice made a rush for the door, shoving Kevin out of the way but Pauline was right behind her, grabbing the back of her sweatshirt, saying, 'Alice, wait! What about the pizzas?' Alice was pulled round, and for black moments all three were struggling together in the narrow hallway in a tangle of bodies and knife. Then the knife got shoved in. Five inches of stainless steel straight to the heart.

They looked at her lying there. There was no question that she was dead.

'Bloody hell,' said Kevin. 'I only come up for a cup of sugar.'

It occurred to neither of them to call the police.

'I'll have to get her bagged-up,' said Kevin then.

The Domestic was red-eyed and shaky in the morning as she handed out the breakfasts. She looked as if she'd been awake all night. She had; the accusing whispers of the Cuddlies had not let up. She could hear them still through her open window as she crossed the grass, the window with the curtain with the knot in it. Her hair was lank and uncombed under her scrunched rufflette of gingham, but nobody gave her a glance anyway.

'Come on, Dolly Daydream, let's be having you,' she said with her abrupt mirthless laugh. 'Tea up. Nice milky one, two sugars.'

Once, not so long ago, Alice's father, the former Detective Inspector, who was trained to observe, would have looked up with a pleased, though puzzled, smile, sensing something amiss as she handed him his tea. She had always had a soft spot for him too, but now he didn't know her from a bar of soap.

Cloud-Cuckoo-Land

The Rowleys glowed in the dark. On wet winter mornings Muriel was fluorescent, streaming in the rain like a lifeboatperson with a lollipop guiding children over the big crossroads where the lights, when they were working, controlled twelve streams of traffic. As often as not there was an adhesive lifeboat somewhere about her person, for her coat and cap were studded with stickers, bright and new, peeling and indecipherable, of any good cause you could mention, and grey smudges were the ghosts of charities which had achieved their aims, given up or been disbanded in disgrace. Her husband Roy had reflective strips on his bicycle pedals, and his orange cape and phosphorescent armbands, his rattling collection tins of all denominations were a familiar sight outside supermarkets, at car boot sales and in the station forecourt. There were neighbours who doused the lights and television and dropped to the floor if they had warning of his approach, but most people preferred to give, if only a few pesetas or drachmas, because everyone knew the Rowleys would do anything for anybody. A landslide victory in the local radio station poll had earned them its Hearts of Gold Award, and they had been presented with a box of Terry's All Gold Chocolates, a catering-size jar of Gold Blend coffee and a bouquet of yellow lilies with pollen like curry powder. In a different household the permanence of the stamens' dye, staining the wall behind the vase, a heap of books, a clutch of raffle tickets and a pile of laundry might have been a minor disaster.

Visitors to number 35 Hollydale Road, having cleared the assault course of the little hall, Roy and Muriel's stiff PVC and nylon coats, the bicycles which still wore the red noses of that charitable bonanza, Red Nose Day of a few years back, boxes of books, dented tins of catfood and jumble and birdseed, stacks of newspaper tied with string, turned left into the front room, where Roy was, this early afternoon, occupied in sorting through a pile of *National Geographics*. Since his retirement from the buses he had been so busy that now he joked about going back to work for a holiday, although he did put in two mornings a week at the Sue Ryder shop. One of his regular passengers had written a letter once to the *Evening Standard* praising his cheerfulness and he had enjoyed a brief fame as 'the whistling conductor'; people had queued up to ride on his bus. 'The Lily of Laguna' had been his favourite, and 'I Believe', and 'What a Wonderful World', until a polyp on his throat had put paid to that. Roy was an autodidact who had left school at fourteen and was now a gaunt man whose hair stuck up in black and grey tufts; his teeth protruded and his bare ankles, between the cuffs of his navy blue jogging pants and his brogues, were bony. There were traces in him still of the little boy in the balaclava waiting for the library to open, and the skinny eager student at the WEA. He was squinting at the close print of the magazines through a pair of glasses picked from a pile awaiting dispatch to the Third World and now and then a brown breast zonked him in the eye. There was not a surface in the room uncovered by papers, propaganda and paraphernalia.

He was distracted by a movement past the window and glanced up to see old Mr and Mrs Wood from 43 creeping along to the shops with their bags inflated by the late October nor'easter. He noted how frail they had become with the end of summer. The clocks went back that weekend.

'"The Woods decay, the Woods decay and" – Muriel!' He shouted her name. 'Muriel! The Woods have had a fall!'

Muriel rushed through from the kitchen, was tripped up by a bale of newspapers and kicked on the ankle by a bicycle, and saw Roy kneeling beside the Woods who were stretched out on the pavement, as two white plastic bags drifting along were inflated by a gust of wind and tossed like balloons into the branches of an ornamental maple. Punching the familiar digits on her mobile phone, Muriel summoned an ambulance, and hurried, her blue acrylic thighs striking sparks off each other, to wrench open Walter Wood's beige jacket with a sound of ripping velcro, and pinch his purple nose and clamp her mouth to his blue lips. Roy was attending to Evelyn Wood.

'Don't try to struggle,' he soothed her, 'the ambulance is on its way.'

When it arrived, the Woods were covered with a grubby double duvet and a scattering of yellow leaves.

'Got the Babes in the Wood for you, Keith,' Muriel called out to the ambulance crew, who were old friends and soon had the Woods strapped comfortably on board.

'He slipped on – something slippery,' Roy explained, 'and took her down with him. They came a fearful cropper. I saw it happen.' As Keith closed the doors a voice came from within:

'Monstrous . . . two world wars . . . Passchendaele, Givenchy, Vimy Ridge . . .' – and was cut off by the siren.

The onlookers went indoors, three subdued young mothers with pushchairs ambled on and curtains fell back into place as the blue light turned the corner. Muriel gave the duvet a shake and headed home to replace it in the bedroom as Roy surreptitiously scuffed a few more leaves over the condom he kicked into the gutter, the slimy cause of Walter's downfall. He felt sick. It was not the sort of thing you expected in Hollydale Road, a pallid invader from a diseased and alien culture.

'Don't suppose we'll be seeing them back in Hollydale,' Roy predicted in the kitchen.

'No. Here – I've made us some nice hot Bovril – I expect they'll be sent to Selsdon Court eventually. Hopefully. Still, perhaps it's a blessing it happened when it did, before the bad weather. I do worry about the old folk in the winter, when the pavements are icy.'

Roy dunked a flapjack into his Bovril and sucked it. The Rowleys were such good sports that if anyone found a half-baked raffle ticket or a paper rose or a lifeboat in one of Muriel's cakes they took it in good part, although among the cognoscenti it was a case of 'once bitten . . .'

'No word, I suppose, Mummy?'

Roy nodded towards the breadbin, where they stuffed the daily post. 'I would have said. Still, she may have tried to ring – you know how busy the phone is.'

A subdued hooting came from the bathroom.

'Drat that barn owl!' exclaimed Muriel. 'Doesn't seem to know it's supposed to be nocturnal! Where does it think I'm going to get fresh vermin from at this time of day? That's something they don't tell you in those wildlife documentaries. Its beak's well mended now, thanks to that superglue, but it obviously has no intention of taking itself off, thank you very much! Knows which side *its* bread's buttered – well, I suppose I'd better fetch him down,' she concluded with maternal resignation.

As Muriel went upstairs the portable phone rang from the draining board.

'Helpline Helpline. My name's Roy. Is there a problem you'd like to talk about? Something you want to share?'

A gruff throat was cleared.

'Take your time,' Roy encouraged. 'I'm here to listen when you're ready to talk . . .'

Helpline Helpline had been established to counsel people addicted to ringing, or setting up, Helplines. Roy and Muriel had been roped in to man the local branch.

'When did you first begin to think you might have a problem?' As Muriel came in with Barney on her shoulder, and Roy motioned her to be quiet, a hoarse monotone was saying truculently,

'The Bisexual Helpline was busy, so I dialled this number.'

'I'm glad you did – um – could you tell me your name, any name will do, this is all in the strictest confidence of course – it just makes it easier for us to communicate. I said I'm Roy, didn't I?'

Barney was swooping towards him, sinking talons into his shoulder. Roy winced.

'Leslie.'

'So, Leslie – is that with an "ie" or a "y" by the way? Not important – you're having a bit of trouble with your bicycle are you? What's the problem, gears lights, mudguards? Well, we can get that sorted, and then, if you feel up to it, we can address the subtext of your cry for help, i.e., why are you hooked on helplines, and how we at Helpline Helpline can – excuse me a moment, Lesley don't go away – I've got a barn owl on my shoulder –'

'And I've got a monkey on my back,' said the caller and hung up.

'Damn! I was just making the Breakthrough. We'll really have to make a determined effort to return Barney to his own environment. At the weekend, maybe. After the Mini Fun Run.'

He picked up the sandwich Muriel put down on the table and

was opening his mouth when Muriel said, 'Don't eat that, it's Barney's. Worm and Dairylea.'

A silence fell and each knew the other was thinking of their own chick who had flown the nest. Who would have imagined, least of all themselves, that the Rowleys would have a daughter who would be decanted on to the doorstep by disgruntled cab drivers at all hours, and who had now taken up with a Jehovah's Witness? They had fallen out with Petula over the issue of blood transfusion; as operations and transfusions were, so to speak, Roy's and Muriel's lifeblood, it was a vexed question. Giving blood was part of their credo. They had medals for it. There were gallons of Roy's and Muriel's blood walking around in other folk.

Roy put his arms round Muriel, feeling pleasant stirrings of desire as man, wife and owl formed an affectionate tableau, until Muriel felt sharp claws rake her trouser-leg.

'Look who's feeling left-out, then. Come on, Stumpy. Come on, darling.'

She sat down with the cat on her knee. Roy adjusted the draw-string of his jogging pants.

'We're not allowed to call him Stumpy any more, according to the Politically Correct lobby. No, we must henceforth refer to our truncated companion as "horizontally challenged . . ."'

'What *is* your daddy on about now?' Muriel asked the cat.

'Like calling him Nigger.'

'Why on earth would we? He's a tabby tomtom, aren't you pet? Nigger was *black*, you daft thing. Well, this won't get the baby a new frock . . . I promised to pick up Mrs B's prescription and pension before lollipop time.'

As Muriel popped on her mac the phone went and she heard Roy answer, 'Helpline Helpline.'

Petula Rowley had once told her father that whenever she heard him explain to a new acquaintance or a reporter from the local media how he had been 'bitten by the Charity Bug', she saw a large striped glossy beetle rattling a collecting tin at her. She had added that she felt like stamping on that antlered stag and Colorado hybrid; but she herself had been the unwitting cause of her parents' metamorphosis from an unremarkable, well-disposed but uncommitted youngish couple into the baggy-trousered philanthropists of the present day.

When Petula was five the Educational Psychologist, called in by her worried headmistress, had diagnosed a boredom threshold at danger level, and it was as therapy that Muriel and Roy had enrolled their little daughter, all the more precious now for her handicap, in a dancing class which put on shows in old people's homes and hospitals. Not very long after the family had been barred from Anello & Davide where they bought Petula's ballet shoes, those expensive pale pink pumps like two halves of a seashell, Petula had refused to attend the class. Muriel took her to the Tate to see Degas' *Little Dancer* in her immortal zinc tulle to no avail and they were requested to leave the gallery. Muriel had Petula's ballet shoes cast in bronze anyway. They posed on top of the television for years until somehow, without anybody really noticing, they became an ashtray, and later a repository for paperclips and elastic bands.

Petula had defected, but her parents were well and truly hooked on Charity. Was it the smell of hospitals or of tea steaming from battered urns that got them; the smiles on old people's faces or the laughter of sad children, or the cut-and-thrust of the committee meeting where Roy could be relied on to come up with 'Any Other Business' or one more Point of Order, just when folk were putting on their coats with thoughts of the adjacent hostelry? He was proud to share his initials with Ralph Reader of *Gang Show* fame; the Rowleys had ridden along on the crest of a wave, and Petula was dragged behind in the undertow, her boredom threshold quite forgotten.

As Roy returned to the task of sorting the magazines, contributions to the next car boot at Stella Maris, the school whose pupils Muriel escorted across the road, he was conscious of the discomfort in his chest; the pain of estrangement from his daughter that Milk of Magnesia couldn't shift. The Third World spectacles slid down his nose and fell to the floor, and as he picked them up a tiny screw rolled out and the tortoiseshell leg came away in his hand. Roy groped another pair with heavy black frames from the pile and put them on. The room lurched at him, furniture, window glass and frame and the trees outside zooming into his face as he turned his head. He sat down, seasick, in a huge armchair.

When the nausea passed Roy became aware of a thick grey cobweb slowly spiralling from the lightshade in the centre of the ceiling, saw that the shade itself, which he remembered as maroon, was furred by dust and trimmed with dead woolly bear caterpillars, and that loops and swags of cobweb garlanded the picture rails, tags of sellotape marked Christmases past and a balloon had perished and melted long ago, and soot and dust had drifted undisturbed into every cornice and embossment of the anaglypta wallpaper. Curled, yellowing leaflets and pamphlets and press-cuttings ringed with coffee stains were all about him, a pile of grubby laundry on the stained sofa, something nasty on the sleeve of the Live Aid record, unplayed because they had nothing on which to play it; his knees were blue mountains with a growth of Stumpy's fur, and downy featherlets caught in a dried-up stream of Bovril. Then his ankles! Roy could not believe the knobs and nodules below the fringe of black-grey foliage, the wormcasts and bits of dead elastic, the anatomical red and blue threads and purple starbursts. 'These aren't my feet,' he said. 'Some old man has made off with Roy Rowley's feet while he wasn't looking and dumped these on me.'

Other people's babies – that's my life.
Mother to do-ozens but nobody's wife!

Roy heard a voice singing at the front door and then a key in the lock, and then a yoo-hoo and then some old girl was in the room shrugging off a sulphurous yellow coat banded with silver, and waving a virulent green lollipop, like a traffic light on a stick, under his nose.

'Yum yum, piggy's bum, you can't have none,' she taunted in imitation of a child's voice, popping the green glassy ball into her mouth, with the stick protruding. She crunched glass and glooped the ball out with a pop.

'One of my little boyfwends gave it to me,' she lisped, and started to sing 'We are the Lollipop League' like an overgrown Munchkin, then stopped. Roy was staring at the great, bobbly pink and grey diamonds on her jumper, the greasy grey elf-locks on her shoulders. It was he who had made her promise never to cut her hair short – how long ago had that been?

'Why are you staring at me like that? You look as if you've seen a ghost – or have I got something on my face?'

'No – not really. I've seen it advertised in the paper, you can get some shampoo-stuff – I mean a gadget for shaving sweaters. It removes all the pills and bobbles – it brings them up like new . . .'

'What pills and bobbles? What are you talking about now? What does?' He had made her feel silly about the lollipop.

'This gizmo I was telling you about.'

All her pleasure in the sweet was gone.

'I reckon it's you who could do with a shave,' she said and waddled – no, this was his beloved Muriel – walked out of the room.

'Mummy,' he called after her.

'I'm going to see about Barney's tea.'

Roy walked over to the mirror which hung on a chain on the wall above the cluttered mantelpiece and breathed on it and rubbed a clear patch on its clouded glass. Grey quills were breaking the surface of his skin and there was an untidy tuft halfway down his neck; he was scrawny and granular, his nose was pitted like a pumice stone; and hadn't he seen an ad for another gadget too, for trimming the ears and nose?

'I look a disgrace,' he observed wonderingly. 'A tramp. A scare-crow in a pigsty – that I thought was a palace.' It was like some fairy-tale featuring a swineherd or a simpleton who, ungrateful for his sudden riches, found himself back in his squalid hut; but was the world he saw through the black glasses a distortion, or reality to which he had been blind?

'Getting vain in our old age, are we?' Muriel, good humour evidently restored, had returned. 'When you've finished titivating yourself, I've brought you a cup of tea.'

A hand like a cracked gardening glove seamed with earth was thrusting a pink mug·at him; he saw the stained chip on its lip and the tea oozing through the crack that ran down its side.

'Ta muchly, love,' he said weakly, lowering himself carefully on to the chair.

'You look different,' commented Muriel.

So do you, he thought.

'I can't put my finger on it.'

She studied him, her great face in cruel close-up going from side to side. Roy was beginning to get a headache. Muriel had slipped her feet into a pair of pompommed mules and the rosehip-scarlet dabs of varnish which time had pushed to the tips of her big toenails marked the end of summer.

'When I've had this, I'd better get the rest of those Save Our Hospital leaflets through some more doors,' he said. 'Shouldn't take too long. What are we having for supper?'

Muriel's mouth concertinaed in hurt wrinkles. Friday night was Dial-A-Pizza and early-to-bed night; a bottle of Black Tower was chilling in the fridge above the owl food.

'Is there any aspirin, love? I think I'm getting one of my heads.'

Muriel dipped into her pockets and tore off a strip of Aspro. He swallowed two tablets the size of extra-strong peppermints. By the time Roy was walking back up Hollydale, his leaflets distributed by lamplight without the aid of spectacles, his head was clear.

'I've got a bone to pick with you!'

It was Mr Wood shouting from the doorway of forty-three. Roy hurried across, surprised and pleased to see the old boy home and on his feet but guilty that he hadn't telephoned the hospital to enquire. Walter Wood's face was purple in the porchlight and he was gesticulating at a padded neck brace which held his head erect.

'I hold you responsible for this!' he was shouting.

'Me?'

The french letter slithered into Roy's mind.

'Me?' Roy repeated. Not guilty, surely?

'Yes you! If you and your do-gooding wife hadn't been so keen to bundle us off to the knacker's yard – we were just a bit shaken, getting our breaths back – and you might advise your better half to lay off the vindaloo if she's going to make a habit of giving the so-called kiss of life! They kept us lying on trolleys in the corridor for hours, like a pair of salt cod – couldn't even go to the toilet. I got such a crick in my neck they had to issue me with this!' he thumped his surgical collar. 'The wife's got one too. She's worse off than I am because they had to commandeer a trolley from the kitchen for her. She's up in the bathroom now, trying to wash the smell of soup and custard out of her hair. I doubt she'll ever look a cooked dinner in the face again.'

He pointed to the frosted bathroom window and Roy became aware of the sound of water gurgling down the drainpipe.

'You and your everlasting charity! You want to come down to earth and do something about that front garden of yours, it's a disgrace to the street! You're living in Cloud-Cuckoo-Land, my friend!'

A Save Our Hospital leaflet was flung as Roy retreated, and was sucked back into the purple vortex of Walter Wood's rage, plastering itself across his face.

Indoors, having slunk through the fluffy Michaelmas daisy seed-heads of his shamed garden, Roy resolved to try a different pair of spectacles, but the multi-eyed heap of insects was gone.

'The Brownies came for them while you were out,' Muriel told him.

A fey image of little folk batting at the window with tiny hands and fleeing with their haul through the falling leaves startled him. I'd better watch my denture in case the Tooth Fairy gets any ideas, he thought, but said that he was going to have a quick bath before the pizzas came. If the Rowleys had been less charitable, a visit to the optician would have been taken for granted; as finances stood, Roy decided to buy a pair off the peg at the chemist as soon as he had time. He put on the black-framed glasses to go upstairs and felt at once the strain as his eyes were pulled towards the huge lenses, and the giant staircase reared in front of him.

He surveyed the bathroom – a locker room after the worst rugby team in the league had departed to relegation, he thought, as he picked at the guano of owl droppings and toothpaste on the mirror. Once immersed with antiseptic Radox emeralds dissolving around him, he felt better, lifted the dripping sponge, squeezed it over his head and began to sing, gruffly:

> I believe for every drop of rain that falls,
> A flower grows.
> I believe that somewhere in the darkest night
> A candle glows . . .
> Every time I see a newborn baby die . . .

Good God! He started again.

Every time I hear a newborn baby cry,
Or touch a leaf, or see the sky –
Then I know why
I believe.

Roy Rowley with a packet of seeds and a bundle of gardening tools versus desert sands unfertilised by innumerable millions of bones.

'I believe that every time I take a bath,
A river dries.
I believe . . . NO!
I believe that Someone in that Great Somewhere hears – how absurd!'

Terrified, he stuffed the sponge into his mouth.

'Never mind, lovey, there's always next Friday,' Muriel consoled him in bed. 'It happens, or doesn't if you get my meaning, to the best of men at times.'

How would she know? Roy wondered bitterly. Barney's great glassy yellow eyes winked lewdly from the top of the wardrobe. Stumpy was sniffing a circle of pepperoni stuck to the lid of the box beside the bed.

'He likes it but it doesn't like him!' Muriel informed Roy.

'I know.'

Roy woke late with a headache and the fleeing remnants of a dream in which he and Muriel were being turned down as foster parents. The smell of frying bacon curled round his nose and he could hear Muriel's and Barney's muted voices.

Tu-whit, tu-whoo – a merry note, while greasy Joan doth keel the pot, he thought.

When he barged into the kitchen wearing the glasses the phone rang. Sidestepping Muriel's morning kiss, Roy picked it up.

'Yes?'

'Oh. Um, I must've got the wrong number. I thought this was the Helpline . . .'

'It is. Got a problem ringing helplines have you, pal? Well, try a bit of aversion therapy – piss off! There that should put you off wasting your own time and everybody else's!'

Muriel was open-mouthed with a rasher sliding from the fork suspended in her hand. Roy removed the spectacles; he had seen that the kitchen, the heart of the home, was splattered with the grease of thousands of marital breakfasts, and shoals of salmonella swam upstream to mate and lay their eggs. Anxiety from his oneiric ordeal crackled in static electricity from the viscose stripes of his dressing gown, caused horripilation of the pyjama-ed limbs, itching of the feet in furry socks and irritation of the scalp. He and Muriel had been unpleasantly accused, judged, condemned in his dream, he remembered with shock that he had been sentenced to some kind of heavy-labouring Community Service for which he had been late, miles away, attempting to read the time on somebody's large upside-down watch. He had been trying to conceal his disgrace from Petula, desperate not to lose her respect, so that she might still turn to him as a daughter to a father. Owl's beak chomped unspeakable morsels, Muriel departed in yellow to take a partially-sighted friend shopping, Saturday got under way.

He had to put the glasses on to examine the pile of post. The fowls of the air, the fish and mammals of the sea, the North Sea itself, besought Roy Rowley of Hollydale Road to save them. An ancient Eastern European face under a headscarf howled in grief and told Roy that winter was coming and there was no end to the killing and no food and no shelter from the snow. Roy thrust all their pleadings into the breadbin. Nothing of course from Petula. Stumpy was importuning for a second breakfast. As Roy spooned a lump of catfood into his bowl, some slithered over his hand. It felt curiously warm to the touch although the tin was almost at its sell-by date. The red buttocks of a tomato squatting on a saucer caught his eye. Roy sliced and ate it quickly, for if his new vision were to encompass lascivious thoughts towards fruit and veg he was lost. He could see Petula in a pink dress standing by the piano in a church hall piping 'Jesus bids us shine with a pure clear light, like a little candle burning in the night. In this world of darkness, we must shine. You in your small corner, and I in mine.' There was a ten-bob note in her heart-shaped pocket, but it had been worth it to hear the collective 'Aaah' when she skipped on to the stage.

There was no possibility of a visit to the chemist that day. The

Mini Fun Run took over entirely. 'Why do they do it?' Roy questioned in the autumnal park, stopwatch in hand, as agonised red and purple thighs juddered past him, and breasts were thrown about in coloured vests. 'The world need never have known. Whatever happened to feminine mystique?'

To his left an aerobics class in very silly costumes was performing a display. How sad to think of them entering sports shops to purchase those garments and then, in the privacy of their own homes, dressing up in those clinging silver suits under magenta bathing costumes, and matching headbands and wristlets, to step on and off jogging machines and hone their muscles on mailorder Abdomenisers and Thighmasters. A police dog was trying to rip the padded arm off an officer disguised as a criminal in a rival attraction; sales of curried goat and rice, burgers, kebabs and Muriel's Rice Krispie cakes were steady; the event was a success even though the mini hot-air balloon Roy had booked let him down. Muriel, in the grey livery of the St John Ambulance Brigade was tending to a bungee jumper who had come to grief. Soon be Guy Fawkes, and she'd be on the Front Line again. Roy was booked for the Scouts' Sausage Sizzle. Suddenly he had no taste for it. He'd rather just stay indoors, worrying about other people's pets.

At the last moment, that evening, Muriel felt that she could not face the rehabilitation of Barney, and Roy set out alone on his bicycle with the owl in a duffel bag and an ersatz Tupperware box of bits and pieces that were to be scattered around the new habitat.

'I'll just stay here and have a good 'owl,' Muriel had told him, 'I only hope he gets acclimatised before Bonfire Night,' and bravely waved a scrunched Kleenex as he pedalled away. She had sent her annual letter to the local paper reminding people to check their bonfires for slumbering hedgehogs.

'He was out of that duffel bag like a cork from a bottle, Mummy, was our boy. I caught hold of him for a moment and he looked me right in the eye as if to say, "Thank you, Uncle Roy and Aunty Muriel, for having me, but I'm an endangered species and it's up to me now to do my bit in the conservation and breeding stakes." I tossed him gently into the air and he took to it like – a duck to water! I don't mind admitting, Mummy, I was quite moved – that poem, you know, "Everyone suddenly burst out singing", came into my mind when I saw him rise above the treetops, silhouetted against the crescent moon.'

'What's that tapping sound? That tap tap tap on the window?' Muriel said sharply.

It was a strand of jasmine, come loose from its pin.

Then he saw that she had all Petula's old photos out, the baby pictures and school portraits and holiday snaps.

That night Roy couldn't sleep. 'Do-Gooders', Walter Wood had called them, tarnishing the Hearts of Gold Award. I do try to do good, he thought, is that so wrong? Then he was in the day room of the Sunshine Ward at the threatened hospital, tickling the yellowed ivories of the old joanna: 'The way you wear your hat, the way you sip your tea . . . the memory of all that . . . no, no, they can't take that away from me . . .' and he looked around his captive audience, hatless and uncomprehending, and at the spouted feeding cup from which an old boy sucked his tea and knew that, yes, they could take everything away.

If they took away his charity work, if he were to stop running from errand of mercy to good deed and stand still, what would Roy Rowley be? An empty tracksuit filled with air? He snuggled up to Muriel's back and his bony fingers rested on gently rising and falling pneumatic flesh, aware of her dedicated, pledged-for-donation organs working a quiet night-shift. But what if that pump which drove them should suddenly stop and he feel no movement under his terrified hand?

Sunday, and an urban cockerel, gardens away, dissolved brick and asphalt in the morning mist as Roy lay in bed, reluctant to leave its safety, and took him back to the muddy green rural outskirts of Orpington of his boyhood. Sometimes in late autumn the birds sing as if they were on the verge of spring rather than winter, and Roy listened dully to their songs thinking about the city built in the air by the birds, where Walter Wood had accused him of living. If only. He could see, on the chair, an empty blue-grey nylon harness and a deflated pair of Y-fronts. O black lace and shiny ribboned rayon and white cotton, when that Lloyd Loom linen basket with the glazed lid was new! The sheets in which he lay, once yellow, had come, like the fibreglass curtains, from Brentford Nylons in the days when he and Muriel had thought it posh, when they had paused for a moment each time they entered the bedroom to admire that flounced valance and the kidney-shaped dressing table's matching skirt. He itched, and longed for the touch and scent of sun-and-wind-dried cotton. Soon he must face the day through those dystopic lenses.

He was not going to church this morning, although Muriel was, having a standing arrangement to push one of the old girls from Selsdon Court, the sheltered accommodation to which she had prematurely consigned the Woods. Roy would be on parade in a couple of weeks, on Remembrance Sunday, in his Rover Scouts uniform, and Walter Wood would be there in his medals. Roy had been demobbed undecorated from his National Service. His memories were of boils on the neck and skin chafed to a raw rash by khaki, and blisters. Walter Wood's protest as he was carried away to the ambulance came back to Roy as he shaved – the roll call of Great War battles. Roy dreaded the service at the war memorial now; feared that the fallen might look down on those they had died to defend and reckon their sacrifice futile: Fall in, you rusty tins of Andrews with your lids jammed half-open in an eternal grin; Present Arms, you broken-handled verdigrised half-spoons and clogged-up combs; To the left, wheel!, Optrex eyebaths and tubigrips and old blue unopened rolls of bandage. Atten-shun Germolene and Brolene and haemorrhoid cream and Dentu-Creme, the packet of razor blades rotted to the shelf, the nest of Kirbigrips, the melted square of Ex-lax, the cloudy dregs of Aqua-Velva.

He went to breakfast to find that some small girls had brought Muriel an injured woodpigeon in a box. She handed Roy a plate of bacon, eggs and beans. She was dressed for church in a turquoise leisure suit. A deckle-edged snapshot of his parents was flashed past his eyes: Mother in a grey costume with white gloves, Father in pinstripes, both wearing hats. He acknowledged his own Sunday attire, a clownish suit which would have baffled them and cost them about a month's wages.

'I'll pop Woody in the old rabbit hutch when I go out,' she said.

'We should call him Herman or Guthrie,' said Roy, fighting his vision of humankind as worth no more than the contents of its collective bathroom cabinet, the grey underwear hiding under its bright uniforms. Muriel smiled.

'Or Allen,' he added.

'Ooh no! You won't forget the boot sale, will you lovey?' Roy could feel the dull pain of Petula's loss as he ate, and stifled a burp in his kitchen-roll serviette.

'Pardon me for being rude, it was not me, it was my food,' he said mechanically.

The bare twiggy branches of the trees stuck up in witches' brooms as Roy walked down the road, the fallen leaves of a magnolia grandiflora lay like bits of brown leather; old shoes. A van was parking in the forecourt of the council estate and two masked men in yellow protective clothing got out carrying fumigating equipment. There was a mattress lying on top of a heap of rags and Roy saw, and recoiled from, had to look again in hopeful disbelief then horror, the sodden outline of what had once been a human being rotted to the stained ticking. Those men in yellow; they and their kind were the ones who really knew how the world worked, and kept it going. He stood, what else could he do, a well-intentioned bloke in an anorak; a drone. And of course they, those yellow ones, were the most respected and rewarded members of the community for what they did, weren't they? Like hell they were.

At the car boot he delivered his magazines and sundry other goods and strolled round the playground with a notion of picking up a better pair of glasses, and stopped in front of a blanket on the ground. It was a thin tartan car rug and the goods displayed were a baby's dummy, two feeding bottles with perished teats, a splayed-out wire and nylon bottle brush, some Anne French cleansing milk, two pairs of pop-sox in unopened packs, a pair of jeans and a tube of coloured bath pearls. Roy paid for the bath pearls with a five-pound note, guessing the young woman would be unable to change it. Three children with purple smudges under their eyes and the necks of baby birds watched silently.

'Don't worry about it. Some other time,' he said and hurried away blushing to the roots of his tufty hair, with the bath pearls in his hand. Petula used to like the red ones; when she was little she would burst one and squash it against her arm or leg in the bath, and then scream, 'Help! Help! I've cut myself really badly!' and bring Mummy and Daddy rushing in panic. They fell for it every time.

'Royston!' the matey misnomer caught him as he made for the exit, past a selection of plastic balls for dispensing liquid detergent, a battered Cluedo, a doll in a dingy knitted dress, and a blur of similar merchandise. Roy went over to the stall where an old acquaint-ance, Arnie, was doing a brisk trade in Christmas wrapping paper, counterfeit French perfume and watches.

'Like the bins,' said Arnie, indicating Roy's glasses. 'Very high-profile executive whizz-kid.'

You wouldn't if you could see the magnification of your face, Roy thought. 'A temporary expedient,' he said. 'I don't think they're quite me.'

'Pathetic, isn't it, what some people have the nerve to try to flog. It's an insult really.' Arnie nodded at the plastic balls, which the vendor was piling into a pyramid, to increase their allure. Roy could only agree.

At home, after telephoning its founder to regret that he must renounce his commitment to Helpline Helpline, and hearing that the service had been discontinued, Roy wandered into the back garden. He was sitting hunched on the old swing, kicking a half-buried tambourine or timbrel, sunk under a wodge of once-sprouted birdseed. A relic of Petula's brief post-punk stint as a Salvation Army Songster.

'You look like a garden gnome sitting there.'

'Petula!'

'Hello, Dad. I like the face furniture.'

Roy wrenched off the glasses. He did not want to see Petula through them, and they had misted up besides.

'Pet. My little Pet. Is it really you? Let me look at you.'

He was hugging her so tightly that he could see nothing, but smelled the fruity tang of her shining hair.

'What's in the hutch this time?' she asked. 'Oh, it's a wood-pigeon. Hello, Woody. Remember that time we made the *Blue*

Peter bird pudding, Dad? Yuk, it was 'orrible, wasn't it? I was really sick. Still, I suppose we shouldn't have eaten it all ourselves. Mum went spare. Where is she, by the way, church? Shouldn't you be getting the dinner ready? I'll give you a hand. It's freezing out here. Can we go in and have some coffee? And I must put these flowers in water.'

'I can't wait to see your mother's face when she walks in!' said Roy, in the kitchen, groping at the coffee.

'Put your specs on,' advised Petula.

'No, I'm better without them. They're the wrong prescription. They're giving me gyp.'

'Try these.'

Petula took a rhinestone butterfly-winged pair from her bag. 'I don't need them – they're from my fifties period. Found them at a car boot,' she said. Her father's daughter.

They took their coffee into the front room.

'What a tip,' said Petula affectionately. She hooked the glasses over Roy's ears before sweeping aside a box of recycled envelopes and Christmas gift catalogues and sitting down. 'They suit you. How are they?'

'Perfect. They're brilliant – might have been made for me. Everything's right in focus. Marvellous! Just the ticket. Let me look at you properly.'

He saw a striking young woman in her thirties, with dark feathered hair and big silver ear-rings, a bright patterned chunky sweater above black leggings and red boots.

'A sight for sore eyes,' he said.

He studied himself in the mirror through the sparkling upswept frames, and wondered if he might introduce a little tasteful drag into his next entertainment. Then he saw that Petula had arranged a bunch of red carnations in a vase, and forbore to remind her that women in Colombia gave their fingers, even their lives, to the cultivation of those scentless blooms that deck our garage forecourts and corner shops.

Walter Wood passed the window, and shook a fist.

'We had a bit of a misunderstanding –' Roy started to explain in unhappy embarrassment as the plastic carriers fluttered in the tree outside.

'Miserable old scrote. The thing is, Dad, I want to come home. I've left Barrington. And I've had it up to here with the Witnesses – all that dragging round doorsteps flogging *AWAKE!* and other boring literature, honestly I might just as well have stayed at home with your interminable Flag Days! I was bored to sobs after a fortnight.' She began to sing, to the tune of 'Born to Lose' – 'Bored to sobs, I've lived my life in vain. Every dream has only brought me pain. All my life, I've always been so blue. Bored to sobs, And now I'm bo-ored with you! Not you, Daddy. I know I've disappointed you in the past – I couldn't be cute like Petula Clark or develop an adult larynx like Julie Andrews, but I'll make you proud of me one day.'

'Darling, I've always been so proud – when we went out with you in your little coat, and your doll's pram, and people used to say "she's just like a little doll," and I was as proud as a peacock when your mother brought you down to the bus garage to meet me and I used to show you off to all my mates – and later –'

He had been going to say that he loved her in all her reincarnations and admired her independence of spirit but she cut in defensively with, 'It wasn't easy for me either, you know, you and Mum always being so involved in other people's problems. Sometimes I used to think that you could only relate to someone if they were disabled in some way – sorry, Stumpy, no offence. I had fantasies about wheelchairs and kidney machines. I was in therapy for a while – well it was group I went to – but I had to leave when it transpired that I was the only person there who hadn't been abused by her father. Amazing how it came back to them one by one. God, it was embarrassing – I felt so inferior. I must have been a singularly unattractive kid . . . sorry, Dad, only kidding – I never fancied you either. Joke. Anyway, we'd better rattle those pots and pans, Mum'll be home any minute, even allowing for coffee in the crypt. "What's the recipe today, Jim?" Pigeon pie? Only kidding.'

Tears, laughter and lunch coming to an end, Woody who had joined the party perking up in his box, Friday night's white wine quaffed, Muriel posed the question that Roy had not liked to put.

'Have you had any thoughts of what you might do next, Pet? Careerwise, I mean?'

'Well, I had thought of becoming a therapist. I read somewhere that any screwed-up, pathetic inadequate with no qualifications can set themselves up, so I thought – that's for me! I could use the front room – it would be money for jam. Then again, I thought I might have a baby. Sometime around next March the first seems like as good a time as any . . .'

'Oh . . . Pet!'

Petula looked her mother straight in the eye.

'I'm afraid I must warn you, Mummy, that there's a fifty per cent chance that the baby will be dyslexic – it runs in Barrington's family.'

'Oh, the poor little mite! We must do everything – hang on, I've got a leaflet somewhere . . .'

Petula settled back comfortably against the cushion Roy had just placed at her back and held out her cup for more coffee.

Late that afternoon as Roy set out on his bike to fetch some things that Petula had forgotten to bring, he saw that as the light faded, the western sky was white above layers of cloud, pale grey and dark grey, barred like cuckoos' wings, and he rode on towards them, the reflective strips on his pedals spinning starry arcs from his feet in the gathering dusk.

The Laughing Academy

After he had closed the door of his mother's flat for the last time McCloud took a taxi to Glasgow Airport to catch the shuttle back to London. The driver turned his head and said through the metal grille, 'I know you. You used to be that, ehh . . .' he broke off, not just because he couldn't remember the name but because the burly blond man in the back had his head in his hands and was greeting like a wean, or a boxer who had just lost a fight and knows it was his last. He concentrated on getting through the rush-hour traffic but when a hold-up forced them to a crawl, a glance in the mirror showed that the blond curls were tarnished and the cashmere coat had seen better days. As the smell of whisky filtered through, he recognised his passenger as Vincent McCloud the singer.

Looks like the end of the road for you, pal, he thought. The end of the pier. Re-runs of ancient *Celebrity Squares*, and guesting on some fellow fallen star's *This Is Your Life*; he could see it all, the blazers and slacks and brave Dentu-Creme smiles and jokes about Bernard Delfont and the golf course, that only the old cronies in their ill-fitting toupees would get. Like veterans at the Cenotaph they were, their ranks a little thinner every year. That mandatory bit of business they all did, the bear-hugging, backslapping, look-at-you-you-old-rascal, isn't-he-wonderful-ladies-and-gentlemen finger-pointing routine – as if the milked applause could drown the tinkle of coloured light bulbs popping one by one against the darkness and the desolate swishing of the sea. As the taxi driver pondered the intrinsic sadness of English showbiz, he thought he remembered that McCloud had been in some bother. Fiddling the taxman, if he minded right. They were all at it.

McCloud was trying not to remember. He'd stood at his mother's bed in the ward, slapping the long thick envelope whose contents brought information about a *Reader's Digest* Grand Prize Draw that her eyes were too dim to read.

'Made it, Ma! Top of the world! This is it, the big yin! A recording contract and an American tour!'

He didn't want to recall all those black and white movies they'd watched together on the television, the smiles and tears of two-bit hoofers and over-the-hill vaudevillians and burlesque queens who were told, 'You'll never play the Palace,' and did. His mother had thought he'd be another Kenneth McKellar.

'That's you, Jimmy.'

McCloud realised that the cab was standing at the airport and the driver was waiting to be paid. Old habits die hard, and McCloud was grateful that the man had failed to recognise him and had not proved to be of a philosophical bent. He gave him a handsome tip.

'Enjoy your flight!' the cabbie called out after him as McCloud went through the door carrying a heavy suitcase of his mother's things.

On his way to the plane McCloud bought a newspaper, a box of Edinburgh rock and a tartan tin of Soor Plooms, acidic boiled sweets which he used to buy in a paper poke when he was a boy. He felt like a tourist. There was nobody left in Scotland for him now.

'Do you mind?' said an indignant English voice.

It seemed he had barged into someone. He glowered. In his heart he had been swinging his fist into the treacherous features of his former manager, Delves Winthrop, that nose divided into two fat garlic cloves at the tip and the chin with the dark dimple that the razor couldn't penetrate.

'Don't be bitter, Vinny,' Delves had counselled him on the telephone after the trial. 'That's showbiz – you win some, you lose some. Swings and roundabouts. And you know what they say, no publicity is bad publicity . . .'

In that, as in his management of McCloud's career, Delves had been wrong. The Sunday paper which had expressed interest in McCloud's story had gone cold on the idea, and his appearance on *Wogan* had been cancelled at the last minute. Box Office Poison. McCloud, branded more fool than knave, had narrowly escaped prison and bankruptcy, and had – the taxi driver's surmise had been correct – a guest appearance on a forgotten comedian's *This*

Is Your Life to look forward to, and a one-night stand at the De La Warr Pavilion, Bexhill-on-Sea. The small amount of money he'd managed to hold on to was diminishing at a frightening rate.

While McCloud was homing through the gloaming to a flat with rusting green aluminium windows in a vast block in Streatham, Delves was soaking up the sun on the Costa del Crime with some bikinied floozie. McCloud hoped it would snow on them. Bitter? You bet Vinny was bitter. He sat on the plane contemplating the English seaside in February, his heart a rotting oyster marinated in brackish sea-water. Wormwood and gall, sloes, aloes, lemons were not as bitter. His teeth were set on edge as if by sour green plums. It came to him that Delves Winthrop owned a house on the south coast, not a million miles away from Bexhill.

At Heathrow he lit a cigarette, great for a singer's throat, and telephoned his former wife, Roberta. She was friendly enough at first, and then he lost it.

'Is either of the weans with you? I'd like a word.'

'The weans? What is this? Sorting out your mother's things, the perfect excuse to get legless and sentimental, eh Vinny? I might have known you'd come back lapsing into the Doric. I'm glad *we* flew straight back after the funeral.'

'Is Catriona there, or Craig? Put them on, I've a right to speak to them. I'm their father, as far as I know.'

'Ach, away'n bile yer heid, Tammy Troot!' Roberta put the phone down.

Tongue like a rusty razor blade, she'd always had it, since they'd met when he'd been a Redcoat at Butlins in Ayr, and she a holiday-maker hanging round the shows, Frank Codona's funfair it was, thinking herself in love with the greasy boy who worked the waltzer. The Billy Bigelow of Barassie. Well, at least he hadn't gone round to her house, as he'd half intended, the emissary from the Land O' Cakes standing on the doorstep in a tartan scarf to match his breath, with sweeties for his twenty-seven- and twenty-eight-year-olds, the door opened by Roberta's husband. Of course he knew they'd left home years ago. He'd rung on the off chance that one of them might be there. They'd always been closer to their mother.

McCloud let himself into his stale and dusty fourth-floor flat and found two messages waiting on his machine, the first from his daughter Catriona sending love, the second from Stacey, a young dancer he'd been seeing for the past six months.

'Hiya darling, guess what? I got the job!!! Knew you'd be proud of me. Listen babes, we leave on Wednesday so I've got masses to get ready. Oh, hope everything went OK and you're not feeling blue. You know I'd be with you if I could. Call you later. Love you.'

'Dazzle Them at Sea' the ad in the *Stage* had read. Royal Caribbean Cruises. He'd spoken to Stacey yesterday on the phone, just catching her before she trotted off to the audition at the Pineapple Studios in Covent Garden. He could tell from her voice, which sounded as if it were transmitted over miles of ocean by a ship's telephone, that in her heart she was already hoofing under sequined tropical stars.

Her neon-red words hung in the air, then faded as grey silence drifted and extinguished them.

McCloud stowed the bag of his mother's things on top of the wardrobe, feeling guilty at leaving them there but knowing it would be some time before he could bear to look at them. There were objects in that bag he had known all his life, pieces that were older then he was. Desolation suffused him as he stood on the strip of rented carpet. With Mother gone, nobody would know who he really was ever again.

He found the copy of the *Stage* and read the ad again. Stacey had joined the company of Strong Female Dancers who Sing Well. McCloud could testify to her strength, he thought, but reserved judgement on the singing.

He sat in the living room with framed and unframed posters and playbills stacked against the wall, a glass of whisky in his hand, studying the Directory, the gallery of eccentrics like himself who lived on hope and disappointment: 'Look at me!' they begged. 'Let me entertain you!' Clowns, acrobats, stilt-walkers, magicians, belly-dancers, once-famous pop groups, one-hit wonders, reincarnated George Formbys still cleaning windows, fire-eaters, Hilarious Hypnotists, Glenn Millers swinging yet and the Dagenham Girl Pipers defying time. Then there were the

Look-alikes, fated to impersonate the famous, and those whose tragedy lay in a true or imagined resemblance to somebody so faded or obscure that it was inconceivable that the most desperate supermarket manager or stag-night would dream of hiring them. McCloud read on, keeping at bay with little sips of whisky the thought that his own face would soon be grinning desperately there, until he came to the Apartments column.

'Sunny room in friendly Hastings house. Long or short stay. Full English breakfast, evening meal available. Owner in the profession.'

A sunny room in February? McCloud was tempted, although there were three weeks to go before his Bexhill booking. The lime-green fluorescent flyers piled on the table filled him with fear every time they caught his eye, and he worried that his accompanist was going to let him down. The last time he'd seen Joe Ogilvy in the Pizza Express in Dean Street, the boiled blue yolks of his eyes and red-threaded filaments in the whites had not inspired confidence. He could go down and case the joint, get a bit of sea air. He put the thought of Sherry Winthrop, Delves's crazy wife, out of his mind, and dialled the number.

However, as he drove down the following morning, crawling along in the old red Cavalier with a windscreen starred by sleet, and Melody Radio, the taxi-drivers' friend, buzzing through the faulty speaker, he imagined Delves's house, to which he had never been invited. Neither had anybody else as far as he knew. It was common knowledge, among those who knew Delves had a wife, that Sherry had been in the bin and she was never allowed to come to London or to be seen in public. She had been Delves's PA, but now he was ashamed of her. She was younger than Delves, of course, and had been quite lively once. In McCloud's mind's eye the Sussex house was tile-hung, its old bricks mellowed with lichen and moss, standing in a sheltered walled garden with a prospect of the sea, and grey-green branches of the southernwood which gave it its name half-hiding the stone toadstools either side of its five-barred gate.

If you listened to Melody Radio, you'd think that love were all, that the world was full of people falling in love and the sky raining cupid's little arrows. And McCloud liked gutsy songs sung from the heart by people who'd been through the mill, that made you feel life was worth living despite everything. Take the rhinestone cowboy singing now, for example, he hadn't a hope in hell of riding a horse in that star-spangled rodeo, but there he was with his subway token and dollar in his shoe, bloody but unbowed. Tragic if you thought about his future, but it cheered you up, the song. It was not in McCloud's repertoire, he was expected to wester home via the low road to Mairi's wedding and his ain folk, but he sang along lustily.

His spirits lifted as he left London's suburbs behind. 'Seagull House, Rock-A-Nore Road, Hastings'; the address had a carefree, striped-candy, rock-a-bye, holiday look about it, and he felt almost as if he were going on holiday with a painted tin spade and pail. The memory of his mother, holding her dress bunched above her bare knees, laughing and running back from the frill of foam at the tide's edge, pulling him with her, was more bittersweet than painful, and he resolved to remember only happy times. That was the best he could do for her now. She had told him a poem about fairies who 'live on crispy pancakes of yellow tide-foam', and he'd tried to remember it for his own children, Catriona and Craig, with their little legs, paddling in their wee stripy pants. Catriona worked in a building society now, and had assured him that it had been for the best, really, that she'd had to leave the Arts Educational Trust when he couldn't find the fees. Craig hadn't found his niche yet and was employed on a casual basis behind the scenes at the National. Great kids, the pair of them. McCloud was not ready yet to admit that whatever he had done as a father was done for good or ill and he was now peripheral to their lives, and the thought of his little girl out in the dark in a dangerous city was too painful to dwell on. He was eager to hit the coast, and so hungry that he could have eaten a pile of those crispy pancakes.

Sherry Winthrop stood at the lounge window of the 1930s bungalow, 'Southernwood'. Flanked by two tall dogs, in her pale-green fluted nightdress with her short auburn hair, she might have been a figurine of the period. She was watching the sails of the model windmill on the lawn whirling and whirling in the icy wind, and old gnomes skulking under the shivering bushes. Beyond the front garden's high chain-link fence was a tangle of sloes and briars on a stretch of frostbitten cliff top, narrower every year as boulders of chalk broke off and fell, and beyond that, the sea. A hand on each Dobermann's head, she stood, her mind whirring as purposely as the windmill's sails in the crashing sound of the waves. At length, knowing that she must get dressed and take Duke and Prince for a run, she went to make a cup of coffee. The kitchen, modernised by previous owners and untouched since, was decorated and furnished in late-fifties Contemporary style. Sherry would have preferred to go back to bed and lose herself in the murder mystery she was reading but she felt guilty about the dogs' dull lives with her and would force herself for their sakes. Was she not afraid, living alone as she did, to read, late into the night, those gruesome accounts of the fates of solitary women? The dogs were her guards, although sometimes she imagined they might tire of their hostage and kill her, and sometimes she felt it would be almost a relief when the actual murderer turned up at last. There was never one around when you needed him, she had learned. Like plumbers. She just hoped that when he did show up he'd only drug the dogs, not hurt them, and it would be quick and the contents of her stomach not too embarrassing at the autopsy. Had Sherry cared to watch them, her husband's stack of videos would have shown her deeds done to women and children beyond her worst nightmares.

She was conscious of the thin skin of her ankles and her bare feet as she unlocked the back door and let the dogs into the garden. There was a freezer packed with shins and shanks and plastic bags of meat in the garage. Crime novels apart, Sherry was quite partial to stories about nobby people who were always cutting up the dogs' meat and visiting rectors with worn carpets in their studies, and American fiction where they drank orange juice and black coffee in kitchens with very white surfaces.

The time she had needed a murderer most was after she'd lost the baby in an early miscarriage. Delves hadn't wanted children anyway, so he didn't care, and she'd ended up in the bin. It had taken her years to get off the tranquillisers but she was all right now, just half-dead. Sometimes, for no reason, she'd get a peculiar smell in her nose, a sort of stale amyl-nitratey whiff, a sniff of sad, sour institutional air or a thick meaty odour that frightened her. She had woken with it this morning, a taint in the air that made her afraid to open her wardrobe lest she find it full of stained dressing gowns.

She would have done something about her life ages ago, if it hadn't been for the dogs. When Delves had brought them home as svelte one-year-olds, they had spied on her and reported her every movement to Delves on portable telephones hidden in their leather muzzles, but Delves had lost all interest in her long since and her relationship with Duke and Prince was much better. It was just that it would be impossible to leave with two great Dobermanns in tow, or towing her. Delves had no wish to remarry – why should he when there was always some girl stupid enough to give him what he wanted – and he said it was cheaper to keep her than divorce her.

There was nothing of the thirties figurine about her when, in boots and padded jacket, she crunched the gravel path past 'Spindrift', 'South Wind', 'Trade Winds', 'Kittiwakes' and 'Miramar', with Duke and Prince setting off the dogs in each bungalow in turn.

It was three o'clock when McCloud, having found a parking space, walked up the steep path, through wintry plants on either side and past a rockery where snowdrops bloomed among flints and shells, and rang the bell of Seagull House. It was tall, painted grey with white windows, a deeper grey door, bare wistaria stems, and a gull shrieking from one of the chimneys. He felt some trepidation now, wishing he'd checked into an anonymous B and B or a sleazy hotel with a scumbag who didn't know him from Adam behind the desk. His fears proved groundless. The ageing Phil Everly look-alike who opened the door showed no sign of recognition. Later, McCloud would learn that he was the remaining half of an Everly Brothers duo whose partner had died recently from AIDS, but for the present Phil simply showed him to a pleasant attic room and asked if he would be in for the evening meal. McCloud decided that he might as well. Left alone, looking out over the jumbled slate and tiled roofs, a few lighted windows and roosting gulls, he wondered what he was doing here. Then he unpacked and walked down to the front and ate a bag of chips in the cold wind among the fishing debris that littered the ground around the old, tall tarred net shops along the Stade. Not very far away, Sherry Winthrop was drifting round Superdrug with an empty basket to the muzak of 'The Girl From Ipanema', avoiding her reflection in the mirror behind the display of sunglasses.

The following day McCloud drove over to Bexhill. Bexhill Bexhill, so good they named it twice. McCloud sat nursing a cup of bitter tea in the cafeteria of the De La Warr Pavilion. He had opened the doors of the theatre and taken a quick look, at the rows of seats and the wooden stage and his throat had constricted, his heart flung itself around in his tight chest and his skin crawled with fear. He had closed the doors quickly on the scene, shabby and terrifying in the February daylight. Then, like the fool he was, clammily he'd asked the woman in the box office how the tickets for the Vincent McCloud show were going.

'Oh, well it's early days yet. Everything's slow just now. Mind you, we were turning people away for Norman Wisdom, but that's different. Anyhow, we can usually rely on a few regulars who'll turn out for anything. Did you want to book some seats?' she concluded hopefully.

McCloud sat among the scattering of elderly tea-drinkers, his prospective audience if he were lucky, with *Let's call the whole thing off* going through his head. The woman in the box office must have taken him for a loony. Maybe he was. Maybe that's where he was headed, the Funny Farm. He saw the inmates racing round a farmyard in big papier-mâché animal heads, butting each other mirthlessly and falling over waving their legs in the air. Or the Laughing Academy. He'd heard the bin called that too, a grander establishment obviously, and then he remembered reading of someone setting up a school for clowns. He pictured the Laughing Academy as a white classical building with columns, and saw its pupils sitting at rows of desks in a classroom with their red noses, all going 'Ha ha ha ha, ho ho ho' like those sinister mechanical clowns at funfairs. He cursed Delves Winthrop for all the bookings not made, the poor publicity, the wasted opportunities, the wonky contracts, the criminally negligent financial management, and he cursed himself for not having broken away while his voice and his hair was still golden.

He thought about Norman Wisdom who travelled with his entourage in a forty-seater luxury coach, with a cardboard cut-out of himself propped up in one of them, and he remembered the child, a mini-Norman look-alike in a 'gump suit' who followed Norman round the country with his parents, and speculated on their weird family life; father driving, mother stitching a new urchin cap for the boy's expanding head and the kid in the back working on his dimples, mentally rehearsing a comic pratfall; a star waiting to be born. The hell with it. He was down, but not out yet. McCloud finished his tea, stubbed out his cigarette and went out into the sea fog which had swirled up suddenly, and found a ticket on his windscreen. He had forgotten to pay and display.

When he had arrived he had been momentarily cheered by the De La Warr Pavilion, that Modernist gem rising above the shingle with its splendour damaged but not entirely gone, the white colonnade and the odd houses with their little domes and minarets and gardens and white painted wooden steps, but now he saw that Bexhill-on-Sea was a town without pity. He bought a bottle of whisky and drove back to Hastings.

Phil was in the hall of Seagull House talking to a woman with a little dog.

'Let me introduce you,' he said. 'Mr McCloud – Miss Bowser, and her schnauzer Towser. Miss Bowser has the flatlet on the first floor.'

Beatrix Bowser, a gaunt grizzled girl in her sixties with hair like a wind-bitten coastal shrub, wearing a skirt and jersey, held out a rough, shy hand.

'I did so enjoy hearing you sing that lovely old Tom Moore song on *Desert Island Discs* recently, Mr McCloud,' she said gruffly, and fled upstairs with the little grinning brindled chap at her heels.

'Is she in the profession?' asked McCloud, imagining a novelty act with Towser wearing a paper ruff and pierrot cap whizzing round the stage accompanied by Miss Bowser on the accordion.

'Retired schoolmistress. Classics. Beatrix is one of the old school. I'm sorry, should I have recognised you?'

'No,' McCloud said. 'I'm out for dinner, by the way.'

On the way to his room he took a glass from the bathroom, and he poured himself a shot and lay on his bed thinking about the grip of Stacey's strong dancer's legs.

The sea fog seeped through Southernwood's windows and the dogs were restless in the dank, chilly air, making Sherry uneasy with their pacing, clicking claws on the lino as she lay in bed reading.

'Settle down, you two!' she commanded. 'Come on, up on the bed with Mummy!' She patted the old peach-coloured eiderdown. As she did, the dogs hurled themselves towards the front door barking dementedly. Sherry froze in terror. The door bell rang. The dogs were going mad, leaping and battering the door. The murderer had come and she didn't want him. The bell sent another charge through her rigid body. Unable to move, to creep to the telephone, she sat upright, praying that the dogs would frighten him off.

A man's voice came through the door, distorted by the barking. Sherry looked round wildly for a weapon, her mind lurching towards the back door, the garden fence and the flight through darkness to 'Spindrift', seeing herself beating on its door while its inhabitants, as she had done, cowered in fear, refusing to open. Feeling the hands round her throat.

'Vincent McCloud —' The voice was snapped off by the letterbox and dogs' teeth.

Half-aware of feeling like someone in a film, Sherry slid her legs to the floor, and slipped on her dressing gown. The front door was unlocked and opened a crack. McCloud saw a bit of her face, a brass poker, two thrusting muzzles with the upper lip, lifted over snarling teeth.

'I'm terribly sorry to disturb you. Can I come in a minute?'

'Friend!' said Sherry, keeping the dogs, who had no conception of the word, at bay with the poker. 'Lie down!'

Slavering, they sank growling to the floor.

'Delves isn't here,' Sherry said. 'In fact he's hardly ever here. What do you want?'

'Oh — I was just passing.' McCloud attempted a disarming grin.

'Pull the other one,' said Sherry, tightening the belt of her dressing gown. 'If you're hoping to get at Delves by doing anything to me, forget it. I'm his least valued possession.'

'I wasn't, I swear. Look, the truth is, I had to be in Bexhill and I thought I'd look you up. And take a look at the Winthrop lifestyle, I must admit.'

'Well, now you've seen it. Bit different from what you expected, eh? The heart of the evil empire. You might have telephoned first.'

'And you'd have told me not to come. Look, here's my bona fides.' He took a lime-green flyer announcing his concert from his pocket.

Sherry studied it and handed it back without comment. She was beginning to experience an odd, long-forgotten sense of having the upper hand, and enjoying it.

'Do you want a drink?' she asked. 'Before you go. Another drink, perhaps I should say.'

They were sitting in the front room, Sherry with her feet tucked up under her on the sofa, and McCloud in a chair. A bottle of Cloudy Bay stood opened on the table, a rectangular slice of onyx on curlicued gilt legs. McCloud put out a tentative hand to Prince, who didn't bite it off.

'This is Delves's wine,' Sherry said. 'I don't often touch his precious cellar. It's too dangerous, living on your own. And it's horrible replacing it. I feel so guilty that I'm sure they think I'm an alkie, and if they think you really need the stuff, they just fling it at you without even a bit of coloured tissue round it. That blue tissue always makes me think of fireworks – light the blue touch paper and retire. Sorry, I'm rabbiting on. I'm not used to having anyone to talk to and I got a bit carried away.'

'It's nice to hear you talk. We never got a chance to get to know each other, did we?'

'No. But I never get the chance to know anybody. People round here keep themselves to themselves, well, I suppose I do too. I've sort of lost touch with my family. After I was ill, you know, after I – my baby – well, I think they were embarrassed, didn't know what to say to me. And they never liked Delves. Or vice versa.'

As Vincent clicked the table-lighter, an onyx ball, at a cigarette, Sherry was thinking that she might get in touch now. Suddenly she missed them dreadfully. McCloud was thinking how pretty she looked, now that the wine and the gas fire had flushed her pale face. He was thinking too that, if he drank any more, he wouldn't be able to drive. He'd had a good snort or two before setting out, as Sherry had noticed.

'May I?' He refilled their glasses.

'Do you want some stale nuts or crisps?'

'That would be nice. I am a bit hungry.'

'I could make you a sandwich. It will have to be Marmite.'

'My favourite,' said McCloud.

'Vincent,' she said, as he ate his sandwiches, 'are you on your own? I mean, is there anybody in your, you know, life?'

He shook his head. 'There was, a girl, a dancer. She was young enough to be my daughter. I don't know what she saw in me. Well, not much, evidently.'

Sherry's dislike of the glamorous nubile cavorter was appeased when Vincent added, 'A two-bit hoofer who'll never play the Palace.'

He found himself telling Sherry about his mother, and how he had deceived her about the recording contract.

'I wanted to make her happy. Or proud of me. I don't really know for whose sake I did it. Anyway, either she can see me and know the truth, or she can't.'

'She would just want you to be happy. And I bet she *was* proud of you.'

Vincent saw his young self against a painted backdrop of loch and mountains. 'Och, aye,' he said flatly. 'Look, Sherry, I ought to be going. After all, I got you out of bed.'

A deep blush overtook the rosy flush on her face. Motes of embarrassment swarmed in the air around them, settling on her dressing gown.

'You shouldn't really be driving. You must be over the limit.'

'Probably.'

'There is a spare room. Only we'd have to air some sheets. Everything gets really damp here. I think it's the sea. Everything rusts.' Including me, she thought, not knowing if she wanted him to make a move towards her. She knew she was lousy in bed. Delves had told her.

'May I really stay? Thank you. Please don't worry about the sheets, I'm sure I've slept in worse.'

'I could give you a hot-water bottle.'

'Real men don't use hot-water bottles. Have you got any music? The night's still young.'

He flicked through the few albums. Tape and CD had not arrived at Southernwood. He held out his arms. They danced awkwardly, to 'La vie en rose', watched by the dogs with Duke howling along to the song.

'They think we've gone mad,' said Sherry, invoking a memory of the bin, and remembering her own inadequacy. She broke away from Vincent and sat down abruptly.

'Look, Sherry, I don't know what upset you but I'm sorry.' He was disturbed by the feel of her body through the dressing gown and nightdress. She shivered at the loss of his body close to her.

'If you think I was trying to use you to get back at Delves, you're quite, quite wrong. This is nothing whatsoever to do with him.' He knelt beside her and took her hand. 'We'll leave it for tonight. Maybe we can go out somewhere tomorrow. Would you like that?'

Sherry nodded. Then remembered that she had started out calling the shots and said, 'We'll take the dogs to Camber and give them a good run over the sands. OK?' she added a little uncertainly.

'Fine. And I'll take you out to lunch.'

He dismissed the thought of his dwindling bank balance, and realised he should call Seagull House, to let them know he hadn't done a runner or gone over a cliff.

Sometime later, lying wakefully with his cold hot-water bottle in sheets that smelled faintly mildewed, having refused a pair of Delves's damp pyjamas and wearing the tartan boxer shorts Stacey had given him – 'Tartan breath' was one of her names for him – he sensed his door opening slowly. Sherry. Two shapes leapt through the gloom and landed on the bed and made themselves comfortable either side of him.

'Thanks, boys. You're pals.'

He eased himself out and padded to Sherry's room. 'The dogs have taken over my bed,' he said, shutting the door behind him.

She was soft and warm as he took her in his arms, and inert.

He kissed her gently and then harder when a fluttering response came from her lips.

'I don't do this . . .' she struggled to say.

'No. Only with me.'

'I've forgotten how. Rusty . . .' she was saying into his mouth, feeling herself to be as attractive as an old gate. She was warm and soft. His lips grazed breasts like little seashells just visible in the darkness. They made love gently. It was nothing like being in bed with Stacey, he thought, which sometimes felt more like an aerobics session than passion.

'I thought you'd forgotten how,' he teased her, and said, 'You are quite wonderful, and beautiful.'

After a late breakfast of toast and Marmite they drove to Camber. A pair of firecrests flashed past them, bright against dun tangles, as they climbed the path between prickly bushes to the dunes.

'Oh look, aren't they pretty!' said Sherry. Then she screamed. She saw a dead bird impaled on the thorns, and then another and another. All around them hundreds of little birds were stuck on the thorns, netted in the wire diamonds of a broken fence; grey-brown sodden masses of feathers glued and pinned to every bush.

'What's the matter?'

She was paralysed with horror. 'We've got to go back!'

'Why?'

'Can't you see them? Look! Everywhere. Songbirds. Trapped. Pierced with thorns. Please, please, we've got to get out of here!' She was crying, tugging his arm violently.

As he saw them it flashed through Vincent's mind that this was some horrible local custom perpetrated by the people who owned the closed pub they had passed and he felt that they were in an evil, barren place. Then he looked harder as the dogs came bounding back to find them.

'They're not birds, darling! Look! They're some sort of, of natural, vegetable phenomenon. Cast up by the sea perhaps, just bits of – matter, dead foliage or something.'

Sherry was not convinced. The shape and colour of them were so dead-birdlike. Vincent pulled one off a bush.

'See?'

331

It lay, disgusting, in his hand. She did see now that the matted hanks had never been birds, but still the place seemed the scene of a thousand crucifixions. She was trembling with the thorny impact of it. Vincent wrapped the two sides of his coat round her, pulling her tightly to his chest.

'"Come, rest in this bosom, my own stricken deer, Though the herd have fled from thee, thy home is still here."' Then he said, 'You're frozen. Come back to Seagull House with me. There are some kind people there, and then we can decide what we're going to do next.'

And there's a little dog, he realised, but decided to worry about that when they got there. They walked back past the shuttered chalets and beach shops to the car, Vincent trying not to think about the De La Warr Pavilion, shuddering at the image of himself on the stage, hanging on to the mike for support, belting out 'My Way'. '"Regrets, I've had a few . . ."' and a heckling voice shouting 'More than a few, mate!'

Maybe he would give the rest of the whisky to Phil or Miss Bowser. Sherry was suddenly reminded of an afternoon near Christmas some years ago when she had delivered some presents to her sister's house. The three children had been sitting in a row on the sofa with a big bowl on the low table in front of them, threading popcorn on strings for the birds. Like children in a story book, except they were watching television. The picture of them made her happy.

Till the Cows Come Home

It is quarter to five on the Fifth of November, and as the year is 1954, when chocolate Matchmakers have yet to be invented, Ruby Smithers is arranging a little pile of pink-headed Swan Vestas on top of her bonfire cake. Dreamy with chocolate buttercream, she sits on the rim of the newly installed bath to admire her masterpiece. Behind her, a Sadia water heater dangles a silver arm that can swivel over the stone sink under the window, and when Eric, Ruby's husband, has his wash in the morning, with much honking and splashing, droplets of water and soap bubbles sizzle in the breakfast bacon and eggs frying on the cooker. Ruby's hair, rolled into a golden sausage on her wide forehead, falls to her shoulders in a perfect pageboy that suggests an unfulfilled desire to be a GI bride. The straps of her petticoat have slipped from the sleeveless low-cut blouse under her flowery overall, restricting her creamy plump arms; her skirt is tight, her bare feet arched in high-heeled shoes.

Light from the window set deep in the wall of the flint cottage shines feebly over Brussels sprouts, tumbledown rabbit hutches and a perilously built bonfire.

> Guy, Guy, poke 'im in the eye!
> Stick 'im up the lamp post
> And there let 'im die!

The voices of children come faintly from the garden. There are no lamp posts in the village but the kids have got their big guy, slumped waiting to burn on the Smithers's bonfire. A mask lunges at the windowpane and a tongue pokes through its mouth. Ruby suspects that the tongue belongs to her daughter Garnet, an idolised only child. Garnet is not really designed to leap and run and climb trees, but she has been like a firework ready to go off since she

333

got home from school today. At nine years old she is a smaller
edition of her mother, with a paler blonde pageboy and full calves
which taper into white socks and patent leather ankle-strapped
shoes. She ought to be wearing her gumboots. Garnet is usually
found with her nose in a book, but she likes handicraft sets in
boxes too, and she embroidered the crinoline ladies watering holly-
hocks on the chairbacks in the front room all by herself. She is
going to be an air hostess when she grows up.

Ruby, listening out for the sound of Eric's motorbike, carries
her cake through to the middle room where Eric's mother, Mabel,
is sitting by the range smoking her millionth Woodbine, and
listening to the wireless, with Trixie the dog snoring across her
feet. Stained by hops, permeated with their smell, furrowed, and
seamed with earth after a lifetime's work in the fields, her back
bent, the old lady seldom stirs further than the outside lavatory
now and is known to all the children in the lane as Garnet's Nanny
Indoors. Two woodpigeons wrapped in a *Daily Worker* are lying
on the table; Nanny Indoors likes a nice pigeon pie and is partial
to a bit of rook when she can get it. Which would be never if
Ruby had her way.

'What's that supposed to be when it's at home?' Mabel says as
Ruby puts down the cake.

'Bonfire cake,' says Ruby, 'for the kiddies. Are you going to pluck
them horrible things?'

She hates the way their broken necks flop, and their beady eyes
and feet. She can't stick dead things. Garnet had had a club once,
for finding dead things. Morbid. Ruby had put her foot down.

'Whoever heard of putting live matches on a cake!' says Mabel.
'It'll all go up in flames.'

'You'll go up in flames, the amount you smoke. Come to think
of it, if we was in India, you'd've gone up in flames years ago,
when your old man copped it. Put you on a settee on top of the
funeral pyre, that's what they do with widows out there.'

'You'll be a widow yourself one day,' Mabel says. 'Eric's late. He
ought to be home by now.'

'Gis a fag, Mabel, and I'll make us a cup of tea while we're
waiting.'

Ruby takes the kettle from the range where Mabel keeps it

simmering and pours water into the metal teapot. She would like to have the black range ripped out and replaced by a stove that burns anthracite, with mica windowpanes. She would like a contemporary dining set in black and yellow.

'Where's Garnet got to?' asks Nanny Indoors.

'Playing out of doors with little Janey and the others.'

Ruby cleans for Jane's mother. When Jane's mother was taken into hospital her husband was abroad on business, so Ruby has taken Jane in for a week or so. She is mistaken in her belief that Jane is outside waiting eagerly for Eric and the fireworks.

Jane is upstairs, lying on the mattress that has been wedged between Garnet's bed and the door, writing a letter.

'Dear Mummy,' she writes, 'I hop you are well this house is purgertree . . .'

That was what Nanny Indoors had said last night. Jane didn't know what purgertree was but she agreed with Nanny Indoors for once. The paper over which her pencil hovers is marked *TOP SECRET* in red. Uncle Eric – he told her to call him that – brings stacks of it home from work for Garnet to write and draw on or print with her John Bull printing outfit, and *TOP SECRET* pages are often found blowing about the village or pasted to hedges. Eric Smithers, like many local people, works at Fort Belstead, a Government Defence establishment for research into weapons, hidden behind security walls in the hills some miles away.

Jane is stuck. She wants to pour out her heart to her mother, but there is a heavy grey cloud in her chest which will not burst. She wishes *her* daddy worked at the Fort, and was coming home. She pictures the Fort as a larger version of the toy owned by Danny next door. 'In 1944 the soldiers went to war. They had no guns, they used their bums, in 1944', that's what Garnet shouts when Danny won't let them touch his toy soldiers. Jane is going to tell Mummy that Garnet Smithers is the rudest girl in the whole world.

'Boo! Made you look, made you stare, made you lose your underwear!'

Garnet, devilish in a red mask, jumps on to the mattress and snatches the letter. '"Dear Mummy I hop you are well . . ."!'

Muffled mocking laughter comes through the mask's mouth as Jane's mouth opens on the pent-up howl of desolation, then at the sound of Eric's motorbike, Garnet flings the paper at Jane. 'Have your bloody letter!'

Jane is shocked into playground righteous indignation, 'Oh, um! I'm reporting you for swearing, Garnet Smithers!'

'Bloody's in the Bible, Bloody's in the Book, If you don't believe me, go there and look!' taunts the red mask and Garnet hops out and hurtles downstairs.

Jane folds the crumpled letter and hides it in her autograph book. Garnet has spoiled that too:

> Albums I've seen
> Of red and blue and green,
> But in Africa where I've been
> All . . .

The rest of the rhyme was so rude that Jane had to cross it out.

Garnet's French knitting, a cotton reel with four nails hammered into the top and a long multi-coloured snake coiling through the hole in the middle, is lying on her bed. As Jane slips the wool off the nails and gives the knitting, which was to have been a lead for Trixie, a savage jerk, she catches the eye of Mildred, Garnet's best doll who is the size of a fully-grown baby.

'Tell-tale tit,' says Jane to Mildred in Garnet's voice, 'your tongue shall be split, and all the little puppy-dogs shall have a little bit!' She hates that rhyme; the cruel picture it brings always makes her want to cry. Cry, baby, cry, stick your finger in your eye. Jane puts on her yellow mask and goes slowly downstairs. Avoiding Trixie's eye, she says to Nanny Indoors, 'When I was upstairs just now, a big jackdaw flew in the window and pulled all Garnet's French knitting off.'

'Speak up, I can't hear you, with that thing on your face!' Jane notices that Nanny Indoors is unwrapping a Plain Jane toffee. She takes her coat from the peg on the back of the door.

'Put your gumboots on, Jane,' says Ruby, carrying a bag of potatoes out to the fire. Jane hasn't brought them, and she is lifted into a cobwebbed pair belonging to Nanny Indoors.

Uncle Eric's face is pale and sweaty, glazed with the drizzle that has started; an arc of paraffin leaps from the can in his hand and sloshes over the bonfire. 'Wotcher, Tuppence!' he says to Jane, but she stomps to the bottom of the garden, by the chicken run, and leans against the wall, holding her sparkler at arm's length with its stars fizzling into the mud. The cold is seeping through Nanny Indoors's gumboots, the eyeholes of her mask don't fit and she can hardly see the dark huddle of grown-ups and flickering children. She hates cocoa, they have drinking chocolate at home, and she hates this flint wall with bits of broken bottles cemented along its top which reminds her of Garnet chanting 'Pounds shillings and pence, The cow jumped over the fence. He pricked his – rude word – on a piece of glass, Pounds shillings and pence.' Poor cow, and anyway, cows are ladies, not hes. She wants to rescue the guy. She can feel his terror. She tears off her mask and stamps on it.

The bonfire goes up with a whoosh and shrieks and crack-crack gunshots of jumping jacks, and two rockets zoom oooh into the sky, and fall in aaahs of green and purple stars. Then a massive, deafening blast, with a blazing flash from the hills lighting up the garden, where the screaming people fling themselves to the ground, extinguishing the bonfire, every bonfire, as the Fort explodes in a gigantic pyrotechnical display like all the fireworks in the world going off, setting the sky on fire.

Nanny Indoors rushes out, snatching up a baby, dragging Garnet to the Anderson shelter that used to be down the garden, and Eric, half-blinded, is kicking his motorbike into action and Ruby has jumped up behind him, her dazzled face ecstatic, as if something worth seeing has happened at last, as they roar off to the scene of the disaster.

It is the Fifth of November, 1993. I bet you thought all that was written by Jane, thinly disguised autobiography, but it's me, rude Garnet, taking the Olympian view. Jane, wherever you are, I hop you are well. I never did become an air hostess. I'm a poet, don't I know it. I went back to our old house the other day; there was a Volvo parked outside, and plaque on the wall that said 'Ancient Lights', made me think of the meat we used to get from Mr Smallbone for old Trixie, and a sign on the gate saying 'Organic Vegetables and Free-Range Eggs'. I still don't know what really happened that night the Fort went up; it was all very hush-hush afterwards, but I've been thinking a lot lately about lives lived out in boundaries of fields and flint and chicken wire, that were illuminated briefly by peacetime catastrophe. My dad, who took the *Daily Worker*, did he want to change the world? And Nanny Indoors, who thought the War had broken out again.

I hear my mother's voice, 'Hurry up, Garnet! We'll be here till the cows come home!', and see her picking her way through the cowpats down our lane in her high heels, and the fall-out from the explosion drifts over me, sepia-coloured, clinging, bringing tears to the eyes. But I'm not really one for all this Hovis-hued nostalgia you get nowadays; I've been quite restrained here, sprinkling the brand names lightly, like Mum with the chocolate vermicelli when she made that Green's Sponge Mix bonfire cake, that Trixie ate, matches and all, in the confusion; and I won't even mention how sometimes, when my answerphone beeps, I half-expect a voice to announce: 'This is the BBC Home Service. Here is the news.'

The Worlds Smallest Unicorn

'There's a parcel for you, Fan.'

'It'll be the toad lilies from the Spalding's catalogue,' she replied listlessly.

Teddy put the package addressed to his sister-in-law on the kitchen table, disappointed in his hope that some pleasure or good will might rub off it on to him and redeem his failure in the gift-bearing stakes. He hovered uneasily in the hostility emanating from Fan, aware of an antagonism caused by something more than his arrival the night before, with only two suitcases to show for his twenty years in Hong Kong. One contained his clothes, and the smaller held papers, a few books and socks and the sort of gewgaws you could find in any Chinese supermarket in London.

'Do stop hovering, Teddy. Sit down and I'll make some fresh toast. Tea or coffee? There's some green tea somewhere if you'd prefer. Or jasmine.'

'Coffee, please.'

Teddy sat on a chair too small for him, a fat man in a kingfisher-blue shantung suit. Fan's reaction to the parcel reminded him uncomfortably of a brown envelope and a clip round the ear long ago.

'Daddy! Dad! There's a letter for you.'

It was the raw noon of a motherless, shapeless Saturday. Teddy tugged his father awake from tangled sheets, while his younger brother watched from the doorway, thumb in his mouth. Willie swore, snatching the letter. It turned out to be the final demand for the electricity bill and he ripped it in two, caught Teddy a stinging blow to the head and buried his face in his pillow again. In the light of experience, and Teddy wasn't feeling too good himself this morning, he could see that Willie had a hangover, but the stupid thing was, he had known at the time that he was being disingenuous, a sly eleven-year-old who ought to have known better. He had hoped to earn his father's thanks by posing as a well-intentioned, if mistaken, lad, and he had got what he deserved.

After Delia, the boys' mother, had left, the house was always cold, a snivelling cold that made them pull the sleeves of their jumpers over their hands and drag their cuffs across their noses, cold that chapped their lips and hurt their hair when they brushed it. Nothing was ever quite clean. The towels were damp and sticky and didn't dry you properly. Dirty clothes piled up in corners and homework was not done. Women came and went, and now and then the boys were treated to a slap-up meal at Bunjie's, that haunt of hobbits and folkies from time immemorial, but it wasn't the same.

Teddy and Webster Shelmerdine were the children of two musicians, Willie 'the Weeper' Shelmerdine and Delia MacFarlane. They grew up in the English jazz and folk revival of the fifties and early sixties, and although they had been named after Teddy Wilson and Ben Webster, they were weaned on skiffle and cut their teeth on Trad. Willie played the clarinet and sang, while Delia was primarily a singer who accompanied herself on washboard. She was also a semi-skilled harpist and harmonica player who could break your heart in the Gaelic at a ceilidh and twang out mouth-music when required. Willie and Delia were part of the scene, minor household names along with Pete and Peggy Seeger, Chas McDevitt and Nancy Whisky, Chris Barber and Ottilie Patterson, partners in the tightly knit world of performers and fans on the jazz and folk circuit of gigs, festivals and clubs. Everybody knew all the gossip, and there was not a dry eye in the Green Man the night Willie bawled out 'Delia Gone' for the first time after she had run off with the jew's harp player from the Colin Clark City Stompers. Beryl Bryden, who was topping the bill, enfolded the weeping boys, Teddy and Webster, in the wings of her striped tent-dress like a hen comforting her chicks, but when they got home bleakness drifted like dust; 'Delia Gone' remained a crowd-pleaser, though.

> He comes down our alley and whistles me out.
> Before I get down there, he knocks me about.
> Still I love him, I'll forgive him,
> I'll go with him wherever he goes . . .

Delia used to sing, before Willie hit her one time too many and she rode that freight train, the 5.15 to Charing Cross, out of his life for ever.

'Don't bother with toast, Fan,' Teddy was saying, just as the bread jumped.

'You should have said if you didn't want it. I've made it now.'

'I do want it, thanks. I was just trying to save you the trouble.'

'It's hardly any trouble to bung two bits of bread in a toaster.' Her tone hinted at a hundred toastracks stretching as far back as the eye could see, all stacked with troubles caused by Teddy.

'I guess Web's gone to work. What about the girls?'

'Still in bed. Wasting the day.'

Fan wiped down the Dualit toaster and snapped at the cat as he came warily through his door, trying not to let it flap.

'And where do you think you've been, Mister? Sneaking in with your tail full of burrs, demanding breakfast at all hours.'

The cat, Rastus, attempted to catch Teddy's eye with a blokish wink, but he wasn't having any.

'Selfish little beasts, aren't they? Still, I suppose that's why we love them. The Cat that Walks by Himself and all that. Takes me back, I remember reading it to the kids years ago, last time I was home on leave. They've grown up into beautiful young ladies, Fan. A credit to you. A pair of real stunners, with the brains to match. You must be very proud of them.'

'I am.'

Fan ripped the lid from a tin of cat food, leaving Teddy feeling that he had said the wrong thing again. Of course, this time he was not home on leave, but redundant, an ex-employee of the Pink Panda Stationery Company billeted on Fan for the foreseeable, until he got back on his feet.

The summer holidays were almost over for Fan, a school secretary, and the girls, Bethan and Megan. Bethan was camping in Megan's room because bad Uncle Teddy had taken over hers. The spare room, where Teddy had slept nine years ago, was now a study filled with the family's computers and files and Webster's rowing machine. Teddy felt so tired as he replaced the lid on the Marmite and carried his plate and mug to the sink that he longed to crawl back into Bethan's bed, beneath the posters of vapid white boy bands and angry black gangstas, pull the duvet over his head, and sleep for a year. Perhaps for eternity.

'What are your plans for today?' Fan asked. 'You can leave those, I'll stick them in the dishwasher.'

Couldn't a man be allowed five minutes' jet lag after flying a quarter of the way round the globe? Did she have to make him feel completely useless by not even letting him wash up a few dishes?

'I – well, I thought I'd just – reorientate myself for a day or two – or re-occidentate myself, perhaps I should say. Put out a few feelers.'

'Like a beetle.'

Fan stared at Teddy in his suit, shot and nubbled with peacock threads.

'I suppose you had that suit made. In Honkers. I always wanted to do that, you know. Go shopping in Hong Kong and choose the material and have something made up just for me, to my own design. Something unique. Oh well, silly of me, I suppose. The paper's there if you want to have a look at it.'

'Thanks.'

Teddy picked up the newspaper obediently as Fan left the kitchen. What was he meant to do, turn straight to the Situations Vacant? How was he to have guessed that Fan had expected to be invited to stay? Perhaps that was what was eating her. Well, the stupid cow had had twenty years in which to suggest it. He wasn't a mind-reader. Just as well, though. Honkers! They would have wanted to eat in fancy restaurants and nightspots, demanded to see the 'real' Hong Kong and hoped to be taken to the Jockey Club or the FCC, where there was a waiting list for membership and where Teddy had dined only once as a guest in all the years he had lived there. He certainly wouldn't have wanted to introduce them to his own watering hole, the Hong Kong Skittles Club, a sporting establishment mostly in name, with its sour clientele of disappointed ex-pats. The Skittles' dullness suited him; he had become accustomed to it, and protective of it, and he shuddered at the thought of Web and Fan fumbling with their chopsticks in its little dining room, before contracting food poisoning, or sitting at the bar in shorts and sandals, Fan sipping some touristy cocktail with a parasol and Web droning on about small-bore cooling systems for automatic hand-dryers and hustling for orders for his light-engineering firm.

Even so, Teddy could kick himself for not having brought Fan a dress or a jacket, or even a length of silk. A bad move to present her with that plastic fan last night, whipping it open with a flourish, 'A fan for Fan, from your greatest fan.' He winced at the memory, and that obsolete Pink Panda stock, the rulers and rubbers and little notebooks and cute panda stickers, had proved quite unsuitable for two young ladies who had done so spectacularly well in their exams, although they'd liked the miniature cameras with scenes of Hong Kong by night and the fortune cookies, waterflowers and joss sticks, unless they were just being kind or sending him up.

'How sad to think of people spending their lives making these things,' Fan had remarked.

Even if he had brought Fan something to wear, he'd have got the size wrong, knowing his luck, because he couldn't help noticing she'd put on the beef a bit. Fan was fair and slimmish now rather than skinny, and still favoured the droopy English look of faded Aertex blouse, or polo shirt, cotton skirt and cardy. Teddy could never quite decide whether it was sexy or not. It was a world away from the gloss and gilt and sharp edges of the women he was used to. He turned the pages of the *Independent* abstractedly. Maybe he could pick something up for Fan in Chinatown and pretend he'd had it in his suitcase, although he'd have to be careful; his pitiful pay-off from the Pink Panda Stationery Company wouldn't stretch far. Teddy's only lasting contribution to the firm which had 'rationalised' him in preparation for the Chinese take-over was to be found in its name.

'With respect, Mr Tang, a company that designates itself "stationary" is a company that is going nowhere,' he had told the firm's founder at his interview. 'No wonder Pink Panda's profits are at a standstill.' Well, he could see it was a tinpot outfit, but gradually they had turned it round and moved the factory into better premises. The trouble was, as young Tangs, sons, daughters, and cousins, grew up and the extended family was brought into the business, Teddy was passed over for promotion time and time

343

again. It was only Mr Tang's residual loyalty that kept him in the office at all, and by the time he left he was an anachronism known simply as 'the *Gweilo*', a word meaning ghost as well as foreigner; a bad spirit to be exorcised.

Fan's head poked round the door, saying, 'If you've got any washing, dump it in the dirty-linen basket in the bathroom. I'll be doing a mixed load later.'

Notes from a flute spiralled down the stairs.

'Who's playing? Not the kids, surely?' said Teddy.

'Oh, the twins have been tootling on their flutes since they were two jampots high.' Fan was dismissive, as though he ought, as an uncle, to have known that.

'Ah well, blood will out,' said Teddy.

Delia's grandfather had been a Nigerian-Scots seaman from Port Glasgow, and her granddaughters Bethan and Megan had taken her pale delicate features and replicated her dark eyes and char-coal cloud of hair in blue and gold. They wore their own hair in cascades of long thin braids, but, as Fan's father had put it at their christening, you would never guess that those two little English rosebuds had a touch of the tarbrush. Unless you had a more educated eye than his. Webster was green-eyed and freckled, while Teddy was white, with disconcertingly opaque eyes like black olives under heavy lids, and their hair, the russet and the black, kinked into wool from unravelled jumpers if it was not kept short.

Teddy was thinking about his nieces. Sixteen years old. It didn't seem possible. So many birthdays he had missed. He couldn't get over how they'd changed, the sheer length of the pale golden legs and thighs in tiny black shorts and the briefest swirl of skirt, the smooth distances of flesh between croptop and navel and waistband, the long, long slender arms flailing from tight-ribbed short sleeves. Even for twins, between them they seemed to have more than their allocation of limbs, and was there really any need for them to be so tall, he wondered. After all, it was not as though they had to reach up to pull the topmost leaves from a drought-stricken tree in order to survive, was it? 'How tall they've grown,' he had said on meeting them last night, and reminded them how he had once read *The Jumblies* to them, one perched on each knee in their pyjamas.

And in twenty years they all came back,
In twenty years or more,
And every one said, 'How tall they've grown! . . .

Except that it was he who had come back after twenty years,
minus a couple of short breaks, he who was the Jumbly, or some
poor toeless Pobble or wandering luminous-nosed Dong, shuffling
home like a disgraced Behemoth. And everyone thought, how fat
he's grown. There was an Edward Lear print, of a salmon-crested
cockatoo, in the dining room. He had remarked on it during one
of the silences which had fallen between the clash of eating implements and the twins' fits of the giggles.

'What's it like in Hong Kong, Uncle Teddy?'

'Well, depends where you mean. There's Hong Kong side and
Kowloon side and –'

'Can you speak Chinese, Uncle Teddy? Cantonese and Mandarin?'

'And Satsuma and Clementine? And Grapefruit?'

'That's enough,' said Fan. 'Be your age.'

Teddy said, 'In Wan Chai, where I live, lived –'

'That's the old Suzy Wong district, isn't it?' put in Webster, with
what Fan perceived as a leer.

'That's right. You've got lots of narrow streets and bars and clubs.
There's the Pussy Cat and the Hotlips, they're mainly pick-up
joints, topless, I believe, and the Wanch, which is a mock pub run
by *gweilos*, foreigners, for *gweilos*.'

The girls were stuffing napkins into their mouths.

Fan said, 'There must be more to it than that. A more salu-
brious side. It can't all be sleaze.'

She heard the tinkle of temple bells above the traffic's roar in
a street teeming with limousines, rickshaws, buffalo-carts and bicycles ridden by people in conical hats under skyscrapers festooned
with ideographed banners.

'Oh, of course. There are the artisans' streets where you can buy
anything in the world you might want. The street of the coffin-
makers for example, the street of the metal-beaters, the street of
the tailors, all sorts. And people sitting on chairs on the pavement
who do every kind of repair, shoes, rattan furniture, clothes; and
old grandmothers selling matches, watchstraps . . .'

'Fake Rolexes,' said the twins.

Teddy glanced at his watch, acknowledging his dereliction of avuncular duty.

'The architecture's fascinating, Fan, you'd love it. And it's a very safe city to walk about in.'

'Oh, good.'

'What about the Triads?' Megan asked.

'We've got Triads at our school,' said Bethan.

'Don't be so ridiculous!' Fan lost patience. 'As if Miss O'Nions would tolerate such a thing! I don't know why you're showing off like a couple of three-year-olds.'

The twins rolled their eyes heavenwards with pitying sighs.

'So have you got many Chinese friends now or did you mostly hang out with the ex-pats?' said Webster.

'Well, a few. The Chinese don't really like us much. And most of the ex-pats are a pretty dull bunch. The sort of people who knew they would never make it here and imagined they'd be big fish in a small pool, and then became embittered and turned to hard drinking when they weren't.'

Teddy realised that they might think he was describing himself. Fan thought of fish bumping each other in crowded tanks in Chinese takeaways. She burst out harshly, 'But they're a cruel people, aren't they, the Chinese? Cruel to each other, and to animals. I mean, look at all those endangered species they grind up for their herbal medicines.'

'They're very fond of birds,' Teddy told her. 'Devoted to them. Everywhere you go, in the streets, on buses and the MTR and the ferries, you see people with their pet birds. Little finches mostly.'

'You mean they carry them on their shoulders, or walk them on leads? I suppose they have to, if they've eaten all the dogs.'

'In cages,' said Teddy.

'Mum rests her case,' said Megan.

Bethan said, 'Mum, I never knew you were such a racist.'

Now, in the bedroom, Fan stared out of the window and remembered the unpleasant evening. The girls had been at their silliest, embarrassingly middle class. Not that she thought they *should* be working in a sweatshop or topless bar like girls half their age in

Hong Kong, but you never knew where you were with them these days; one minute they were clamouring to be allowed to stay at clubs until six o'clock in the morning, the next behaving like spoiled brats. She didn't know what Teddy would think, not that she cared about impressing him. She saw that the Michaelmas daisies, those harbingers of autumn, were in flower and it occurred to her that they always seemed to be out nowadays. Everywhere you looked, people were going on about the melting of the polar ice-cap, and hurtling towards the Millennium, but maybe the Michaelmas daisies only indicated the swift passing of her own years. Whatever, it appeared likely that she would spend her personal *fin de siècle* picking up other folks' dirty clothes. No sooner had she shaken the sand of Cyprus from the holiday suitcases, than along came Teddy, the bad penny, the hole in the head, to dump another peck of dirt on her. She had returned from their self-catering villa looking forward to pottering about in a leisurely way before the start of term, and now here was this succubus squatting in her kitchen, expecting to be fed. She wondered if he had found yet the item in the paper which she hoped he would encounter with a shock. A double-take of disbelief. A stab of grief. A pang of guilt.

She watched Rastus shredding the trunk of the lilac tree with his claws. The garden was full of seed-heads, thistledown, parachutes, exploded pods and burnt-out rockets. The green bunches of ash keys were tinged with red and mildewed damsons lay scattered on the grass. It would soon be time to put the bulbs in. 'Forever Autumn', she thought, but another song was playing insistently through her head, one she had always hated, about Willie the Weeper who made his living as a chimney sweeper. Well, if Willie Shelmerdine had ever swept his own chimney, that terraced house in Blackheath, so convenient for the Green Man, might be standing now. As might Willie. What a dead loss as a grandfather he had been. And as for that reprobate runaway grandma, Delia Gone, the old trout, now finally departed and good riddance, she had become a romantic figure to the twins, who insisted on claiming their one-sixteenth part of African heritage, apeing the hairstyles and speech of their black classmates and spelling Africa with a k.

Fan sat on the bed, averting her glance from her reflection in the wardrobe door. Trust Teddy to pitch up when sun, salt and sand had frayed her hair to rope, and haloumi and feta and Cypriot wine had taken their toll. The irony was, she had been feeling relaxed and attractive, languorous and at ease with Webster in their late-summer lovemaking, until Teddy had arrived to diminish her. And yet he was no oil painting himself, no spring chicken either. She had been practically at screaming point last night, waiting for a moment alone with him, and had gone bitterly to bed at last, leaving him and Webster chortling over old times with the bottle of duty-free Jack Daniels, and Teddy stubbing out cigarettes in the saucer Webster had provided, one of the few left from their wedding tea service.

And this morning, when they were at last alone, he had just sat there eating toast in that bright blue suit. Enraged as she was by Teddy, Fan despised herself more, because she had to admit that if Teddy had shown by a word or a look or a covert touch of his hand that he desired her still, she would have forgiven him. He was pathetic. All the fat fool had to do was to tell her she hadn't changed a bit, or that she was more beautiful than ever, and he was too dumb to realise it. Of course she was proud of the girls, but to have Teddy Shelmerdine, an adulterer who had slept with his own brother's wife, treat her like some mumsy hausfrau was more than she could bear.

It was a sultry day, nine years ago, the grey sky full of static electricity and little grumbles of thunder. The children had been taken to the cinema by the mother of one of their friends. With the passing of time, Fan had managed to put that afternoon out of her mind, but every now and then her conscience, responding to some stimulus, flashed an ugly scene into her mind. In a red desert landscape, two beasts, coarse-haired, four-footed, ungulant, were pawing the dust, raising their snouts to sniff the scent of distant rain, circling and circling a tree, whose uneasy leaves shivered in the dry wind that ruffled a ridge of bristles along their spines. They got closer and closer, tusk to flank, until with a grunt they were coupling blindly in a stinging red sandstorm of tumbleweed and broken cactus spikes, and raindrops as flat and heavy as stones.

But it hadn't really been like that at all, ochreous, ruttish, with nostrils dilating in the sulphurous air, splayed hooves, and curved tusks gripping her back, the afternoon that two palish mammals had sheltered from the storm in the spare-room bed. Teddy had been tender and sweet; Fan had cried, and for a while imagined that she had married the wrong brother.

The following day Teddy had been driven to the airport by the doubly betrayed and unsuspecting Webster, with the kids in the back singing along to an old ABBA tape. Fan waited in vain for a phone call, she searched for a coded message in the postcard that arrived at last, thanking them for having him to stay, she half-dreaded but yearned for a mysterious bouquet from Interflora, with no card. Then she fell into a dark and unexplainable depression. Teddy had forced her to reappraise herself and to discover that she was not the high-principled person she had thought herself to be, caring and competent and so clever in presenting her husband with a pair of bright-as-a-button twins. She had slept with two people in her life, both of them Shelmerdines. What a track record. Why not make it a hat trick with old Willie? A grey year passed before she seemed to be her old self again. Teddy Shelmerdine had stolen a year from her, and from her family, while she wore those fog-tinted spectacles of despair, and he was not gentleman enough to pretend that he was still carrying a torch, or that the episode had meant anything to him at all.

The girls had switched on the radio in their room, with the sound considerably low.

'For God's sake turn up that bloody noise!' Fan shouted. 'I can hear myself think!'

'Sorry, Mum.'

And the volume was turned down.

Fan kicked one of Webster's unassuming shoes under the bed, furious with him for being so pleased to see his big brother, as if he had been the failure of the family and Teddy the success. Webster had looked so hurt and disappointed in her last night when, needled beyond endurance, she had taken advantage of Teddy's trip to the bathroom to remark, 'Typical of Teddy to turn tail and run as soon as things get a bit rough out there.'

'When the going gets tough, the tough get going. Isn't that

what your Mrs Thatcher used to say?' Teddy came back into the room.

'She was never "our" Mrs Thatcher. If it comes to that, she was yours as much as ours.'

'Fan! Have you seen this, in the paper?'

Teddy ran up the stairs, holding on to the banister on the landing to get his breath.

'Did you see this about Lola Henriques?'

'The singer? Wasn't she an old flame of yours? What about her?'

Teddy saw Lola's face in the flare of a cigarette lighter. Yes, she was an old flame of his.

'She's dead. The funeral's today, at Golders Green. Has Web got a black tie I can borrow?'

The girls had come out on to the landing, wearing the big T-shirts they slept in, which scarcely covered their minuscule pants.

'For goodness sake put some clothes on,' said Fan, 'lolling around half-naked at this time of day.'

To Teddy, she said, 'I saw her on the telly a few months ago, in some documentary, can't remember what it was about, but I do recall remarking to Webster at the time that she didn't look well.'

'Lola never looked well. It was part of her charm.'

'There's a black tie somewhere, I think.'

Fan went into the marital bedroom and came back dangling a black knotted noose.

'Here you are. Actually, I believe it was your father's.'

'Uncle Teddy,' said Megan, 'we're like really sorry about – you know, the funeral – and that.'

'Thank you, Megan.'

Fan followed Teddy into his room.

'Do you think this shirt's all right? Not too tight?' he asked.

'Let me look. Hmmm. Have you tried the pencil test?'

'The pencil test?'

'Oh, it's just something people used to do, to see if they could go without a bra. You put a pencil under your breast, and if it falls out, you're OK.'

Teddy looked at her with his black olive eyes whose expression she could never read.

'I'd better get going. Don't bother about lunch, I'll pick something up on the way.'

'This isn't Hong Kong, you know, with noodle-sellers on every street corner and people ringing little bells to advertise their wares.'

After he had gone, Fan booked herself a hair appointment and decided to go into school the following day to prepare for the new term. The thought of the bewildered new intake in their big blazers calmed her down.

Teddy was sitting on the red bench at the bus stop outside Chik'N'Ribs, waiting for a bus to Brixton tube station, and watching three pigeons playing spillikins with somebody's lunch on the pavement, taking turns to stab a chip with their beaks and send it flying into the gutter. Spillikins, Jack Straws, Pik-a-stik, whatever you called the game, the ratio of potato to effort was minimal. Teddy saw that one of the players was handicapped by the loss of a foot, and he wondered if the number of discarded takeaways at such a short distance from Chik'N'Ribs was an indictment of its cuisine, or whether most of its clientèle were simply too drunk to finish their meals. To his left sat a man of about his own age with the rough red skin and tormented, boiled-sweet stare of the heavy drinker, and to his right, as far away as possible, a young black woman glanced up from time to time from the gospel text she was reading to see if a bus was coming. The greasy smell of warm meat drove any thought of his own lunch from Teddy's mind.

It was hot now, and traffic and people pushing buggies hung about with children toiled up and down the hill in fumy sunshine splintered by the drills of roadworks and thumped by music from passing cars. The engine of a parked lorry throbbed like a thousand headaches and the sirens of a posse of police cars swooped and looped the loop; the leaden air had an aggressive edge. This had never been a wealthy area, but Teddy could not help noticing the general atmosphere of defeat, how much poorer and shabbier the people looked since he was last there, how many shops were boarded up. Evidently the news that the recession was over had not reached these parts yet.

A bus marked 'Sorry Not In Service' raised false hopes for a

351

moment. Teddy lit a cigarette. A small crowd had formed at the bus stop. Apparently queueing was a thing of the past. He had been waiting fifteen minutes now and he remembered how often he had set out on some journey in good spirits, only to have his heart broken by the transport system of south London. They ordered these things much better in Hong Kong. Teddy suddenly felt homesick, an exile in his own land. He dared not think about the future. He did not want to think about Lola; time enough for that at the crematorium. He thought about Fan. How bad-tempered she had become. Perhaps she was getting menopausal, that might explain it. They'd hit it off so well last time he was home. Her attitude of sarcasm and contempt couldn't, surely it couldn't, have anything to do with that afternoon when they'd been alone in the house? So far as he recalled, it had been great. A bit of fun. She'd had no complaints then. Surely she didn't expect – surely she was as anxious to forget the whole thing as he was? After all, they'd both been a lot younger then. So much water had flowed under the bridge for all of them, and his life was complicated enough already without dragging up the past.

If a train came right away at Brixton, and if he didn't have to wait long for a Golders Green train at Euston, he might still just make it. Two useless buses came and went. Ought he to get some flowers? Why were there no taxis? No wonder everybody looked so ground down. Twenty-five minutes now. Didn't anybody give a damn that there might be someone in a hurry to see an old flame consigned to – to pay his last respects? It was when a funeral cortège going up the hill to Norwood Cemetery stopped at the lights, displaying a floral tribute which spelled out NAN in pink and white letters, that Teddy gave up hope and turned away from the bus stop. What did he know of Lola's life anyway, and there would be people there he didn't want to meet, who would think him fat and seedy and wonder what Lola had ever seen in him, and remember that he had treated her shabbily. Just as well he hadn't bought any flowers, but then again, he supposed he could have given them to Fan. Teddy went into a florist's shop, and on his way out, his eye was caught by a brightly coloured poster for Zippos Circus on the boarded-up shop next door. Across the bottom of the poster was written, SEE THE WORLDS

SMALLEST UNICORN & THE FANTASTIC CONTORTION OF MADAME
ZSA–ZSA!

Teddy felt he could live without Madame Zsa–Zsa's contortion,
but the world's smallest unicorn, that would be something to
behold. How big would it be? He pictured a miniature beast, milk-
white, with a horn fluted like a conical seashell, nestling in the
palm of the ringmaster's hand. Or perhaps it would be larger, trot-
ting round the ring, wearing the golden medieval collar of a
unicorn kneeling beside a maiden in a tapestry. Then he thought,
you fool. The unicorn is a mythical beast. There is no such animal
as the unicorn, big or small. It is heraldic, it battles with lions in
nursery rhymes, it is rampant on shields and attracted to virgins.
Disappointed, and feeling foolish, he turned away. Zippo's unicorn
would turn out to be a Shetland pony with something glued to
its head, or a bonsai-ed goat whose horns had gone wrong, and
fused into one protuberance. Just as well he had realised his mistake
before buying a family ticket and trundling them all off to Streatham
Common.

A convoy of buses passed him, the 196, two 2s and a 322, all
going to Brixton. He sat for a while in Norwood Cemetery, out
of sight of the funeral, and asked Lola to forgive him for not making
it to hers, the flowers he had bought to placate Fan beside him on
the bench. The Chinese sent their dead off into the afterlife equipped
with everything they might need, cars, computers, fridges, stereos,
microwaves, you name it, all made of paper, and he hadn't even
managed a flower for Lola. Sitting there, psyching himself up to
return to the house, he felt as much of a *gweilo* as he ever had in
Hong Kong, as lonely as a ghost. He dreaded the thought of a
succession of nights in Bethan's room with her posters and makeup
and cuddly toys. The Chinese were probably right, the smaller and
more crowded the room, the less space there was for ghosts.

Teddy let himself in with the spare key Webster had given him,
and went straight upstairs. There, in the doorway of Bethan's room,
with a bunch of funereal white gladioli in his hand, he confronted
an extraordinary tableau. Megan stood with a sandwich halfway
to her mouth, Bethan was kneeling, stilled in the act of scrabbling
through an untidy drawer, and beside his open suitcase was Fan

353

with a tiny black silk slip in one hand and a framed photograph in the other.

'What's this?' she said.

'No idea – mix-up at the laundry I suppose. Never seen it before in my life.'

'No, this! Who's this in the photograph?'

The girls crowded her to look. The picture was of a boy, a smiling boy about ten years old with almond-shaped eyes. A beautiful boy.

'His name's William,' Teddy said.

'He's your son, isn't he?'

Fan sat down on the bed, still holding the photograph.

'You bastard,' she said. 'I was looking for your dirty washing and I found it.'

Bethan took the picture from her.

'You mean, he's like – our cousin?'

'He is your cousin,' Teddy said.

Fan burst into tears, weeping like a monarch who has been brought the news of the loss of a colony, but the twins were staring at Teddy over the photograph frame as if at a shining island rising out of the sea on the horizon.

Crossing the Border

Flora had never been so far south. She was driving past sari shops, silk wholesalers, sweetshops and sweatshops, restaurants and jewellers, through a low-rise landscape broken by spires and temples and mosques, in Sunday afternoon traffic puffing out bouquets of January gloom. Her own second-hand Metro was fuelled by a mixture of anticipation and doubt. Long streets of stuccoed terraced houses curved away on either side of the road, and then the red-brick pagoda of a Tesco superstore reared up and blue galvanised warehouses and DIY emporia, and now she was in the half-timbered hinterland, where London ebbs into the pampas grass and mock-Tudor of the edge of Kent, taking the wrong turning at a roundabout.

When Flora had left home, the dark bobbles of the plane trees in the square where she lived were draggling like trimmings of frowsty curtains in a sky of mushroom soup. Now, as the road petered out into a rutted track and she stopped the car, the sun licked through the glutinous grey, revealing streaks of pale-blue glaze and linking a gold necklace of dazzling puddles. Across a small field, behind the bare twigs of oak trees, Flora could see what must be the backs of the houses in the road she had missed, Bourne Avenue. At the field's edge, an angler was fishing in a pond encircled with barbed wire where white geese swam, and two booted and anoraked women walked past with seven or eight dogs leaping between them. Flora stepped out into a mild composty wind and locked the car. Elders and wooden fence posts were emerald with winter damp. She picked her way over gravel and mud, telling herself that ten minutes more would make no differ-ence to Great-Uncle Lorimer after all these years. To her left, in a thin tangled wood, here and there the massive trunk of a felled oak sported a crown of new pale antlers. Flora tripped on a root and reflected that she was, in a sense, seeking her own roots, tracing a branch of her family tree. There was a tape recorder in the bag on her shoulder.

Her chief interest lay in her late Great-Uncle Laurence, the poet, and she was hoping that his brother Lorimer would give her insights into and anecdotes from the shared childhood of the two sons of the manse who had taken such different paths. She, like her great-uncles, was among those of the large Looney family who had dropped the second 'o' from their name. Uncle Lorimer had reverted to the original for reasons of his own. Flora, whose father was a poet of a different kind from Laurence, a corduroy-jacketed, much-married journeyman, had determined to write the biography of Laurence Loney, who had died alone in a trailer park in Nevada, and she had got as far as her title, *Tumbleweed and Whin*. It encapsulated, she felt, the unhappy, contradictory character of the author of *Poor Pink Trash* and *Behind the Scones at the Tattoo*. Like Laurence, she was moved by ephemera and junk and saw eternity in a plastic flower and the human condition in the brittle pink Little Princess Vanity Set in the supermarket, whose tiny mirror flashed a fragment of dream. The bleached bones of a bird or a skull in the heather spoke to her too, as plaintively as a peewit or the pale torso of a lost Barbie doll.

The tips of birches made a rosy haze in the distance against a sky growing colder and Flora could hear the chilly sound of running water. Squelching into the wood, she discovered a swift stream carrying leaves and little gnarled alder fruits between its steep banks. A middle-aged man with a red setter was approaching and, surmising that he was not a murderer, Flora called out, 'Is there a bridge across this stream?'

'Stream? This is the Ravensbourne river!'

A stalwart local historian, Flora recognised, as the dog scrambled into the water, splashing against the current in a whirligig of red feathery ears and tail and radiant droplets, and the man followed it upstream. Flora returned to the path and walked on, encountering several more of these unfriendly, not-quite-country folk, until she found herself on the verge of a pick-your-own smallholding, where strawberry plants huddled in rain-spangled furrows of black plastic, by a makeshift shelter of corrugated tin and polythene where the strawberries were weighed in the summer. Time to turn back, but there was something shimmering and dazzling at the end of the track, with bright flashes of moving colours.

It was a heap, a low mountain, of shining straw mucked out from stables, glinting gilt and copper and brass in the sun as Flora drew near, its stalks clogged with horse manure, and on its peak stood a cockerel, red-gold and viridescent. Guinea fowl, turkeys, cocks and hens and ornamental pheasants pecked about on the pungent slopes and ridges of the magic midden, astonishing and entrancing Flora with their display of drooping shot-silk tail feathers, yellow chinoiserie, scarlet and coral combs and cloisonné plumage.

While she had been wandering in that strange landscape, Flora had been able to forget herself, and to flinch only slightly when her rebuffed smiles fell like dying butterflies into the mud, but the mirror in the car brought her abruptly back to Flora Loney, aged twenty-seven, wind-smudged and damp, lips chafed, blue eyes watering, fair hair in clumps of straw on the shoulders of her coat, black ankle boots stained and black tights speckled and a smear of dirt across one unusually pink cheekbone. Yes, she looked inescapably like Flora, blurred, anxious, untidy and late, with new footwear ruined by a careless impulse. If Great-Uncle Lorimer had not been expecting her, she would have gone straight home, carrying with her the picture of those exotic birds on the golden dunghill as sufficient adventure for one day. She reversed along the track, splashing a sullen couple in woolly hats, negotiated the turning into Bourne Avenue and found a parking space. She walked up the path on her long black legs under her short black coat as nervously as a little girl going to a party, with her tape recorder in her bag, clutching a paper cone of orange spray carnations.

The house looked ordinary enough, Edwardian, double-fronted, with dull green paint and windows looking out on to wintry shrubs and the tips of bulbs, but what had she expected, a bunch of balloons bobbing on the gate, a bucket of whitewash balanced on the porch? She took a deep breath and pushed the bell, heard its tired voice in the interior, and waited, contemplating an umbrella like an injured fruitbat. Footsteps shuffled and the door was opened by an old woman in purple pompommed slippers, with her hair piled in an elaborate confection of peroxide peaks and swirls on top of her head, circles of rouge on white powdered cheeks and a crimson mouth in which her own lips were lost somewhere. Giggling with relief, Flora said, 'I can see I've come to the right house!'

'What do you mean?'

'Grimaldi House. The Home for Retired Clowns.'

'Next door,' said the woman, shutting her own in Flora's face, which burst into flames of embarrassment and guilt.

Flora could have wept at her own ill-judged verbal custard pie. Me and my big mouth, she thought, fishing in her pocket for a stub of lipsalve and applying it to her frayed lips. She could no more make amends than she could have eaten her words at the dinner party the night before, when she had remarked, 'A fettucine worse than death,' as her hostess put down the dish. After that everything, including the soufflé that followed, had fallen rather flat. Flora was almost at the gate when she heard, 'Miss!'

She turned, ready to attempt an apology.

'I doubt if they'll take you. Why don't you try a different career instead? Apply for one of those government retraining schemes?'

'Yes, thanks. I might do that. Good idea,' Flora was bleating as the door snapped shut again.

The name on the gate was Grimsby Lodge. Grimaldi House was indeed the house next door. But the false clowness had been nearer the mark than she knew. A few years earlier Flora had been one of only two students, in a class of thirty-five studying circus skills, who had failed to graduate. Just one more smallish shame in a lifetime of fumbled catches and dropped opportunities. How right Daddy had been to suggest that Flora was a little unbalanced even to contemplate the high wire, and how smug he had been when she had fallen off. Since she had flunked circus skills, she had seen former classmates coining it in from the crowds in Covent Garden, and once, broke, desperate and behind with the rent, Flora had set up with her juggling balls on someone else's pitch, only to be pelted from the Piazza. Her fellow-failure, a young woman named Ziggy Deville, with whom Flora was superficially friendly, now had her own column on a newspaper which paid her vast sums of money to write about her hangovers, discarded diets, disastrous love life and the drug-related deaths of her flatmates.

A sad-faced visitor was leaving Grimaldi House as Flora arrived and he held the front door open for her, admitting her to the hall, where she tinkled the ceramic handbell that stood under a vase of beige silk roses next to the visitors' book. Flora glanced at the page, hoping to recognise some illustrious showbiz name, and saw that somebody had drawn a smiley face by way of signature. She waited apprehensively, inhaling a potpourri of late-afternoon ennui, tea in plastic beakers and air-freshener. A portrait of the great Grimaldi hung on the wall, opposite a garish and rather tactless print of a clown with a downturned mouth and a teardrop oozing from his painted eye. Televisions rumbled behind doors, cutlery clashed in a distant steel sink. Eventually a small woman of Far-Eastern mien, in a pink overall, appeared.

'Can I help you?'

'Oh, yes, thank you. I've come to see my Great-Uncle Lorimer. He's expecting me. I wrote.'

The woman stared at Flora.

'Looney the Clown,' Flora added helpfully.

'Oh dear. If you'd like to just take a seat in the visitors' lounge.'

A white door was closed behind Flora. She sat on the chintz sofa wondering what the pink-overalled woman had meant: *if* Flora just took a seat, would Great-Uncle Lorimer be wheeled in to her in a chair like the one she had seen folded in the hall; would she be led into a roomful of clowns in full motley and be expected to pick out the right one? She hadn't seen Looney since she was three and had been carried screaming back to her seat after she had rushed into the circus ring to batter with her tiny fists the clown who tipped a bucket of yellow paint down Looney's trousers. Would she just be left sitting here until she was old enough to be wheeled away herself? Not daring to try the door in case it was locked, Flora combated her panic by deep breathing. Nobody knew she was here. She had told nobody of her mission that afternoon. She tried to concentrate on the hand-stitched Serenity Prayer on the wall, but found herself thinking about a friend who had lost a toe in the throes of a charismatic church service in the Brompton Road, and she turned to study a signed poster of the Cottle Sisters' Circus. Grimaldi House was, she knew, a benevolent institution founded by a famous circus family and maintained by voluntary contributions and fundraising activities. Flora recalled seeing a minibus without wheels in the front garden. The residents of Grimaldi House weren't going anywhere, it seemed. She began to worry about the woman in the pink overall, and wondered if she were a prisoner too. A Filipina child-prostitute, tricked into a fake marriage, and held as a suburban slave, possibly even a sex-slave, in a house of dotard clowns.

Was it her duty to help the woman to escape? Ziggy Deville would know what to do, if she were here, and she could then expose the whole racket in her newspaper column. If only she had a mobile, she could call Ziggy now. Except that she'd probably be asleep or too hungover to speak or in bed with somebody, or dead or something. Flora heard the desolate buzzing and thumping of a vacuum cleaner, such a bleak sound on a Sunday afternoon, and an old man droning out, 'If you don't want the whelks, don't muck 'em abaht,' over and over again, until Flora felt lost on a timeless foreshore made up of whelk shells ceaselessly shifting with the tide. She was about to try the door when it opened and a tall, fair woman in a brown and beige jacquard dress came in.

'I'm Mrs Endersby. Sit down again, won't you, my dear? That's right. I'm afraid I've got some rather sad news for you. Your poor dear uncle slipped away from us in the early hours of this morning.'

'How?' said Flora, dazedly picturing a clown sliding like a shadow under a sash window into the pre-dawn darkness and shinning down a drainpipe. 'He was expecting me. I wrote. I really need to talk to him. I'm his brother's official biographer. Sort of.'

'I'm afraid he just couldn't hang on any longer, dear. He was already very frail, and an infection in somebody of his age – well . . . Of course the sixty cigarettes a day for all those years, until he came to us, had taken their toll . . .'

Flora gazed at Mrs Endersby. It was the first time she had actually seen somebody wearing that dress advertised on the back pages of tabloid Sunday supplements, with smart gilt-effect buttons and matching belt-buckle trim. She realised that she was sitting on her flowers.

'Am I being thick?' she asked. 'I mean, are you trying to tell me that Great-Uncle Lorimer is dead?'

'I'm so sorry, my dear. I would have hoped that you might have been saved a journey – some of the other relatives have collected his bits and pieces, and the gentlemen from Messrs Chappell are in charge of the Arrangements. They gave one of our long-term "Grimaldis" a lovely circus send-off recently, with a dear little baby elephant pulling the hearse. Perhaps you saw it on *Newsroom South-East*? Oh, no, you wouldn't have, you've come all the way down from Scotland, haven't you? Such a shame.'

'Indirectly,' said Flora. There was no way she was going to ask which of the relatives had collected Lorimer's 'bits and pieces'. There were so many, and any one of them was capable of pipping her at the post in the biography stakes, given half a chance. Poor old Looney. She knew his funeral would not make the local news and that Mrs Endersby knew it too and despised them all accordingly. She hadn't even let him smoke, poor old bugger, probably not even an exploding cigar for old times' sake.

'He wouldn't want you to upset yourself,' said Mrs Endersby. 'Dear old Looney, we'll miss him. He was always such a merry soul, never complained. Are you in the profession yourself? No, I thought not. Never mind, I'm sure our Looney's got them all in fits up in heaven now!'

'I bet you say that to all the girls,' Flora muttered as Mrs Endersby cocked an ear ceilingwards as if to catch the gales of angelic laughter. All Flora could hear was, 'If you don't want the whelks, don't muck 'em abaht.'

'Doesn't that man ever sing anything else?' she asked, taking a tissue from a conveniently sited box.

'Oh, that's our Corky. Quite a card is our Corky. Keeps us on our toes, bless him,' she added grimly. 'Oh, I almost forgot. Looney left something for you. He was most particular you should have it. I'll just ask Mrs Ho to fetch it before you go.'

She left the door open as she went into the hall and shook the little bell. Flora heard an exasperated female voice say, 'Put it away now, Chippy. It's not clever and it's not funny.'

Flora's heart was beating faster. Great-Uncle Lorimer had thought of her at the last. If only she hadn't put off the visit.

Mrs Endersby returned, followed by the sex-slave, now identified as Mrs Ho, carrying a white cardboard box. Flora took it awkwardly.

'Aren't you going to open it?' asked Mrs Endersby.

'See what your uncle give you,' Mrs Ho encouraged.

Flora hesitated. Mrs Ho was probably very keen on ancestors and would think that Flora was dishonouring Great-Uncle Lorimer by her lack of enthusiasm, but she was afraid to open the box. It was as if she might find Uncle Lorimer inside, shrunk to the size of a doll or a mummified monkey in a clown's costume. She prised up a corner, then lifted the lid. On a bed of faded pink tissue paper lay a pair of clown's shoes.

Cradling the box like a baby she hadn't wanted, Flora said, 'I wonder why . . .'

A younger woman, in pale blue, hurried in, saying, 'Sorry to butt in, but could you come please, Mrs Endersby? There's been an incident in the Big Top!'

Flora followed them into the hall and saw, through a half-open door at the end of the corridor, old men in dressing gowns slumped on a circle of chairs under the bright circus mural running round the walls.

Mrs Endersby, excusing herself, strode towards the Big Top. Mrs Ho showed Flora out.

As she sat in the car, hoping that her orange carnations, which she had left on the sofa in the visitors' lounge, would perk up in water and give pleasure to the poor souls in the Big Top, but suspecting that they would find a home in Mrs Endersby's sanctum, a minicab drew up beside her. As it reversed, Flora glimpsed a white masklike face at the passenger window. She pulled away quickly. So it had been Great-Uncle Lorimer's room that they were hoovering. She remembered a children's television programme showing how clowns register their makeup by painting it on eggs which are then stored in the vault of a special clowns' church in the East End of London. What was the copyright on a greasepaint smile, Flora wondered, ten years, fifty years, a hundred years, eternity? Or, in an East End crypt tonight, would an eggshell be ceremoniously smashed?

'Oh no, not clown shoes! I must be in for some pretty bad news!' Flora's mother, Ella, said when Flora telephoned her that evening.

'What do you mean, Mother? I've just *given* you some pretty bad news.'

'It's a song, "Clown Shoes". I've been trying to remember the words for years, and who it was by. Was it Johnny Burnett? Anyway, darling, of course it's sad about Lorimer, but he had a good innings, or whatever clowns have, and I hardly knew him. He *was* your *father*'s uncle, you know. Anyway, in the song, this girl sends her boyfriend a pair of clown shoes to tell him they're through. It's hilarious – as if sending clown shoes was standard dating protocol. Do you think there was a special clowns' shoe department in the shoe store, or that they had to buy them from a circus? Anyway, it ends up with the boy putting the clown shoes on. Sad. Can't you just see the High School Hop, with all the Jilted Johns bopping around in clown shoes?'

'No, Mother. I'd better ring Daddy.'

'Poor Looney. I wonder what they did with his wig. It was green. Looney was a punk before his time. I wonder if that's where Keith got it from.'

'Of course he didn't.'

One of Flora's cousins had enjoyed brief local fame, in Maybole, as Keith Grief, lead singer with the Kieftans.

Flora, lying on her sofa bed, with a packet of Marks and Spencer's cream cheese and chives crisps to hand, Mozart's Requiem playing quietly, dialled Aberdeen, picturing her father in a claret-coloured corduroy jacket which, in fact, his third wife had thrown out years before. He was on his fourth marriage now. Flora was the child of his second. When Flora had been a little girl, she had wanted to be a poet in a jacket with leather elbow patches. She had had her own study in the kneehole of Daddy's desk, where she had written her poems on a toy typewriter, but Daddy had left when she was five and her brother Hamish was three. Flora's third stepmother, Ishbel, picked up the phone.

'Hello, Flora, how are you? Have you got snow down there too? What's the weather like?'

'Dreich,' said Flora. 'Foggy. A real mushroom-souper.'

'You'll be wanting a word with your father. Hang on, I'll give him a shout. He's just sorting out the boys' computers.'

'Don't bother,' Flora almost said, bitterly, but remembering that she was the bearer of bad news, forbore to hang up. Ishbel had taken to calling herself Bel since she had published her volume of verses on childbirth, *Drupes and Pomes*. Wedding photographs showed long brown hair cut in a fringe, under an Alice band of ice-blue roses, huge hazel eyes swimming behind hexagonal spectacles, dangling ear-rings, a gift from the groom, an outfit with too many lapels and a blue carnation in silver paper and a blouse with gilt-trimmed buttons the size of quails' eggs. The mail order catalogue bride, Ella had called her, but marriage had altered Ishbel. With all his faults, nobody could deny that George 'Dod' Loney was a worker, a grafter. That was what they said of him. He was a fanatical supporter of his football team, the Dons, and he had dreamed once of captaining Scotland in the Poetic League, so to speak. Now, here he is, turning out in all weathers for third-division fixtures, stiff-legged in his impeccable old-fashioned kit, bringing a whiff of brilliantine, starch and dubbin to the field of younger players, and the price tag for all those goalless draws, lost matches and substitutions could be read in the lines of his face. As if the usual fouls and penalties of literary life were not enough to contend with, Dod had a wife who was in greater demand on the poetry circuit than he was, a son who was making a name in the books pages of the English papers, and a daughter who was threatening to write a biography of a talent greater than himself, a profligate who had squandered his gifts, scored over and over again with an effortless arc of the ball from an impossible angle, and then been stretchered off in disgrace before half-time. Dod sucked on a bitter wedge of lemon.

Flora heard his feet on creaking stairs, loping up from the basement den, thought of the boys' computers and her tin typewriter, and hardened her heart against his craggy charm and iron-blue hair.

'Aye, aye, Flora. Fit like?'

'I'm well, thank you, Father. But the bearer of bad news, I'm afraid.'

'I've heard.'

'Oh. Anyway, it was surreal, I went there, to Grimaldi House, and it was full of ancient clowns. Great-Uncle Lorimer had left me something, you'll never guess . . .'

From his study window Dod could see the statue of Wallace in Union Terrace Gardens with a bonnet of snow. He interrupted Flora.

'Ah well, he had a good – clownings. I suppose that puts paid to your notion of attempting the Life, then?'

'On the contrary, Father. I'll see you at the funeral. I've ordered black balloons, and a little baby elephant to lead the cortège, as a mark of respect.'

Death by Art Deco

In shop windows all along the King's Road, pale spring clothes struck optimistic attitudes, gesturing behind wet glass to the people hurrying past in their winter black, with umbrellas blowing inside out and heads bowed against the February wind that came straight off the North Atlantic seaboard loaded with melting ice. Those pastel linens make you long for sunshine as yellow as the daffodils shivering on the flower stalls, Lily thought, for coral, sand, silver, turquoise, and spicy ochres bleached by the heat. She was on her way home from work, one of the crowd pouring in and out of Sloane Square tube station. Lily was seventeen and had just become aware of the importance of wearing colours appropriate to the seasons. She had only recently got the point of turquoise. True turquoise, not peacock blue or eau-de-nil or aquamarine or the debased hues of lacy bedjackets and babies' cardigans and velour leisure-suits that call themselves turquoise, but the vibrant stone of scarab and torque and misshapen ancient beads and Islamic glaze.

Pulling down the brim of the hat skewered to her rain-frizzled hair with a Bakelite pin in the shape of two Scottie dogs with rhinestone eyes, she quickened her pace, almost certain that tonight the letter would be waiting for her. She had to leave the house in Finchley, where she lived with her parents, before the post arrived in the morning, and it was tantalising to think of that envelope lying on the hallstand all day, unopened. Surely the winner of the Untapped Talent Short Story Competition, sponsored by *Contour* magazine, with a first prize of two hundred pounds and guaranteed publication, must be notified soon.

Her story, 'Death by Art Deco', was gaudily painted, glittering and flamboyant, but would the judges appreciate that? Should she have made it more Fortuny and Arpège? As she passed the man selling the *Big Issue*, she was struck by the queasy thought that she ought to have mentioned the homeless. Or brought in drugs. Did a story about a serial killer have street cred now? She wished that she had taken the trouble to check out the judges, and read some of their work to see what they would go for. She had never even heard of two of them, but Andrea Heysham was famous. It was awesome to think of Andrea Heysham reading her story. Absorbed in that thought, Lily went through the ticket barrier and down the steps, and as she descended her conviction that her story was a winner rose again. Her job, as assistant to the miserable Welsh proprietors of Bizarre Bazaar, a tiny shop which specialised in jewellery and artefacts of the twenties and thirties, had proved inspirational in supplying authentic detail, and to avert the horror of Mr and Mrs Pritchard recognising themselves in print as victims of the serial killer, she had turned them into a miserable Welsh gay couple, look you. There's cunning.

In a pink-washed terrace house not far from Sloane Square, Andrea Heysham was lying on the floor of her study surrounded by jiffy bags, paperclips, scrunched-up balls of paper and manuscripts. She had regretted agreeing to judge this competition as soon as the blasted stories arrived some weeks ago, hundreds of them it seemed, and now she could put off the disagreeable task no longer. She had to find her Untapped Talent tonight. Andrea was a tall woman in her late forties dressed in dusty black leggings and tunic that emphasised the top-heaviness they were meant to disguise. A fraught coronet of yellow hair stuck up in points from her working bandeau of black Lycra above her wide forehead, and a cigarette dropped ash. Reading glasses, resting on rounded cheekbones and a slightly retroussé nose, magnified her brown eyes.

On the desk below the shelves of her own books in several languages – Andrea thought of herself as a dependable shrub which flowered every second summer – a word processor sat in a plastic mac: wisely, for a coffee stain testified to the uncertain climate of the room. Andrea ought to have been working at it now, but the screen had been blank for weeks. Big coloured paperclips held wodges of unopened post and several invitations were stuck behind a bowl of sepia scentless rosebuds, fluff and cat fur, among the jumble of china and glass on the mantelpiece.

Tarnished silver-framed photographs of her parents, both dead now, and her son Kit's progression from beautiful babyhood through shining schooldays to handsome graduation. Kit was living somewhere in Camberwell now with a transpontine vampire called Melissa, wasting his education, not calling his mother, who found their estrangement almost unbearable. Andrea's elbow caught a glass of red wine, tipping it over the pages she was riffling through.

'Bugger.'

She ripped off a handful of sodden text and aimed it at an over-flowing black bin liner. Pouring herself another drink, she read on for a couple of minutes before lobbing the remainder of it into the sack. An orange tabby cat came mewing in from the paved back garden out of the rain, running across the room to rub its wet back across her face. It left a trail of smudged pawprints across the papers.

'For goodness' sake, Pumpkin,' said Andrea, picking him up and kissing him, with the cigarette clamped in the side of her mouth. 'Those are somebody's dreams you're treading on.'

She crossed another name off her list and poured another drink. The haphazard pile of unread scripts was dwindling: any which contained the sentence 'That summer I sprouted breasts', or featured pubescent boys measuring their manhoods with school rulers, went straight into the bin bag, along with half a dozen old clockmakers who had escaped the Nazis, all the homeless, a dozen giros, and several pounds of prize leeks and marrows. Andrea picked a cold baked bean from the transparent sleeve of 'Death by Art Deco' by Lily Richards, and ate it as she skimmed the pages. Pretty name, Lily.

'Pumpkin. I think we've found our winner!'

Good characterisation. Those Welsh fairies, Dai and Dafydd, were remarkably like that ghastly couple at Bizarre Bazaar, who had overcharged her for a Lalique scent spray, some rather splendid ear-rings and a few bits and pieces of amusing tat. Neat plot too. Dai and Dafydd are poisoned by a rare Amazonian venom injected into matching pairs of faux pearl cufflinks. Andrea noted some minor critical points: 1. The opening sentence suggests a story about a ruthless serial killer yet the only victims are Dai (intentional pun?) and Dafydd. 2. Check spelling of Dafydd. Shd it be Dyffydd? 3. Writer has used the word 'faux' thirteen times.

Never mind, it would do. Now for two runners up. Andrea rooted around for three OK-looking manuscripts, the first of which turned out to be about a sensitive little boy who was rescued from his brutal stepfather by a talking dolphin. Then it was a toss-up for third place between a peeping Tom and a woman who wrote poison-pen letters. Poison pen won on points because Pumpkin had plumped down on the penultimate page of peeping Tom, preventing Andrea from finishing it. She Tippexed a smear of cigarette ash from 'Boy with a Dolphin', wondering why men were so in love with themselves as little boys, and as she rose stiffly and slightly unsteadily to place her choices on her desk, red drops spattered them, from a finger cut on the sharp staple of a jiffy bag.

'Blood,' said Andrea. 'That's what they want, Pumpkin, blood.'

At the working lunch the following day the groomed and soignée public Andrea found herself in fierce disagreement with her two fellow judges, both of whom had binned 'Death by Art Deco' as decisively as she had selected it. Swallowing her astonishment that they appeared to take the whole thing seriously, she felt it incumbent on her to champion her choice. The wispy Angelica Dodder favoured some account of a young girl's mental breakdown, which Andrea had missed. Well, as the author of *Mistletoe in a Dirty Glass*, a remaindered Virago Classic depicting her own descent into the netherworld, Angelica would, wouldn't she? Anybody could go into a loony bin and write about it, but that didn't make it Art: God knows Andrea had been tempted at times herself, and who didn't feel like cracking up at Christmas? It was only normal. Maldwyn Evans, with the tightly knotted tie, rimless glasses and neatly trimmed beard of the fanatic, agreed with Angelica and rejected 'Death by Art Deco' on political as well as aesthetic grounds.

'What do you mean, racist?' Andrea demanded, agitating an annoying thread of anchovy wound round a molar.

'It's anti-Welsh.'

'Don't be ridiculous. It's perfectly OK to hate the Welsh. They're white − well, white-ish. Everybody does.'

'I'm Welsh.'

'Oh, but I never think of you as Welsh, Maldwyn. I mean, you're not exactly Organ Morgan, are you?'

He flushed and pulled the knot of his tie even tighter. 'I'm sorry, Andrea. "Death by Art Deco" is disallowed by a majority decision, and that's final.'

'Well, screw you,' said Andrea and, turning to the waitress, demanded, 'Who snuck an anchovy on to this bruschetta?'

Angelica smiled placatingly at the waitress and looked anxiously from one to the other of the opponents, thrilled to be in a majority but fearful of unpleasantness. Why did everything always have to be spoiled? Andrea rounded on her, angrily projecting the image of the vampire Melissa on to their chosen winner. 'If you're determined to raise false hopes in the pierced breast of some tattooed neo-Goth with magenta dreadlocks and dirty fingernails poking out of torn lace gloves, on your own head be it. I resign.'

Her literary judgement had been questioned, that was what really rankled, and she had given up her time for free, for nothing. There was no way that she would admit now that her powers of discrimination might not have been quite up to par when she made her choice. She strode along the King's Road with an armful of scarlet amaryllis and a mouthful of chocolate; treats to console a hurt little girl, even if she had had to buy them herself. Andrea's longing to see Kit swelled and burst like bubblegum, leaving an empty hole as she noticed that the sun was shining on clouds like cold spring lambs. She went into Waitrose and bought a couple of little chops. Then, finding herself outside Bizarre Bazaar, she decided to put her bruised writer's instinct to the test. It was really only half a shop: the other side, which sold candles, was all purples and yellows and wafted the scent of wax lemons and violets and primroses over the cluttered shelves and glass cases of art deco true and faux.

A girl with eyes that were almost violet and a great bunch of hair the colour some call Titian, smiled at Andrea.

'Can I help you, or are you just browsing?'

'Browsing be buggered,' came a Welsh mutter. 'Sun's shinin', she's got wine on 'er breath, she's 'ad a good lunch, make a sale, girl! We done no bloody business all mornin'.'

Andrea looked round, at two heads bent over price lists, and back at the red-faced assistant. She had come to detest long hair, and you could make a coir doormat out of this lot, with enough left over for a set of coasters.

'I'm looking for something overpriced and preferably fake,' she said. 'Something faux. No, actually, I think it might be you I've come to see. You're not by any chance Lily Richards, the writer, are you?'

'Oh my God,' Lily said. 'It's you, isn't it?'

'Lily, you've had your two warnings about social calls!' came the voice of Mr Pritchard again, before the girl could answer.

'Right then. I'll get my coat,' said Lily. 'Mr and Mrs Pritchard, you have just witnessed the beginning of my real life.'

Ten minutes later she was sitting opposite Andrea in Picasso's with a spoon of knickerbocker glory halfway to her quivering lips, and a big glacé cherry of grief stuck in her throat. Opposite Andrea Heysham, the famous novelist, who had come to seek her out only to half-break her heart.

'Do take your hair out of your ice cream.' Andrea took an irritated sip at her espresso. 'I've got a proposition to put to you.'

'It all sounds rather dubious, Lily,' her mother said, touching a petal of the amaryllis flaunting itself from a vase on the green oilcloth of their kitchen table, where she and Lily sat opposite each other. 'I never thought of these as cut flowers. You say she's offered you a job, but doing what, precisely? This Andrea Heysham may be a brilliant writer as you say, but it's not as though you're a trained secretary, is it? I mean, you may not have liked the Pritchards, but at least that was a proper job.'

'Mum, I'm an amanuensis–cum–PA now, whether you like it or not!'

The strange word bloomed between them like one of the alien red lilies that woman had pressed on her gullible daughter. Janet Richards, who worked as a home help, blamed Lily's father, a telephone engineer who had fantasised about being a pop star until an audition for *New Faces* smashed his dreams, for not having backed her up in her bid to persuade Lily to go to college. She sat on at the table worrying after Lily left the kitchen. Writing was all very well as a hobby, she herself went to an art class once a week, but she couldn't see it as a career for a young girl with a handful of mediocre GCSEs. If she was serious in her ambition to be a writer, Lily should have applied herself at school and gone to university to study English. Janet accused a certain authoress too, whose name she had forgotten, who had come to Lily's school in her final term to run a series of creative writing workshops, putting ideas into Lily's head. She could have reminded Lily of that essay on *To Kill a Mockingbird* that she had got her dad to write for her, and in her conversation with Lily just now she had managed to bite back the truth, that Lily's story had actually been rejected. She had seen Andrea Heysham's books in the library but had somehow never got round to taking one out. Now she almost hated her, as if Andrea Heysham were trying to take her daughter away from her. The Chelsea Set, she thought, her lips pursed in a sneer.

Lily, who that afternoon had seen her hopes and ambitions melting in a tall glass, only to be reglorified by Andrea, went out to the hall to telephone her boyfriend through a blur of disappointed tears. In the silence that followed her news she picked a nodule of paint from her mother's 'View of Finchley Rooftops' that hung above the phone. Then he said, 'You want to watch out. She probably fancies you. You know what those literary types are like.'

'If that's what you think, Damian, I've nothing further to say to you.'

Janet's doubts would have been confirmed if Lily had told her that she had spent her first morning in her new job taking Pumpkin to the vet for his booster flu jab, and part of the afternoon shopping in Marks and Spencer for Andrea's dinner party. Lily kept her fingers crossed that she would be invited to stay and meet some of Andrea's writer friends, as she was a literary type herself now, but after she had hoovered and dusted and polished the drawing room Andrea told her she could go home. She was between cleaners, she explained, and had been too busy to do any house-work for a couple of weeks.

'Is this your son?' Lily asked, picking up Kit's graduation photograph in its shining silver frame. 'He's really good-looking, isn't he? What's he doing now?'

'Shacking up with some troglodyte south of the river,' replied Andrea. 'You know where the dusters and things live, don't you?' Lily's snubbed look reminded her of the job description she had concocted.

'We'll make a start on some of the backlog of post tomorrow,' she promised.

Lily sat in her bedroom with a notebook, at the white melamine child's desk Dad had got her from MFI years ago and made a start on her novel, *True Turquoise*. Mum's voice came from the hall.

'Who's picked the smoke off my chimney? Lily, don't you want to watch *Brookside*?'

'*Brookside* schmookside!' said Lily.

She wished she were in a room in Chelsea with paintings by real artists on the yellow walls and an iridescent classical CD spin-ning round, at work on a word processor, with a drinkypoo at hand. That was what Andrea had called her lunchtime Bloody Mary, using invisible inverted commas to indicate irony.

At one o'clock in the morning Andrea started clearing plates in a half-hearted way.

'You should get a dishwasher, Andrea,' her best friend remarked, taking the hint to ring for a cab.

'I have,' said Andrea. 'In a manner of speaking.'

After they had all gone Andrea sat on, smoking, thinking about Lily. Admittedly, pique at Angelica and Maldwyn had prompted her to tell the girl that she had chosen her story, but some impulse had made her take Lily on. It wasn't just because her latest cleaning lady had walked out. Perhaps, unconsciously, she had planned to replace Kit's Gothic girlfriend with an untainted flower. Was she then a procuress manqué? Why was she so unhappy? She had success, even if it meant people making all sorts of demands, all take and no give; she had Pumpkin, her friends, her house; she could afford to travel, but she was finding it increasingly difficult to motivate herself, with only the cat to turn to for advice, to make her feel real. Having Lily around would avert the danger of becoming a recluse, she thought, with her roots growing out until her hair looked like burnt toast spread with margarine, and of being found dead one day beneath an avalanche of paper, while the answerphone exploded with piled-up messages.

Andrea tried to be positive: she knew she would get Kit back again. Nothing could break that bond. And she genuinely liked Lily, who reminded her a little of herself when young, before her genius had turned out to be a middle-brow talent. But in admitting Lily to her life she would make herself vulnerable by exposing the reality of it, so different from the dreams of a starstruck amateur. She knew so much about so many things: mother love, love, the deaths of parents, of friends, divorce. She had lived so long that her work should have achieved the profound stateliness of a mature symphony, and yet she had nothing to say. It was out of the question that she would fail to deliver on time, but at this rate she would soon be reduced to dashing off a novel set in Chelsea, about a novelist with writer's block. Perhaps she should get out of town for a bit and bring back a sack of fertiliser for her imagination.

Kit Heysham was lying awake beside Melissa, who was curled up with her face to the wall. Moonlight and streetlight diffused by the cotton bedspread tacked over the window glittered on the crystals suspended on threads from the ceiling. Melissa had taken them from Phantasmagorica, the shop in Covent Garden where she had worked until recently. He heard her mutter in her sleep, the swooping sound of police cars, the tap in the shared kitchen dripping, the nocturnal sounds of a decaying house in multiple occupation, and shifted his position carefully, negotiating the wire sticking through the mattress. He thought about his mother. He hadn't read any of her books but he had witnessed enough of her hard work to respect her for them, even if he *had* sold her typewriter when he was nine years old. His father had married again and although Kit quite liked his half-sisters, he didn't visit very often. His mother and stepmother had something in common, besides Dad, Kit thought bitterly; both of them had been horrible to Melissa when they'd met her. He decided to take her round to Mum's again, if he could persuade her, so that Andrea could see how wrong she had been. He wanted them to be friends. Trying to get comfortable, he pulled the rubber band painfully from his ponytail and let his hair fan loose over his bare shoulders, releasing its vapours into the night air. It would be nice to have a bath at Mum's too.

'There's no way I'm going round there to be insulted,' said Melissa in the morning when he suggested calling on Andrea. 'Snobby cow.'

'We could have a bath there, she wouldn't mind,' he cajoled her.

'Yes she would. What's wrong with our bathroom here, if you're so keen on the idea?'

'It's filthy, and it's not really our bathroom, is it?'

'Oh, poor little Kitty, does he want his own bathroom den? I thought public school was meant to make you tough and enjoy bathing in other people's dirty bathwater?'

'It was only a very minor public school.'

'What's she call you Kit for, anyway? Why couldn't she just call you Chris like anybody else?'

The visit to Andrea's was deferred.

Like a child with a new best doll, Andrea started to take Lily about with her. Dressed in ice-cream colours, they went shopping, to a couple of private views and a few publishing parties. People began to speculate whether they were an item. Andrea also introduced Lily to her hairdresser, and the annoying mass of hair slithered to the floor in a heap of snakes. Lily's mother cried when she saw the result, but had to concede that it showed off Lily's cheekbones. Her father said he supposed it would grow back for the winter and asked how much it had cost, and Lily, who had no idea, had to lie, and then she felt guilty. The whole atmosphere of the house was upset by her new look. Meanwhile, *True Turquoise* almost filled two notebooks; admittedly, she hadn't managed to work in any turquoise yet, but Andrea had approved of the title. She was going to put it on Andrea's word processor when it was finished. 'Death by

Art Deco' she filed away, for the collection of stories which would follow the novel. It was so brilliant having Andrea to advise her; the only thing was, Andrea herself never seemed to write anything, even though she was always dressed in her writing outfit of leggings, tunic and headband when Lily arrived in the morning. She spent much of her time talking on the telephone, reading and going out to lunch and the opera or the theatre. 'I'm working in my head all the time,' she explained when Lily plucked up the courage to voice her fear that the next addition to Andrea's oeuvre might be late in delivery. 'And in my dreams. Putting words on paper is the easy part. Don't you find?'

'Oh, yes!' Lily agreed.

Each morning Lily, as amanuensis, had to deal with the quantities of post which came through Andrea's door. 'Refuse all requests to perform for nothing and bin anything upsetting from charities, everything from charities, in fact,' Andrea had instructed, 'and brown envelopes addressed in purple, green or red biro. They are from loonies and shouldn't be opened. Just use your initiative and get rid of anything that looks dreary or claims to be from somebody I was at school with. Manuscripts, and they are without exception unsolicited, come under that heading, and first novels hoping for a quote, unless you want them yourself. Vet the fan letters and give me only those that really merit a reply. I'll give you a list of the people I'm in to on the telephone. Oh, and tell any students writing theses to do their own bloody research, that's what they get grants for.'

Lily felt honoured at being asked to protect Andrea from all those awful people. She bought herself a stretchy working bandeau like Andrea's, even though her hair was too short to need one, and found it really helped. She was reading her way through Andrea's books, which were as brilliant as she had expected. Her admiration was soured only by jealousy of the characters who had lived in Andrea's head and heart, especially the girls, and she scrutinised herself anxiously for any of the faults which Andrea had criticised. It seemed that she had little in common with any of her friends now. She asked her mother to do bagels with cream cheese and scallions for breakfast, and she took up smoking at work and learned to enjoy a weak Bloody Mary. Andrea was getting through at least a hundred cigarettes a day. 'Why does that blasted son of mine never ring?' she growled. Kit must be mad, Lily thought: if she had a mother like Andrea, she'd be round there all the time.

'I've decided to go away for the weekend,' Andrea told her one Friday morning. 'To some friends in the country. Pick up some local colour, sort of thing. Do you think you could possibly –'

'Babysit Pumpkin? Yes of course. I'd love to! You have a nice break, you really deserve one.'

On the Saturday morning, Kit let himself and Melissa into the house. They could hear a Hoover upstairs.

'Mum?' he called.

There was no answer, and he led the way up to the study. The sound of the Hoover died. Kit pushed open the door and someone sprang across the room at him with a dagger. Melissa screamed. He grabbed a wrist, and saw it belonged to a mad-looking girl with her hair sticking out of a black band, clutching a silver paperknife.

'What are you doing here? Why are you wearing my mother's headband?'

'You're Kit, aren't you? I'm sorry. I thought you were a burglar.'

He let go of her.

'Who are you? Does my mother know you're here?'

'I'm Andrea's amanuensis. Lily.'

'What?'

'She's the cleaner, Chris!' said Melissa. 'What a crap job.'

'I recognised you from your photos,' Lily told Kit, ignoring Melissa. 'Your mother's really upset that you haven't been in touch. She'll be devastated to have missed you.'

She tried to smile at him, but they were intruders in the yellow room that now belonged to her and Andrea. They smelled of – mildew and Camel cigarettes, and Melissa, who looked like something malevolent from beyond the grave, with several silver rings in each ear, one long purple glass teardrop, and two rings in her nose, had picked up a Victorian figurine and was examining her lacy porcelain drawers with a tattooed talon.

'Yeah, well,' said Kit, 'we haven't got a phone, and you know

378

how it is with call-boxes, all vandalised or out of order when you want one.'

'Not any more,' said Lily. 'My father's a telephone engineer and he says that —'

'Where is my mother, anyway?' Kit interrupted her.

'She's gone to the country for the weekend, to see some friends.'

'Typical,' said Melissa. 'Well, might as well have a bath since we've come all this way.'

'Would you like some coffee?' Lily asked Kit when Melissa had gone. She remembered that she wanted to make friends with him, to be the one who brought him and Andrea together again. She tried not to mind his unwashed hair, fair like Andrea's but dull with the grease of a hundred burgers and chips.

'I'll make it. Mustn't keep you from your work.'

Kit was deflated and disappointed, and he had bribed Melissa needlessly.

He picked up the Hoover hose and handed it to Lily with a courteous, distancing smile and left the room, with the treacherous Pumpkin squawking at his heels. Lily burst into tears.

'I'm not the bloody cleaner. I'm a writer!'

To think she had often secretly fantasised about sitting round the kitchen table with Kit and Andrea, like a family, Melissa having been dumped.

It took her ages to clear up the kitchen after they had gone, and she had to remove a sickening nest of brown and magenta hairs from the plughole of the bath, in a piece of loo paper, with her eyes closed, and flush the toilet twice before it disappeared. Then she found a note from Kit to his mother on Andrea's desk, giving his address. 'Love ya, Mels' was scrawled across the bottom. Lily, still feeling violated and diminished by them, and sick after disposing of their hair, ripped the note furiously into little pieces and then, horrified at what she had done, hid the evidence under the debris of their lunch in the bin.

'You look terrible,' said Andrea on her return, dripping bluebells and red campion and cow-parsley. 'Has anything happened to Pumpkin?'

'No, no, he's fine. Good as gold. I just don't feel very well. I think I'd better go home.'

Andrea felt cheated of her homecoming, but said, 'Poor baby. OK then, off you go. Take a cab. I've had a wonderful time. Can't wait to get down to some work, actually, you'll be delighted to hear, and I've got lots of plans for tubs for the garden. We can go plant shopping tomorrow, when you're feeling better.'

For three days Lily lay in bed, listlessly watching soaps on the little portable television with her own guilty drama playing in her head, and sleeping fitfully while a film of dust formed on the Lucozade her mother brought each morning before she left for work. Andrea might never see Kit again, and all because of her. In her dreams, she found Kit's note, restored, and Andrea threw her arms round her and hugged and kissed her. Lily woke in tears, sweating in the sunshine assaulting her through the window. She made desperate plans to haunt Camberwell until she ran into Kit, so that she could explain that the note had been sucked into the vacuum cleaner and then beg him to ring Andrea, without mentioning his visit. She would do anything he asked in return. But how could she find him? There wasn't even a tube station in Camberwell where she could lurk. *True Turquoise* lay untouched under her bed. On the fourth day she got dressed, but it was even worse wandering round the small house like a tormented ghost. How could she have done that to Andrea? How could she have been such a spiteful, jealous coward? Andrea would hate her when she found out. What lies could she tell her to make her go on liking her? Her mother had telephoned Andrea for her, to explain that Lily was suffering from a nasty bug, and had been won over by Andrea's warm concern for Lily. Pumpkin sent a funny Get Well postcard. Lily could hardly look at it.

After a week Lily, faint with apprehension, rang the Chelsea door bell. Andrea let her into a house smelling of bluebells gone bad, kissing her on the cheek for the first time. Lily recoiled, unworthy, remembering her dreams.

'Sorry, I am a bit garlicky. Had people round last night. I'm afraid we've left a bit of a mess. Come and have some coffee. Do you feel up to a bit of gardening? This weather's too divine to waste, isn't it? I've managed to get quite a bit of work done this last week too – it hasn't been all partying. You're shivering! That d. and v. really takes it out of you, doesn't it?'

Lily felt unable to thank Pumpkin for his postcard. She piled up dirty plates in a silent miserable confusion of wanting to confess and terror of the consequences, while Andrea opened a fresh jar of coffee. She plunged the spoon through the foil with a crack that made Lily jump.

'By the way, Lily –'

Lily's heart lurched. Andrea knew of her crime.

Andrea kept her back to Lily, spooning coffee into two mugs, keeping it casual.

'Have you got my ear-rings?'

'Ear-rings?'

Relief, then a new panic, left Lily hot and cold. The kettle boiled and switched itself off. Andrea turned round, and saw guilt written all over Lily's face.

'The dangly black Bakelite ones, with faux pearls? I don't mind you borrowing my things, only I wish you'd ask. They are rather precious to me, and worth a bit and I would like them back.'

Andrea, picturing the naked branch of the little velvet tree where the ear-rings should have hung, and remembering her search for them, and the shocking realisation that they had been taken, nevertheless was still hoping that the matter could be settled without further embarrassment.

'I never touched your personal things,' said Lily. 'Any of them. I wouldn't! I've got too much respect.'

'Look, Lily, there's no point in prolonging this. We both know you did, so why not just say so?'

'But I didn't. I didn't! You can't say I did. You must have lost them yourself, in a taxi or somewhere, without noticing at the time. You often lose things when you've been – when you've been out. You know you do.'

At that Andrea wanted to slap the lies and defiance off Lily's white, tearful face. She felt a fool for having missed her. Her plans for the garden were collapsing in a stupid heap of compost. That silly postcard she'd sent from the cat.

'Oh, come on,' she said. 'I told you I don't mind. Just put them back and we'll forget the whole thing.'

Put them back. Like a thief.

'You've got to believe me. I swear I never touched your ear-rings.'

Lily stared back at an Andrea turned ugly, with no makeup and little puckers of skin under her eyes, arms folded across her enormous cat-furred chest, and a voice gone hard and posher, as if she were accusing a servant.

'This is ridiculous,' came out of thick pale lips like the rind of ham. 'I was willing to turn a blind eye to the fact that you helped yourself to most of my vodka and my bath oil, but this has gone too far!'

'Melissa!' Revelation flooded over Lily. 'Melissa took them! It must have been Melissa! They were here, her and Kit, while you were away. It must have been her. She had a bath. They both did. And they were drinking vodka!'

Andrea screwed up her eyes to shut out the image of Kit and Melissa splashing about in scented oil in her bath, glugging vodka from the bottle.

'How can you stand there, in my kitchen, telling such disgusting lies? How dare you use my son to manufacture an alibi to get yourself off the hook? If Kit was here, where's his note? I know my own son, he would at least have left a note. How could you be so cruel?'

'I'm not cruel,' Lily sobbed.

'No? What about that story you wrote, ridiculing your employers, wasn't that cruel? You betrayed them as you have betrayed me. I expect I'll be your next victim. Grist to your mill.'

'Kit did leave a note.'

'Oh yes? Where is it then? Why didn't you give it to me?'

'I – I – forgot.'

'You forgot,' Andrea repeated heavily. 'My only son who I haven't seen for months just happens to turn up the one weekend I'm away and leaves me a note, and you "forgot" to give it to me. How very convenient. I suppose you'll come up with some cock-and-bull story about Pumpkin eating it next. And putting the blame on poor little Melissa. How *low* of you, Lily.'

Her chin quivered into a pitted lemon and crumpled. Tears spurted from her eyes and she wiped her hand across her nose, giving a choking snort. 'First Kit and now you.'

At seeing Andrea broken, by her, and in the impossibility of saying anything at all, Lily picked up her bag and started backing through the door.

'Yes, go!' Andrea was shouting. 'Go! Get out of my house! And those ear-rings had better be in tomorrow's post or we'll see what your mother has to say! My friends warned me against you. "Remember that film *All About Eve*," they said. My God, I wish I'd listened to them. And your racist little story wasn't up to much anyway. Did you know you'd used the word "faux" thirteen times? Is that the mark of a writer? Is it? And serial killers are of no interest whatsoever, not that yours was too successful with only two victims, was he? They're old hat, stale buns, nerds in elastic-waisted anoraks! How many serial killers have *you* met? Your story's phoney, fake. It's all false, false, false, like you, Lily Richards! Faux faux faux faux faux faux . . .'

Lily rushes out into the glare of the street, groping blindly in her bag as she runs, flinging her writing bandeau away in a black circle that loops the aerial of a passing car. Then she is running along the King's Road, bashing into people, in the glitter and noise, streaked with the shame of her writing, her life, her whole self that Andrea had torn into pieces and dumped like garbage from a bin over her head, running until an insurmountable barrier of loss suddenly slams down ahead of her and she stops abruptly in the middle of the pavement, knocking an ice cream out of a child's hand.

Trouser Ladies

One by one the pumpkins, heavy orange lamps glowing against the deepening blue dusk, are carried into the shop and extinguished. Oranges, lemons, satsumas, pomegranates follow in procession, and when the greengrocer's grass, bleached now by the street lights, is rolled up in a strip of muddy turf, the woman watching from her window turns away into her own life in a room lit by tangerine glass globes and fans. A low band of sound runs past her like a pattern etched into the glass, a dado on the wallpaper, so familiar that she hasn't heard it for years and, besides, Beatrice at seventy-six is becoming a little deaf. Her white hair is still thick, while the embroidered kimono she is wearing, for she is in the process of getting ready to go out, has faded from peacock to azure and worn to patches of gossamer grids and loose hammocks of threads slung between blossoms and birds. She has let herself be diverted by the street because she is apprehensive about the evening, fearing that it will be an uneasy walk down a memory lane signposted by someone else's reminiscences, made strange like a road in a dream. As a journalist she had been photographed in battledress and safari suit in theatres of war, but she is in a blue funk at the thought of meeting the daughter of her best and dearest, now dead, friend in the neutral territory of a restaurant. Catriona Ling had seen the announcement of Beatrice Alloway's birthday in the paper, had telephoned her, and was probably regretting her impulse as much as Beatrice rued her surprised acceptance.

Chinese lanterns and bronze and yellow chrysanthemums, birthday tokens, are crammed into a Bizarre jug on a low table and a glass rectangle in front of the tiny black grate-basket; and on the mantelpiece, at the centre of a jumble of cards and invitations, is a branch of spindle-berries in a conical blue vase. Beatrice bought them herself, making her birthday the excuse for extravagance. They cost her six pounds, but she had to have them. She catches her breath each time she sees the pinkish-red four-lobed fruits opening in the warmth of the room like a flight of wing-cases across the cobalt-blue wall, flaunting their orange seeds. One of her birthday cards, the one from Catriona's twin sisters, had cast a blight of unease over her birthday, and although it is hidden by another card, it obtrudes as she gazes at the spray of spindle and remembers Betty's excitement when they came upon a spindle tree, the first either of them had seen, at the edge of a little wood in Kent more than forty years ago.

It had been the afternoon of Beatrice's ill-conceived visit to Canterbury. What she had hoped or imagined would come from a descent on Betty's domesticity she did not know then and couldn't say now, just that she had been overcome by longing to see her again. Beatrice Alloway and Betty Gemmell had grown up together in Ardrossan, gone to school and university together, and then Betty had married Alec Ling, the boy next door. Betty and Alec, and their son, wee Donald, went to London to seek their fortune, found that the streets were not paved with gold, and now Alec was a miner, digging away in the Kent coalfield to support a growing family. Beatrice's unannounced arrival that Sunday had caused a confusion that had sent them all, Alec, Betty, Donald, the twins Heather and Erica and four-year-old Catriona, out on this awkward walk. Suddenly there was the spindle tree, exotic and English, with red leaves and pink fruit trembling on delicate stalks in the blue autumn sky. Heather and Erica held up the baby dolls Beatrice had brought, to admire the berries, and Beatrice wished that the whole lot of them, Alec and the children, would prick their fingers on a spindle and fall asleep, like the Sleeping Beauty's court, so that she and Betty could be alone together.

Then, like the good sport she was, Auntie Bee was instigating a game of hide-and-seek, whooping through falling leaves, bobbing up behind bushes and letting the children pelt her with damp handfuls of red and brown and yellow, chasing them round tree trunks.

The smell of kicked-up leaves, fungus and lichen is pungent in her head as she opens her wardrobe and takes out the black suit in which she will face the evening. The trouble was, and is, Betty Gemmell was the love of her life, and she was Betty's best friend.

Ting-a-ling-ling goes the old-fashioned black bell on the shop door, saying our names because it belongs to us, the Ling twins, Heather and Erica, Erica and Heather – our names were Father's little joke. He loved all the *Ericaceae*, and sprinkled sand on our cloddy garden to make them feel at home. When we moved into our brand-new council house in Canterbury, all the gardens were raw, shining clay; like everybody else, we planted vegetables and chrysanthemums and Esther Reeds, big white daisies or marguerites that we children took to Harvest Festival in the solid bunches with a blob of carnations at the centre like the jam on semolina, but only Father grew heathers and dwarf conifers in crazy paving. Mother preferred heather growing wild, in Scotland, where our family came from. She hated dwarf conifers.

We had come down south in 1948, first to dismal lodgings where we were all very unhappy, and then to our new house, east of the Martyrs' Memorial, near a railway bridge where you could stand and let the trains puff great cornets of pink and white steam and smoke over you so that it was like being at the heart of an ice cream. Canterbury had been badly bombed in the war, and when you were out playing you came on half-houses, with staircases leading nowhere, rising from the rubble of buddleia, willowherb and toadflax, smashed bricks and glass and porcelain, and rolls of brambles and barbed wire. You squeezed through the corrugated iron that fenced off the wasteland and found heaps of jagged slates for tomahawks lying among the nettles, and once a gang of us discovered a shining pile of aluminium offcuts that made swords and arrows beyond our wildest dreams. A boy called Goldfish was shot in the tongue, but lived to tell the tale.

Of course, it's all changed a lot now, but we can still see it as it was, the streets of little houses behind privet hedges and hydrangeas, with beds visible in front rooms, and old men with two sticks sitting on walls, and people limping along on one big black surgical boot, with a steel stirrup to make their legs the same length. And even now one of us just has to say 'Remember' and the smell of our house comes back in whiffs of pastel distemper,

bright patterned carpet, the new wood and varnish of the furniture smelling like Lefevre's, where we bought it, and the ploughed
earth of the garden glittering with bits of bottle glass, fragments
of pottery and oyster shells.

We can remember school too, vividly, and it's quite strange when
one of our old schoolmates comes into the shop accompanied by
children or grandchildren, but mostly we get tourists. Our little
shop is near the cathedral and we sell pretty things, angels and
illustrated bibles, silver Canterbury crosses and Celtic jewellery,
cards, bookmarks, gargoyles and so forth, and we live in the flat
above, overlooking the River Stour and the Westgate Towers and
gardens. It seems as though people don't really change, they just
grow bigger, and when some middle-aged voice asks for this or
that, they might as well be saying, 'Got any fag cards, twin?'

We had. Fat bundles of them, in rubber bands.

'Got any film stars? Who's your favourite film star, twin?'

Doris Day, we said. We hadn't seen any of her films, but you
had to have a favourite film star. Some children queued up after
the register for National Savings stamps with pictures of Prince
Charles and Princess Anne, and had scrapbooks of the royal family.
Our brother Donald belonged to a stamp club, Catriona collected
bits of coloured glass which she called her jewels, and woolly
caterpillars whom she called her friends; and we latched on to
Doris Day. One day our made-up love for her became real.
Mother's best friend Beatrice, whom we always called Auntie
Bee, although we hadn't met her and we only knew her from
the Christmas presents she sent us, was a journalist and sometimes she sent Mother magazines and we would fall on them
with our blunt scissors in the hopes of finding a picture of Doris
Day inside. Pink and white, gingham and golden, laughing eyes
as blue as speedwells or periwinkles, with her wide, eager, cream-
cheese smile, Doris Day was our goddess. Not an ideal to aspire
to, for we knew that we, with our ginger hair and scratched legs
and floppy cotton socks, hadn't a hope of growing into anything
resembling Doris. Film stars were an entirely different species
then, a race apart; we couldn't tell one from another of this
current lot if we wanted to, no grace, no style, no glamour, no
charm, no charisma, no quality, and we're still waiting for the

real film stars to come back, to descend from Valhalla and reclaim Hollywood.

It must have been about 1951, the year of the Festival of Britain, when we finally got to meet Auntie Bee. At that time, women wearing trousers were a comparatively rare sight, apart from bus conductresses and the occasional brown landgirl in a brown landscape, glimpsed through a bus window. Catriona used to call them 'trouser ladies'. It was a dull autumn Sunday afternoon, and we were sitting reading on the windowsill of our front room, Heather sitting on the left as usual, Erica on the right-hand side and Catriona was standing in the middle, on the little sea-grass stool, when suddenly she said, 'Here comes a trouser lady. And she's coming to our house!'

It was true. A trouser lady was coming up our path. She was in our porch, knocking at our door.

'Beatrice! What a wonderful surprise! I can't believe it's really you!' Mother was laughing and almost crying, hugging the trouser lady. 'Children, this is your Auntie Bee, at long last!'

'Let me look at you all!' said Auntie Bee. 'Donald, Heather, Erica, Catriona! They've all got your red hair, Betty! Alec, hello!'

'Just the one bag, Beatrice?' said Father. 'I do hope that this doesn't mean you're not planning a good long stay with us?'

A cold shiver ran through us. Father was smiling, but only the family could tell when he was just pretending to be nice, and sometimes even we got it wrong.

'Come away in, pet,' he said. Something had made him cross; perhaps it was that Bee had said we all had Mother's hair.

'Dad's got red hair too,' said Donald. His own was dark red like Father's; Mother's, ours and Catriona's was fiery and crinkly and leapt and sparked at the hairbrush's strokes. We were always losing our ribbons and Kirbigrips.

Bee had brought us all presents; Meccano for Donald, a teddy bear for Catriona, and twin dolls for us. They were delicate featured, with rosebud mouths and blue eyes that opened and closed, and feathery painted light brown hair. One of them had a soft green knitted dress and bonnet tied with ribbons, the other was dressed in lavender blue. We called them Suzannah and Maria. They were very pale, and when we took them to the baby clinic – Jamie was born about nine months after Bee's visit – the nurse weighed Suzannah and Maria and told us to give them more porridge. We did.

Auntie Bee stayed for five days, and we would race home from school at dinner time and in the afternoon to see her, and she would let us all get into her bed when we took her a cup of tea in the morning. The only thing that spoiled it was Father. He was in a bad mood all the time and argued continuously with Bee. If she had said the coal was black, he would have sworn it was white. One teatime he threw his food at the wall and he hit Donald around the head for spilling his milk. The trouble was, Bee didn't know that you had to agree with everything Father said.

Bee tried to put things right. 'Let's all go to the pictures,' she said. At that Father stormed out to the lodge – which was what everybody used to call the big garden sheds – and Mother couldn't come because Catriona was too little. So Bee and Donald and we two set out. It was thrilling; we had never been to the cinema at night, and we twins held tight to Bee's hands. It was like entering a palace, and the curtains across the screen, rippling with magical, ever-changing colours, were the most beautiful things we had ever seen. To make our happiness complete – or it would have been if we hadn't been worried about Father and Mother missing the treat – the film was *On Moonlight Bay* starring Doris Day. We staggered out, drunk with pleasure, into the middle of the night. But there was more; Bee bought us chips on the way home. Drizzle was making haloes around the street lights, we had seen Doris Day, and our choice of favourite film star and our collection of cigarette cards was vindicated; we were real people, with lips and fingers stinging with salt and vinegar.

'What the bloody hell time of night do you call this?'

Father was waiting in the hall, wearing a sleeveless pullover and pyjama trousers, waving an alarm clock.

The house seemed dark when we got home from school the next day. It was cold. Mother was kneeling in front of the fire trying to blaze up the wet coal with a newspaper. She had cut her finger on the bread knife and a thick drop of blood splashed on to the tiled fireplace. Bee had gone.

Suzannah and Maria are still with us, as reminders of Auntie

Bee. In a manner of speaking. You see, their heads and limbs were attached to their bodies with elastic bands and over the years they had many adventures, until somehow there were just enough parts to make up one doll. We call her Zan-Mri now. It does seem a shame that Auntie Bee, who gave her to us, never married. She was wonderful with children.

As she leaves the office Catriona Ling swallows two Quiet Life tablets and drops her paper cup into a wastebin full of crumpled paper and cigarette butts. She is feeling sick with the apprehension that curdles her life like sour milk. Bee, she remembers, used to smoke some exotic brand, De Reszke or Du Maurier or Black Cat, screwing a cigarette into a green and black holder banded in marcasite with her red-tipped nails, flicking her lighter at Mother's Woodbine. Catriona wishes that she had not lost the deco cigarette case that somebody once gave her because it is important that she appears to be a success. She is afraid that she will regress to a four year old, blurting out her troubles to Bee. She is regretting her impulse to telephone her, and is worried about her choice of restaurant, which, convenient for her, will mean that Bee will probably have to take a taxi. Anxiety buzzes away, under the grief of a recent bereavement; there is her old uncle, her father's only surviving brother for whom Catriona has somehow become responsible; the women's publishing co-operative in which she is a partner is in dire financial straits; there are friends in hospital she should be visiting, calls she is too tired and dispirited to return when she gets home in the evenings, the heating in her flat is on the blink, ready to fail at the first really cold weather, the Hoover is broken, the mortgage huge, the car due for a service, her cat is on tablets, hence the scratches on her hands, and her lover, Rachel, has volunteered to take part in a late-night television programme where unattractive people talk frankly about their sexual practices. And she had meant to have her hair cut before seeing Bee.

A wind whips her across Covent Garden, and the sight of people bedded down in doorways does not make her count her blessings; instead the dark shapes are absorbed into her despair. At least she has arrived before Bee, but her relief is swamped by terror that she has got the wrong place, the wrong time. Noise bounces off the tiled walls as she sips a glass of wine and she knows that she should have chosen somewhere more *intime*. But for what? To tell Bee that she was sorry that they hadn't invited her to Mother's funeral? To say that she, Catriona, had never forgotten her first sight of Bee swinging along the road, of her turbaned head and houndstooth jacket flaring from padded shoulders, her red lipsticked mouth, and wide black trousers skimming thickly high-heeled black suede shoes? To mumble how Bee's risky glamour set her above the respectable neighbours and teachers with their hair in buns like dried figs, and that she had always had a thing about trouser ladies? Or to confess how, later, any old collar-and-tie job hunched over a pint of Guinness would set her young heart racing as if one of those pinstriped pockets held the key to the world she was desperate to enter, and how, in her teens, she had lurked outside clubs, not daring to ask anybody to take her in? Should she risk confiding that only she, of all the family, could guess what hell that visit to Canterbury had been for Bee? Then she sees Bee, walking a bit stiffly, leaning on a silver-topped cane, being led by a waiter towards her table.

Bee, treading carefully so as not to slip on the floor, which feels like an ice rink as pain flares around her hip joints, has a sudden memory of Alec slamming down his miner's helmet with its lamp on the kitchen table, and his snap tin and dudley – metal lunch box and water bottle – in hard, shiny, male challenge to her, and sees his eyes glaring out of the grimy face, which he has left unwashed, and the blue coal-dust scars under the skin of his arms. And Betty is standing up and waving to her across the restaurant, the light catching the crinkle-crankle, zig-zag, rick-rack hair; except that it is Catriona, of course, who is kissing her awkwardly on both cheeks now, bumping her nose.

Bee hadn't meant to say it so soon, but putting down her glass, while they are waiting for the starters, she hears herself, 'I was rather puzzled – and very upset to tell the truth – to get a birthday card from the twins. Signed by them both. When, you know, you told me the dreadful news on the telephone – that Erica has died. I didn't know what to think. I'm sorry, I didn't mean to upset you, my dear . . .'

'No, it's all right. I mean, it isn't really at all. But you haven't upset me. It's difficult to explain. We're all upset, Donald and Jamie and their families, but you remember how the twins were always a bit – odd. Different. They never – I mean, I don't suppose you recall those dolls you gave them, Suzannah and Maria – well, anyway, over the years they, Heather and Erica, sort of – amalgamated. As far as Erica's, I mean, Heather's concerned, they're both still there, nothing has changed. So we go along with it . . .'

Catriona is looking helplessly at Bee when the food arrives. Neither of them wants it.

'Are the twins still crazy about Doris Day?' Bee asks resolutely, dipping a bit of bread into olive oil.

'Oh yes!'

In fact, Catriona and Rachel have a tape of Doris Day's greatest hits, which they like to play full blast in the car. She doesn't tell Bee how Father took them all to see *By the Light of the Silvery Moon*, the sequel to *On Moonlight Bay*, a couple of years after Bee's flight from Canterbury, or how she and Mother had wept, each for her own reasons, while watching *Calamity Jane* on television not long before Mother died, or say that the scene where Calamity and Adelaide Adams transform Calam's filthy cabin into a pretty love-nest for two always breaks her heart. 'A woman and a whisk broom can accomplish oh so much, so never underestimate a woman's touch!' The film should have ended there, with the two of them so obviously in love. 'With the magic of a broom she can mesmerise a room.' Catriona resolves to try to put the romance back in her marriage when she gets home tonight by the light of the silvery moon. Then, aware that a long silence is hanging over their table in the clamour all around them, she looks up.

Bee, the birthday girl, is raising her glass in salute, smiling across glistening strips of red and yellow peppers on painted plates, saying, 'This is fun!', and Catriona sees that Bee, the good old trouper, is going to make the evening all right.

The Index of Embarrassment

We were in my uncle's study, Bob, his dog Fido and I, when he started telling me about a visit from his next-door neighbour Martha earlier that morning. Uncle Bob sprawled in his chair like a slack-bodied snake digesting some live prey, his eyes flickering off the Harvey Nicks carrier bag in my hand.

'Martha said, with uncharacteristic delicacy, "We noticed the — odour."'

'She said *what?*'

Uncle Bob believes that soap and water destroy the skin's essential oils. His plump pink cheeks, the long beard which he sometimes wears in a plait and the white ponytail sticking out of his baseball cap have a tallowy gleam, and as he considers household chores to be women's work and there wasn't one around, things had got a bit out of hand. Was it Bob's drains, his dustbin, his dog, his socks or his person which had provoked this insult? I was surprised by a rush of family loyalty, but luckily, before I could put my foot in it, he went on, 'He must have been in the bath for a while, if he was — stinking.'

Bob masticated the word. Everything has to be oblique with him; his pronouncements can be difficult to decipher. His master-work, *The Definitive Index of Embarrassment*, was ranged in files on the shelves of the study, which was the front room of his ground-floor flat. Newspapers and magazines were stacked on the floor. I had always been a bit scared of him, and it was only now that I was no spring chicken myself that I felt grown-up enough to dare to say,

'I don't understand. Who was in his bath, and why did he stink? Surely whoever it was would be very clean if he'd been there a long time?'

Uncle Bob's lips tightened, working themselves up to express a conventional sentiment. Martha is a pillar or something smaller, such as a hassock, of a local evangelical church; she's tiny, knee-high to a grasshopper, like me. Her porch is usually crammed with cash-and-carry cases of soft drinks for post-service refreshments, and it was her piety which made me think of Lazarus in the Bible – 'by this time he stinketh'. But presumably this guy, whoever he was, had simply been accused of shower-gel pollution or bath-essence abuse, or so I hoped. I imagined Martha wrinkling her nose at a drifting cluster of malodorous pink bubbles. Nobody but Bob could have charged her with indelicacy.

'I'm sorry to report, nephew o' mine,' Uncle Bob said, 'that we have lost Neighbour Dennis. The police had to break in to take him away.'

'Why?'

Dennis lived in the upstairs flat of the house on the other side of Martha's. I only knew him to say hello.

Then the blood rushed from my head and I sat down, picturing Dennis white and bloated, decomposing in a bathtub of red water.

'Martha said, and she didn't make any other comment, that it was never women who came to call. Friend Dennis's visitors were all men. The implication, I very much regret, seemed to be that our Mr Jennings was a bit of a lowlife.'

Fido settled on my feet like a mildewed chenille bathmat.

'Do the police think it was suicide then – or murder?'

I was uncomfortable, a voyeur spying through the keyhole at Dennis naked in his bath, and I felt like a ghoul presuming on my slight acquaintance with him in suggesting that Dennis might have been killed. Yet as I uttered the word 'murder', which the television news and drama has robbed of its power to shock, it took on its true shape and hung ghastly and terrifying in that quiet room with a dog snoring in a pool of February sunshine.

'Could it have been – natural causes?' I asked then, in the faint hope that a congenital weakness might make the death of a man in his forties somehow, well, less – unnatural, even though I had known lots of people younger than Dennis who'd gone. Bob shook his head.

'Didn't he have a mother? When he borrowed your stepladder, wasn't he fixing the place up for her to come to stay?'

'One might be forgiven for trusting a chap to have the decency to put his affairs in order if he intended to do away with himself, don't you think, Freddy? I let him take that ladder, against my better judgement, a good six weeks ago and I haven't heard a peep out of him since. Nor will again, I suppose. In fact, the more consideration I give to his story, the less I am inclined to believe that he had a mother at all. However, should such a person exist, no doubt she is ensconced in Number Fifteen now, clawing through the deceased's effects and making such arrangements as are required for the disposal of a body in unhallowed ground.'

'Fair dos, Uncle Bob,' I bleated, despising myself for not walking out on the old bastard. My sister Iris would have been halfway down the street by now.

I had probably attended more funerals than Uncle Bob had had hot dinners; his Meals on Wheels foil dishes were on the floor. Sometimes I ate the puddings, but today Fido had got there first. It seemed so sad that a mother should have had a little baby way back in the fifties, and named him Dennis, only for it all to end like this. She must have written his name in biro in his wellies, Dennis Jennings, and hung his gloves on elastic through his coat sleeves, and called him Dennis the Menace when he was naughty. I could see that Bob was more concerned with the loss of his ladder than of his neighbour, so I said that I'd better be going to the shops, before he could send me round to the house of horror to reclaim it, offering my condolences to a grieving mother as I clattered out with the aluminium legs high-kicking under my arm.

I took the shopping bag and list and set off, with Fido waddling in front of me. The wind lifted his ears and rippled his coat, so that for a moment he looked quite lively, and I wondered briefly what was the point of him and whether he had any race-memory of running in a pack with his wild ancestors, and I felt a stab of pity for his debased existence. It was a long time since this splay-footed eater of processed food had felt grass beneath his pads, or any surface but the pavement between Colley Gardens and Albion Minimart. Uncle Bob had named him Fido as a sort of joke, for of course the poor mutt had no option; cats can clear off if they like, but infidelity isn't in a dog's nature. There used to be loads of dogs here, pit bulls and Rottweilers and Dobermanns, bandy-legged scarred dogs used for fighting, but the government stuck them all on death row, family pets, convicted maulers and drug dealers' bodyguards alike, and now you see hardly any except the long-haired Alsatians in the shops. Fido and I had to pass Dennis's house. I averted my eyes, and he lifted his leg over the gatepost.

Uncle Bob is virtually a recluse now; age and his natural misanthropy making it difficult for him to leave the house. I don't mind doing his shopping because other people's shops are always more interesting than one's own, and I am a hotel night porter, and don't sleep much during the day. In fact, I usually manage to snatch a catnap or two at the desk, despite the video camera trained on the lobby. Vincents Hotel, off Chelsea Green, advertises itself as one of London's best-kept secrets; it's chintzy, discreet and overpriced, and I fit in there very well.

When I was a boy, I assumed that I would grow up into the sort of person who listens to Radio Three and goes to concerts at the Wigmore Hall or St John's, Smith Square, yet here I am, my mind permanently tuned to Capital Gold and Country 10.35 AM, the opera buff inside me still trying to get out. Although Bob despises me as a physical and intellectual lightweight, I'm the only one of the family with whom he hasn't quarrelled, and I'm useful in that I've been able to help him out with many an embarrassing line from a song which should never have been allowed within a mile of a recording studio. It's my proud boast that I never forget a phrase.

Only last week, I'd provided Bob with a couple of corkers for the food section of his Embarrassing Lyrics file – the oldies but goodies, 'Frankfurter Sandwiches' and 'Pineapple Princess', and he has me to thank for 'Johnny Get Angry' and 'Friendly Persuasion' ('Thee pleasures me in a thousand ways') of the same era, and many a golden turkey plucked from the pages of Sir Cliff's songbook. My personal *bête noire* is the phrase 'keep me satisfied'; it really makes my skin crawl, conjuring up an exhausted sex-slave in thrall to lusts which have nothing to do with love. Be that as it may, Bob's tragedy is that despite having lived through the Radio

Luxemburg years and being the Casaubon of Colley Gardens, he has a tin ear, a poor memory and lacks the fundamental ability to differentiate between the poignant and the embarrassing. 'I heard a good one on the wireless today, Freddy,' he told me once, '"Nobody Loves a Fairy When She's Forty."'

'That's not embarrassing, it's sad,' I said. 'Anyway, Mum's still got our old fairy dolly; Christmas wouldn't be Christmas without fairy dolly perched on top of the tree.' And I'd had to delete Dolly Parton's 'The Bargain Store' from the *Index* when I was inserting 'Rabbit, Rabbit, Rabbit' by those chirpy cockney sparrows (ain't it a shame sparrers can't sing?) Chas and Dave. That's rabbit as in rabbit and pork – talk, and this geezer's bird's 'got more rabbit than Sainsbury's', whereas in all my wide retail experience I've never encountered a single member of the family Leporidae, unless you admit the petfood display, which actually I don't, in any of Mr Sainsbury's establishments.

Perhaps fortunately, the Internet had come too late for Uncle Bob; true, he was at risk from drowning in newsprint, but access to the Web would have driven him right over the edge, like a mad spider. Nevertheless, it was kind of melancholy to visualise his magnum opus heaped in a skip outside Number Eleven, or in the black sacks of the vultures who clear the houses of the dead. The worst-case scenario, though, would be that he left the lot to me. It might seem strange that Bob, who has on more than one occasion been spotted in Albion Road in his pyjamas, and secures his beard with a rubber band or a twist of plastic wire, should have set himself up as an authority on embarrassment, but there it is. He was a fighter pilot in the war, risking his life to make the world a safe place for wimps like me, and thereafter a civil servant, so I guess he is entitled to spend his retirement as he wishes.

The *Index* started out as a hobby, a scrapbook of humorous and humiliating stories gleaned from the media, became a sort of thesis entitled *Seven Types of Embarrassment*, and then like Topsy (see under *Clichés*), it just growed. Into an obsession. The man's a fool, though; he's got *Magnificent Obsession* listed in the Hollywood file, whereas I'm a total Douglas Sirk freak. As for personal embarrassment, my sister and I ingested it with our mother's milk (Cow & Gate naturally). Iris was twenty-five before she could walk across a room.

But she beat it and now she's a gynaecologist, married with two great kids. Anyway, as I've come to realise, embarrassmentology is an inexact science, it's all relative – and uncles can be the most embarrassing relatives of all. Minimart was doing a nice line in square silver scourers, so I bought a couple, as well as Bob's groceries and the local paper. Bob had checked out the nationals, but I thought there might be something about Dennis there. I did feel slightly ashamed, even if it was the best way of finding out without engaging in gossip with the shop people or Martha. A depressed-looking woman was choosing five valentines, probably for her daughters; that would have tickled Uncle Bob, but I wasn't going to share it with him. Walking back along Colley Gardens, and the address is something of a misnomer now, Fido got tangled up in loops of the cassette tape that always seems to be blowing about. Again I avoided looking at Dennis's house; I didn't want to know what was going on inside, or to imagine his state of mind as he died. A rook was going 'carp carp carp' on a chimney across the street and I noticed the tips of bulbs pushing up through a crushed polystyrene cup beside Bob's dustbin.

'Here it is,' I said to Bob, opening the paper, 'MAN FOUND DEAD.'

'Hold the front page. That should sell a lot of copies round here. *Man Found Alive*, now that would be a story.'

'It's the wrong bloke,' I said, reading on about a pensioner dis-covered in a maggoty condition. 'It's not him.'

'Just another sad little south London death,' said Bob, adding, 'it is not *he*.'

I crumpled the newspaper into the bin, not wanting Bob to read it. It struck me that people in our family, after lives filled with love affairs and adventure and admirers, have an unfortunate habit of ending up alone in rented rooms. At least I owned my place, be it never so humble, but there was somebody else living there with me whom I had begun to neglect. It's awful, isn't it, how that happens; as if you bid for a beautiful plate in an auction, and then after a few months, you risk bunging it in the dishwasher, telling yourself it won't hurt just the once, and before you know it, it becomes a habit and your plate's chipped and the pattern faded. A lurking fear, unformed until now, that I would turn into Uncle

Bob, settled heavily on me, and I decided to stop off at M&S for an American-style cheesecake that Jacob liked – I'd been nagging him about his weight recently – and pick up some flowers at the tube station.

Bob had his finger in the pot of Gentleman's Relish I'd brought. It turned my stomach to look at him.

'I forgot to give you a gobbet of embarrassing information,' I said, 'a mere titbit, a *bonne bouche*, an *amuse gueule* . . .'

'Spit it out,' said Bob.

'On my way here I noticed that the name of the Duke of Clarence pub has been changed to the Ant and Artichoke.'

Bob, a self-appointed recording angel with a red biro, noted down grimly this latest example of human folly.

'What a cheap trick,' he said.

'Who is?' I quipped.

'What kind of a scoundrel would invent a mother to get his hands on an elderly and not at all robust chap's stepladder?'

'You tell me,' I said. 'Well, Bob, I suppose I'd better be making tracks.'

Panic flashed in his eyes as he said, 'Like a snail. Couldn't you manage another cuppa? Perhaps you'd like to wash your hands? You've got a long journey.'

'I'm fine thanks.'

Uncle Bob always managed to imply that he had no use for a lavatory himself, but kept one purely for the convenience of incontinent visitors such as myself.

'Well, I mustn't keep you from your work.'

He plaited his beard nervously, dismissing my job with a bitter smile that suggested some house of ill-repute. He never asked me about my life, either from lack of interest or because he didn't want to know, but as his misogyny equalled his homophobia it suited me not to subject any of my friends to his scorn even at a distance. Take Lady Brenda, for example. He would have had a field day with her.

Lady Brenda is a permanent resident at Vincents and has lived in a suite of two rooms on the fourth floor since the year dot. I have to fetch her fur coat, chilled and smelling of mothballs, from the fridge when she goes out in the evenings and help her into it. She's ninety if she's a day, and her legs are heavily bandaged and she walks with two sticks. She looks a right old *roué*, rouged and decked with paste jewellery, but I have a lot of time for her. You don't find many nonagenarians making the effort to go down the pub every night, and as I often tell Jacob, she is an example to us all. She only has a couple of Guinnesses, but she's well away when she gets back, and we have some brilliant conversations, and she's given me some of her late husband's cufflinks. I only hope I'm half as good as she is when I'm her age.

'We're two of a kind, Freddy,' she said once.

After I'd put her in the lift, I studied myself in the mirror above the desk, and I saw what I might become; one of those bad-tempered elderly elves working behind a bar, with a cinched-in waist and tiny bum and the lined face of a disgraced jockey. Actually, I did start out in the racing game, after I was invited to leave school, as a stable lad at Lamberhurst, but I fell from grace on my first day. Grace was a mean donkey, the travelling companion of a nervous gelding, and she ended my career on the turf.

My father was a second violinist. He was run over by a taxi while nipping out for an interval drink, and it was a struggle for my mother to provide for us. We were always keeping up appearances. She was a needlework teacher, and she felt the shame of my father's demise deeply. I don't recall her brother, Uncle Bob, being around much to help. He usually had some woman in tow, some poor sap who thought she would be the one to tame him; for a man who despised women he certainly had a lot of mistresses, but that's often the way. The last one, Audrey, who knitted him socks, had thrown in the tea towel a month ago; perhaps she had found her file. Bob's pet name for her was Tawdry. I was pretty sure he had a file on me too, stashed behind *The Greengrocer's Apostrophe* and *The Human Body*.

'Have you noticed, Freddy,' he asked me once, 'the ugliness of anatomical terminology? Perhaps justifiably so. Tastebuds,' he enunciated, 'gland. Membrane. Tonsils. Toenails. Scrotum.' His mouth was moist with distaste.

★　★　★

So why did I go on visiting him? I think it was because I felt sorry for him, although Iris said he was just using me and Jacob insisted it was a symbiotic relationship of parasite and host, though I wouldn't know who was which.

'See you next week, then,' I said, and a wave of dreariness swept over me as I reflected how my pleasure in snouting out snippets for the *Index* had long since palled. The truth was, the older I got, the less embarrassing I found everything; life, people, words. I mean, I can exchange a quip with the best of them now and employ expressions like 'the year dot' without turning a hair or batting a proverbial.

Martha was going into her house as I came out of Bob's.

'How did you find Uncle today?' she asked.

'Oh, not too bad, thanks, Martha. But not too good, either, if you know what I mean.'

'I know what you mean! We're none of us *too* good, eh? But we try, we keep on trying.'

She was laughing as she shut her door. And then I saw a woman standing in the front garden of Dennis's house.

My instinct was to cross the road, but I made myself walk towards her.

'Mrs Jennings?'

She was smartly dressed in chainstore pastels, with pale blue eyeshadow on swollen lids and coral lipstick and a perky daffodil yellow scarf. She looked as if she had her hair done for the occasion of identifying her son's body. Dennis's mother was a type of woman for whom I have a lot of respect; the sort who works in a shoe shop all her life and makes the best of herself, smiling at the customer when her own feet are killing her.

'I just want to say how sorry I am.'

'Thank you.'

'If there's anything I can do . . .'

'Not really, I don't suppose. But thanks anyway. Did you know – my son?'

'Not well. We met once or twice, in passing. But my uncle, at Number Eleven, knew Dennis and he always spoke very highly of him.'

'So Bob's your uncle?'

That's how somebody caught up in a hideous tragedy smiles, I thought, that's the crooked way the mouth goes.

''Fraid so.'

'I believe there's a ladder belongs to him, indoors. I'll fetch it round later.'

'No, don't. You mustn't. I'll take it.'

It was imperative to keep this woman as far away from Uncle Bob as possible. She must not set foot over his threshold. His sharp nose would sniff out the loneliness masked by her rather shrill perfume and he would home in on the vulnerable heart beneath the peachskin mac, biding his time before going for the jugular hidden by that brave yellow scarf.

'It's no trouble,' she said.

'No, really, I insist. I'll do it now.'

'I wasn't going to run off with it, you know. I'm sure Dennis would have returned it himself, if –'

'Oh God – I didn't mean – I'm so sorry, so sorry.'

'Don't,' she said. 'You'll start me off again. Here.'

She opened her handbag and gave me a mauve tissue.

'This is so embarrassing. It's all the wrong way round –'

I wiped my eyes.

'I'd offer you a cup of tea,' she said, 'only . . .'

I thought she meant that I might be squeamish about going into the flat.

'That would be great. I could murder a cup of tea!'

'Only, there isn't any, I was going to say. Not one single solitary teabag.'

Barbarians

When Ian and Barbara Donaldson started the mail-order children's clothes company Barbarians, operating from the family home in one of those parts of London that thinks itself a village, their own brood of four modelled Barbara's designs. As the business expanded, the offspring of some of their home workers were co-opted, to bring a bit of light and shade to the catalogue, and despite Barbara's initial *faux pas* of forcing a little Sikh boy with his hair in a mobcap into a dress with matching tights, the results were so charming that the orders flowed in and Ian was negotiating the purchase of new factory premises. The Donaldson boys' hair was cut in shiny pudding-basin style and ranged in tones from conker brown, through sun-streaked blond to white; it was Amber, the oldest at eleven, who was the problem. As her mother often remarked, Amber had been born on a bad-hair day, and now, with her string-coloured frizz scraped back in a scrunchie, scowling through the Cutler and Gross frames that didn't help much, she stuck out in the photographs like a sore thumb. She often *had* a sore thumb, or a bandage or Elastoplast somewhere about her person, and managed to look like a refugee in the snazziest Barbarian togs.

'We're supposed to be promoting "Fun Fashions for Real Kids", not soliciting donations for some Third World charity,' Ian complained, slapping down a pile of prints on the table in the breakfast room, where he and Barbara were lingering over coffee and brioches at eleven o'clock on a spring half-term Tuesday morning, having decided not to go down to their Suffolk cottage. Ian was a big, jovial man, ruddy-faced with white curls tumbling on to the collar of his denim shirt and springing through the gaps between the buttons. Holidays in the French farmhouse they were renovating had taught him to prefer his chips fried in horse fat and he was spearheading a campaign to get Dobbie's, the local butchers, to stock it.

'But Amber *is* a real kid,' her mother felt obliged to point out, then conceded, 'poor lamb, she's not quite Barbarian, is she, bless her little cotton socks.'

She shook her head over the photographs, rattling the beads that had been plaited into her fair hair on a recent buying trip to the Caribbean. She had an emergency appointment at the hairdresser's that afternoon to have them cut out.

'Daddy.' Amber came into the room with her friend Rukhsana in tow. Her yellow cotton socks flopped, as if there was no Lycra in them at all. 'Daddy,' she demanded, 'do you believe in a minimum wage policy?'

'I do not, Pop Tart, and I'll tell you for why. Sit yourself down, and have some juice. *Et tu, ma petite Rucksack, un jus de pomme pour toi aussi, hein?*'

Rukhsana giggled dutifully as Ian poured from the bottle labelled Château Donaldson. His favourite daydream was of a *fête champêtre* beneath the blossom, with all his family, including his two ex-wives, their children and assorted partners, seated at a long table in the orchard, and himself at the head, standing to carve. Babies toddled through the daisies and crawled under the white cloth that was weighted with meats, fishes, fruit, cheeses, green walnuts, jugs of young wine and cobwebbed bottles of the finest vintage, platters piled with bones and rinds and shells; and at last, as the first stars pricked the evening sky and fireflies sparked and glowworms glimmered, an enormous cake was carried in triumph over the darkening dewy grass, tremulous with the flames of sixty candles.

'Well, Daddy?' said Amber.

'I do not support the theory of the minimum wage for two reasons, Pop Tart. The first being that it is simply unworkable, and the second that enforcement of such a policy in a market economy would mean that your papa would be unable to employ such estimable ladies as our young friend here's delightful mama, and what would poor Rucksack do then, poor thing, and all her little brothers and sisters, eh? You wouldn't want to see your friends out on the street, would you? And your old mum and dad in the debtors' prison?'

'But, Dad, it doesn't seem fair that we —'

'That's enough, Amber!' Barbara cut her off. 'Your father's

explained. Go and find Marie-Claude and see if she needs any help with the boys. And Amber, do please change into a Mood Indigo Tee with those saffron leggings. If I've told you once, that range is mix'n'match! Do *try* to remember that you are an ambassador for Barbarians at all times.'

Amber slammed down her glass, and the girls left the room just as Barbara was saying to Ian, 'Saffron can be so draining on a sallow skin.'

'That's all I need, my own kid turning into a barrack-room lawyer. She'll be manning a picket line outside the front gate next. Little Roxanne's getting to be quite a looker though, isn't she? I suppose they'll be finding a husband for her soon.'

'Don't be so ridiculous, Ian. The child's still in primary school,' snapped Barbara, scratching her thigh, where a line of sunburn marked the hem of her beach shorts. Beneath her clothes she was as pink and white as a Battenberg cake, and starting to peel.

As they went upstairs, Rukhsana asked, 'Why does your dad call you Pop Tart?'

'Same reason as he calls you Rucksack, because he's a dickhead.'

Amber's bedroom smelled mustily of the mice who lived in Mouse Palace, the brightly coloured perspex construction that sat on top of her bookcase like a miniature Pompidou Centre. These piebald pets served two purposes: Amber adored them, and they kept Marie-Claude out of her room, as well as Barbara, who could tolerate rodents only when they were made of felt and dressed in Victorian clothes. Amber and her brother Diggory, the next in line, had a contract; he would not let Willow the cat in as long as she refrained from popping the blisters on his collection of bubble wrap.

'You're sad you know, Diggory. It's like you really love that stuff. I mean, I wouldn't keep clingfilm for a pet, would I?' Rukhsana told him once. Then she went on to cajole, 'Let me pop one, just one, go on Digg, *please, please, please*. I'll give you a whole packet of Jolly Ranchers for just one pop.'

Diggory shook his head, smiling and backing away with a roll of bubble wrap clutched to his chest. 'Get a life, Diggory,' said Rukhsana in disgust.

Now, the voices of the two younger boys and Marie-Claude, who was the daughter of the schoolmaster in the village where the Donaldsons had bought their farmhouse, came plaintively from the garden, which backed on to a small wood. Beyond that was the railway line which carried commuter trains, Eurostar and nuclear waste along the edge of the Donaldsons' lives; in summer the line was screened by the leaves of the trees which were now putting out a fuzz of catkins and buds. The children were forbidden to play in the Coppice, as the wood had been named by a local estate agent – Ian called it the Codpiece – and so naturally they had a secret entrance through the fence to the fox-runs and the railway bank.

'What do you want to do?' Amber asked. 'Shall we watch a video of *Ab Fab*?'

The two girls were word-perfect, even though Rukhsana had not been allowed to watch the series at home. They sprawled on cushions on the floor. Spitting crisp crumbs as they laughed, oblivious to Siobhan the cleaner, who came in to vacuum listlessly around them.

Ian had been married to Nell, his second wife and the mother of his twins, when Barbara, then a fashion student on vacation, came to work as a waitress in the restaurant they were running. Ian moved in with Barbara as soon as she graduated. Nell changed the name of the restaurant from Le Boeuf sur le Toit to Déjeuner sur l'Herbe, and was operating it still, as a successful wholefood café, while Daniel and Damien were building a reputation as chefs elsewhere. They came into Barbara's mind, duelling gracefully with a pair of knife-sharpeners, as she leafed through the Divertimenti catalogue, accepting regretfully that there was no piece of equipment, however desirable, that her own kitchen really needed. Once Barbara had enjoyed fiction and biographies, but now her bedside table was piled with magazines, brochures and catalogues even though she rationed the children's comics and had claimed to have sleepless nights over Jack's refusal to read at seven and a half. She looked at the clock and groaned.

'Is that really the time? Half-term is so disorientating; we might as well have gone down to the cottage. Be a love and get Wills for me, would you?'

'OK, *mon ange*. I'd better get on the road. Don't wait lunch,' said Ian, and was through the door, roaring 'Wills!', before Barbara could ask where he was going. She felt the premonition of a headache and wondered if it was those damn beads weighing her down.

When Amber came into the garden room, she found her mother lying on the sofa with her eyes closed and Wills on his little milking-stool, glued to a *Thomas the Tank Engine* video.

'What do you want now?' Barbara snarled. 'You know this is my Quality Time with Wills.'

Amber went out through the french windows, waiting until she was in the garden before she said, 'Who needs a Fat Controller with her around?'

Marie-Claude was hunched on the seat of the swing, rubbing her eyes with a tissue, while Diggory pushed.

'I bet if we both pushed really, really hard, we could push her all the way over the rooftops, up into the sky, all the way back to *la belle France*,' said Amber.

Ian, having left Barbara without explanation, was in a Portuguese café a couple of miles from home, drinking an espresso while he waited at a corner table for two. Sunshine freckled the floor and chrome and glass and the display case of spun-sugar storks and cradles for christening cakes. Two old men sat playing chess and mothers with *bambini*, or whatever they called them, came in to buy bread and choose from the array of cakes and *pasteis de nanta*. Ian stretched his legs contentedly in his little patch of Abroad, kicking the table next to him.

'Do you mind?'

'I beg your pardon, madam.'

Ian saw a woman, invisible until now, glaring at him as he apologised. She was a skinny, faded blonde, intrusively English, wearing a grey sweatshirt over leggings. She lit a cigarette, and coughed, one of those neurotic crones who smoke themselves to death and then expect the NHS to provide a bed for them to die in. No wonder the country was in such a state, with an ever-increasing population of no-hopers draining its resources from the cradle to the grave. Ian could see it all, the funeral procession holding up the traffic with its sanctimonious floral tributes spelling out MUM and NAN. There was something vaguely familiar about the woman and he wondered if she had worked for him in some capacity. She had one of those red, white and blue striped shopping bags, which common people take to the supermarket or launderette. He hoped that she was not going to claim acquaintance with him, and closed his eyes to let the Portuguese music drift over him.

He opened them as a chair was scraped back and the table wobbled, and he half-rose with a smile as Laura sat down. She was eighteen, training to be a nurse and had filled in as a mother's help between the departure of the Donaldsons' last nanny and the arrival of Marie-Claude.

'I'm late,' she said.

'Only ten minutes. It couldn't matter less, sweetie, only I am a bit pushed. Cappuccino, and how about one of those delicious-looking cakes? I'm going to, although I know I shouldn't. Cholesterol nightmare, what?'

Ian went up to the counter and ordered coffee and a cream horn oozing custard and a glistening layered confection decorated with swirls of red and yellow.

'I feel like a naughty schoolboy playing truant,' he said setting down the tray. 'Reminds me of my prep school days. Tuck in, and then we'll hotfoot it back to yours.' He glanced at his watch. 'I take it Mum's safely out of the way?'

'I mean, I'm late. You know, late! As in overdue.'

Froth spilled into the saucer as Ian sat down, feeling desire draining away. Those words again. One more woman's stricken face staring at his. There was something embarrassingly old-fashioned about the scenario.

'Are you sure? I mean, couldn't you have miscalculated?' He knew his lines.

Laura shook her head. Her hair was dragged into a ponytail, and she wore no makeup. Funny how women adopt the least-becoming hairstyles when they're out to trap a bloke. Bad tactics.

'It's nearly two weeks.'

'Oh well, a fortnight's nothing. That eating disorder you told me about probably buggered up your cycle. Here, eat your cake like a good girl and stop worrying.'

'That was ages ago.' Laura pushed away the tray. 'If you'd bothered to ask, I only wanted a glass of water.'

'Oh, for God's sake.' Ian stuck a fork into the cake. 'How could you have been so stupid as to take a risk? I thought –'

'It takes two to tango,' put in the woman at the next table.

Ian turned on her, 'Who asked your opinion? What bloody business is it of yours and what makes you think you have the right to eavesdrop and butt in on a private conversation?'

'This is my mum, Mrs Kelly,' said Laura. 'Mum, Mr Donaldson.'

'I said, it takes two to tango,' repeated Mrs Kelly, ignoring her daughter's introduction.

Ian thumped the table in disbelief and fury at being set up.

'Madam,' he said, 'it may well take two to tango, as you so originally put it, but what makes you think I was your daughter's only dancing partner?'

'You bastard.' Laura burst into tears.

Ian shoved the table out of his way and blundered towards the door.

'You haven't heard the last of this. Not by a long chalk!' Mrs Kelly's voice pursued him. 'Sitting there like Lord Muck, with cream on your chin and your high-and-mighty talk of cycles and prep school . . . and who's paying for this lot, eh? My daughter never ordered those pastries.'

'The woman always pays, that's what they say, isn't it?' Ian slammed the café door behind him.

He regretted his words as soon as he was back in the car; it had probably been a dangerous mistake to outsmart the stupid mare. He leaned across to look in the vanity mirror. Ma Kelly had been right about the cream. Ian watched his tongue licking his chin, and saw one eye closing in a wink that said, 'Uh-oh, who's been a bad lad, then? Playing away from home again eh, you old devil.'

Responding with a rueful grin, he started the engine. There might be life in the old dog yet, but he had broken the eleventh commandment: Thou shalt not be found out.

★　　★　　★

'Any calls while I was out?' Ian asked Amber when he got home.

'Only Granny Molly. She's coming on Sunday. There's an antiques fair at the college and she says I can go with her.'

Amber gave an irritating skip of pleasure. Piggotts College, Ian's alma mater, one of London's oldest public schools, stood in its park ten minutes' walk away. The two older boys attended Piggotts prep and Wills was at the nursery. It annoyed Ian to imagine Molly poking through junk in the Great Hall.

'And me,' said Diggory. 'Granny Molly said I could come too.'

'Only because you begged,' Amber told him.

'Where's your mother? At the hairdresser?'

'She didn't go. She wasn't feeling well, so she cancelled her appointment. She's gone to lie down.'

Ian went upstairs. Jack was sitting against the wall outside the master bedroom, wrapped in his duvet.

'What on earth are you doing? Get up at once, you look like some homeless layabout in a shop doorway begging for change. Take that thing off and go and play in the garden, or read a book or do something useful. When I was your age, I'd have been ashamed to waste my half-term skulking in a quilt, sucking my thumb.'

'I want Mummy and she won't let me in. Anyway, you know I can't read.'

Ian was the first to look away. Jack's hazel eyes were defiant under his glossy fringe, his little legs in jeans drawn up to his chest. Oh well, if you have eight sons, perhaps it doesn't really matter that much if one of them is illiterate. Ian supposed it would sort itself out in time. He went into the bedroom. All that was visible of Barbara was a spray of beaded plaits on the pillow beside the sleeping cat.

'Where've you been?' her muffled voice accused.

'To the factory. I told you I had an appointment with the vendors. Sorry you're not feeling well, Pudding. I hope you didn't pick up some bug on that trip of yours. You've been looking a bit green round the gills since you got back.'

'Thanks. Don't bother to contact the Institute for Tropical Diseases yet, though. It's only a headache.'

'Try to get some rest, then. I'll bring you some tea in a bit.'

He found Jack still crouching outside. He had pulled the hood of his sweatshirt over his face.

Ian sighed. 'Come on then, Jackanory. I'm going to make Mums some tea later, and you can take it up. How's that?'

'Daddy?'

'My son?'

'*Have* you got any spare change?'

One of the many things that Ian held against his mother-in-law was that she was about his own age, but he resented more her indifference to his charm; even after giving her four grand-children, and the success of Barbarians, Molly still managed to suggest that he was some sort of dilettante who could not be trusted with her daughter's happiness. Molly dealt in vintage clothes, 'rags' as she herself termed them, from a booth in an indoor antiques market in Highgate. Widowed when Barbara was a child of six, she had stayed true to the memory of her husband, which irritated Ian too: it seemed a waste and a reproach. He hated the smell and touch of old material, flaccid gauzy stuff, and velvets that set his teeth on edge and made him feel grubby. Most of all, he disliked Granny Molly's advocacy of Amber; she was always ready to leap to her defence, on the lookout for an imagined slight to her darling. Not that she didn't love the boys too, but her atti-tude to Amber implied some dereliction of duty on her parents' part; it was typical of Molly that it was she who had discovered that the kid needed glasses just before they realised she was short-sighted. None of his other kids wore specs. As far as Ian could see, Molly just sat in that arcade all day, sewing beads on old evening bags, smoking, gossiping and eating baked potatoes from the take-away upstairs. He decided to impress her with Sunday lunch *en famille*, and began planning the menu. It was ages since he'd made his Calvados apple tart.

Amber was in the kitchen, spooning flour into a bowl. Ian peered at the mixture. 'What's cooking, Pop Tart? More play dough for Wills? Tell him to try to keep it out of the carpet this time. Where's your better half?'

'If you must know, it's a practice run for my simnel cake. Rukhsana had to go home.'

413

'At least use a sieve for that flour then,' Ian said heavily. 'Here, Jackanory, there's a spoon for you. You can help your sister. You should take a leaf out of Rukhsana's book, Amber, and pay a bit more attention to your brothers. Leave the phone on answer, I'm not taking any calls.'

'As it happens, she's got to work. Her mum was up all night on the Easter order.'

When Ian had gone, Jack asked, 'What's a Jackanory mean?'

'It was a TV programme in the olden days. I expect he used to watch it with his other kids. Give me that, you're not sticking a licked spoon into my cake mixture.'

'I haven't even licked it yet. What's a sinimel cake?'

Amber looked at him. 'You're really going to have to get your act together, you know, Jack.'

Jack decided it must mean cinnamon, and pulled down his hood again.

Merde, merde et trois fois merde, Ian thought, that's all I need, some kid buggering up the new range. The outworkers really were the end, letting their brats loose on the machines. No wonder they were constantly under repair. The sooner the factory was up and running the better. He switched on his computer to do a few sums, and paused to wonder what the going rate for a termination was these days and whether it could be done on plastic, then poured himself a shot of Calvados. Women. They'd be the ruination of him yet. Why was it his fate to attract the unfailingly fertile of the fair sex? Or was it perhaps a clever ruse on old Dame Nature's part, to equip the gene pool with superior breeding stock? God knows that was needed nowadays and he wouldn't be without his sprogs, any of them. He took another shot. Not excluding Amber, even if she was a poke-nosed clever-clogs who'd palled up out of contrariness with the wrong sort, instead of one of the more suitable girls from her own school; she might not have the looks he would have liked in his only daughter, but academically she knocked spots off the boys. Probably turn out to be more of an asset to the company than dreamy old Diggs, with his bubble wrap. Still, he supposed it showed the lad had a feel for texture. There was a piece of the stuff on his desk and Ian popped the blisters systematically, as if he were on a strand at low tide, bursting a ribbon of bladderwrack. A memory was niggling at him, of a woman with whom he'd had a casual fling some years ago. The telephone had rung while he'd been in the kitchen cooking for a dinner party.

'Ian, I've found a lump in my . . .'

'And I've just found a lump in my béchamel. I'll call you back.'

He had rung her back, eventually, but she was dead.

Now he made himself focus on the Laura problem, but it was all unthinkable and he couldn't face any of it. Scenes from various *ménages* flashed through his mind; women, children, ranks of largely forgotten in-laws and a procession of hamsters, stick insects, gold-fish, cats. Pussy Cat Willum, Orlando, Kit Cat, Tigger, Bilbo Baggins. No, Bilbo Baggins had been a Volkswagen Beetle. Any incorpor-ation of Laura, not to mention Mum Kelly with her sharp knees pointing through her leggings and black court shoes, into the picture was out of the question. He saw them sitting bitterly apart from the rest of the family, with a howling infant, turning the cream sour and the champagne flat at his *fête champêtre*. No, there was no way he could go through any of it again. Besides, Laura wasn't that much older than Amber; ought to be concentrating on her studies, the silly girl. Ian leaned back, lost in a reverie of Laura modelling the silk underwear he'd given her at Christmas. A smile softened his face, and he reached for the bottle. The ladies, God bless 'em!

Upstairs, Pussy Willow, bored, began to bat the beads on Barbara's pillow with his paw. She groaned. 'Leave me alone, you beast. Ouch, that was a claw! Get out of my hair. Why don't you go and catch a mouse or something?'

Barbara didn't need Willow to tell her the beads had been a mistake. The entire trip had been disastrous. Mercifully, Ian hadn't questioned her too closely, beyond remarking that she had brought back very little and he hoped the whole thing hadn't been an expensive waste of time.

'I admit Jamaica was a bit of a let-down, but these samples might turn out to be brilliant and I've made some very useful contacts. And that's partly what it's all about, isn't it?' she had told him. A length of bougainvillea-coloured cloth was churning round in the washing machine, on its third go, still pumping magenta dye into the system. Barbara had the Tropixie fashion shoot all planned; she was going to get a load of silver sand from a builders' merchant and have it tipped into the kids' old sandpit. She would stick in a branch of the hibiscus from the garden room and a palm frond or two from the florist. One of the women had a pair of divine twins, Taneesha and Tenara, who were so totally Tropixie that Barbara could just see them, with their hair in corn rows, and perhaps a blossom behind the ear, kneeling on either side of her own white-maned, blue-eyed palomino Wills, who, scrumptious as a vanilla ice, was smiling beatifically as he turned out a perfect sandcastle.

Queasily she turned over in bed, pushing away a coconut pierced by two straws, brimming with a foaming cocktail of guilt and longing. Her body was tingling and she was reminded of one of the children's toys, a magic wand, imported from God knew where and bought off a market stall. This transparent tube, tipped at either end with red plastic, was filled with a thousand floating rainbow specks and, although disappointingly powerless, was spellbinding in its mesmeric shiftings as it was turned first one way and then another. Barbara felt as if she had become that magic wand, weightless and swarming with polychromatic organisms, while pinpricks and flashes of light sparked the blackness behind her closed eyelids. Phosphorescent with desire, she had to deal with the knowledge that she had been unfaithful, and that she was lying in bed pretending to be ill. Perhaps she *was* ill, she hoped. Her head did ache and she was feverish.

One of the worst things she had to face was that Ian had been so proud of her going off on Barbarian business that he had bought her a new set of luggage, and all she'd done in return was drink too much rum punch with a bartender half her age, and grab a few rolls of cloth from the market on her way to the airport. They had been careful, Berris and she, as far as she could remember. With hindsight, she knew that Berris had forgotten her by now, that she had been the classic English dupe on holiday. It made her realise how much she loved Ian, but it caused her to wonder too how he could have borne the anxiety of infidelity so many times before he had found her. Recalling that he had just called her

Pudding, his pet name for his former wives, made her feel a mite less anguish, although her heart beat too fast if she thought about their deception of Nell all those years ago, even if the end had justified the means, and now her own betrayal of Ian was doing her head in. Never, never again. A good wife and mother and business partner was what she would be from now on. But where was the tea Ian had promised her? She was so thirsty. Had he found out somehow? Where were the children? Why had they deserted her? Was Ian keeping them from her? Had she become a spectre in her own house, condemned to wander from room to room searching for them, in the blue beads of shame?

'Jack,' she called, 'you can come in now.'

There was no answer. She sweated and itched and peeled, not knowing what to do with herself, unable to find a comfortable position. She had never wanted to before, not in her wildest dreams, had thought herself incapable of such an act – making love with somebody younger and prettier than herself. Barbara writhed, sick with detestation of her charming, funny, beautiful young lover.

Molly was elated by the early blossom as she drove to her daughter's house. There is nothing in this world so lovely as London in the spring, she thought. It was almost nine o'clock, and the plan was that Molly should collect the two children and take them to the fair before the public was let in at eleven. She was looking forward to seeing Barbara and hearing all about her trip, and was prepared to feel benign towards Ian on this beautiful morning of church bells and daffodils and people looking cheerful in the sunshine. Even if he *was* a serial adulterer who would give you the derivation of the word denim at the drop of a hat; she, of all people, had nothing against second-hand goods or used merchandise, but a rorty, rollicking old foodie of a father-figure wasn't necessarily what you wanted for your only child. The thought of the children gave her pleasure too; Molly was in the privileged position of favourite grandparent, as Grandma and Grandpa Donaldson were pretty gaga now, and had long ago lost count of their grandchildren. Nevertheless, she often had to bite her tongue at the way the youngsters were being brought up, and she did feel intensely protective towards Amber. Molly was of the opinion that every child needs an adult who thinks she is the best thing since sliced bread, and she saw herself fulfilling that rôle for Amber, as if by taking it for granted that Amber was pretty and popular, she could make her so.

All the curtains were closed when Molly drew up outside the house. Diggory let her in, after the third ring.

'How's my best boy?' she asked, hugging him, catching a whiff of garlic on his breath.

'Everybody's still in bed, excepting me and Amber,' he told her.

'Have you had any breakfast?'

'Yes, we had some pitta bread and hummus.'

The house smelled of unopened windows and sleep. Amber came down the stairs, without her glasses on, looking pale and as vulnerable as one of her pet mice. Molly realised that not so long ago, Amber would have hurled herself into her arms, and said briskly, 'You'll need your specs, if you're going to be my picker.' She tapped her own frames in a businesslike way, and Diggory felt excluded.

'I hate them. I want to get contacts,' said Amber.

'I'm sure you will, when you're old enough. Let's get going, or all the decent stuff will be taken.'

Amber took her glasses from her pocket and put them on.

As they walked through the college gates, Molly looking vernal in her Balenciaga green linen dress and jacket, between the two unkempt and garlicky ambassadors for Barbarians, Amber said, 'Mum's not well. She picked up something on her trip, Dad thinks.'

'My mum went to the West Indies,' said Diggory.

'Jamaica?' Molly obliged.

'No, she went of her own accordion.'

Amber heaved a deep sigh.

'Diggory, do you have to get everything wrong? I think he does it deliberately, you know,' she said to Molly, woman to woman.

'Now, now,' said Molly. She almost said nobody likes a smart-ass, but asked, 'Tell me about poor Mum. How long has she been ill?'

'Only since yesterday, but she was hallucinating last night, I think. She was lying there going, "Too much loose dye, too much loose dye," like the tailor of Gloucester when he went, "No more twist. No more twist."'

Ian was in the kitchen, wearing his butcher's apron and a chef's hat given to him by Daniel and Damien, when they returned. Diggory was clutching a roll of bubble wrap and Amber was sporting a garish fifties' necklace. Molly had a couple of fusty-looking carrier bags. She stood on tiptoe to kiss Ian's jowls.

'Dad, if you knew what you looked like in that hat . . .' said Amber.

Molly sighed. Ian, obviously hurt, said, 'Your slip's showing, Ma-in-law.'

Molly looked down. An edge of old lace was peeking from under her skirt. Annoyed, she said gaily, 'It's raining in Paris! That's what we used to say at school, didn't we, when somebody's petticoat was showing?'

'Not at Piggotts, we didn't,' Ian replied stiffly. She always had to rub it in that they were near contemporaries.

'How's Barbara? Should I go up and see her?'

'It's OK, I'm down. Hello Mum, good to see you. Hi, guys. Amber, where did that ghastly necklace come from? It really doesn't go with a hooded sweat.'

Molly saw her child, looking wan in a dressing gown, with touristy beads in her hair, and embraced her, winking at Amber, who had flinched.

'She's got an eye, you know. To some, that necklace is a collector's piece. Those braids are very amusing, but darling you look awful! Have you had the doctor?'

'No, I'm fine now. It was just one of those twenty-four-hour things. Probably something I ate.' She grimaced.

'I'm the one who deserves your sympathy, Molly. Tossing and turning all night, she was, sweating like the proverbial – if I didn't know better, I'd have thought she was having hot flushes. I didn't get a wink. Then the bloody foxes started their mating – sounded like a chainsaw massacre. I suppose they must enjoy it but –'

'Please, Ian, *pas devant les enfants* . . .' Molly remembered how Ian used to line the children up and make them each say three rude words before breakfast, whether they wanted to or not. 'Gets it out of their system,' he would say.

'Oh, come on, Ma-in-law, there's nothing they haven't seen on those wildlife TV programmes. Probably know more about it than we do!' He took a slurp from a glass of white wine. 'Cook's perks. What can I get you, Molly? Barbie Doll? Up to a snort yet?'

'Perhaps a little wine, topped up with lots of mineral water,' Barbara said bravely.

'I'll have a G&T, thank you, Ian,' Molly said. 'Where are Jack and William? I haven't seen them yet.'

'They'll be with Marie-Claude.'

'I hate that smell, of meat when it's just starting to cook,' said Amber. 'Granny Molly, did you know I'm a vegetarian?' She picked a slice of apple from a dish and ate it.

'Ignore her, we do. She's just copying her little Asian friend,' Ian commented. 'Personally, I love it when the juices start to run. Gets my own juices running. Shall we take our drinks into the garden room? This will take some time. Amber, I hope you heard that apple scream when you bit into it?'

He took off his apron.

'You'd already killed it, stupid.'

Molly winced; she was so weary of being the referee. It would be immoral of course to wish the child would learn some feminine wiles, but she had to clench her fingers to stop them from removing the scrawny, scraggly − scrunchie, that was it − from Amber's hair.

Jack and Wills were in the garden room, watching television.

'How are my best boys?' cried Granny Molly. 'Still in their jimjams at nearly two o'clock? Where's Marie-Claude?'

'In the garden. All she ever does is sit on the swing and cry every time Eurostar goes past,' said Jack.

'Oorostar! Oorostar!' wailed Wills, and everybody laughed.

'I think she might be a bit homesick,' said Amber.

'We ought to try harder with her, Ian. I know she isn't easy, but she could blacken our characters to the whole *village*, if she's unhappy,' Barbara said.

'I have tried,' said Ian.

He thought suddenly, It's after two. There's been no word from

Laura or her mum. No heavies have come looking for me. It must have been a false alarm. Thank you, God.

'Perhaps she's missing her horsemeat,' Amber suggested. 'Such a shame we can't get it at Dobbie's in the village.'

In the release from tension that washed over him, Ian exploded. 'Amber, I've had about as much as I can take from you with your constant sniping and undermining. If you despise us all so much, why don't you just pack your bags and go? And take your smelly mice with you! If you ever gave a thought to anybody but yourself, you'd get down on your knees every day and thank your mother and me. You don't know just how fortunate you are to live in a household like this. It's a jungle out there. You may sneer at my chef's hat, which of course you know has great sentimental value for me, but most of the kids you pass on the street have never watched their parents cook a proper meal, never seen them lift a needle or a hammer and chisel. They live on Pot Noodles and crack cocaine, savages in a new Dark Age, without hope, without pride, without skills. Is that what you want, eh? If it is, you can check out of that fancy school as soon as you like, and I won't waste any more thought or money on you. My God, those pampered pets of yours have a better lifestyle than half the world's population, how do you justify that? I doubt your friend Roxana has so much as a mousetrap to call her own, let alone a state-of-the-art mouse cage or an architect-designed bedroom to herself like you, but at least she does a bit of work to earn her keep. It's all take, take, take, gimme, gimme, gimme, with you, isn't it? You're not even any use to the catalogue, are you? Just a flaming liability!'

Barbara and Molly had both been attempting to remonstrate during this tirade as Ian delivered verbal blow after blow, but he was unstoppable. Throughout it, Amber had attempted to hold a supercilious expression, but the reference to a mousetrap broke her. She bolted for the door, her face twisted, eyes spouting angry, humiliated tears behind her glasses. Molly caught her and struggled to hold her tight.

'There, there. Daddy didn't mean it. Darling, don't fight me, don't cry, he didn't mean any of those things, you just rubbed him up the wrong way.' Molly was crying too. 'People say things they don't mean in the heat of the moment.'

'Of course, I didn't mean it, Amber knows I didn't mean it, don't you, Pop Tart? Silly old Daddy lost his rag back there for a minute, didn't he? Just got a bit stressed out because he's been under a lot of pressure. Come on, Pop Tart, give your old Popsicle a hug and tell him you forgive him, eh? Please? Pretty please!'

'Go on, darling. Kiss and make up, eh? Daddy's said he's sorry.'

Molly, kneeling with her arms round Amber, glared at her son-in-law's loins packed into denim, his trainers like two dead pigeons on the carpet, even as she pushed the girl forward.

'Yes, go on, sweetheart,' Barbara urged. 'Look the boys are crying, we're all crying. Let's stop all this silliness now.'

Ian fell to his knees now, pleading, striking his forehead with his fist. 'Forgive me, forgive me, or I shall surely die.'

Molly stood up, and Amber said, 'Dad, you are *so* embarrassing. OK, I forgive you. Even though I know you did mean every word. Just get up, all right?'

Amber walked towards him and Ian hoisted himself up to hug her. Amber avoided his kiss and, in a gesture that chilled her grandmother, held out a small, disdainful hand for him to shake.

'There, that's better. Now we can all forget all about it and get on with enjoying this lovely day,' said Granny Molly. 'Which of you boys is going to find Marie-Claude and bring her in to join us? Thank you, Diggory. Switch off the television and let's sit down like civilised people and have a conversation. Barbara, darling, when am I going to hear all your adventures? I'm all agog. Not now? Oh well, over lunch then, when you're feeling a bit more like yourself. Now, did anybody else see that very disturbing programme about the child carpet weavers of Bhutan last night? No, perhaps not . . . what pretty daffodils.'

'I picked them for Mummy because she was ill,' said Jack.

'They're lovely and they made Mummy better.' Barbara blew her nose hard.

Molly lit a cigarette and walked over to the open french windows. The garden was still wintry, except for one forsythia, and bleached plastic vehicles were scattered in the grass.

'You'll be able to get your first cut in soon, if this weather holds,' she said to Ian, not without a touch of malice. Then she saw, with a jolt to her heart, that the garden was quite bare of daffodils, but the railway bank was ablaze with them. Diggory was coming out of the Coppice, followed by Marie-Claude. He was sucking the edge of a piece of bubble wrap, and Molly recognised it for what it was, a comfort blanket.

'Look, a magpie!' she exclaimed.

'Oh, there are masses around,' said Barbara. 'Loads more than there used to be.'

'Roadkill,' said Ian. 'The increase of carrion has led to a magpie population explosion. Breeding like rabbits, and taking over the cities. There will have to be a cull soon, they're decimating the local song-birds. Have you come across that book, Ma-in-law, *The Roadkill Cookbook*? Some surprisingly appetising recipes.'

'Oh, good. A pair, that's lucky! Two for joy. And another!' said Molly.

'Three for a girl!' shouted Jack. 'Yuk. Where's four for a boy?'

Neither of his parents answered him.